A History of Forgetting

Other books by Caroline Adderson:

Bad Imaginings

A
HISTORY
OF
FORGETTING

Caroline Adderson

Caroline Adderson

For Keith and JoAnn

best wishes

PATRICK CREAN EDITIONS

an imprint of

KEY PORTER BOOKS

Lines from the song "Heureuse" reprinted by permission of Réné Rouzaud/Marguerite Monnot copyright © 1954 Editions Salabert

---

Canadian Cataloguing in Publication Data

Adderson, Caroline, 1963-
    A history of forgetting

ISBN 1-894433-01-7

I.   Title.

PS8551.D3267H57 1999   C813'.54   C99-931309-6
PR9199.3.A33H57 1999

The publisher gratefully acknowledges the support of the Canada Council for the Arts and the Ontario Arts Council for its publishing program.

We acknowledge the financial support of the Government of Canada through the Book Publishing Industry Development Program (BPIDP) for our publishing activities.

Canadä

Key Porter Books Limited
70 The Esplanade
Toronto, Ontario
Canada M5E 1R2

www.keyporter.com

Electronic formatting: Rena D. Potter
Design: Peter Maher

Printed and bound in Canada

99 00 01 02 03   6 5 4 3 2 1

For Bruce Sweeney

CONTENTS

The first of the taxi drivers in the line is wearing mirrored sunglasses that reflect back in miniature and reverse the entrance to the Muzeum. It looks, in fact, as if he's thinking about the Muzeum as he sits there smoking and waiting for a fare. Open the door and he immediately starts the engine, but does not turn around to ask where you want to go, just looks at you in the rearview mirror—at least, you think he's looking at you. You can't see his eyes. Tell him you want to go to the train station, "The train station," and before you have a chance to look up how to say it in the guidebook, the taxi pulls away from the curb.

Even now, this late in the day, the parking lot is filled with tour buses and cars. Look at your watch. You have been here for almost seven hours and at some point it must have rained, for the asphalt is a darker black and water pools between the cars. Strange you didn't notice when you were in the Muzeum walking from block to block. It was a bully wind that dominated, that sucked and gusted up and down the avenues. Something fittingly menacing about it, but now the wind has died away and under the sky's grey shroud, everything feels colourless and completely still.

The taxi driver turns onto the main road, the cigarette between the fingers of his hand on the wheel. Smoke thickens in the small space you occupy together, yet if you coughed, if you unrolled the window even a slit, his contempt would be too much for you. Almost a tyranny, the power they have over you, the downtrodden cabbies and discourteous waiters, the surly tellers and aggrieved clerks. What are you doing here? they seem to ask with their glowers and their sighs. Who in their right mind would come here? In truth, you see a point to their indignation. What have you come for but to rake up the horrors of their past? Where you are fervent about remembering, they, living at the wrought iron gate to hell, they just want to forget.

But look at his jacket. Black leather, it is so new that when he turns the steering wheel, the leather speaks. And his cigarettes are American, Camels, you know because he has been careful to display the package on the dash. How downtrodden can he be driving this lucrative route, barely ten minutes back and forth? He will likely earn more today shuttling passengers than you will for the months that will turn out to be years that you will spend writing about this day.

Over your shoulder, glance and see the Muzeum receding. Turn back and see the spiky grey hairs on the back of his neck disappearing down the brand new collar of his jacket. What does he think about all day as he drives? Does he believe in the Muzeum and the lessons that it teaches? Ask him because you're curious. Ask: "Have you ever been inside?"

He seems to understand you. Heaving burly shoulders, he grunts, "Tak."

He's just the right age, mid-fiftyish, to have stood and stared through the barbed and electric wire into the Muzeum before it was a Muzeum. He knows exactly what it means, more than the average visitor who can only imagine how it was. So do you pity him for the way he has to keep on coming back, or do you despise him for making his living off tourists? All at once, you find you want to despise him. He may have lost family here; it is more than likely, yet you discount it because you have already judged him and found him deserving of your contempt. It is a conscious decision, entirely wilful and self-righteous and, of course, misplaced. By the time the taxi pulls up at the station, you have not once looked out the window, but sat the entire ride staring with a fixed loathing at the furrows made by the comb on the oily back of the driver's head.

He quotes you his outrageous fare in English, not really that much, only that the currency is so devalued. Toss him the bills with disdain and watch him drive away, back to the Muzeum again.

Left standing in front of the train station, all you have for baggage is this sudden, acid shame and a line remembered, though you can't think from where: At the start of every nightmare waits a train. The Oświęcim town station is a glass-and-concrete box, circa 1950. You have just come from the Muzeum, the old station. The old station was called Auschwitz.

THE PROBLEM IN THE MIRROR

1

Something woke Malcolm in the night. For that one instant, as his eyes opened in the dark, he understood how Denis felt, not knowing what city he was waking in, or what room for that matter. The ceiling above him, an unremarkable square of grey, could have been any of the ceilings he had stared up at through the years from different beds. Utter disorientation, but after a moment his eyes adjusted. He saw where he was and remembered. He remembered that he wished waking were the dream.

For Denis, though, it just went on and on. Yesterday, doing the laundry, Malcolm checked his pockets and found yet another note. *Je m'appelle Denis Cassel. J'habite à Paris. Je suis coiffeur.* Discouraged, he crumpled it, squeezed it tightly in his palm. Every night of the last three months they had stood on the balcony together, Malcolm pointing to where the river funnelled to the ocean, the Fraser, not the Seine. The ocean looked static at that distance. "The Pacific," he explained. But Denis did not remember from one day to the next, or even an hour later. "What do you see?" Malcolm asked once and

Denis had replied, as if by rote from a French primer, *"Voilà la Tour Eiffel."*

Rubbish, Malcolm had thought. In Paris, they had never lived anywhere near it.

Now, in the middle of the night, Denis was up again and walking around the apartment. Malcolm heard footsteps and a bump against what must have been the china cabinet—the dishes tinkled—then something was picked up and set back down ungently. In a different life, Malcolm might have thought it was a break-in, could imagine the scenario, a tragicomedy like everything else: the intruder running smack into Denis in the dark and blurting, "What the fuck?" as Denis asked in genteel French who he was and, once on that tangent, what time his appointment was.

An unholy crash. Malcolm sat up with a start. All at once, he remembered it was Christmas. *"Père Noël?"* he called out. "Is that you, *mon vieux?"*

"Merde," came the faint reply.

He felt around with his feet for his slippers, then down the unlit hall he went. The living room, when he reached it, was completely dark, more so for its contents—the dark wood and upholstery, the paintings with their black backgrounds. The winking coloured lights on the tree had been unplugged for the night. In this dimness, Denis appeared slight and spectral, his hair silvery, his skin white. He was completely naked, restless, padding his luminescent way around the room. He touched everything, patted it, the ashtray now, the Egyptian head on the coffee table, trying to make it all familiar. When he turned and looked at Malcolm, the hair on Malcolm's arms and the back of his neck lifted— as if Malcolm had seen a ghost and now the ghost saw him. His great, great fear was that Denis would not remember him and, thinking that he must have been standing too far in the shadows, that this was why Denis didn't speak, Malcolm took a step toward him, but Denis remained mute, staring on with an expression Malcolm could not make out until he drew nearer.

There it was: the half-smile broadening, the spark behind the eyes. It was the same delighted expression he would have put on if they had met by chance in the street.

"*Chéri,*" he told Malcolm. "I'm so glad to see you."

Relieved, Malcolm extended his hand for Denis to come and take. Lately Denis had adopted this vaguely simian posture, arms heavy in their sockets; he moved as if he were carrying the weight of a large stone in each hand. "Come on, King Kong," Malcolm said as he led him back down the hall to the bedroom. He switched on the light and almost got him to the bed when suddenly Denis drew his hand from Malcolm's and backed away.

"What is it?"

"*Il y a quelqu'un là-bas!*"

"Where?" asked Malcolm. "In here?"

"*J'ai vu quelqu'un!*"

"There's no one here but me."

In the doorway, still squinting from the light, Denis looked young. Despite decades of dishes laced with butter and, yes, even lard, Denis had never gone to fat. Almost imperceptible, his transition from blond to grey. And his hair had barely thinned and was worn the same way, short all around with a thicker lock between the two crescents of a high hairline, like a comma punctuating his glowing forehead. At sixty-nine, he was more boyish than ever, his penis retracting to thumb length in the cold air.

"There's a man there. I saw him. I tell you, he's hiding in there."

Malcolm went over to the window and drew the cord on the drapes. Red velvet, they jerked open like a theatre curtain; no one was on stage.

Denis was unconvinced. Sighing, tugging his pyjama legs at the thighs, Malcolm got down stiffly on one knee and flipped aside the brocaded bedskirt. Under the bed, dust congregated on the hardwood floor in little bales. He went over to the closet, too, made a great show of scraping the hangers back and forth, crossed to the wardrobe, opened the mirrored door and called inside, "Yoo-hoo?"

He invited Denis to come and look himself. Stepping nervously into the room, Denis craned to see inside the closet without daring to go near it. "But I saw him," he muttered, all the more confused. "*Je l'ai vu.* I swear it." Shaking his head, he allowed Malcolm to lead him to the bed.

"What did he look like?" Malcolm asked, drawing back the covers on Denis's side.

"Skinny with white hair. A shrivelled little cock." He pursed his lips in disgust.

"Why, you twit," said Malcolm. "That was you!"

He went back to the wardrobe and, shutting the door, beckoned to Denis who came and stood with Malcolm before the mirror. Pale eyes narrowing sceptically, one hand pressed against his hairless chest, the other felt down and squeezed his cock. Warming, it swelled a little and, all at once, Denis chuckled.

"So it is," he said. "So it is."

In the morning, despite his nocturnal bumpings, Denis was first up and making coffee. The aroma woke Malcolm, who remembered right away that it was Christmas Day, but didn't give a ho ho ho or a sweet fuck, would have liked to forget the whole charade except that Yvette had decked out the apartment like a department-store display to keep Denis on the calendar. He brought to the breakfast table a gift. Denis came over with the coffee pot and the carafe of hot milk, his shirt buttoned incorrectly, but other than that, dressed for success.

"*Qu'est-ce que c'est?*" he asked, seeing the gift next to his bowl.

"Merry Christmas."

He met Malcolm's eyes, a blank blue stare.

"It's Christmas," Malcolm said.

"*Je ne crois pas,*" he said. "I would have remembered that."

So it would have been better not to mention it at all. As for the Styrofoam snowman centrepiece in the middle of the table—they could just go on ignoring it, as well as the cut-out paper snowflakes taped to the window. That a man as cultured as Denis sat there every morning doing what Yvette called "crafts" was, as far as Malcolm was concerned, the truest symptom of his decline.

"*C'est impossible,*" Denis muttered, taking his place across the table.

"What is?" asked Malcolm.

"What is what?"

"Exactly. Here. Let me pour yours."

He took the coffee pot back to the kitchen, but when he returned to the table, Denis was turning the damn present around and around in his hands. "What's this?"

"A present."

"*Pourquoi?*"

"Because you're special."

"Bah!" said Denis, pleased.

"Open it."

He tore away the paper. Inside was a hairbrush with a blond wood handle. Denis took it out of the case and, stroking his palm with the bristles, nodded his professional approval. He stood, came around the table and, one hand on Malcolm's shoulder, drew the brush through Malcolm's hair. Malcolm, head bowed, felt all atingle with Denis's small hot hand on his shoulder and the hard bristles against his scalp.

"*Où est Yvette?*"

"She's not coming today."

Denis stopped brushing. "*Pourquoi pas?*" and Malcolm lifted his head. Pressing his fingers briefly to the corners of his eyes, squeezing the bridge of his nose, he sipped from the bowl of coffee.

"*Pourquoi pas?*" Denis demanded.

"She is spending the day with her family. We are not the only ones she loves."

"*Quel jour est-il?*"

"Tuesday." Mistake. He should have lied. He should have said Saturday or Sunday and the whole matter would have been forgotten. But he couldn't seem to start lying after all these years.

Off Denis staggered. From the kitchen came the commotion of slamming drawers and cupboards.

"What are you doing?" Malcolm called.

"*Je cherche quelque chose!*"

"What?"

The noise ceased. All was quiet. Malcolm finished his coffee and got up.

He found Denis in the living room, running one hand through his hair. He looked drunk, but it was only that he was stuck. He couldn't remember what he was looking for. Malcolm knew—it was a calendar—but Malcolm was not about to tell him that it was hanging

above the toilet so that Denis could refer to it throughout the day. Instead, Malcolm crossed over to the stereo,
lifted the lid and, seeing a record already on the
turntable, lowered the needle.

Heureuse, comme tout. Heureuse, malgré tout.

He approached Denis, who was listening and at last
remembering, something from long ago.

Heureuse, heureuse, heureuse!

Their palms touched, fingers laced and Malcolm put
his other hand on Denis's waist. Close together, he realized neither of them had shaved. There was the rough-
ness of whisker against whisker and the softness of
Denis's breath inside his ear. "*Il le faut, je le veux, mon
amour, pour nous deux.* Around the carpet, they turned, its
pattern marking their steps, and Malcolm saw over
Denis's shoulder what made that racket the night
before—the Christmas tree toppling, the coloured balls
rolling in the grate.

Heureuse d'avoir, enfin, une part ...

"Is it really Christmas?" Denis whispered.

"No," said Malcolm. "Indeed it's not."

Denis pulled his hand out of Malcolm's grip. "Then
where is Yvette?"

De ciel, d'amour, de joie.

Malcolm sang along so as not to answer, "*Dans tes
yeux, dans tes bras ...*"

Heureuse, comme tout,
Heureuse, n'importe où,
Par toi!

Denis drew back his arm and struck Malcolm in the
face, his fist meeting Malcolm's mouth—two parts that
had never been acquainted even after thirty years. So
unexpected and out of character; Malcolm immediately struck back. An impulse, an instinct, blinded by tears

that sprang up, he simply swung out, then stumbled back against the stereo, setting the record skipping. Instead of "happy" she began singing "hour, hour, hour" impassionedly.

His hand over his mouth, his mouth filling up with blood, Malcolm stared at Denis, aghast. On the floor, blood streaming from his nose, Denis was begging, "Please don't hurt me! How could you hurt me?"

"How?" asked Malcolm, stunned.

"What have I ever done to you!"

"Christ!" Malcolm made a move toward Denis, to help him up, to embrace him, but Denis shrieked and crawled away.

"I'm sorry, Denis. Please forgive me."

Denis squeezed behind the couch.

"I can't believe I did that," said Malcolm. "Denis. Darling. Please come out."

A long condemning silence, then Denis sniffed. Malcolm came hopefully over and peered behind the couch. Denis was curled fetal, bleeding on the carpet. "Come out, Denis. Come out. *Je t'en prie.*"

"*Où est Yvette?*" he asked churlishly. "*Je veux Yvette.*"

He sighed. "She's coming, darling. She'll be here."

Christmas was in full swing chez Yvette, or so it sounded when Malcolm called. He heard the screech of het-up children, the television, women in the kitchen speaking the gravelly French so different from what Malcolm and Denis spoke. "*Âllo,*" Yvette answered when the phone was handed to her.

"Merry Christmas."

Hearing it was Malcolm, she switched immediately to English. "It's the day after for us, eh? We celebrate the twenty-fourth. Is Denis having a good day?"

"How should I put it?" said Malcolm. "Things are not so much merry here as catastrophic."

In the background, the oven door yawned and slammed, a knife struck staccato against a block, the tap ran: a meal being prepared by many hands. Yvette was smoking. Despite all the noise, he heard the faint pop of her lips releasing the filter the second before she asked, "What happened?"

"Denis is behind the couch and won't come out."

"Leave him there," said Yvette. "He'll forget all about it."

"He's bleeding."

"Eh?"

"We had a little punch-up. You know us," he quipped.

"You pig."

"Why do you assume it's my fault?"

"Because Denis is ill. He's not responsible. Is he hurt bad?"

"A nosebleed. Can you come over?"

"What? Now?" She snorted. "The house is full up. Did you try distracting him?"

He sighed very loudly, in case Yvette didn't hear him over the unlistened-to child who had begun needling in the background. Somebody wouldn't let him play with something. Over and over he repeated it at a higher and higher pitch. His complaint was in English and the female hubbub he was trying to penetrate was French.

"Malcolm? Just a sec." She cupped the receiver and snapped at the child whose siren of indignation finally gained him the attention he'd been seeking. He was interrogated briefly, then Yvette was scolded. "I'm trying to have a conversation here, *câlisse*," she retorted. "*Câlisse*, I can't hear myself think."

"Sorry, Yvette," said Malcolm. "I shouldn't have called."

"You know what? I'm gonna come just to get away from this."

"I appreciate it," he said.

"Yeah, yeah. It's not a Christmas present. You know holidays are time and a half."

"Of course."

Back in the living room, he called to Denis still behind the couch. "Come out, darling. Yvette is on her way."

No reply. Denis was sobbing like a child.

This was not how things usually were with them. They rarely fought and if they did, forgiveness was not usually hoarded, but graciously bestowed. In the bathroom, Malcolm rinsed the taste of nails out of his mouth. His upper lip inflating, he drew it carefully back to inspect the soft inside of his mouth cut by his teeth. So this was what love comes to. It comes to blows, he thought.

He couldn't bear to return to the living room, so stayed at the table finishing Denis's coffee as he listened numbly to his weeping. His hands shook as he lifted the bowl. It stung to drink. It stung. This was perhaps the worse thing that had ever happened between them.

Thankfully, Yvette was on her way, Yvette their homemaker, their saviour. When the agency had first sent her, their only employee who spoke fluent French, Yvette, a Québécoise, took one look around, jaw locked, eyes narrowing, sussing out the situation.

Straight out, Malcolm told her, "You won't have to bathe him."

"Ugh!" she said. "I suppose you do."

"You also won't have to cook. Denis does."

Her eyebrows arched; the promise of less work was tempting. What clinched it though, was Denis himself shambling into the living room on cue. He saw Yvette planted there on the couch and he slew her with that smile of his, the left corner of his mouth lifting a second before the right, making him seem perpetually guileless and bemused—which he was. Another of the extraordinary things about Denis was that he appeared to be exactly what he was.

Yvette's clenched jaw softened. "Oh," she said. Malcolm knew the look, knew the breathy sigh; he'd seen and heard it a thousand times. She was already in love with Denis standing there twinkling in his unmatched socks. And Denis, bless his heart, loved her back. Denis loved everyone.

"I don't usually like the French," she said, but since then Denis had risen quickly through her ranks. Most days Malcolm came home and found him brushing out her hair, Yvette sitting there, complacent and slit-eyed as a cat in a cloud of her own dry dead ends breaking off. They never met or parted without a profuse exchange of kisses. Denis probably got more kisses out of her than did Mr. Yvette.

In twenty minutes she was buzzing to get into the apartment—never just once, three impatient blasts, as if in a code they'd previously established.

"We got my gang with us again this year," she told him at the apartment door. "The three sisters, the hubbies, all the kids, my dad. They come out for the skiing, eh? Continuous fucking fighting. I'm glad to get away for an hour."

Malcolm, relieving her of her coat, made reference to the child he heard in the background when he phoned. "I cannot bear whining."

"It's not the kids! It's the adults!" And Mr. Yvette, an Anglo, didn't understand a word. "I dunno if that's better for him or worse!"

"Thank you again for coming," he said.

She heaved her heavy shoulders, dismissing his appreciation, and in the mirror patted her hair. It was an adjectiveless brown, crisp from overperming, swept back with girlish barrettes on both sides of her broad face. "So what did you do to him?"

"He became agitated when I told him it was Christmas. I mean, don't we all? I woke up this morning and very nearly vomited."

She frowned, which was half her repertoire of facial expressions; she also puckered when she smoked. As for smiling, Malcolm had never observed her at it. He suspected she didn't have a molar in her head because every time she opened her mouth to slang at Denis, he glimpsed a deep black hole.

"You didn't celebrate last night?"

"I had driven it from my own mind, frankly."

"Then it *is* your fault."

She started down the hall, Malcolm following her caboose in tight cotton leggings, sighing that it always, always was.

He stood in the doorway while Yvette went over to the couch. "Denis!" she bellowed, as if the problem was his hearing. To him, she spoke her twangy French. "What's going on?" When he didn't reply, she knelt on the couch and reached over the back. "Come on. Up you get."

It pained Malcolm to see Denis obey her and pull himself to his knees. To see the blood smeared on his face.

"There's a good boy. Up we go. Jesus Christ, what happened to you? It looks like someone hit you."

"*M'a frappé?*" Denis laughed and shook his head—an absurd suggestion. When he made a move to kiss her cheek, she put out her hand in a policeman's halt.

"Let's wash your face first, eh?"

She led him out of the room, passing Malcolm in the doorway. "Who would do that to you, Denis? You're such a dear."

Denis told Malcolm, *"Yvette est arrivée!"*

"Yes, I see that."

"Shame, shame, shame," she hissed in English. "I'd like to clobber you back. How would you like that?"

Sheepishly, he followed to the bathroom where Yvette left Denis while she went to get a clean cloth from the linen cupboard. Denis, standing in front of the basin, staring in the mirror, was clearly alarmed by what he saw: the blood clotting in one nostril, blood sticky on his lips and chin. He reached out and lightly touched the mirror, looked at his fingers, shook his head.

"Denis, I'm sorry."

Denis didn't seem to hear. He pulled a hand towel off the rack, wet it, then did the oddest thing. Instead of wiping his face, he began cleaning his reflection, scrubbing, scrubbing, then blinking at himself, perplexed.

He wasn't coming clean.

2

Malcolm brought Denis to Vancouver because it was where he had been born and raised, but when they arrived he found a city so changed as to seem an entirely different place. They might as well have gone to Quebec or Montreal, he realized, but by then it was too late. Even the cityscape was unrecognizable, the right-angled lattice-work of all the construction cranes further altering the view. The Hotel Vancouver still stood downtown, along with a few old churches squatting in the skyscrapers' shadows, but the wrecking ball had demolished so many familiar buildings. Gone was one of his favourites: the Art Deco medical arts building where he'd used to get his teeth filled. They'd resurrected the granite nurses that had adorned the original façade, but these once-grand symbols, Nurse Health and Nurse Hygiene, only looked butch and out of place on their updated pediments. Even the house he'd grown up in had disappeared, the whole block razed, and in its place there was a pink stucco condominium complex streaked with mildew. He marvelled that they had not blasted away the mountains, too.

None of this he really minded, though. He preferred that everything be new. When they lived in Paris he used to stop every afternoon at the same café on the way home with the groceries. Once, early in his first year, he came by in the evening and left his coins as usual on the table. The next day the waiter told him that the prices increased after six. Malcolm said that he hadn't known, that he would make up the difference now, but the waiter waved off the debt. "Yesterday was yesterday. Today is today." This struck him then, as now, as a sensible philosophy.

At certain moments, though, everything did seem as before. When Malcolm stepped across the threshold of the apartment, he could have been stepping into their place in the Marais. The layout was not quite right and neither were the neighbours or the view, but all their furniture was there—it had nearly bankrupted them to bring it over—and the Persian carpet and the paintings, everything in exactly the same arrangement. Except that the ceiling was lower, the kitchen matched; he had been very particular about the kitchen when choosing the apartment. Disassembling the old one, he'd made careful notes in order to put it back together here—no easy feat, what with Denis's hundred unlabelled jars and bizarre implements, some of which Malcolm couldn't begin to presume a use for apart from torture. The kitchen was all Denis's and, once he started to cook, this apartment smelled just like the other, too.

Back in Paris Malcolm would not, when he got home from work, find Yvette smoking at their dining-room table and reading an American tabloid. That was different. But Denis still came to greet him with his only English sentence: "*Are you angry?*"

He meant, "Are you hungry?" the beguilingly dropped "h," the charm in his accent.

"*Très fâché*," Malcolm answered, smiling.

Malcolm, who, as always, left that morning with Denis's list, had returned with a bulging net shopping bag. Taking it, Denis began unloading the packages on the counter. Into a clear glass bowl he emptied the mushrooms from the paper bag.

"Are they all right?"

Denis sniffed at one and shrugged. "They'll have to do."

Nothing Malcolm bought for Denis passed inspection. Ever. He could have planted a garden, run with a dew-drenched lettuce throbbing in its prime and presented it to Denis on a tasselled cushion, and still Denis would have deemed it unfresh, bitter, bruised. There had been a time when this annoyed Malcolm no end. They had had their share of quarrels over an imperceptibly browning fennel bulb, a leek supposedly too packed with grit. Malcolm, rebelling, had even gone so far as to suggest that Denis do the marketing himself, a threat he regretted making, seeing Denis turn away, hurt. It is these little rituals that prolong love, Malcolm knew now, but it had taken him a long time to learn.

The list read one Spanish onion and twenty pearl onions.

"*Un, deux, trois, quatre ...*" Denis expertly shucked their paper skins as he counted.

"There are twenty," Malcolm assured him. "*Il y en a vingt.*"

"*Vingt-et-un,*" Denis continued, "*vingt-deux, vingt-trois ...*"

"Now you've confused him," Yvette said from the table.

"*... vingt—*" He broke off, flustered.

"But I couldn't get juniper berries," said Malcolm quickly, so Denis could save face. "The IGA certainly doesn't stock them. Where could I get them in this city?"

Denis tutted and named the owner of a shop close to where they lived in Paris. "Bernard always has them. Just nip out and get them, will you?"

"Oh, I went there," Malcolm said. "It was closed."

Yvette turned a page in the tabloid. "All the way to France and back? That was quick. He'll never remember where he is if you don't set him straight."

"Don't you have another client to go to?" asked Malcolm, the Queen of Tact.

"I do. It's the old judge."

"He'll be waiting."

"At bath time, he always asks to suck my tit."

Malcolm recoiled, "Yvette!" Yvette laughing at his prudishness. "That would never happen here, Yvette," he said.

"No, it wouldn't, would it? Denis is a gentleman." Still she remained parked at the table, propping herself up on a plump elbow as she interfered.

"May I help?" Malcolm asked Denis.

Denis looked up, the one silver lock flopping in his eyes, and waved Malcolm off politely. He never accepted the first offer. Malcolm would have to ask several times. He'd have to beg and then Denis would give him a menial task to do incorrectly, insult his work and drive him from the kitchen.

"Please."

"*Non, non.*"

"I insist."

The task he granted Malcolm at last, just as Yvette stubbed out her cigarette and lumbered over, expectant-faced, was to open the brown paper package on the counter.

"Ah, your cheque," Malcolm said. "It's on the desk."

He went to get it and, when he returned, he found Denis chopping up a carrot while Yvette tested the weight of the package, squeezing it curiously. She opened the paper wrapping to have a peek. A blue-black coil, a whiskered neck. Eyes. She dropped it on the counter and jumped back. "*Câlisse!*"

Denis was at her side in an instant, wielding the knife. With equal parts comedy and chivalry, he decapitated the thing, the force of the cut sending the head rolling off the counter and onto the floor where it looked up expressionlessly from beside its executioner's slipper.

"*Merde,*" he muttered, bending to scoop the head up on the side of the knife.

Yvette elbowed Malcolm out of the way. He followed her to the door. She must have been terrified to run away without her cheque, without kissing her darling Denis.

"What was that?" she hissed.

"An eel. It's a delicacy, Yvette. You should come for dinner some night."

She snatched the cheque out of his hand. "*Câlisse.*"

Then, as he helped her with her coat, she told him, "I almost forgot. A mirror in the bedroom, the one on the wardrobe? He threw a vase at it."

"Not the blue vase on the dresser?"

"That's right."

Malcolm cringed. "I think it was worth something."

"Not any more. I just closed the door so he wouldn't step in the glass. I don't clean, right?"

"Of course not." He pressed his fingers to his eyes. "Why does he do that?"

"What?"

"Fly off the handle when he sees himself?"

"He expects to see someone younger."

"Don't we all?" Malcolm cried.

Frowning, which, if inverted, could have been a smile, she fished for her keys in her purse. "He's going to get more difficult to handle."

Handle? thought Malcolm.

"Did you talk to him about a dog?"

"Oh, you and your dog." Malcolm opened the door and waved her out.

She stepped into the hall. "You know I love Denis."

"Yvette," he teased. "Is this a confession?"

"No. It's me telling you that the day I get caught in the crossfire, I'm out of here for good."

He closed the door behind her, hoping she didn't see how her warning startled him. She would learn her true worth then and demand more. For this was the great irony of his relationship with Yvette: she thought she was fleecing *him* by getting paid to come here and be preened by a still-beautiful Frenchman and do not a lick of work. But what would they do without Yvette? He could not believe there was anyone like her in the city— bilingual, certified, tolerant at the core. Leaving Denis with someone he couldn't talk to would have been unthinkable. Again, he chided himself for not going to Montreal.

He went back to the kitchen where Denis, at the stove, was melting a great white cube of lard in a casserole. "Now what can I do," asked Malcolm, shamming a smile.

"*Rien du tout.*" Denis took a wooden spoon from the drawer, patted Malcolm's cheek fondly with it, and began pushing around the skating lard.

"Yvette says you threw a vase this morning."

Indignant, he turned to Malcolm. "I did not!"

"She thinks a little dog would help calm you."

"*Un chien?*"

"Would you like that?"

Denis would. He loved all creatures. He used to cup the summer wasps in his bare hands to release out the window and throw bread crumbs down for the courtyard pigeons. If, on the street, he happened to pass a dog tied to a post, he would always stop to offer it encouragement. As for the rabbits hanging like Mussolini in the market—too late. Denis could only help by elevating them to a higher incarnation in a terrine. In a bowl next to the sink the eel, flayed and segmented, soaked in water, waiting its turn at immortality. The decapitated head floated near the surface, the eyes little sightless beads.

"Would I?" He paused in confusion and scratched the very tip of his nose. "*Quoi?*"

"I'll open the wine," Malcolm said.

Three bottles were ready on the counter, one *vin ordinaire* and two Bordeaux. He drew the corks, three soft plosives, as Denis changed the water the eel was soaking in, pouring it off cloudy, then refilling the bowl from the tap. Denis could not always follow a simple conversation, or practise his chosen craft, or find his way out of the apartment on his own, but was able to execute the most complex of recipes without consulting a cookbook. Regrettably, he could not remember what last he cooked.

Drying his hands now, looking extremely pleased, he threw the towel over his shoulder. "*Bon!*" He tried to dismiss Malcolm, but Malcolm went over to the cutting board and picked the onion off it.

"*Non! Non!*" Denis cried.

"*Oui! Oui!*" Malcolm pleaded.

A few exasperated words addressed to the ceiling, Denis threw the towel over his head, sighed loudly, tore it off, then went to hover around Malcolm chopping the onion. First he criticized how Malcolm held the knife, then the size of the pieces that he cut. Malcolm was crying, but it had nothing to do with Denis's carping.

All at once, Denis grew quiet. "Darling." He lifted the towel from his shoulder and, tsking, wiped the onion tears off Malcolm's cheeks.

"*Trop de cuisiniers gâtent la sauce!*"

Snapping the towel, he drove Malcolm off.

With the broom and dustpan, Malcolm went to the bedroom to clean up Denis's latest wreck. Oh, the foreign objects he hurled—a copper pot from Turkey, the Egyptian head! The vase was a Limoges.

He stopped in front of the mirror. The damage was centred on his face. He would not have called it a crack. He would have said it was a web. With each of his features caught between the strands, fragmented and at the same time brought together, he looked positively Cubist.

This was not the first time he had looked into this

very mirror and seen something not quite right. One day years ago Malcolm found himself standing before it after work, blinking and rubbing at his eye, then lifting the lid and with a finger very gently touching the membrane to extract the irritant—a minute particle of hair no longer than a two-day-old whisker. His eye stung from the salt on his finger and he had to purge it with more blinking. Probably because he had never before stood so close to that mirror for so long, he only then noticed that where the glass met the oval frame there was a liquid-looking discoloration, flat and unreflective as molten lead. In the worst of these patches the paint had chipped away entirely, exposing the wood backing and the illusion. Across the whole surface were scattered blemishes like mildew.

The simplest method of repair would have been to replace the mirror, but Malcolm took it first to a man who restored old furniture, nearby on the Rue des Francs-Bourgeois. He unscrewed the door and carried it down the street, suspecting the whole way that resilvering mirrors might be a dead art, like illuminating manuscripts or painting frescoes. But no, the man laid the door on a bench and with a few tools unfastened the mirror. With Malcolm holding it steady, he stood the glass up between them, its reflecting side facing Malcolm, Malcolm looking at himself. He must have been in his early forties then, a few threads of grey just starting to show at his temples, the different-textured strands, less obedient than the darker, springing up as if feeling for the light.

Before his very eyes, he disappeared. In one stroke, his face was swept away.

Then the man took the glass from a very rattled Malcolm, laid it down flat on the bench and began brushing his hands together. Stuck all over him were scales off the mirror, little scintillant flecks of Malcolm's reflection.

In the kitchen, Denis was singing as he cooked, "*Heureuse, comme tout ... Heureuse, malgré tout ...,*" the heady perfume of garlic and onions wafting through. Blue shards of vase lay scattered at Malcolm's feet. So the sky was falling, too, he thought.

3

In Paris, he used to work with Denis in the salon they owned and ran together. Now he worked in the morning for a woman named Faye whose salon, Faye's of Kerrisdale, stood on the avenue between the delicatessen and the Shopper's Drug Mart. Weeks before he actually walked in and asked for a job, he had noticed Faye's, marvelled at it even—the plastic flowers and plastic smocks and the sun-faded sign that read WE ALSO STYLE WIGS. It had seemed to Malcolm that this was where he would have been all along had he trained in Canada in the fifties and stayed.

Faye, stationed behind the desk when he first entered, looked up at him through big rose-tinted lenses, listening and nodding as he explained himself and his credentials. After he had finished, she did a curious thing. She reached out both hands to him, as if imploring. She was showing him her rings, loose and sliding back and forth, trapped between her swollen knuckle joints.

"This is my lucky day. Sometimes I can hardly get my fingers in the scissors. The standing kills me, too. How about working half the day?"

"Perfect," Malcolm said.

She stood and gave him a hobbling tour. "Here are the smocks, as you can see. The dryers are there. With experience like yours—Paris of all places!—I guess you'll want to charge more." They had come to the sinks. "You have to watch the nozzle on this one. It can shoot off to the side and soak you."

"I'll charge what you charge," Malcolm said.

"You are too good to be true."

Malcolm had been thinking the same thing about her.

"Of course, I don't know if they'll agree. They're old, you know, my girls. All of them." Faye, Malcolm had guessed, must be nearing seventy herself. "They don't like change. You can't even get them to change their hairstyle, let alone their hairdresser."

"We can give it a try."

"We'll have to push them. Of course, you're so young, they just might thrill at the attention."

"Young?" He laughed. "I'm fifty-six."

"Fifty-six! Younger than I thought! How long have you been grey?"

The next morning, Faye was there when he arrived, telling him, "Here he is. The answer to my prayers." She had come early to unlock and get the coffee things assembled—the right number of mugs on the tray with Taster's Choice spooned in so Malcolm only had to add the boiling water. She didn't believe him capable of the task. "I'm sure you've had a hundred pretty girls making you coffee all your life." She scheduled the appointments—everyone seemed to know to phone first thing in the morning—did the accounting from the previous day, then left him on his own until the afternoon.

The clients *were* old, some of them very. His first, Mrs. Parker, required motorized assistance to keep her out and about. Malcolm was laying his own tools across a folded towel when she arrived, hammering faintly on the glass door with her fist. As he hurried over to open up, she reversed the scooter, then drove it in, the tremendous whirring sound it made amplified indoors.

"You are he?" she asked in a voice both sceptical and barely there.

"I am. And you must be—"

"—the guinea pig."

Malcolm, who had to lean down to hear what she said, laughed.

"She's made me go first, hasn't she? I said I'd do it, so long as I wasn't first. But all she did was schedule me a little later, thinking I wouldn't notice."

She pulled off her tam. If he had known her better, Malcolm would have shielded his eyes as a joke. Her hair, besides being flattened by the tam, was the exact shade of an apricot. "I have a bone to pick with Faye now," she muttered, whirring over to a station.

"I'll take you here," said Malcolm, referring to where he had his tools already laid out.

Mrs. Parker said, "Faye does me *here*."

So he simply rolled everything up in the towel and carried it over to Mrs. Parker. "Can I give you a hand?" She took his proffered arm, gripping it tightly. She was, he understood now, as much afraid as cranky.

He swung the chair around for her, but she turned toward the sinks. "Please, Mrs. Parker, have a seat."

"What?" she said. "Aren't you going to shampoo me?"

"Of course, but I thought we'd have a little chat first."

Still clinging to him, she shuffled round. "About what?"

"Why you, of course."

"Me? There's nothing to say!"

36

"Now, now," he chided. "No modesty, please. We are in a house of vanity, after all." He patted the chair back. She laughed then and, letting go of Malcolm to clutch the armrest, dropped herself into the chair.

With her permission, he removed her glasses, then very lightly began to comb out her hair. He was careful not to catch a knot, not to cause her any pain. "How long have you been coming here?"

"Years and years," she said. "Faye took over as my bridge partner after Albert passed away."

"Albert was your husband?"

"Yes. It was years ago he died."

"You miss him just the same, I'm sure."

She looked at Malcolm in the mirror, but could probably not see him clearly. "Oh, I do," she said. "It never goes away."

"You have beautiful bones, Mrs. Parker."

"What?"

"Your bones are your best feature, apart from, of course, your eyes. You were probably aristocratic-looking even as a child."

"I don't know," she said.

"As you're wearing it now, your hair detracts from these assets. We can't see your lovely jawline for all this ... fluff. Might we shorten it?"

"What will Faye say?"

"She has given me *carte blanche*, I assure you."

"All right, then."

Next he hinted at changing her colour. "Something more *subtle*, say?" But he had gone too far. She dug her heels in. "I have been this colour for so long, if I changed it now, people would notice." And she clammed right up, holding lips tight over dentures.

He helped her up and over to the sinks, grandly

covering her with the plastic smock. She leaned back; he was very nearly cradling her, bird-light, in his arms. When was the last time a man had held her like that? Shampooing, he saw the smile come and go, and come again, dreamily.

As he cut, he drew her out again by asking about Mr. Parker. Her eyes, which were deep brown, each iris haloed by a fine line of smoky blue, began to tear up as she talked. The loneliness would never go, she said, but at least she had Mitzi.

"Your daughter?"

"My dog! If my daughter were half as good to me as Mitzi, well, that would be another story, wouldn't it?"

At the end of the hour, he felt he had won her over, or at least got back to where he'd been before mistaken-ly mentioning a change of colour. Mrs. Parker looked a different person. If it were not for the fruity colour, she would have looked chic. Chic!—at what? Eighty? Malcolm, pleased with himself, passed her the hand mirror so she could see herself from all angles as he slowly turned the chair.

"Oh, no," she said. "This is not me at all! I don't like it! Where's my tam?"

The entire morning went like that. They told him in shrill, querulous voices as he worked, "This isn't what Faye does!" their pinched expressions pruning up their faces even more. Though he managed to get each of them to budge a little, each one despaired of the results. It was not going to work out.

Faye's greeting the next morning was the same. "Here he is, the answer to my prayers. The phone has been ringing off the hook."

"Ah," he said, crestfallen. "Complaints."

"They gushed all over Mrs. Parker at the seniors'

centre. She said she hasn't received a compliment in years. She said to tell you that she feels every inch a member of the aristocracy."

That was what brought them back: objective praise for what had seemed to them too radical and strange. And Malcolm's chairside manner, of course, which was impeccable.

"I hear you're hiding a young man in here, Faye!" Mrs. Szabo bellowed later in the week. She crashed her walker through the door. "Where is he, Faye? Let him at me!"

Within the month Malcolm was as worried about Faye's feelings as she had been worried about his. They all wanted him now. "You don't seem to understand," Faye reassured him. "I'm tired."

He came to truly enjoy them, his doting girls clucking their pains over a mug of Taster's Choice. As their hairdresser, he couldn't help but consider them "his." Particularly now that friends were far away and things were so difficult at home, a passionate fondness for them filled him. He had his favourites, a few he cared about especially. Mrs. Parker, the first to be won over, was one of them. Mrs. Soloff was another—dignity personified, her white hair, filamentous, floating in a nimbus around her head. Of course, he adored Faye.

He came in one day and, after hearing that he was the answer to Faye's prayers, swept over on a whim and asked permission to do something he had wanted to do since he'd met her. He reached out and touched the white plastic frames of her glasses with their pink lenses, so outrageous.

"May I?"

"Try them on? Of course."

Gently, he lifted them off her face and slipped them on his own. Turning to the mirror, he let out a cry of mock astonishment, though some of his astonishment was real. Everything *did* look better through rose-coloured glasses. Faye glowed youthfully. The vat of Barbicide blinded him with its blueness. In the mirror, he saw a pimp, but a healthy one, who might pimp another fifty years.

"Faye, this explains a lot about you," he said, handing the glasses back. "I thought you were on Prozac."

"Oh, no! I look on the bright side, Malcolm."

He put a finger on *Monday* in the appointment book. Mrs. Soloff's name was at the top—crossed out. "Did Mrs. Soloff cancel?"

"Yes. Her niece called."

"She's not ill, is she?"

"No. Mr. Soloff passed away."

"Oh, no," said Malcolm, thinking of Mrs. Soloff's fragile form. Made all the more diminutive by an arthritic stoop, she always gave the impression by her pitched-forward posture of listening intently to everything he said. "This is terrible." Soon all his girls would be widows.

They agreed right then that Malcolm would go next door to the delicatessen, have a gift basket made up and take it over. When his next client came in, if Malcolm wasn't back, she'd just have to make do with Faye like she used to.

The neighbourhood had a lot of trees. The streets were named after them and lined with them. Full and leafy when Malcolm and Denis had arrived, they were in their February nakedness now, their branches like a network of veins, the clots of once-hidden nests exposed.

Malcolm rang at Mrs. Soloff's door. Intending only to

leave the basket, he turned and was walking back down the steps when a plump woman of about forty opened the door. "Come in," she called, beckoning to him. Malcolm, coming back up the steps, said, "Really, I just wanted to leave this for Mrs. Soloff."

"Come in," she said again and, passing her in the doorway, Malcolm brushed against her and smelled the clashing scents of hair spray and perfume.

"I'm Elaine, the niece. Who are you?"

"Malcolm. The—"

"Did I see you at the funeral?"

"No. I didn't hear the news until today."

"I didn't think I saw you. I would have remembered."

There was a slight pause while he looked curiously at her. She beamed back, then set the basket on the hall table and helped him with his coat.

"It happened on Friday."

"The funeral?"

"The stroke."

He thought of tiny Mrs. Soloff in the throes of tragedy yet still remembering to get her niece to call her hairdresser and cancel her appointment.

The coat stand was already full, so she laid his overcoat carefully on a pile on an armchair next to the table. Hanging above the armchair, Malcolm noticed a large picture hidden now under a dark cloth. From where he was standing he could see into both the kitchen and the living room where Mrs. Soloff was sitting by the window. He'd never seen her in black. It contrasted sharply with her hair and made her look very pale, almost powdery, as if an exhalation of grief might blow her away. Other people gathered round, children, too, all of them talking in subdued tones. Louder voices came from the kitchen crowded with women preparing food. Suddenly he felt like an intruder and wished he'd been allowed just to leave his offering and go.

"He had a good long life, but that doesn't make it any less sad. You know what a lovely man he was. And what a sense of humour! What he used to say about meeting my aunt? 'A skinny girl at the time.'" She laughed, too loudly. "After all they'd been through, imagine saying that? You know how they met, right?"

"No," said Malcolm.

"In the camps."

"Christ!" He turned away, pressing his eyes. He'd had no idea. She never talked about herself, only her grand-children. He thought of all his ridiculous prattle and felt sick.

"He was a bit of a patron of the arts, too, my uncle. He had this friend Phil Epstein, his accountant or something, who was always telling my uncle that he was throwing good money away. So my uncle started using this guy's name as a synonym for 'Philistine. ' In our family we never said 'Philistine. ' It was always, 'He's such a Phil Epstein. ' You probably know all this, right?"

"No," said Malcolm. "I didn't know him. My connection is to your aunt."

A woman came out of the kitchen and said, "There you are, Elaine." They were mother and daughter, Malcolm could tell. They shared a broad pleasant face and a shade of hair dye.

Elaine introduced him. "This is Malcolm."

"Hello, Malcolm." She took the basket off the hall table. "Did you bring this?"

"Yes."

"That's very nice of you. Elaine? Maybe he wants to

say something to Auntie Rachel. Maybe he wants a cup of coffee."

"I was just going to get you coffee!" Elaine squealed.

"Actually, I don't have the time."

"Well, say something to my aunt at least." She hooked his arm and led him to the living room where everyone turned to look at him.

"Malcolm," said Mrs. Soloff, lifting her head as far as it would go. "You got the message? I'm sorry I couldn't make it."

"I was just telling him about Phil Epstein," said Elaine and laughter filled the room.

"Phil sent flowers," said Mrs. Soloff.

"Get out!" a woman sitting on the carpet said. "He isn't real, is he?"

From the couch, a man began, "While we're on the subject, here's the last joke Dad told me," and everyone turned to listen.

"This little old lady is walking down the street when who does she meet but this little old man she once knew. 'Mr. Epstein!' she cries—" He paused until the laughter had subsided. "'Mr. Epstein! I haven't seen you in years! Where have you been?' 'To tell you the truth,' says Mr. Epstein, 'I've been in prison.' 'Prison!' she exclaims. 'What did you do to get yourself in prison?' 'To tell you the truth, I killed my wife with an axe.' 'Oh, Mr. Epstein,' she says. 'So you're single?'"

Two contradictory emotions coinciding, the whole room cracked up as the box of tissues made its way from hand to hand. Malcolm turned to look at Mrs. Soloff who was laughing and crying, too. He took the opportunity to cross the room, held her small hand, mottled like a bird's egg, and as light. Bending, he whispered, "I'm sorry for your loss."

"Thank you, Malcolm. You're a dear for coming."

Elaine followed him back to the door. "Sure you don't want to stay for coffee?"

"I really can't. I have to get back to work."

She tilted her hair to one side and put on a face of unfeigned disappointment. "We might meet again?" she suggested.

"Yes," said Malcolm. "We might."

She smiled, helping him on with his coat, then brushing at something on the arm, an intimate, caring gesture. "What do you do?"

"I'm a hairdresser."

Instantly, her face fell. Her smile literally slid away. Flushing, she clapped both hands over her mouth—ten long brick-red nails—and made an alarming noise, half snuffle, half squeal, as she leaned into Malcolm's chest. Horrified, glancing back to see if Mrs. Soloff saw her niece in his arms, he hissed, "What is it?"

"I'm embarrassed!"

"Whatever for?"

When she lifted her face, he saw she was trying not to laugh. "I didn't realize you were a ... hairdresser! Oh, God." She took a step back and looked him up and down. "It's so obvious! How stupid could I be? And I even phoned and left a message for you! That was you, wasn't it?"

"Yes."

"You're not Jewish, are you?"

"No," said Malcolm.

She seemed relieved. "At least I didn't get *that* wrong." At ease now, she was suddenly what she really was, a handsome woman who tried too hard. "Never mind," she said, opening the door for him. "Maybe I'll get your card from my aunt. My hair's not right, is it? It's too big, right?"

"It's not doing you justice," admitted the Queen of Tact.

She pressed against him again, in fun now. "I like the way you put that," and Malcolm laughed.

"Can I ask you something?" He pointed to the draped picture above the chair. "Is that your uncle's portrait?"

For a second, she was confused. "Where? That? Oh, no. It's not a picture. It's a mirror."

4

He finished shaving and rinsed the razor under the tap. Lifting off the towel, tucked up for the moment so he could see himself, he dried his face, then carefully refolded the towel around the door of the medicine chest. Every mirror in the apartment draped now with a towel or cloth, like they were in mourning, sitting shivah on the death of their former life.

The sky, too, had a grey cloth tossed over it, he noticed from the bedroom window as he dressed. An inconsolable sky, drab with tragedy. So green, so green, was what they always said about Vancouver, but in perpetual half-light he seemed to lose his ability to distinguish colour. All winter he had felt as if they'd been living in monochrome.

In the dining room, Denis brought him his coffee with unsteady hands and sat down with his list. "I was thinking about *matelote d'anguille* for tonight. It's been years."

"Denis," said Malcolm, valiantly patient, endeavoring not to gag. "*Matelote d'anguille* requires three bottles of Bordeaux."

"It does not. Two Bordeaux, one *vin ordinaire*. And

twenty pearl onions," Denis wrote. He was having difficulty with the pencil and it moved stiffly in his hand.

"Denis! It's too expensive!"

"*Trop cher?*" He looked at Malcolm with pale, mocking eyes and half a smile, then said what he always said when expenses were brought up, "Aren't we worth it?" Malcolm, fingers pressed to his eyes, sighed.

"One Spanish onion," Denis wrote. "Twenty button mushrooms. On the small side. Will you remember or should I write it down?"

"See you in the poorhouse," was Malcolm's offhanded comment. "Of course, you'll still fancy yourself in the City of Light."

He didn't think Denis would catch his meaning, but evidently he did. He let the pencil drop and, after a long stunned moment, turned to Malcolm and asked, "Where am I?" as if only now he had noticed. Abruptly, he rose and stumbled over to the window. "Where are my pigeons? Where are my cats?" He meant the feral courtyard cats that he had used to feed leftovers in newspaper nests. Throwing open the window, he shouted down, "Where are my cats?"

Malcolm hurried over. "Darling, we moved. I told you that." Three sharp blasts—Yvette, *thank Christ*. "Who could that be?" he asked.

"How the hell should I know!" Denis roared.

"It's Yvette, you twit! Come. Let's meet her at the door."

"I don't know any Yvette," Denis muttered. "I don't want to know any Yvette. I don't like the name Yvette."

Malcolm buzzed her in and began coaxing Denis down the hall.

"Where are we going?"

"To let Yvette in."

"Who is Yvette?"

A cursory knock, she opened the door herself, surprised to see them standing there. "Denis." She took a step toward him, ignoring Malcolm as usual and frowning when Denis stepped back.

"Who is that?" Malcolm asked, pointing at Yvette, giddy with dread. "Who is it, Denis?"

"I am not a child," Denis told him coldly. "Do not speak to me in that tone." And like a stubborn child he refused to answer who Yvette was, refused even to look at her. He crossed his arms and shrank up small, ruining his face with petulance.

"Now what?" Malcolm asked in English.

Yvette dropped her purse; it thudded to the floor. She was not about to be refused—denied, thwarted, forgotten. She opened her arms to Denis and drew him close. "I'm Yvette," she told him firmly. "Yvette. Don't you forget it."

He began to sob. "Please. Whoever you are. Take me home."

Malcolm had to go and Yvette waved him off. His presence was not required as far as she was concerned. Even so, he left with reluctance—needlessly, as it turned out. He phoned when he got to Faye's, but the morning's tribulations had already been forgotten. "Nothing is the matter," Denis said brightly, "but it's kind of you to call."

"You wouldn't ever forget me, would you?" asked Malcolm.

"*T'oublier?* Don't be silly."

"Who is there with you?" Malcolm tested.

"*Qui?*" A long pause. "*Un instant.*" Denis set down the receiver; it knocked against the table. And while he was waiting for Denis to come back, Faye tapped him on the shoulder.

"Malcolm, look."

Turning to the window, he had to shut his eyes. Already the words "Faye's of Kerrisdale" were burned in negative on his retina from where the writing on the glass blocked the sun. Denis was not going to remember to come back to the phone, so Malcolm hung up and took Faye's hand, a clutch of knobby sticks in a skin glove.

"Where are we going?" she giggled.

"To a spectacle. Step right up. Hurry. It won't last."

They stepped out onto the sidewalk and turned their white faces to the sun, tilted them to the warmth. Eyes closed, they stood that way for minutes, holding hands. Like the time he had tried on Faye's rose-coloured glasses and felt more hopeful, so too, the sun's effect.

It was still shining when he left work. What Denis needed, Malcolm decided, was to get out into the air, so he went home deliberately empty-handed and announced that he was taking Denis to do the shopping. "I wish you'd take him out from time to time, too," he hinted to Yvette, though he was already familiar with her views on exercise: she wouldn't walk any farther than to and from the car.

Afraid to step over the threshold, Denis clung to the door frame. He reached one foot very tentatively into the hall, as a cat reaching for a goldfish would loathingly dip its paw in water. Yvette and Malcolm each took an arm and led him to the stairs, but on the landing he stiffened. "Down we go, Denis," said Yvette, who was allowed to talk to him like a child. Denis wouldn't budge. He looked like a man being asked to step into oblivion. They had to pry his fingers off the banister. "Ahhhhhhhh," he moaned as they led him down; in his mind, he was plunging.

"What is that awful smell?" he asked when they had finally got him out of the building.

"Spring," Malcolm answered. For months they had been breathing air heady with garlic and wine reducing, and the reek of Yvette's combustibles.

They said goodbye to Yvette, Denis kissing both her cheeks. "A nice woman," he commented after she had driven off. "We must invite her again." Turning, he began his shuffle back toward the apartment, but stopped short when he saw the building. "This is not our place!"

"We're going shopping. Come."

"Shopping?"

"The walk will do you good."

If Denis kept his eyes down and his hands in the pockets of his coat so his arms did not hang down so troglodytically, they looked like any other couple out for a walk on the first sunny day in weeks. The cherry trees were beginning to bloom, the clumps of crocuses open. Robins paced the lawns and yanked stubbornly on worms. But if Denis lifted his eyes and, squinting, looked around, he grew fretful and claimed that they were lost. "No. We're going shopping," Malcolm told him, marvelling that he did not notice any difference between Paris sidewalks and these, free of any obstacle course of dog shit. They passed the seniors' centre and Malcolm spotted Mrs. Parker bombing through the parking lot on her scooter. She didn't see him. She didn't see that far.

"*Nous sommes perdus!*"

He patted Denis's shoulder, then picked a crocus for his lapel. "I know exactly where we're going."

They neared the corner where they would turn onto the avenue of stores. In front of the bank, Denis nudged Malcolm. "Look who's here!" he hissed. Inside, a line of people waited for a teller, none of them familiar. But Malcolm was looking in the bank while Denis was staring at his own nemesis reflected in the smoked glass, a mauve crocus perking in the buttonhole of his coat.

"We'll give him the slip." He took Denis's elbow and hustled him around the corner. "Is he following?"

Denis looked over his shoulder. "*Non.*"

They went first into the bakery where Denis seemed immediately less anxious. Around food, he felt at home. He began chatting to the girl behind the counter, a young thing susceptible to charm, who stood listening, rapt and comprehending not a word. To Malcolm she said, "It's French, right? I took French in school, but only remember a few words."

"Say something to him."

"I can't."

"Go on. Try."

"*Je t'aime beaucoup,*" she blurted, then reddened.

Delighted by this impromptu declaration, Denis reached across the counter for her hand. He pressed it to his lips, murmuring, "*Je vous aime aussi,*" and when they left, Denis with a baguette under his arm, everyone smiled after them.

"*Au revoir!*" chimed the girl.

"Must you always do that?" Malcolm asked, pretending to be annoyed.

"*Quoi?*"

"Collect admirers everywhere we go. I can't take you anywhere it seems."

"Bah," said Denis, smiling. "*Elle est bête, la pauvre.*"

Outside the fish store they found a dog tied to a parking meter, a golden Labrador deep in mourning with its muzzle stretched out long on its yellow paws. When Denis stopped to console it, it lifted its despairing wet brown eyes.

Malcolm stepped inside, for the first time noticing how many reflective surfaces there were in the shop: the chrome edging and the glass on the cases, the black counters, the mirror behind the cash register. In any one of them Denis might see himself, so Malcolm stuck his head out the door where Denis was standing with hands on his hips talking to the dog.

"And does she often tie you up like this?"

The dog was sitting up now. It jerked its muzzle.

"Denis? Will you wait right there?"

He didn't seem to hear. Anyway, Malcolm would be able to keep one eye on him from inside the store. Another customer ahead of him, he had to wait. Then the fish seller turned to Malcolm and, clapping his hands together, said, "Have I got a beaut for you today."

He beckoned Malcolm over to the far case where, on a bed of crushed ice, next to a jumble of smiling clams, the eel lay, slick and black with an ostentatious ruff of gills. "A dandy," Malcolm agreed.

"Close to five pounds," said the fish seller and he whistled a long downhill note.

"Nothing smaller?" asked Malcolm.

The man looked disappointed. "I thought you'd go crazy for it."

"Wrap it up then."

He lifted the thing out of the case by the scruff and carried it dangling over to the scale. "Four and three quarters."

"Christ," Malcolm said.

Paying, he saw from the corner of his eye the owner of the dog untying it from the parking meter, but by the time he'd got his change and left the store, Denis was nowhere to be seen.

Next door was a lingerie shop, which seemed a logical place for Denis to have stepped into. "Did a man come in here?" Malcolm asked the woman sorting brassieres on hangers.

"When?"

"Just a second ago. Smallish with silver hair. A lock hanging in his eyes. Gorgeous, really. Doesn't ring a bell?"

She started to laugh.

He entered every shop, every café on that side of the street and asked if Denis had been in. It seemed impossible that a man who paused again and again for bearings he would never retrieve could have gotten very far. Yet he was gone, vanished.

"He was carrying a loaf of French bread and had a crocus in his lapel."

"Sorry."

"He would have been speaking French."

They all shook their heads.

Then he couldn't be on the avenue. Probably he'd wandered off down a side street, likely following the dog. As soon as Malcolm realized this, he stopped looking for Denis and began searching for the dog, for the yellow flag of its tail. He retraced his steps back to the fish store, turned down the closest street, walking fast. He would get a dog for Denis. Why hadn't he got one before?

At the corner, he stopped to ask a man digging in his garden if he'd seen it.

"A golden Lab?" He shrugged. "Lost? That's too bad."

Lost, but really, was there any need for Malcolm to be sweating so profusely, for his heart to be in his throat? They would be used to wanderers in a neighbourhood home to so many elderly. What was the worst thing that could happen to Denis? True, he could be hit by a car, but more than likely he'd charm his way into someone's kitchen. Probably he was this very moment asking where they kept the lard.

He kept looking for the yellow dog, looking, and after he had walked up and down for an hour he went back home and called Yvette.

No one answered. She would, he remembered, be breast-feeding the judge.

He phoned the police and in thirty minutes they returned his call. "We've got your man," the officer chuckled, "but we can't seem to convince him to get into the car."

"I'll be right there," said Malcolm. "Are you far?"

They were barely four blocks away, on the train track, sitting on the rail. In his lap, all that was left of the baguette was the heel.

"What in the world are you doing?"

Denis couldn't answer. He seemed completely dazed.

"You've gone and eaten all the bread!" chided Malcolm, who couldn't have cared less about it.

"*Non, non.* I was feeding the pigeons."

He took Denis's arm, helped him to his feet and thanked the officer who seemed bemused by the scene.

"Need a lift home?"

"We'll walk."

They made their slow way back, in silence, beside the tracks. Soon they came to a bit of bread, and then another. Then Malcolm saw that Denis had been breaking off pieces to mark a trail. Here, on the ties, a crow, so black it looked dyed, was choking down a piece.

Hands on his hips, he stood watching Grace snuffle the perimeter of the sandbox, watching with distaste. She had been with them weeks now, at their table perched on Denis's lap accepting morsels off his fork, burrowing between them in their bed, curling next to Denis's neck, her stump in Malcolm's face. The sound of Mrs. Parker's motorized scooter came into earshot, nearly drowning out her faint hail.

"Malcolm!"

On colder days, Mrs. Parker wore her chenille tam at a rakish angle, but now she had taken it off, revealing hair Malcolm had finally been allowed to rid of its apricot tint. Mitzi, her chihuahua, rode in the scooter basket. Malcolm lifted down the dog, then offered Mrs. Parker assistance in dismounting.

"We must stop meeting like this, Mrs. P."

She gripped his forearm, fixing on him a flirty look. Within minutes the elegant Mrs. Rodeck joined them with Hugh, her epileptic pug. Mrs. Rodeck used to wear a fall, but Malcolm had changed all that as well. Then Miss Velve arrived, Miss Velve who looked like some necky waterbird. For decades she had run an antique shop on the boulevard, specializing in not quite complete sets of English china and Coronation mugs. "Gone to walk the dog," read the card taped on her shop door at this time every day.

The dogs sniffed each other's backsides—they did it in a ring—and the ladies didn't seem to find this behaviour smutty in the least. "Look," said Miss Velve. "Look what Malcolm's done to Grace."

Mrs. Rodeck clucked. "Isn't that the cutest thing?"

He had put on her a rhinestone collar and combed

up and tied with a bow the wiry hairs that fell into her eyes, not so much to prettify her as to play up the ridiculous kind of dog she was. When Grace's eyes didn't show, you couldn't see the brown matter that they wept.

"Adorable," said Mrs. Parker and Grace's ears pricked up. She answered to flattery of any kind. Malcolm could even summon her by calling, "Vanity, Vanity," in a saccharine voice. Bouncing over to Mrs. Parker, she began her grotesque little jig, rising onto her hind legs, pawing the air. The stump in back of her—the size of a man's thumb severed at the knuckle, covered with long dun hairs—wiggled as she peed.

"Aren't you precious? Aren't you precious?" cooed Mrs. Parker.

Mrs. Rodeck's pug thundered over, pop-eyed with jealousy, slathering, and knocked Grace aside. The ladies laughed and groaned and the pug looked around, confused. His lips were too large, loosest at the corners, almost fluted, pebbly-textured, moist. The pug's mouth at the corners reminded Malcolm of blackened female genitalia. He looked away, to Grace splayed pornographically as she cleaned herself. He avoided ever looking at Miss Velve's Lady; she had an outrageous growth dangling underneath. The chihuahua wandered in a seemingly inoffensive circle, except that in the few short weeks that Malcolm had been a dog walker, he'd learned to recognize the signs preliminary to defecation. He had a moment like this every day, when he didn't know *where* to look.

"Malcolm?" Miss Velve asked girlishly. "Could you pretty Lady up, do you think?"

"He could take his scissors and cut off that—"

"Mrs. Rodeck!" Miss Velve roared in her real voice,

the one that evicted over-browsers from her store. "You know that it's benign!"

When the dogs had finished what they were there for, the pug kicking out behind himself with pride, plastic bags were produced from coat pockets and purses and Malcolm, ever the gallant, offered to do Mrs. Parker's dirty work. It was so difficult for her to stoop. Their rendezvous over, they said goodbye until tomorrow.

Last week Mrs. Soloff had told him, "This group you meet when you walk your dog? They think you love dogs, too. They think you feel the same way they do. But you don't. You are an impostor. Am I right or am I wrong?"

Mrs. Soloff was long ago a Russian, before worse things happened to her; this lent some gravity to her words. Malcolm, feeling both guilty and accused, asked, "Do you think I should confess?"

He had been bad-mouthing Grace, casting himself and the dog in comic anecdotes—some outright lies, others mere hyperbole—with Malcolm playing a world-weary Jeeves catering to the childish and self-indulgent whims of Grace. He was no kinder to her canine friends.

"Confess?" She shook her head slowly, a pinched look on her face. "Why disappoint them? They're old and alone. Probably you make their day. But you *are* an impostor. Yes?"

"Mrs. Soloff, you always call a spade a spade."

She shrugged, then asked to know what happened during walkies that week and seemed amused by what he said. At least she smiled and did not annul it, as she so often did, by shaking her head and wincing. Mrs. Soloff was barely out of mourning. Because of this, Malcolm saved the high jinks for Faye.

"Here he is, the answer to my prayers. How are you this morning, Malcolm?"

"Elated."

Her pencilled-in eyebrows lifted curiously above the big white squares of her glasses frames. "What happened?"

"It's Grace," he said. "She has come through for me at last."

"Explain," said Faye.

He hung up his coat. "You remember Mitzi?"

"Elsa Parker's dog?"

"Right. Well, you know she's legally blind."

"I didn't. Do you want a coffee? I think you have time."

"Do I? All right."

Faye started to rise.

"I'll get it. You sit right there." The coffee stand was in the reception area. Malcolm plugged in the kettle. "And you remember Hugh."

"The pug."

"Epileptic, or so Mrs. Rodeck claims. We have yet to witness a seizure. And then there's Lady with her growth."

"Where is this growth you're always talking about?"

"On Lady."

"Where on Lady?"

"Don't make me say. Suffice it to know that its placement brings into question her very name."

Faye stared at him.

"It's pendulous," he hinted.

"Malcolm."

The kettle started to shriek. "There's the kettle!" he sang and turned away.

Already Faye was laughing. The phone rang and she answered, telling whoever was calling, "Is tomorrow all right? No, it's not you, dear. It's Malcolm. He's got me in stitches here." Hanging up, she hissed, "That was Gwen Velve!"

"Miss Velve! Get away!"

"Her ears must have been burning!"

"Not hers. Lady's!" He brought over the coffee and Faye lifted her glasses and daubed her eyes before she took a sip. "Please, Malcolm," she begged. "Tell me where it is."

He made a show of relenting. "All right, but don't ever mention it to Miss V. It's a teat gone berserk. A rear teat. It hangs almost to the ground."

Faye grimaced. "Why doesn't she have it taken off?"

"It's benign! I don't believe that's the reason. She wants to fuss. Hugh has his supposed epilepsy."

"Aren't they silly?" said Faye. "What about Grace? What's the matter with her?"

"This is why I'm so overjoyed. Up until now I've had to stand there every day adding nothing to the conversation. You can imagine how difficult that is for me. 'Poor Hugh,' says Mrs. Rodeck." He imitated Mrs. Rodeck's Britishness. "'He had another fit.' 'What about Mitzi?' Mrs. Parker counters. 'She fell down the stairs.' You get the picture? Well, Grace, she has an annoying habit, but it never occurred to me before that I might elevate it to a condition."

He paused, toying.

"What?" asked Faye.

"She piddles," he said.

Faye slapped her knobby hand down on the desk and snorted.

"Particularly when she's happy. She dribbles everywhere. When you call her name, she positively gushes. I'd put it down to youth or excitability, but now I see it's much more serious. Grace is incontinent, Faye. Incontinent. She simply cannot hold it."

"Oh, Malcolm," said Faye, wiping the tears off her cheeks.

"I plan to make an announcement this afternoon and eclipse them all."

But he didn't say anything to them. He would never have risked hurting their feelings. For all he knew, they might be similarly inconvenienced. And after Mrs. Rodeck and Miss Velve had left and he was helping Mrs. Parker back on her scooter, he was especially glad he hadn't.

Balanced in her rear basket was a garbage bag stuffed full. "What's that?" he asked.

"Just a few old clothes I'm giving away."

"Ah," he said, offering her his hand.

"I thought I might give them to you."

"To me?"

"Yes. You're about his height. I can't throw them out, you see? I'd like to think someone nice got some use out of them."

He untied the bag, reached in and pulled out a tail of yellowed silk. It was an aviator's scarf. As he wound it around his neck, Mrs. Parker's smiled.

"It's monogrammed. Here, see? A.E.P."

"Albert?" said Malcolm.

"That's right. How sweet of you to remember."

He found Denis and Yvette as he'd left them when he'd picked up the dog a half-hour before—Yvette reclining on the couch, her doughy feet in Denis's lap, Denis rubbing worms of dead skin and dirt out from between her toes. She always wore a badge now, with her name and a surely ironic happy face.

Denis looked up, saw Grace and immediately let Yvette's feet fall. "What have we here?" his delighted cry, Grace responding in a volley of yaps and dampening the doormat.

"*Elle est mignonne!* Who does she belong to?"

"You."

"*Moi?*" cried Denis. He swept her, still trickling, off her clawed feet. "*Mais tu n'aimes pas les chiens.* What in the world possessed you?"

"I did it for you."

"*Tu n'aimes pas les chiens.*"

He let her lick his face all over with her pink tongue and Malcolm, watching, felt a tinge of jealousy.

"Who does she belong to?" Denis asked.

"You. What are you going to name her?"

He clutched her shaggy muzzle and turned it left and right. Grace whimpered. "She looks like a Mireille."

"Very nice," said Malcolm. "Grace suits her."

"*Oui.* Grace."

Denis took her into the living room to show Yvette. "*Regarde. Voici Annabelle. Elle est mignonne, n'est-ce pas?*"

Which reminded Malcolm that Denis's condition did have its element of bliss. Every time Denis saw Grace, he saw her for the first time. With each encounter, he was freshly smitten. And the mileage Malcolm had gotten out of the Phil Epstein joke! He told it to Denis in translation almost every night. At the punch line, "So Mr. Epstein? You're single?" Denis nearly died laughing.

Malcolm took the bag of clothes to the bedroom where he found the bed, as usual, unmade—no hope that Yvette might have, on a whim, straightened it. Out of the bag he pulled a camel-hair overcoat and laid it on the rumpled covers, then a cashmere sweater ruined by moths. He could put a finger in a hole and have it go right through, as if Albert Parker had met his demise by being strafed by bullets. Ties and shirts, camphorous, but otherwise in good condition, a maroon dressing gown with broad quilted lapels, then something really fine. Peering into the bottom of the bag, he saw the tangled black sleeves and legs and tails of what turned out to be a tuxedo.

"Malcolm?" Denis was calling. "Malcolm? *Où es-tu?*"

"In the bedroom."

He heard Denis in the hallway opening the door to the linen cupboard because he didn't remember where the bedroom was.

"*Ici!*" Malcolm called and when Denis appeared in the doorway, he was just slipping the dressing gown on over his clothes.

"My!" said Denis. "Where did you get that? *Mon Dieu, que tu es beau!*"

He lifted the towel off the dresser mirror and saw for himself how distinguishing a garment it was. All he needed now was a pipe and a leather-bound copy of Proust.

"Did Yvette leave?"

"*Oui.* Are you angry?"

"Not yet. Try something on, why don't you?"

Because of the clumsiness that had infected Denis's fingers, Malcolm undid his buttons for him, lifted the shirt off his shoulders and helped slide his arms out of the sleeves. He could still get out of his pants on his own, but didn't know when to stop, kept on going, stepping awkwardly out of his briefs. Trying to shake the snare of them off one ankle, he teetered and Malcolm reached out to steady him.

"My God. What happened to your ass?"

"*Quoi?*" asked Denis.

"It's disappeared!" He had noticed the same thing about himself a few months ago getting out of the shower. "First we lose our looks, then we lose what's left behind."

Denis looked over his shoulder at his flattened, diminished buttocks reflected in the uncovered mirror—so it was only his face he objected to. He grabbed a cheek in each hand, pumping them like bellows, the asterisk of his anus winking.

The shirt that Malcolm lifted off the bed was much too large for Denis. He had to roll the sleeves and, with Denis balancing against his shoulder, help him step into the trousers.

"*A gauche, n'est-ce pas?*"

He tucked the long shirt tails in, then, surprised, he drew back his hand from inside the band.

"Denis."

This had not happened in such a long time, not during waking hours, only early in the morning as Denis slept against Malcolm's back. If Malcolm happened to wake to that gentle, involuntary nudge, he would grapple with himself, then smear his own semen on his face. If he had had fewer scruples, he could have involved Denis in the tussle, but how to exact consent from a person who, in a moment, might forget what he'd consented to? He tried not to hope now, tried to put it out of his mind, yet the thought of being tenderly buggered by a man in a tuxedo, while wearing a dressing gown of maroon silk, simply engorged him with hope.

He went on dressing Denis, got down on his hands and knees to roll the trouser cuffs, his hands trembling as he touched Denis's feet. His feet were the only part of him that really showed his age. Crusted around the heels with flaky rinds, toe knuckles like knobs, each inordinately hairy, they were the feet of an ancient. Clutching each slender ankle, Malcolm pressed his lips to Denis's insteps.

The first time he saw Denis was in a Paris train station in 1959. He was coming over from London, where he'd trained, on a recommendation from a friend who knew a certain Denis opening a new salon. If, back then, Malcolm ever found himself in a crowd, he would scan it and in his imagination pick someone out to love. He saw among the throng there a man of boyish build with a woman's wrists and fair hair cow-licked up, then falling over one eye. He did not know he was the very man he'd come to see. Then, like in all Malcolm's romantic dreams, the one he had picked chose him too, came right up and said, "Ello," the dropped "h" an indulgence Malcolm would never have allowed himself in his already too dubious dreams.

Gallantly, Denis lifted up his suitcase. He jangled when he walked. It was the music of loose change in his pockets. Leaving the station, he fished out the coins and gave them to a beggar girl. Malcolm would remember that they left in a procession, Denis radiantly in the lead sowing his beneficence, Malcolm, already besotted, trailing, while stray dogs joined the queue behind. Denis was beautiful. Denis was good. He was touchingly hairless. He taught Malcolm how to love.

And there was Malcolm still—on his hands and knees grovelling. He didn't dare look up. Dizzily, he rose, took the tuxedo jacket with its wide silk lapels and the black pleated cummerbund from the bed. Once Denis was in it and the dangling sleeves tucked up, the black bow tie knotted, he was transformed. He looked Continental again, instead of like a man who had no idea what continent he lived on.

Straightening the tie, Malcolm met Denis's gaze. "My, you look dapper," he said. Denis smiled and it seemed that he was all there.

"A glass of port?" Malcolm suggested.

"*Certainement.*"

In the living room, Malcolm stepped out of his pants, left them in a heap before the sideboard as he walked off with the decanter. Already he'd sprung out of the dressing gown, could possibly have carried the tray on his tumid cock. He couldn't recall ever being that magnificent.

They simply had to smoke; in those costumes, it was obligatory. They used to, Denis straddling Malcolm's thighs, holding his exhausted cock up by the head, making as if to torture it with the lit end of his Gitane. Each time he brought the burning end up close, Malcolm stiffened with an exquisite terror. In minutes, they were back at it again.

He picked through Yvette's butts in the saucers, searching for something not smoked to the filter. Down the hallway with the tray, on the way he slipped into the bathroom for a jar of something once purchased on a whim in Boulevard de Clichy. The whole contents of the medicine cabinet clattered into the sink, knocked by the towel draping the mirror.

In the bedroom, Denis was standing exactly where he had been, looking marvellous, but clearly he'd forgotten what they were up to. He was gazing around blankly, but as soon as he saw Malcolm in the robe, he brightened. "Where did you get that? *Mon Dieu, que tu es beau!*"

"*Asseyez-vous.*" Malcolm gestured to the unmade bed and Denis sat down. "*Cigarette?*"

"*Oui.*"

Malcolm puffed at it first to fill the atmosphere with

atmosphere, then handed it to Denis and bowed close with the other unlit between his own lips. The spark transferred, the port poured, he joined Denis on the bed where, ringingly, they touched their glasses together.

Denis picked up something that was lying on the crumpled sheet between them. By the colour, it belonged to Malcolm. Holding it close to his face, squinting, Denis said, "*Quel trésor.*" They both laughed, remembering, and Denis abandoned the cigarette in the ashtray and began sucking on the pubic hair instead.

"*Monsieur?*" Malcolm let his hand graze Denis's lap, but to his crushing disappointment, nothing rose to meet it.

Denis shone upon on him nonetheless. "*Après vous,*" he urged.

"*Êtes-vous certain?*"

"*Oui, oui. C'est mon plaisir.*" Invitingly, he lifted his arms and lay back on the bed. Malcolm undid the tuxedo waistband, with difficulty now that his hands were shaking. And the recalcitrant lid of the jar taken from his pocket—at first he couldn't budge it, then it flew off and rolled ticking across the floor never to be recovered. No matter, he would not need it in the future. This would be their last time, Malcolm knew it.

Enter the bitch. Yapping shrilly, she charged, Denis's whole body tightening when he heard her, and Malcolm, gripped, coming. Coming to a ruined moment—to little needle teeth in his calf, to Denis calling out a name that wasn't his.

6

Each question the doctor asked, Malcolm translated. "Where are we now?"

"Paris," Denis answered, and the doctor, after muttering that he wished that were the case, asked him the date.

"I've never known the date without looking at the appointment book." He turned to Malcolm. "Isn't that so?"

"How old are you?"

"Fifty," his smug reply, and Malcolm let loose a laugh.

"Count with me," said the doctor. "Backward, by sevens. One hundred, ninety-three, eighty-six, seventy-nine ..."

"*Soixante-dix-neuf* ..." said Malcolm.

"*Quatre-vingts*," continued Denis, "*quatre-vingt-un, quatre-vingt-deux, quatre-vingt-trois—*"

"Thank you."

Denis flashed a triumphant look at Malcolm.

"Tell me, Mr. Cassel, what does the expression, 'Where there's smoke, there's fire,' bring to mind?"

Malcolm translated this as, "*Point de feu sans fumée.*"

"Well, that's evident," said Denis. "Smoke, yes. Fire."

They sat waiting for him to elaborate, and by the way his nearly transparent eyebrows came together and his gaze rested in middle space, he seemed to be thinking. But no, he was only looking at something on the desk. Leaning forward in his chair, he picked up the doctor's coffee mug.

"What is that you've got there?" the doctor asked, and Denis really began to think. A plain blue mug, luckily it was empty, because Denis began to turn it around and over in his hands, studying it from below, looking down inside it, even touching the unglazed ring on the bottom, feeling for the answer. The handle's purpose eluded him completely. He held it to his eye and peered through it. Malcolm, watching with shocked fascination, had to bite his tongue to stop himself from blurting, "It's a mug, you twit." And all at once there rose in him an intense paternal urge to protect Denis—from his own foolishness, and from the doctor, the sadist who had set him up like this. When he turned to confront the doctor though, he had to admit there was nothing mocking in his manner. He was younger than both Malcolm and Denis and had an intensely sympathetic face.

Shrugging, Denis set the mug back down on the desk. "I don't know what it is. It doesn't say."

Malcolm translated this for the doctor, who didn't laugh or smirk or react in any way, simply resumed his questioning. "How about, 'Too many cooks spoil the broth'?"

"*Trop de cuisiniers gâtent la sauce.*"

Denis laughed and turned to Malcolm. "You know how I like to be alone in the kitchen!"

"'Love me, love my dog'?"

It took Malcolm a moment before he could remember the equivalent expression. "*Qui aime Bertrand, aime son chien.*"

That the doctor thought was funny.

"Who is Bertrand?" Denis asked.

"It's uncanny," said Malcolm, "You've picked proverbs that seem to resonate for us."

"Really? I just take them from a book. Do you notice how he's unable to interpret them? His thinking has become quite literal."

Strange that he would need this pointed out to him, but he did. Malcolm stared at the doctor for a second. So his life's companion was now a literal thinker. Was literal thinking any worse than, say, wandering the apartment half the night or hurling things at mirrors? Yes, it was. He knew it was. On Denis's behalf, he felt bereft. He could not imagine a life without metaphor.

Disregarding the presence of the doctor, he reached over and took Denis's hand. Although he didn't know it yet, it would be the last time he felt for him an unadulterated pity.

Denis had always been an elegant dresser. He would spend half of what he made on wine and food, the other half on clothes; what was left they lived on—Malcolm's share. But now he needed to be told what to do. Getting dressed an abstruse procedure, an enigma of arm and leg holes, of baffling fasteners; he needed Malcolm to pass him each article in the right order with clear instructions on how to get into it and a hand on his shoulder for support. Some mornings he would send Malcolm pridefully away, then make his appearance in an ingenious permutation of dress.

The morning when everything really began to come apart, Malcolm heard Denis moving up and down the hall, opening and closing all the doors. This went on for many minutes, so by the time Denis stumbled upon the kitchen, he was simmering with frustration. Instead of his usual lost, endearing look, he wore a glare—and his undershorts over top of his trousers, his sweater backwards and inside out, seams showing, the label under his chin, as if he'd been sewn into it and tagged.

Malcolm laughed. He couldn't help it. It was his sense of humour, after all, that kept him sane. "You look dapper," he told Denis.

"*Qui-êtes vous?*" Denis replied.

Malcolm started, though he'd known about this moment years before. You see the pin, you see the balloon and know there will be an explosion, and yet you jump. He opened his mouth to answer: if Denis didn't

68

recognize him, at least he would know his voice. But his mouth was suddenly too dry, his tongue a desiccated leather tongue out of an old shoe; no words issued forth. Numerous times he swallowed before he was able to whisper his own name. "Malcolm. The love of your life." His voice was quavering with dread.

"*Menteur*," said Denis, backing away. "Malcolm!" he shouted. "Malcolm!"

"It's me! I'm right here!" But Denis did not believe him. "Smell me," said Malcolm, coming over.

Denis retreated to the corner, looking wildly around for a place to run. Malcolm thought they would come to blows again, the way Denis was holding his hands out to protect himself, but Grace heard him and came to his call, yammering hysterically at his feet, distracting him, her sole purpose in their lives. Denis stared down at her a second, which allowed Malcolm to get his wrist under Denis's nose.

Denis pushed his hand away. So? said his eyes. "You use the same cologne. Malcolm isn't old. *Malcolm n'est pas vieux.*"

He got to the salon and, after hanging up Albert Parker's camel-hair overcoat, went directly to the mirror. It had been years since he'd really seen himself. Certainly he had looked in the mirror—to shave, to dress; he'd even stood on this very spot and laughed at himself wearing Faye's glasses, but he had been looking at the glasses. The years he'd been caring for Denis, he'd tried very hard to understand how he perceived things, to live the nightmare with him and make it less frightening for them both. But in doing so he'd forgotten about himself, and now it did seem as if a stranger was standing there on the silver side of the glass.

It must have been going on for years. Half the brown hair had converted. And what the hell had happened to his face? With his fingertips, he propped up the loosened flesh, leaned close to the mirror, fogging it with his breath. On Sunday nights he had used to lie with his head in Denis's lap, a steaming cloth over his face. Denis would bend and extract with a deft clean-fingered tenderness the dark plugs from Malcolm's pores. Now Malcolm looked a wreck.

He went to the back room and found Faye there sorting a heap of clothes into two cardboard boxes. "Oh. Hello, Malcolm," she said. "You're early."

"I need you to do a favour for me, Faye."

"Certainly," she said, quietly, without reservation.

Malcolm scanned the cluttered shelves. A rinse would do, he thought. He handed Faye the box.

"What? You think brunette would suit me better?" she asked.

"Me. I'm suddenly feeling my age."

When she realized what he was asking, she shook her head. "I'm used to working on the ladies, but all right."

He got himself into a smock, sat at the sink, a plastic daisy field across his front, and leaned back. Faye looked down on him long and hard, elderly from that vantage. Faye, she was old.

"Are you sure you want to do this?" she asked.

"I have no choice really."

"Malcolm," she tsked, "you say the strangest things."

She turned on the faucet, touching his head at the same time as the warm water, so it seemed as if a tremendous warmth was emanating from her hands. He closed his eyes, feeling her stroking fingers wet down his scalp. How could they change *her* for *him*, he wondered of his clients. How could they accept a touch less good than this?

The dye, squeezed out of bottle, by contrast felt icy cold.

"All right," she said, and he sat up. She blotted his temples with a tissue to stop the staining. That, too, felt comforting. "There you go." She passed him a hand mirror. "I can't say as I like it. It's harsh."

"Yes," Malcolm agreed. "It is."

A quarter hour later, when Mrs. Parker came in for her weekly wash and set, he'd had time to dry his hair. "You seem different today," she said, recognizing the tie Malcolm was wearing, but not quite putting her arthritic finger on the real change. "You remind me of someone I knew a long time ago."

All morning Faye stayed in the back room. Malcolm did wonder briefly what she was doing, but was too preoccupied worrying whether the dye would appease Denis's doubts to take a minute to go and ask. He ducked back only to say goodbye before he left for the day.

"Can you sit down a minute?" she asked. "I need to talk to you."

He sat.

"Have I ever mentioned George to you?" she asked.

"No," he said, all at once noticing how dispirited she seemed. She was upset. A fine mist clouding her rose-coloured lenses, she removed them, folding the white arms with a click and setting them in her lap. She waved a hand toward one of the boxes. "Those are his clothes, if you want them."

He took her frail hand. "Faye. I'm sorry. When did it happen?"

"It's not what you think. He left years ago and all this time I've had his things. Just in case he came back for them, you know. I didn't want to seem a spoil-sport."

"My God, Faye," said Malcolm. "He must have been mad to leave you."

"You're sweet. Please take them."

Mrs. Parker had started some kind of trend. Faye was the third woman to offer him the clothes of a departed male. "What? You want to see me every day dressed up like the rogue?"

She flushed and could not seem to look at him. "How are your finances, Malcolm?"

The first thing he thought, ever the optimist, ever deluded, was that she was offering him a raise along with her absconded husband's clothes, something he could certainly have used. He made a joke. "I find myself, as usual, teetering on the brink."

"So you couldn't buy the place?"

She lifted her hand out of his and showed him her crooked fingers getting worse. The neighbourhood was turning hip. A buyer, she said, had approached her.

At that moment Malcolm realized just how happy he'd been there, as happy as was possible, considering the circumstances. He'd dedicated himself to his clients, gazed affectionately into their lined and wobbling faces. He owed so much to them; collectively, they had saved him by saving his pride. Just now, how Mrs. Parker had thrilled to see him step into the mirror wearing that familiar ascot. He tried to picture them, grey, white and blue, climbing aboard a city bus for the first time in decades, heading out of Kerrisdale in search of the good, old-fashioned wash and set. Impossible. Mrs. Parker rode a scooter, Mrs. Szabo used a walker, a number required canes.

"You can't abandon them," he said, pressing his eyes, teary not only for himself, but for his biddies, too.

"Absolutely not," said Faye. "I've put a clause in. You'll get to rent a chair."

All the way home—a daze. He couldn't quite take it in. He even forgot he'd dyed his hair until he walked into the apartment and caused Yvette to shriek, "*Câlisse!*"

She thought someone was breaking in.

But Denis knew him at once and threw him a radiant smile. "Oh, hello, Malcolm! It's you! Are you angry?"

Malcolm nearly broke down and wept.

Perhaps everything would work out after all, for the time being at least. He might have lost Faye, but he had won back Denis. That germ, hope, was infecting him again. The leash was attached to the dog waiting to go out. She stood there with her tongue out. Even she was smiling.

They would dine at the oddest hours, depending on when Denis was moved to cook—eleven o'clock at night, three o'clock in the morning—but when they sat down to dinner on that particularly memorable night, it was at a perfectly sensible hour, seven o'clock in the evening. Before each of them was a wide-lipped bowl, a slice of French bread fried in butter waiting in it. Denis ladled out the stew. The bread drank it up.

"*Bon appétit*," he said, lifting his spoon to sip.

Malcolm swirled his wine glass, staring down at the heady, alcoholic broth. This had used to be his favourite dish, but lately it tasted more and more like bile. "Oh, I know!" he said. "Would you like to hear a joke?"

Denis leaned forward to listen.

"This old Jewish lady is walking down the street

when she sees, on the bench at the bus stop, a man she used to know—a Mr. Epstein. 'Mr. Epstein!' she cries out in delight. 'It's me, Mabel Goldberg. I haven't seen you in years!'"

Denis frowned.

"'Mabel,' he tells her. 'It's true. I haven't been around.' 'Where have you been?' 'To prison,' says Mr. Epstein. 'Prison!' cries Mabel. 'What did you do?' 'I killed my wife,' he confesses, and Mabel brightens. 'Killed your wife? Why then Mr. Epstein, you must be single.'"

Malcolm thought he had told it pretty well. Every night, he changed the joke a little, just to amuse himself. But Denis wasn't laughing. He was looking in his bowl, wearing a disgusted expression, as if he'd finally grown sick of everything: the joke, the *matelote d'anguille*.

"What's the matter?" asked Malcolm. "Don't you think it's funny any more?"

"*Non*," Denis said. "I don't like jokes about Jews."

Malcolm was taken aback. Denis had never criticized him that way before and he felt unfairly accused of something. "A very nice man told me that joke," he said. "The son of a client and Jewish himself. He told it in a room probably full of Jews and everyone laughed. No one thought it was offensive in the least."

The way Denis pursed his lips, he looked surprisingly ugly for such a beautiful man.

"What?" asked Malcolm, defensively. "I don't see anything wrong."

"Bah!" Denis said. "I don't like Jews."

YOU ARE ENTERING A PLACE OF
EXCEPTIONAL HORROR AND TRAGEDY.
PLEASE SHOW YOUR RESPECT FOR THOSE
WHO SUFFERED AND DIED HERE BY BEHAVING
IN A MANNER SUITABLE TO THE DIGNITY
OF THEIR MEMORY.

Push open the glass door. You are now face to thin-lipped, blank-socketed white face with a plaster bust in the top tier of a curler trolley. The exterior of the salon is a false front of a Roman temple with columns and VITAE inscribed on the entablature, so this bust must be Augustus or Nero. Someone gives the impassive head a voice.

"Hi."

Over there. Seated behind a desk painted to imitate marble, she's leaning on an open appointment book, smiling, not a forced service-sector smile, but not an entirely sincere smile either, as if smiling might be, somehow, inappropriate. Come in, come closer and tell her you have an appointment with Donna. Her long hair falls on the page, and she pulls it back with both hands, holds it behind her neck as she searches for your name. Take a quick look around. The last place you had your hair cut was postered with hip gelled-up models, but here fourth-century laurel-wreathed emperors hang in profile on platter-sized medallions, their locks as painstakingly arranged.

She reads your name out—hollowly. She stands. In clunky shoes and a long black dress, she leads you through the waiting area where an expressionless Venus with a finger wave is down on one knee covering naked breasts with her arms, to a red curtain strung between a pair of columns of the Corinthian fibreglass order and hands you, surprisingly, a smock, not a toga.

"Would you like coffee? Tea?"

Tell her coffee. "Please. Black."

Enter the changing room and, after you have passed the aptitude test of ties and Velcro tabs, re-emerge to find her already waiting with a mug in hand.

"Donna's ready for you now."

She takes you through another pair of columns to where the stylists work, a fresco on the back wall showing, through a window, lounging nudes. At each station is a plaster replica of a different stiffly coiffured Roman bust. She sets down the mug before an Octavia with a ridiculous candy-floss swell of ringlets.

Do you get it? It's a joke.

Point at the bust. Ask, "This is Donna?"

In the mirror see her smile again, just slightly, before she walks away.

But something here is not funny despite the tongue-in-cheek decor, the dance music running a manic loop in the background, the pump bottles of verve and sass and bounce. Exemplified in the funereally clad receptionist: an incongruity of place and mood, *Julius Caesar* staged on the set of *A Funny Thing Happened on the Way to the Forum*. Two stylists are working at this moment, one silently and mechanically marking a grid with the comb on the pale scalp of his client, whose bowed head suggests a posture of grief. The other, a woman, is telling a long story in whispers. She keeps gesturing in the air with the scissors and closing her eyes and the haircut, the haircut is not progressing. Only the client can you hear, saying over and over, "Oh, Christ, oh, Christ ..."

Then Donna bubbles into the frame of the mirror—shampoo personified. "Oooh, dry, really dry," she chides teasingly, clutching your ends and alternating the tilt of her copper head with a forced perkiness that fails to counterpoise the solemnity. "This is what I recommend. Really close to here. That'll give you really a lot more body. Then cut into the whole thing for more movement. Really."

Tell her not too short.

"Never. Let's get you shampooed." Pointing you to the sink, she calls for Alison, the receptionist in the black dress now sweeping up hair beneath one of the chairs on the other side of the salon, hair that has fallen in perfect brown sickles to the floor. As if she's heard Donna, she stops sweeping, though instead of turning she stares fixedly at the little pile she has made. You are just seating yourself at the sink as this is happening, and naturally you wonder what she sees in the hair that makes her freeze.

Meanwhile Donna stands waiting, hands on the waist of her retro hip-huggers, on her biker's belt, a full minute maybe, before wigging out.

"A-li-son!!!"

Everyone, you too, starts and looks at Donna who, post-shrill, is reddening, then at this girl Alison letting go the broom. The floor is tiled with a ceramic faux marble so the wooden handle hitting it cracks resoundingly, and if it weren't for the music, you might describe what falls over the salon with the broom falling over as a hush.

Alison is the first to move. Stepping over the broom, she comes toward you on her awkward shoes. She does not seem angry or disturbed. In fact, her expression is exactly as it has been all along, blank, her face like a statue's.

She makes you a shawl of a towel, shakes out a cape and fastens it over you. "Lean back," she says.

The chair reclines with you and your head settles in the basin. Try to keep watching her—surely she'll react—but before long you have to give in.

And close your eyes.

The water comes on in a fizzy burst and you know, you can see as if you were floating above yourself, that she is testing the temperature against her wrist as a mother tests a baby's bath water. Breathe in and out, feel your jaw loosen, your neck muscles slacken. For a brief moment your eyelids twitch involuntarily and you perceive, flickering in silhouette over your face, a hand with long spatulate fingers waving away the unpleasantness of two minutes ago. Then water, warm and diffused by the nozzle, gushes against your scalp, swirls tingling over your ears, seemingly down the length of your spine, into the channels of your nerves and down to warm your toes and fingers.

"How are you today?"

Fine. Tell her fine. Ask, "You?"

"Fine." She shuts off the faucet. A squirt, hands brisking together, then she touches you.

Instantly, you are embarrassed. Embarrassed that her fingers will know the private topography of your skull, its lumps and scars, its queer flat places. It is almost the same feeling as standing naked and imperfect before another person the first time you make love. There it is again: the thought of love. And now that you have allowed in the thought of love, the thought of sex, and felt the blood of embarrassment rush to your face and the blood already coursing under your scalp, which she is working in tiny pleasurable circles, it only follows that you will become aroused. Yes, she's a stranger and unremarkable, not even the gender you prefer, but with closed eyes it makes no difference, such is the beauty of darkness, of encounters that take place in darkness.

The sort of dark encounter you prefer.

Eyes closed, it's dark now and this is how it begins, with a moment that seems like tenderness, not so different in sensation from a lolling head lifted and supported, a nape caressed. Quickly though, the mood alters so, all of a sudden and together, you come up against a wall—probably you are already doing it against the wall—and this wall is the barrier that separates what most people consider safe and decent pleasure from a different kind of thrill. Though there is no pause for conference, mutually you crash right through it, not like spirits wafting, but dislodging brickwork, loosening plaster, one of you crying out, a lot of sweat and pain.

And she says, "Every time, I'm surprised."

Surprised? Surprised is not the word. There is no word for what in shocked after-moments sometimes must be pounded back with fists. And if there were, you wouldn't voice it. The secret pact, the unspoken rule of anonymity: you must not speak.

"Surprised what a head weighs," she says.

Ah, so she is hinting. As she bows over you like this, she is telling you something by not saying it, the way real lovers do. She's telling you that she knows what you know, that despite the wince-making existential fact that we are completely alone in our skulls, she has been inside yours while it lay in the palm of her hand. But it's not the head that's heavy. It's what's inside it. What you know.

She opens the faucet again, lowers you into the vortex of rinse water and for almost a minute you are engulfed in surge and gurgle, the sound of your own body externalized, made vulnerable. First she went inside your head; now she has turned you inside out.

Dare. Dare to open your eyes and meet hers. What you see: mercifully not a leer, not contempt, only blue, two discs of sky with a stone falling through them.

She shuts off the faucet and eases you upright in the chair. Blinking, you see a bright salon, a shining afternoon. Someone has finished sweeping up the hair and put away the broom and rolled the unstationed bust on the curler trolley into the middle of the room. Covering your head with a towel, she presses all around it. Naturally, you feel cleaner.

Then the telephone in the reception area starts to ring, but one stylist is occupied in shingling his client's head in foil and the other is blow-drying, so probably cannot hear. Finally, Donna appears and makes a dash for the front just as someone pushes open the glass door of the salon. Halfway there when he picks up the phone and says "Vitae," Donna about-faces and walks right past you again, tight-lipped, though it's not you she's avoiding, of course.

From over the girl's shoulder, see him approaching. He's older, perhaps sixty, or maybe his defeated expression and the stark black of his hair add on the years. If you hadn't heard him on the phone, you might have thought he'd come in to break the mirrors; he could even break them with his look. He stops behind the girl, waiting as she pokes a corner of the towel in your ear. It takes a moment before she realizes he's there.

"What a hassle," she says, for the first time showing some feeling. "It's not an easy place to get to. The stopover is terrible. We need a visa."

"Expect a hassle," he says, "then you won't be inconvenienced."

She lifts the towel off your head. "I booked and paid. It's non-refundable."

"Non-refundable?" He laughs. "Imagine *refundable*." Then he disappears into the back room with her staring after him.

A strange interaction, it has left you wondering how a mean queen like that and a girl with healing hands could accompany one another, and to where, so ask her. Ask, "Are you going some place?"

She turns to you again and, taking a damp lock near your ear, tugs it, making a sound like a rat in your head.

"Yes," she says. "I am going to hell."

HOW IT GOES IN RATLAND

1

The new owner—her name was Amanda—called him at home and invited him in a NutraSweet voice to have lunch with her. Malcolm had already met her when she came in to look around before they'd closed up Faye's. She'd brought with her three minions bearing tape measures and paint samples, and not once did she look at or speak to Malcolm. "We have a lot to talk about," she said now on the phone.

She named the restaurant—right there on the avenue, conveniently—and the time. Malcolm came a little early, then had to wait twenty minutes for her. When she arrived, it was calmly, without a hint of hurry or apology. She was a tall woman, ageless in her too-taut skin.

"Look," she told him as soon as they were seated at a table, "there are other salons nearby. Five, actually. I took the trouble to count. At any of them you might fit in better."

Already Malcolm's back was up and he had not even opened the menu. "Do you include in that number MagiCuts," he asked dryly, "and Wanda's House of Beauty?"

"Okay. Four. Wanda's is okay."

"As far as I can tell, her clientele is exclusively Cantonese-speaking."

"Okay, three. Those are only the ones within walking distance. There's a whole city out there, you know."

He didn't. He rarely sallied forth. The closest he came to adventurousness was to trace his finger along the crest of the North Shore Mountains, as he had used to do as a boy, though now it felt as if he were mimicking his own unstable vital signs on a screen.

The waitress interrupted to take their order. Malcolm didn't really care what he ate any more, so long as it wasn't eel. Amanda ordered the wine. She had a system, he observed: the second most expensive. The only system Malcolm's budget tolerated was that he choose water.

He watched Amanda pose before the menu, exquisite nostrils flaring, her adolescent breasts resting pertly on the table. She was a phoney, Malcolm thought, and not only because of cosmetic surgery. As any hairdresser-philosopher knows, perfection has little to do with beauty. A truly beautiful woman acknowledges her flaws, even flaunts them, for they are what make her unique. They grace her character, which is the real seat of beauty. What was Amanda doing with a salon if she didn't understand something so elementary?

"What is your background?" he asked, hoping to steer the conversation to personal matters, hoping she might say something that would persuade him to change his mind and like her.

"I have an MBA. Have you gone to see it yet?"

"What?"

"The salon. It's almost finished."

"Yes, I walk the dog past it every day. You've given it quite a face-lift." *Wicked*, but she didn't even flinch. She wasn't listening to him. She was only talking, and what she went on to say did change his opinion.

"Your clients won't like it. You won't like it. Best if you take them elsewhere, don't you think?"

Now he thought she was a fool, as well as a phoney, if she believed for a second that he wanted to stay. He fully intended to look around for another position, once he had got Denis settled somewhere. It was taking longer than expected; every facility had a ticker-tape waiting list. In the meantime, he just wanted to work in peace.

The food arrived. He wished she would shut up. On she harped, which only made him dig his heels in. "They're old, my clients. They don't like change," he said. "I can't get them to change their hairstyle, let alone their salon."

"I don't give a damn about your clients." She stabbed petulantly with her fork at the grilled vegetables on her plate. "I don't want a bunch of old ladies tottering around spoiling the concept."

He stiffened in his chair. "You'll be old yourself one day. Sooner than you'd like. Anyway, I believe there's a clause in the contract." She waved it off, so Malcolm said, "I'll have to contact my lawyer." It was a bluff. He'd sooner hire a call girl than a lawyer, but Amanda fell for it. She had no imagination. She thought everyone was like her. Amanda would call a lawyer in a snap.

The bill came on a little William Morris tray. She snatched it up, read it, then tossed it his way. "We'll split it, okay?"

During the renovations he made house calls. Then, when he saw the place and heard the music that they played, he felt sure none of his clients would come any-way. But their diminished hearing proved to his advantage, as well as the daily confusion over which pair of glasses to wear. The one universal complaint was that they had to change. "We didn't change when it was Faye's," they griped. It took their arthritic fingers a quarter-hour to do up their buttons at home, only to have to undo them all again. As for the decor, it offended Malcolm more than it offended them, the outcry over EuroDisney echoing daily in his head. "I have become a snob," he admitted to himself, no different from the snobs he had been decrying all those years.

As for his rapport with the other stylists, something had gone grotesquely wrong from the start. Perhaps he had said something to offend them, or maybe they had simply sensed how he felt—that they were flowers of degeneration, that freakishness and mutilation had replaced beauty as a standard. Theirs was a torture-chamber aesthetic. If he hadn't already ceased to give a damn about the world, he would have shuddered for it. None of this meant he didn't *like* them, of course. It was their values he disapproved of, their grammar, and their clothes. As individuals, however, he was actually fond of one or two. Thi, for example, the manager. She charmed everyone and, apart from the silver knuckles of rings on her every finger, didn't look half so vicious. Even her tattoo he liked, a delicate Celtic interlace around her ankle, as if she had dipped her little foot in the Book of Kells. Jamie had a tattoo, too, and ponytail—a nosegay of bright red curls. He was less a favourite though. He liked to work out, he told Malcolm. "Work what out?" Malcolm had asked, though he only had to look at Jamie's Popeye forearms to know. There were the tattoos, spiral bracelets of song lyrics. Malcolm, who read compulsively, picked out several alarming phrases about rape and hate. Also: *I think I'm dumb* ...Well, *he* said it first.

For the first eight months they had a languid, metallic-headed apprentice named Donna. "So you lived in Paris," she would say, snapping gum through her brown lipstick and smirking as if she did not believe it. "Attitude" was what they termed Donna's affliction. It did not hold her back. They made a stylist out of her nonetheless.

A new girl came instead, Alison, who in one hour did what Donna used to do all day. When Alison was seen sitting down on the job, it was because she was on her break. She spent it in the corner, watching everyone work. Over and over that first day Malcolm heard her say, "I have so much to learn."

From across the street, they looked almost imposing—marble columns rising between the deli and the Shopper's Drug Mart. Alison had no idea what the Latin meant, or that the stone wasn't real; she simply marvelled that her placement had brought her to this temple.

She crossed the street then stood a moment looking in; the whole front of the salon between the columns and under the heavy inscribed entablature was glass. Inside, a beautiful oriental child looked up from behind the desk as Alison entered and asked in an adult voice if she had an appointment.

"I'm the new apprentice," Alison told her.

"I forgot it was today you were coming!" She laid a chiding hand against her cheek, her thumb and every finger reinforced with a silver ring. "We've been so unbelievably busy. Come in. Come in."

Not a child, then. When she stood, Alison saw a grown woman in miniature, looked straight down on the perfect blue-white path of her part, two blue-black fields of hair on either side, as she led Alison through

86

another pair of columns to a gallery where three stylists were working.

"It's Ali, right?"

"Yes."

"I'm Thi, the manager, and this is Donna." Thi stopped beside one of the stylists who, pausing in her work, smiled at Alison, though not exactly in a friendly way. She wore a helmet of platinum hair, chin-length, cut at angles. "Oh, *Ali*." She stressed the first syllable— Aa!—the same sound she'd make if she found a hair in her soup. "Shucks. A-*lee*, we thought. We were expecting a big black bruiser."

Thi kept her moving along. Between each station, a half-column rose from counter to ceiling and a different bust stood, each with eyes rolled back showing whites. On the far wall, trompe l'oeil windows looked out on an idealized garden where nudes of both sexes posed.

They passed a bust in a matted wig and sunglasses. "Christian works at that station. He'll be late. Here's Robert. Robert, Ali."

Roxanne was the stylist with the nose ring at the sinks shampooing her client. "I love your hair," said Alison. Roxanne's was the most hair Alison had ever seen on one person at one time, a great tendriling mass of brown. It seemed impossible that she could support a whole head of it on such a thin neck.

"And Malcolm's in the back," said Thi. "I'll show you the back room, Ali."

"Don't leave her alone with him," Roxanne teased. "He bites."

"What kind of name is Thi?" asked Alison as they moved on.

"Vietnamese. T-H-I. You know, like what the Queen drinks."

The stock, supply, lunch and laundry rooms were combined in a six-by-twelve-foot square; dye samples stacked on style books stacked on the microwave, then on the shelves Pepto Bismol, dishes, a fan, perm solution, sugar cubes, bulk shampoo—all the verticality, squalor and cramming-together of a slum. This was the slum off the Forum.

The man on the bench covered his face to sneeze, then looked at her from behind the tissue with a wet-eyed, sour expression. Thi said, "That's Malcolm. What do you think so far?" She took two mugs from the shelf and filled them, sliding one toward Alison.

When Thi wasn't looking, Alison had rapped her knuckles on the columns and scrutinized the walls. She'd never been close to antiquity, not even in a museum, excepting moss-hung thousand-year-old trees, nothing ancient and made of stone but mountains. She could still feel unjaded awe for replicas and marble mocked up with a sponge. "I like that it looks so old."

"Post-Bankrupt-Italian-Taverna," someone quipped from the doorway just as Alison picked a package of coffee whitener out of the clutter on the counter.

"Here you are, Christian," Thi chided. "Your client's waiting."

Alison saw him framed in the doorway, his face flattened like it was pressed against glass. He was small, bigger than Thi, of course, but tiny for a man. "That's bleach activator you're putting in your coffee," he told her and laughed a grating warble.

Thi shooed him off.

"I love coffee. I love Thi. I love Thi, but she doesn't love me. ..."

The bar fridge, tucked under the counter, was where she would find the cream. It would be a day of little chores, Thi explained, until Alison got to know the place. "The dryer's ready to be unloaded and that's the cupboard for the towels. When you're finished, let me know. I'm up front."

Alison dumped the tainted coffee in the sink and, seeing the caffeine mire, cringed and rolled up her sleeves. Under all the submerged dishes, tea bags clogged the drain. Malcolm was still there on the bench, breathing heavily through his mouth, head lolling against the wall. He didn't look like a stylist. Much older than everyone else, he looked, in those clothes, like an out-of-stylist. An over-stylist—his hair rinsed a lustreless black. Also, there was a musty smell in the tiny room that seemed to be coming from him.

"So, Malcolm. What do you do?" she asked.

His eyes opened. He seemed surprised—by her question, or that she'd talked to him at all. "What do you mean?"

"Do you own the place?"

He started to cough, a deep phlegmatic hacking, and pressed his fingers to his eyes.

She let him alone. He clearly wasn't well. After she had washed the dishes and tamed the static-spitting towels, she tiptoed out, back to the gallery where she found Thi at one of the sinks bowing over a client. Up front the phone started to ring.

"Can you get it, Ali?"

"Vitae," Alison said, assuming that was how she should answer. On the telephone, old people always sounded to her like those old vinyl records, their voices popping and scratchy. She plugged the music in the background out of her other ear and still barely heard the caller say she was the one who cancelled with Malcolm that morning.

"You're afraid?" Alison asked. "You had a fright?"

"*Am* a ..."

In the appointment book Alison pencilled "Mrs. Parker" in a slot for the next day.

"Take her phone number, too," said Thi over Alison's shoulder, smiling approvingly when Alison hung up. "Ninety."

"What?"

"Mrs. Parker. She's ninety. How about sweeping up?"

"What does Vitae mean?"

For a second she pondered. "You know, I haven't got a clue."

"I have so much to learn," said Alison on her way to get the broom.

Passing Christian again, she paused to watch him with his chin steadied on his client's crown. On either side of her face, he drew out a strand to compare the length. The woman was staring at Christian in the mirror, either not aware of or not bothering to conceal her fascination. There was more than one thing wrong with Christian's face: eyes unsynchronized, maybe a birth defect.

She started under Robert's chair, sweeping the whole salon and, moving through the room, hearing omnisciently all the conversations—Christian's client asking, "What could I do? What would you do?" Someone up front coming in late and saying, "Forgive me." When she got to the end of the room, Thi, passing, pointed out the little trap door in the wall. Alison pushed the pile of hair against it, then stood peering into the dark place it fell.

"Where does it go?" she asked, but Thi had gone.

Just before her break, she was given, to her surprise, her first real task—so soon. She was asked whether she was ready to shampoo a client.

At hairdressing school they practised on each other, foaming chatter. Her boyfriend Billy loved it. "Scrub me, baby. Rub-a-dub-dub." But here, perhaps because it was an actual salon or maybe because the decor suggested it, everything seemed at once ancient and symbolic. The client leaned back in the chair. She poured the water over his head, watched his forehead unscoring, the shuttling under his eyelids slowing, his jaw releasing. Suspended in her hand, his head grew heavier. She knew then that whatever concerns he had come in with, she was washing away. Her choice of career, now that Alison had finally made it, she had explained like this: "I want to make people look good. If you look good, you feel good. I want everybody to feel good." Naïve, perhaps, and idealistic, but she was, after all, the daughter of a woman who ran herself ragged for charity and looked it—hair and person frazzled—and a Shriner father. "We hoped you'd be a nurse," said her mother, who to Alison's great regret could not see that hairdressing too was a healing profession. She didn't understand that Alison almost had to take this man in her arms to sit him up again.

She pressed around his head with a towel, then showed him to Robert's chair. Robert, in his crocheted vest, hiply ugly, appeared a moment later. After introducing himself, he asked the man what he could do for him today.

"Something different."

"Good. Who do you want to be?"

The client laughed. He didn't exactly know. Robert, a ring through his knowing brow, advised. Alison watched him moving hands in the air, lightly touching his client's head and hair.

A few minutes later she sat down in the corner to watch Robert through her break. Something was different, though she had missed the transition while she was in the back room getting the client his coffee. Now his expression had turned serious. Already he and Robert were engaged in an intimate conversation, which she could not hear over the music. Perhaps it was not so strange considering the limited time they had: an hour together, ninety minutes at most. At every station, the white faces of the busts stared out with the usual blank, bored dispassion, but Robert was actually listening. Listening was also Robert's work.

"What could I do?" she had heard another client say earlier. "What would you do?" So it was not only to look good that they came. They came to be offered a pierced, sympathetic ear. For advice, for judgement to be reserved. To confess. The snip-snip-snip of the scissors lulling, Robert's client looked up contritely. "Forgive me," someone that morning had distinctly said.

When her break was over, she went back to the reception area. Christian's last client, the woman who had been puzzling over his face, came out of the changing room. Alison said, "Wow! You look great!" The woman beamed as she paid. She paid a lot, but it was worth it. She looked good. She felt good. She had been absolved.

"You're Christian, right?" his next client asked him.

"No. I'm Jewish."

Alison peeked around the column. What little remained of Christian's hair he wore duckling-coloured and shaved down close, and now he was pointing to his bald spot, a perfect yarmulke of flesh. His strange laugh curdled the joke.

At a station beyond she saw Malcolm knuckle-deep in the sea-foam curls of an aging client. This was an older neighbourhood, so perhaps the woman had come in because it was close, but Alison wondered how she stood the music. Even her own parents, much, much younger, preferred their old vinyl records to CDs. Maybe she was deaf. Malcolm, chairside manner elegant and doting, fluttered around the old lady. He had come alive.

"Vee-tay," she practised saying, walking home from the bus stop. "Vee-tay. Vee-tay." It was a word you had to smile to say, drawing up and back the corners of the mouth in the "vee" and showing teeth. She hoped she was pronouncing it correctly.

A figure was crouching at the end of their walk. It was Mrs. Branz, their landlady, come over from the apartment building she owned and lived in across the street. On either side of the walk, and in beds surrounding the house, were the flowers she fanatically tended. There didn't seem to be a Mr. Branz.

As Alison drew near, Mrs. Branz stood. She was wearing, to comical effect, athletic knee pads outside her trousers. Her gloves, lying there on the path, were so stiff-fingered with mud they looked like severed hands. "Different flowers for every season, yes?" she said. "This is Japanese anemone." With a long stem between her fingers, she cupped one of the white blooms for Alison to see.

"Maybe Billy already called you," Alison took the opportunity to say. "The fridge is leaking."

"Yes, he did." She turned back to the flowers.

The house was an old mansion divided into apartments. Alison clumped up the wooden stairs, unlocked the main door and in the vestibule, where the walls were stained with luminous migrating colour from the stained-glass windows, she put her key in the apartment lock. The door opened on a maliciously grinning Billy, flowers clutched in his hands still trailing roots and soil.

"Billy! She's out there! Did she see you pick them?"

Passing her the looted bouquet, he stepped sock-footed onto the porch. "Mrs. Branz?" he called. "Have you ever been to Lake Superior?"

She turned and, shielding her eyes, answered matter-of-factly. "I am German. I have seen only the Lake of Constance."

They ducked back in the house, stifling each other's laughter, and Alison kicked off her killing shoes.

"How was the first day?" Billy asked.

"Wonderful, but my feet hurt. I'm totally beat. It was a lot of work. A lot of fun. I think I'm going to need a tattoo."

She brought the flowers to the kitchen, careful not to step in the puddle seeping out from under the fridge. The kitchen was its usual mess—stacks of unwashed dishes precarious on the counter, dried spaghetti in hardened doodles on the ceiling—Billy's trick.

"How many people work there?"

"Um." She counted on her fingers. "Seven, including me. One I didn't meet. I really liked the manager. She's this cute little Vietnamese girl."

"How many are fags?"

"Billy," she said chidingly and, under the sink, found an empty pickle jar for the flowers.

"I'm just asking. Out of sociological interest."

She had something to ask him. That the scientific names she had learned for scalp disorders were in Latin didn't occur to her. She asked Billy because he seemed to know everything, because he dropped *Rattus norvegicus, Mus domesticus* and *Mesocricetus auratus, ad nauseam.*

"What does Vitae mean?"

He rolled his eyes, flecked like he'd been painting the ceiling a darker shade of grey. "Shit-for-Brains, think." Then, drawing her close, he pressed against her hip so she could feel he was hard. "*Vive l'amour!*" he said.

"That's *vive*, not *vitae*." She propped the flowers up in the jar, muddying the water.

Taking her hand, he began leading her away.

"Where are we going? Oh, Billy, I'm tired. I just got my period."

"Great," he said. "We'll pretend you're a virgin and I'm deflowering you again."

He would never force her to do something she didn't want, but he would coax. He seemed to like her to balk a little, then he'd toy with her and, suddenly, she'd want to. She fell back on the futon, giggling. He ducked under her skirt and began to thrash around, a bagged cat. Houdini-like, he writhed. "Oh!" she shrieked. Billy, backing out of the skirt, emerged with his hair tousled and the pink string of the tampon in his teeth. On all fours, he crawled on top of her, swinging the tampon, purply-brown with her blood, back and forth over her disgusted face, intoning through his teeth. "You are becoming very sleepy. You will let me have my way with you. You won't remember any of this. Nothing that is about to happen to you ..."

2

From that first day, Malcolm was struck by how wide-eyed and eager to please the new girl was, how quaintly sweatered. She was the answer to *his* prayers: someone smiling in the morning and offering him coffee, someone, finally, he could trust his fragile clientele to. She would lead them to the dressing room as if helping them negotiate a busy street. She seemed to know where they were stiff and which ear to speak into, seemed to understand, as well, that Malcolm was suffering. She would actually talk to him, not about anything important—he didn't believe her capable of uttering anything of substance—but her funny questions made him laugh. She was a great dollop of a dear, a Girl Scout in plain clothes. Perhaps the world was full of such young women. Malcolm wouldn't know. He didn't have much to do with the world any more.

"Your cold seems better today," she said as Malcolm was hanging up his coat. He didn't turn or acknowledge her in any way; he seemed not to have heard her. Under the coat, he was wearing a sports jacket that had to be a joke. It was like something her father would put on to go to a Shriners' meeting, minus the fez, of course. But where a jacket might not fit her father across the gut, with Malcolm it was the sleeves that were too short, his shirt cuffs escaping in inches at the wrists. She got the feeling he was actually wearing someone else's jacket.

"Malcolm?"

He swung around. "Were you talking to me?"

"Yes," said Alison. "You're feeling better?"

"Not worse," he conceded.

"You would know, I bet. What does Vitae mean?"

"'Of life' or maybe 'for life'. What that has to do with a hair salon, perhaps you can tell me."

Alison, amused by his tone, said, "I kind of like it. It makes you think."

"It makes me think what a twit that woman is."

"What woman?"

"That Amanda person! This is not her only venture.

96

She has plans for a salon in Kitsilano, too. You've heard of it—the Aztec temple? What will the next one be, I wonder. A Christian Science Reading Room?"

Alison didn't know what he was talking about or why he seemed so annoyed. Then Christian came in. "Mal! I *love* it!" He touched the jacket sleeve. "What is it? Fortrel?"

Malcolm turned and walked away, the smell that hovered around him trailing. Alison identified it now: mothballs.

Left standing there with Christian, she turned to him and said good morning. For no reason, he reached out and touched her hair. "Listen," he whispered, "I saved your life. You should buy me lunch." He meant the bleach activator she'd put in her coffee a few days ago. "Sweetie. It could have *killed* you."

Another busy morning—answering phones, folding towels, sweeping hair. Apparently they were going to teach her something, but in the meantime she performed all these banal tasks with cheer; she was happy just to be there.

At lunch, Christian came to fetch her in the back room. Roxanne stopped them on the way. "Where are you going?" Christian told her, next door to the deli. "I'll meet you there," she said.

Cowbells clanked on the deli door. The young man behind the counter looked up from his newspaper and, smiling at them, slipped a pencil behind his ear. "My," said Christian, seeing he had been doing the crossword puzzle. "An *intellectual*."

The deli man laughed. He was wearing a clean white cap and jacket. Strung in rows above him, cudgels of sausage.

"This is Ali, my assistant," Christian told him and Alison rolled her eyes. "She's the brat in my bratwurst. My little friend."

"What'll you have?" the deli man asked her.

She ordered a bowl of soup, then took a table over by the window, the cloth red-checked, the napkin holder a mock cuckoo-clock chalet. "My fantasy," Christian said, joining her and speaking low so the deli man wouldn't hear, "is that one day he won't be wearing that *smock* thing."

Now that he was across from her, she no longer had to avoid looking at him for fear he would think she was trying to figure out the problem on his face. Where to look, though? When he fixed her with the bright tack of his left eye, the right veered off, distractingly. She followed its dead-end gaze, only to abruptly refocus on the left straight-ahead eye again. The moment she did, *it* veered—a back-and-forth confusion like the old gag where two people jam in a door frame after so many after-yous. Soon she realized she wasn't listening to what he was saying—something about lederhosen and embroidered braces—so she looked elsewhere on his face, to the flattened nose, the nostrils squashed almost to slits. He snuffled when he breathed; he nasalized. The scarred skin above his lip was shiny and pink.

"You have found me out," he said suddenly, covering his nose and mouth with his hand. "I am a hairdresser with a harelip."

Alison was mortified.

"You'll get used to me," Christian said, then pointed behind her where a travel poster hung on the wall. It was a mountain scene—crowded peaks tapering skyward, a tiny napkin holder perched in a stone cleft. "That's the Eagle's Nest," he said. "Hitler's *infamous* hideout." He rubbed his hands together. "*Ja, ja. Who vill be our first victim?* I know! *Mal de coeur!* Malcolm Malcontent. Isn't he *bad?* Isn't he just plain *mal?* He was born that way, you know."

"Born what way?" she asked, still thinking of the harelip.

"Born wearing *slacks.* Later, he spent his formative years in *France*—thus the *supérieur* demeanour. You know Faye's?"

"Whose?" Alison asked.

"Faye's of Kerrisdale? Malcolm *was* Faye." He paused, one eye listing toward the counter where the deli man was ladling out Alison's soup. "But I should tell you about Roxanne before she gets here. She has a little problem." He mimed a finger down his throat.

"She's *really* thin," Alison agreed.

"I bring her vitamins. She'll eat those. You could drop some in her coffee, too. Now, James—"

She had met Jamie that morning. He looked more like a construction worker than a hairdresser, both forearms scribbled to the elbows with tattoos—lyrics in a continuous spiral starting at his wrists. He wore his red hair in a clutch of corkscrew curls.

"It's *real,*" said Christian. "It's *natural.*"

"What is?"

He smoothed both hands over his own yellow down. "James is a *true* redhead whose *sole purpose* is to mate with other *true* redheads and thereby replenish the redhead population which has been in steady decline since the Vikings. When you see him filled with *angst* it is inevitably because he has been fooled by a *pretender.*"

"You'd think a stylist would know."

"Yes, but he's a *bull,* too. When he sees red, he charges. Thi, she's very sweet. What do you make of Donna?"

"I don't think she likes me."

"Oh, she *loathes* you." He reached out and gave her hand a consoling little pat. "She's jealous. *You're* our star apprentice now. Another thing, Donna just got started as a stylist, but—look, don't date clients. You go out on a date with a client and decide you don't like him, think he's going to let you cut his hair again? How's your love life, by the way?"

"Great."

He pinched his nose, blatting like a game-show buzzer rebuking a contestant. "An answer in the *affirmative* is a *negative*. Love and life are one. If you separate out love, you're not living. Instead, live every moment for love."

He was wearing a T-shirt that read "Worship Me," valentine-red Doc Martens and a necklace of dog chain, which he toyed with incessantly. Alison thought he was joking.

"Not at all!"

The deli man set down her bowl swirling with pale vegetable cubes, a grainy slice of bread on the side, and walked off, oblivious to Christian's pursuing gaze.

"What's his name?"

"I don't know. I've never been here."

"Your sweetie."

"Oh!" She laughed. "Billy."

"Billy, Billy, let me guess." Stubby fingers to his temples, he shut his eyes. It was a relief to her; she wouldn't have to wonder where to look. "Blue of eye, blond of hair, buns of steel."

Alison blew the soup right off the spoon. "He's brunette and hardly got buns at all. What about you? Do you have a sweetheart?"

"Ham on rye," the deli man said, appearing as if in answer to her question. He set the sandwich down.

Christian watched him for another moment, then gingerly lifted the corner of the bread, then the lettuce, the cheese and ham, an inventory. He took a bite and didn't wait for the swallow. Sandwich revolved between his words.

"Robert—"

"I know," said Alison, sadly. "Thi told me."

"She did? The little *gossip*."

The goat bells sounded and Christian waved as Roxanne came in. Weaving wraith-like between the tables, she seemed dazed or sleep-walking or ill: there was something deadened or trance-like about her walk. "Can I join you?" she asked in a slow, plaintive voice. "Do you mind?"

"Rox, Rox," Christian assured her. "We were waiting for you."

She sank down on the chair, sank and slumped, folding in on herself, spine and shoulders bowing, a self-protecting posture. Staring at them, sucking on her fingernail, she really looked extremely pretty with her huge eyes and her mane, the delicate gold wire looping one tear-shaped nostril. She took the finger from her mouth to say, "I'm so glad you're working with us, Ali. I like you. I like your sweaters."

Alison was just going to thank her when the tide came in on Roxanne's eyes. They filled with salt water. She blinked and expelled a tear.

"What's the matter?" asked Alison.

"Oh, Rox," said Christian, chidingly. He took a napkin and wiped her cheek, digging in his jeans pocket at the same time.

"I'm just so happy!" Roxanne cried.

"She's hungry," said Christian.

"Who knit it?" she asked, meaning the outsize blue

guernsey that Alison was wearing with boots over a short black sheath dress.

"My mother."

"Have you eaten anything today?" Christian asked.

"I had a coffee. My mother would never knit me a sweater."

"Coffee isn't food," said Christian.

"Does she know how?"

"I don't know. I don't even talk to her any more."

"Here." He found what he had been rooting for in his pocket: a pink oblong bead. A vitamin. He set it in front of her.

"I can't."

"You *can*!"

"I need water."

"Ali?" Christian pointed to the counter and Alison got up and went to ask the deli man for a glass.

When she got back to the table, Roxanne was talking about getting a lip ring. "What do you think, Ali? Should I? Or maybe one through my eyebrow, like Robert's. Which do you guys think?"

Christian took the glass of water from Alison and handed it to Roxanne. For a minute they sat watching her blink petulantly at the vitamin. Who would want to take it? Bright pink, it was like the outrageous pupae of some insect from the sixties. Finally, she picked it up and took a sip of water. Alison heard a tiny clink. Roxanne swallowed the vitamin, gagged, and suddenly, it seemed all a show, a show that both Roxanne and Christian were putting on—not for Alison, for themselves.

Christian leaned over and kissed Roxanne's cheek. "There's a good girl." She sniffed and smiled. "Now go and get yourself a soup or something. Go on. Or we won't let you sit with us any more."

Slowly, Roxanne stood and made her way over to the counter. "See? *She's famished*," said Christian. "She barely has the energy to stand."

They watched her talking to the deli man, teetering on her platform shoes, legs thin as an insect's. She pointed at something, then changed her mind and headed for the bathroom.

"Go after her," said Christian.

"What?"

"Go listen at the door."

"Why?" said Alison.

"In case she pukes."

She felt silly, but she went because he asked her to.

Waiting there, now and then pressing her ear to the door, Alison couldn't hear a thing. Then Roxanne opened the door and, seeing her there, smiled weakly. "I have to go, too," said Alison, blushing at her excuse.

When she returned to the table, Christian was feeding her soup to Roxanne, coaxing. With each mouthful, Alison heard that little metallic click again, and a scrape against the spoon. Against Roxanne's tongue stud, she would learn later, when Roxanne showed her all her piercings. Under her hair and clothes, Roxanne was skewered.

3

"Vitae means life," she told her mother when she and Billy were over for dinner on Sunday night. She was helping peel the potatoes, paring into the sink the spirals of tough brown skin.

"How poetic."

"You don't get it, do you?" said Alison, a little hurt.

Her mother's refusal to approve still felt like pins stuck in.

"I have to say I don't. You could have taken upgrading. You could have gone to college if you wanted."

"I didn't want to go to college!" said Alison, exasperated because they'd talked about this before. Many times before, but for some reason her mother couldn't understand that Alison didn't want anything more to do with books. She wanted to learn from experience. Life would be her school.

From the living room, her father bellowed to her. "Come and show Billy your hands!"

"He's seen my hands!" she called back, but already she was washing them under the tap and going, just to get away from her mother.

"He's probably telling him you have twelve fingers," her mother said, trying too late to be kind.

Her father was in the La-Z-Boy, his gouty feet raised up on the footrest, a can of beer propped in his crotch, Billy on the couch. The TV was on, but the volume muted. "He was asking who plays the piano," her father said, as Alison came over drying her hands on her jeans.

"Jeffy does."

"Yeah, yeah. Let him see."

That her father still showed her off like this even though she was twenty and all grown up didn't bother Alison. She found it endearing. If she really were a freak, she could at least have distinguished herself with freakishness. As it was, she felt she had no special feature, no talents of which to boast, nothing but long thin fingers that widened at the tips like a tree frog's.

She held her hands out to Billy, as if she wanted something from him. "Ooo," he said. "She's an alien. How come I never noticed?"

"We thought she was going to be some kind of Liberace. Started saving for the piano right after she was born. Two, three years of lessons. What sound do those fingers make on the keys? Plunk, plunk, plunk. Plunk, plunk, plunk. Instead she goes and becomes a hairdresser!"

From the kitchen her mother called, "I still think she'd make a terrific nurse!"

"She plays nurse with me!" Billy yelled back and Alison's father guffawed loudly and slapped his knee.

"Anyway, Dad," said Alison. "I'm not a hairdresser yet. I'm an apprentice for a year."

"As long as I get my free haircuts, I don't care what you're called. Go and get your brother, will you? We want to hear a tune."

Jeffy had a friend over for dinner, though neither of them had made an appearance yet. Going down the hall to his room, she looked at her hands again. A hairdresser's hands, she thought, pleased.

His door patchworked with stickers, she paused outside it to listen, heard them inside grunting in the secret guttural of teenage boys. When she knocked, though, something else—a desperate cluck and gurgle. "Jeffy?"

No answer.

She knew she was not supposed to, would undoubtedly meet his wrath, but she opened the door anyway. At first glance they seemed locked in a confusing kind of love pose: on the unmade bed, Kevin Milligan, on all fours, straddled Jeffy who, squirming, arms reaching, held Kevin by the collar bones. A few months ago, she had accidentally barged in on Jeffy in the bathroom, caught him on the edge of the tub jigging, so knew this time not to scream, but to duck out fast, except that just then Kevin looked up. He was a bulky kid with coarse yellow hair, his lips drawn back to show big teeth, his whole mouth stretched wide with straining, his face very, very red. Alison's mouth opened, too, and she pitched forward slightly, but didn't make an utterance or really move. For weeks afterward she would remember this moment as her own near-asphyxiation, the horror and shame of doing nothing cinching off her breath. Kevin was strangling her brother and Alison just stood and stared.

Then he bolted. He hurtled off the bed, knocking her aside, Alison blinking after him, afraid to look back at Jeffy. Afraid for two reasons: first, Jeffy might be dead; second, she might be relieved if he was. Jeffy, at thirteen, was the most infuriating person she knew. Across her back, lash marks from where he still ignobly snapped her bra. "Fatso" was his name for her. Once, right in front of her, he'd swallowed her diary key.

When she did finally turn, he was still flat out, but breathing as if he were inflating a beach ball. "Are you okay?"

"Fuck off," he croaked.

"Dad wants you to play the piano."

Slowly, he began to raise himself from the half-dead. He got off the bed and listed dopily down the hall, Alison following into the living room where their oblivious father heralded his arrival by braying for a tune. When Jeffy walked straight into the piano bench, Alison almost cried out that she loved him and wouldn't let him down again, that she was his big sister and would protect him from now on—but Jeffy was already sitting down to play. He played by ear, and his ears, too, looked less than what they were except if you imagined that ever-present golden smear inside as honey. His normal, musical fingers moved up and down the keys.

A Christmas carol. He was playing a Christmas carol in September. "To save us all from Satan's power when we were gone astray!" sang their soprano mother in the kitchen.

"Where's Kevin?" asked their dad.

Gone home, Alison hoped, but no: there he was, lurking in the hall. Hearing his name, he came brazenly in, swaggered right over to the piano where he sat down next to Jeffy and joined in. A cacophonous, off-kilter duet—Kevin didn't know how to play. He simply pounded his fist on the keyboard so it sounded as if something demonic had entered the piano.

"Stop it, you two. Stop it," said their mother, bringing in a bowl of chips. Immediately, Kevin ceased his assault on the keyboard to go over and grab a handful.

"Kevin, you'll never guess what Billy does," their mother said. "Did you tell him, Jeffy?"

Jeffy had stopped playing, too. He didn't reply. Abruptly, he stood and lurched from the room, everybody staring after him. A moment later, they heard his door slam down the hall.

"What's eating him?" asked their dad.

Alison went after him. She came to his door, hesitating before she knocked. When she opened it, she found him sitting on the bed, staring at the floor. His face in profile—the ski-jump nose, the thick lashes against his still-flawless skin as he squeezed his eyes shut—was prettier than hers.

"What happened?" she asked.

A tear got away. Stunned, she watched him whisk it off his cheek with the back of his hand. As far as she knew, he hadn't cried since he fell out of the tree and broke his arm, back when he was ten, around the time he last spoke to her without sneering. Around the same time he'd stopped saying "please."

"Please." He barely mouthed the words. "Don't say anything."

"But you didn't do anything!" She came over and put her hand on his shoulder, but he looked up suddenly and ran her through with his glare.

"Jeffy?"

"Leave me alone," he said, face crumpling.

She hovered there a moment, anguished for him, confused. Then she left him, closing the door behind her.

No one was in the living room when she returned. "They went out to the garage," her mother called, "to show Kevin the Socred Hotel."

Alison groaned.

Kevin didn't want to be out there with Billy and her dad, she could tell when she joined them. He looked over his shoulder as she came up, edgily, as if expecting his own badness to catch up with him at any moment. He didn't know what the Socred Hotel was, probably didn't even know what Socreds were—the erstwhile right-wing foes of the New Democrats, the party Alison's parents had supported all their voting years. Socreds were scarce now; they'd essentially disbanded after an ignominious defeat, fled, as Alison's father liked to say, "like rats from a sinking ship." Into the arms of the Liberals. "Liberals, my arse," in her father's opinion. "In that case, Hitler was a liberal."

It took him several minutes to find it, the garage a veritable junk room. From behind some stacks of newspapers, he finally lifted it out, a square metal box he'd soldered out of sheet metal, "Socred Hotel" painted on the front. He was a machinist in a shop near the docks, much frequented by rats; the hotel was just a glorified rat trap.

He demonstrated the ingenious workings of the door, triggered to shut when the upward-sloping floor was weighted down. "Open a can of cat food and leave it in there. You can catch three or four at once."

"Tell him what the hole is for," said Billy. The small circular hole at the back.

"Oh, Dad," said Alison as he carried the box over to the station wagon. "It's awful."

Chuckling, he showed Kevin how the exhaust pipe of the station wagon fit exactly into the hole. All at once Kevin stopped twitching and looking around and shifting from foot to foot as if about to dash. He was suddenly able to focus. "You *made* that? *Cool!*"

"Uggh," Alison said, and went back into the house.

Dinner was almost ready. She helped her mother set the table. "Who is that kid anyway?"

"Kevin Milligan. He's in Jeffy's class at school."

"He's a little creep."

"It seems they had a fight."

"I can't believe he stayed," said Alison.

"Boys will be boys. They'll make up, you'll see."

When it was time to gather round the table, their mother had to go get Jeffy from his room. She came back, enjoining them all to sit, sit anywhere, Jeffy looking sullen and withdrawn—looking innocent. He made for his usual place, but when Kevin started for the facing seat, he balked. Instead, Alison and Billy took those chairs, their father his at the head of the table and their mother the one closest to the kitchen. The two remaining seats were across from each other anyway, so Alison stood, intending to invite Jeffy to switch. Just then Kevin stamped down purposely on her stocking foot.

"You little shit!" she hissed.

"Where are you going?" asked her father. "I'm about to say grace."

She sat back down, fuming.

Her father clasped his big hands together. "Thank God supper's ready!"

Then it seemed too awkward to offer to change. Already the mashed potatoes were being passed around and her father had started carving the roast chicken. "Who's a Catholic? Who wants the Pope's nose?" He swashed with the carving knife, like it was a regular Sunday dinner.

Except that a war was going on. At first even Alison didn't notice, serving herself and keeping one protective eye on Jeffy. She saw him grimace as if he were straining or in pain. He braced against the table, making the candles teeter, and Kevin's lips curled back the way they had done when he was trying to kill Jeffy, teeth reminding her now of the big disembodied set the dentist used to demonstrate how to brush properly. Worse, though, was Jeffy suddenly wearing exactly the same expression. "Hey," she said and looked under the table.

Kevin, the bigger boy, had bigger feet; they were wrestling, sole to sole, Jeffy's ankle pinned painfully to the floor. They stopped when their mother scolded, "No roughhousing at the table." But every time Alison looked Kevin's way during the meal, he opened his mouth and showed her his masticated food.

Evil child, she thought. Brat. Demon.

Profound was her astonishment then, when, after dinner, the boys got up and walked off together. She did a double take. How had it happened? Neither had said a word. Had they exchanged some secret sign? Had Kevin been mouthing threats to Jeffy?

She got up and followed to Jeffy's room, hesitating briefly before opening the door. Just a crack. Just to see that Jeffy was all right.

They were turning on the computer. "Jeffy?" she said. "We're going in a minute." He swung around, his off-guard face sweet and brotherly until outrage twisted it up.

"Hey, fatso! Knock, why don't you?"

Then Kevin turned and, suddenly, she realized who he was. It was written all over his sneering, bully face: Kevin Milligan, Future Ruler of the World.

4

The first thing she learned working at Vitae was about history: that the present rests upon layers of the past, but is a stratum so unstable, so shot with fault lines, that now and then the *then* rears up and knocks down the *now*. Platform shoes, for example, disco, the shag—in 1994 they were all back. Vitae, antiquity itself, was built on the ruins of Faye's of Kerrisdale, its sole archaeological trace the still-unrenovated back room.

Six stylists were employed besides Thi and Alison— Donna, Roxanne, Jamie, Christian, Robert, and Malcolm. On average, five stylists worked on any given day; the back room held four. At any time six or more of them might be back there rubbing each other the wrong way.

Malcolm was always there between appointments, squeezing further into the corner when the claustrophobia-inducing space filled. He would be reading— reading a book. No one else ever brought a book in.

"Why does she only have one name?" Alison asked one day, glancing at the author's name on the cover.

"Who?"

She pointed to the book. "Colette."

He dropped it in his lap and threw his head back. This wasn't the first time she'd heard him laugh. He often chuckled to himself as he read and seemed mysteriously to keep his clients in stitches, but it was the first time within her hearing that he'd laughed with one of them.

"Why does Twiggy have one name?" he asked. "Or Minou?"

"Who are they?" asked Alison which, inexplicably, started him laughing again.

"You were reading something different yesterday," she said, picking the book off his knee. "All the books you bring in are old."

"More precisely, all the authors are dead."

"Oh! It's in French!"

"Do you read French?" he asked.

She looked at him sidelong, wondering if he was making fun of her. He was not above sarcasm. She had heard him tell Jamie that Chekhov was a defenceman for the Canucks and Rambo a poet. She had taken French in school, but retained not a syllable beyond the usual phrases already learned from pop songs. "How do I pronounce 'I love you?'" she asked now. "Correctly, I mean."

"*Je vous aime,*" he said.

"Je voo zem. Je voo zem."

"*Je vous déteste,*" Malcolm told her. "You'll need to know how to say that, too."

Christian poked his head in the door. "Listen. Amanda just called. She's on her way. I have a plan. We are going to *revolt.*"

112

It was over the back room. They were going to work to rule. Alison's part, as Christian explained, was quite simple: when Amanda arrived, she was to get her into the back room by any possible means.

She found Thi shampooing a hulk of a man at the sink. "You don't know what a kipper is?" he was asking Thi, incredulously and in a Scottish accent.

"Did Christian tell you?" Thi asked Alison.

"Yes."

"You," said the Scotsman, meaning Alison. "Do you know what a kipper is?"

"Of course. A fish."

He grabbed at her hand and pressed it to his broad chest. "Bless you. You're the first woman in this city to answer me that. Will ye marry me?"

Laughing, Alison pulled her hand away and hurried up to the front to be there when Amanda walked in. Donna was using the phone. When she hung up, she asked Alison, "Did Christian tell you?"

"Yes."

"Is my client ready?"

"Just about." Her client was the Scot.

It was a half-hour before Amanda appeared carrying a cardboard box in her arms. "A new product," she explained when Alison opened the door for her. "Holding *mud*. Isn't that great?" She headed for the back room. Alison was relieved it was so easy.

Walking through the salon, Amanda did not seem to notice each stylist start a little to see her, then lean forward and whisper something to the client in each chair. She did not see how, as soon as she had passed, they left their clients, clipped and dripping and blinking in the mirrors, while they trooped back to protest. Into the back room, the rowdy plebeians crowded in.

113

Except Malcolm, who went right on working. "Malcolm," Alison said. "Come on."

It was not his fight. He predated them all. He was of the *ancien régime*.

"He'll be back in a minute," Alison told his client, taking him firmly by the arm.

"But I am ancient," he protested.

She squeezed into the room with the others, pushed her way back, then took a seat on the steps that descended to the alley parking lot. From there, Alison could see the perfect rounds of Amanda's breasts, her uniform cut-work lace nostrils widening defensively. Parts of her were as authentic as Vitae's columns, but she was the owner, after all.

"These are, as you observe, *intolerable* conditions," said Christian, their self-appointed spokesman. He was doing that nerve-racking thing with his eyes, staring her down with one, then switching. Amanda, who could not seem to adjust to a gaze so demanding and unpredictable, kept looking around at the rest of them.

"What do you want?" she asked indignantly. "Me to renovate again?"

"Why not?" said Christian.

"Money," she said and Malcolm let out a laugh. "I have another salon starting up. The funds just aren't there."

"How about a window then," said Thi, clasping her ringed fingers together, entreating. "Just a window to let some light in."

"Eventually, yes. Everything in good time. Rome, after all, wasn't built in a day, ha ha."

Everyone groaned. They argued on, but eventually gave up. Their clients were waiting. As they filed back out, Christian asked, "Has anyone seen *Satyricon*?" Going over to his station, he hefted the scowling bust there

onto a curler trolley and tore off its wig and glasses.
"Here he is. All hail the Senator." He rolled it once
around like an invalid in a bath chair.

And so an idea was born, that they would re-enact
Rome's decline and fall.

"Weren't they always having orgies?" Jamie asked.

Everyone cheered. Right there on the faux marble,
they would do it. And heat larks' tongues in the
microwave, steal a lion from the zoo and have it prowl
the premises. Robert bemusedly mentioned slaves and
Donna volunteered Alison to be theirs. All day
Christian exhorted stylists and clients alike to remember the fate of the Christians.

Malcolm did not participate in their fantasy. He listened and watched and, for the first time, noticed that
the girl had changed. It was inevitable, of course. She
was too easily influenced. He would not have been surprised if tomorrow she turned up with a tattoo and a
copy of *Ferret World* rolled up under her arm.

Alison, had she heard his thoughts, would only have
agreed. When she had first come to Vitae she'd likened it
to a temple and the stylists to priests, but not any more.
Thi liked to hip-hop to the sink, which was not at all the
way to approach an altar, and the way they dressed—
weird and funky, in clothes that often looked like rags,
but cost a lot more—half of them perforated by rings
and studs and stained subcutaneously with bruise-blue
ink, they would have been driven out of anywhere holy.
No, with the dance music pounding continuously in the
background, the banter and the jokes, it was more like a
party. A month into her apprenticeship, going to work
was like getting paid to go to a party—every day, all day
long, without the punitive hangover.

She told this to Billy who asked her who was who.

"What do you mean?"

"There's a wallflower at every party. A hostess. A guy who throws up in the rec room."

"Okay," said Alison. "Malcolm is the chaperone." Always at the party but never celebrating, watching instead from behind the cover of a book. *Disapproving.* She did an imitation of him for Billy, crossing her legs and turning down the corners of her mouth. Her chin, tucked in, doubled. That upturned crease of flesh was, some days, the closest he came to smiling at any of them.

"And Jamie is the lady's man, of course. He's the only man interested in ladies. Donna's the vamp. Robert's the quiet one in the corner. Roxanne and Thi are the girls giggling in the bathroom, but Thi's the hostess, too. Amanda's the unwelcome guest."

"Who are you?" asked Billy.

Alison didn't know yet.

"You have to come out with us for a drink after work, Billy," she told him. "You have to meet everybody."

"I'm not sure I want to."

Billy was conservative, except in bed, a guy's guy. She hadn't told him the half of it—that Robert's partner had AIDS, that Roxanne was seemingly held together by her cotter-pins of piercings, that Christian's hair was dyed the garish and innocent colour of a duckling. She hadn't told him anything about Christian.

He was the life of their party, their antic impresario. "Quick! Get me a fag!" he would bray to the smokers on the back steps. Not only had he spontaneously organized the revolt in the back room, but for Thi's birthday he assembled them all in the alley and armed Thi with a bottle of Baby Duck, a reference to his hair. Twenty paces off, he stood with a towel over his head. How it resembled a lamp shade! Thi fired the plastic cork and when it struck his chest, he pretended to crumple, while, cheering, they passed around the erupting bottle. An *impractical* joker was Christian, so elaborate and time-consuming were his tricks.

If he was particularly pleased, he would take his embarrassed client by the hand and parade her from chair to chair. "Is she beautiful, or is she beautiful? Am I good, or am I good?" Excellent, Alison thought, and more than that—lightning-bladed. Also, his memory was prodigious. Before sending her off to shampoo, he'd brief her: "He has three small bumps behind his left ear. They don't hurt and they're not *infectious*. I'm just telling you in case you're *squeamish*." Alison had overheard him pick up conversations left off a year before.

Over lunch, always in the deli, though there were cafés up and down the avenue, he would play his favourite game, which was to put on an expression of delighted surprise as he waved to a passing stranger. The passerby, his victim, would casually wave back, then stop in his tracks, stop and peer in at Christian. Sometimes he would visibly start. Always the easily read question on his face, "Do I know you?" would change to, "What *happened* to you?" Christian, behind the glass, seemed to bask masochistically in these reactions. He wanted people to look at him and squirm. As the stranger stalked away, Christian would blow a kiss.

"His name is *Karl*," he told her one afternoon after flummoxing a passing businessman.

"Whose?"

He gestured to the counter where the deli man was making their sandwiches. "I heard someone call him that. Do you think it's *Carl* with a C or *Karl* with a K?"

Alison sighed. "I have no idea."

"I hope it's a C. My name starts with C. But this is a deli. A *German* deli. Karl in German is with a *K*. Do me a favour?"

"What?" asked Ali.

"Ask who cuts his hair."

When she went to get the sandwiches, she said, "It's Karl, right?"

"That's right."

"I'm Ali and that's Christian. We work next door."

"Yes, I know. I see you every morning, flying past my window."

Perhaps she was looking at him too hard, studying him, trying to see what Christian saw. She didn't care for his nose; puggish, it didn't seem full-grown. Under his cap, his hair was fine and straight, the colour of wet sand. Probably in the summer he metamorphosed to blond.

"Who cuts your hair?" she asked.

"Maybe you'd like to?"

"I'm not a stylist yet!" she told him and, blushing, took the sandwiches and hurried back to Christian at the table.

"What did he say?"

She wasn't about to tell him, so she blurted the first thing that came to mind. "His mother."

"His mother!" Christian wailed. "How can I compete with that?"

She felt fortunate in having Billy. Other than Thi, who was happily married, no one else at Vitae seemed to be in a satisfying relationship. Robert had John, yes, but John was dying, so how could they be happy?

Alison actually knew John better now than she knew Robert. A couple of afternoons each week he would come and sit in the reception area and read the magazines. He wasn't working any more, he told her. He was on a disability pension.

"Were you a hairdresser as well?" she asked.

"We're not all hairdressers," he said. "We can do other things, too."

Embarrassed, she tried to stammer something, but couldn't think of what to say. She'd only presumed he was a hairdresser by how he kept coming in week after week.

Then he winked. "We can dance and arrange flowers," he said. "We can't be beat as interior decorators."

"So what did you use to do?"

"I'm a metallurgical engineer. But one with *flair*."

Later, he told her why he came, why he always sat in the same place on the sofa, right next to the kneeling Venus. It gave him the vantage of looking through the columns to Robert's station. John came in to watch Robert. For hours at a time, he only pretended to be reading the magazines. "Watching Robert," he told her, "is more interesting than metallurgy."

Christian was sweet on the unattainable deli man, straighter than the arrow stuck in his heart. Donna was seeing one of her clients—the gargantuan Scotsman who had asked her to marry him when she had correctly answered what a kipper was. "Isn't that cute?" she had told everyone. "It was, like, a skill-testing question." Malcolm, Alison couldn't imagine with a love life, though some days she wondered if he wasn't courting all his clients at once. They were old, yet half of them seemed to regress to girlhood when they saw Malcolm coming out of the back room to greet them. They'd flirt and giggle and bring him mysterious bulky things in bags.

As for Roxanne's views on love, they were decidedly peculiar. She explained them to Alison one day when they went shopping with Donna after work. "What's your boyfriend like?" she asked. "Christian says he's a genius or something. He has, like, a Ph.D?"

"That's next, I guess. He's actually taking a break right now and working in a lab at the university."

"How long have you lived together?"

"About a year."

Donna appeared on the other side of the rack and held up two identical copper-coloured flower-speckled dresses. "Put these on. You'll look like twins."

"Twins?" Alison scoffed, but Roxanne said, "Come on, Ali."

It was a Friday after work, the store crowded, and only one dressing room was free. Roxanne stepped into it, then stood holding the door for Alison. "Come on."

They were all so uninhibited, none of them self-conscious in the least, the salon filled with half-naked plaster statuary and frescoed nudes. Once Donna had taken off her shirt in the back room so that Thi could sew on a button, then sat on the back steps brazenly smoking a cigarette in her brassiere. They would tease her about her modesty if she didn't change with Roxanne. Everyone back at Vitae would hear about it. But Alison wasn't sure what she dreaded most: to take her clothes off in front of Roxanne, or to see Roxanne without hers.

Roxanne didn't wear a bra, Alison saw right away as Roxanne was pulling her T-shirt over her head. Her hair got stuck in the neck band. No, it was her ears. Along the edges, her ears looked brass-tacked, as if she were upholstered. In the lobes were grommets that made holes large enough to see through. All of this was concealed by her hair, as the nipple ring was a secret under her clothes. And the navel ring. And the grooves between her ribs, the bumpy plate of her breast bone bigger than the blebs that were her breasts.

"Why the right one?" asked Alison.

Roxanne turned to look at herself in the mirror, at the steel ring swinging from the centre of her petal-pink aureole. She shrugged. "I don't know. That's the side I'd wear a brooch?"

"It's for sex, right?" That was what Alison had read.

Roxanne shuddered. "I don't like sex." She dropped her voice so they couldn't be heard in the next dressing room, leaning into Alison as she whispered, Alison smelling the mouldering odour of Roxanne's breath. She always smelled of coffee or bile or this faintly rotting scent. "Do you?"

"Sure," said Alison, suppressing a smile, thinking of what had happened last night. She had told Billy she wasn't in the mood, that she felt a little depressed for no particular reason. From the bedroom a dull thud had sounded, then Billy appeared dragging the bed, a futon. He hauled it into the kitchen, but it was larger than the surface area of the floor so he had to roll the sides, forming a padded chute against the cupboard doors and fridge and stove. "Know how, at a party, everybody sticks to the kitchen?" he said. "The kitchen is the comfort room."

Their Half-Tunnel of Love, he called it afterward, dancing around the apartment, ecstatic and nude, the happiest part of him shiny with his own opaline fluid. Unfortunately, they had forgotten about Lake Superior, the puddle from the leaking fridge. It was going to take days for the futon to dry out.

All Alison's life she had been told she was a good girl. That she was helpful and unselfish, with a sunny disposition. That was not necessarily the opposite of someone who liked sex, yet somehow she always felt strangely embarrassed afterwards, as if it wasn't really her who did those things.

"Jamie and I are in love, did he tell you?" Roxanne asked.

"No."

"It's hopeless."

Alison nodded. Roxanne was brunette.

"I don't like to be touched, so we're just friends. Still, when I see him with other women, it just kills me."

"Why don't you like to be touched?" Alison asked.

A sharp rap sounded on the door. "What are you two whispering about in there?" asked Donna.

"Love," Roxanne answered.

"Oh, *that*. Hurry up."

"Once I saw him kissing a girl," Roxanne continued hushedly as she unzipped and stepped out of her pants. "Necking in the car. That's when I did this." She stuck her tongue out, the stud nestled there, as on a velvet cushion. It was Alison's turn to shudder. "Anyway, I have to accept it. It's the way it's got to be. Except for Jamie, all my men friends are gay. You can trust them."

Alison didn't know about that, but she did think it was cool that now she actually knew a few homosexuals personally.

"I like you, Ali. You always listen." She reached out with her bony arm, slinging it limply over Alison's shoulder and turning to face the mirror. Before them was a picture of two women of equal height, one hipless with very thin, slightly bowed legs, a shrunken chest, and voluminous hair; the other not exactly fat, but much, much fuller—rounded, fleshy. With Roxanne's skinny arms around her neck, their heads together, it was strangely clear to Alison that both of them felt they came out ahead in the comparison.

5

"Mrs. Soloff," Alison said, "I'll take you back first because I know Malcolm likes to shampoo you himself."

Holding out her arm for Mrs. Soloff to clutch, Alison looked down on the mat of fine white filaments covering, like a harmless mould, the old woman's head. She drew back the red velvet curtain, saw her into the changing room, then, after a respectful lapse of time, asked through the curtain, "Are you all right? Would you like my help?"

"Yes, dear."

She came in smiling and, taking Mrs. Soloff's blouse, hung it on a hanger and held out the smock for her. It seemed to hurt Mrs. Soloff to creak her arms back; she stiffened halfway, waiting for Alison to bring the sleeves to her instead, and in that brief moment Alison noticed a blue mark on the inside of her arm near her wrist. Pressing the Velcro tabs together, she said, "There's ink or something on your arm, Mrs. Soloff."

Mrs. Soloff didn't reply; she looked away as though she hadn't heard. Alison pulled aside the curtain to let her through and together they stepped out, one of Mrs. Soloff's arms curled arthritically around Alison's, though not as tightly as before. Her handbag hanging from the other arm, where the leather strap crossed her forearm, Alison saw the mark again—this time the blurred digits of a tally.

"Oh, Mrs. Soloff," she blurted in surprise, "there are numbers on your arm."

Mrs. Soloff stopped and for a long moment stood staring at the floor, as if to catch her breath or recover from vertigo. "Mrs. Soloff?" Alison whispered.

She let go of Alison's arm, so Alison knew then that she had made a mistake, a mistake worse even than falling on faux marble and shattering a hip, though what exactly her mistake was, she didn't understand. Mrs. Soloff, bracing herself against the column, not even looking at Alison, said clearly, though not loud enough for anyone else to hear, "You are a very stupid girl."

Alison stood there, stricken. She watched Malcolm sweeping over to help Mrs. Soloff, saw him settle her in the chair and, taking a towel, wrap it dotingly around her diminished shoulders. Though she couldn't hear him across the gallery for the music, Alison knew that when he paused and bent close to Mrs. Soloff, he was asking in a concerned whisper if anything was wrong. Mrs. Soloff didn't answer. She didn't seem able to. Waving her hand weakly, she shut her eyes.

Alison wanted to cry. She took hold of her own hair with both hands and pulled until it stung more than Mrs. Soloff's words, until that, instead of her confusion, was the reason for her eyes welling up with tears. Turning, she went back to the reception area. The woman who had been waiting when Alison first arrived was still there. On any other day, Alison would have offered her a coffee. "Who are you here to see?" she asked dully.

"Christian."

"He should be here any minute. Come with me and I'll get you shampooed."

The woman rose and came to Alison, but Alison didn't move. She looked back distractedly at Mrs. Soloff. Suddenly Alison was sobbing, sobbing with shame; she had hurt the feelings of an old lady.

In walked Christian, right on cue. He didn't say anything to Alison, simply took her hand and, looking at his client said, "We have an *emergency* here, as you can see. I'm going to be later than usual."

"I'll wait," said the woman.

"Sal, you are a *dear.*"

He whisked Alison out the door. Embracing her on the sidewalk, he soothed her all the more for being small; Alison, who hadn't felt so rebuked since childhood, clutched Christian like a doll. In her arms, he felt sinewy and compact and good.

"I said a stupid thing to Mrs. Soloff."

"Mrs. Soloff is a sweetheart. It will be all right."

"*Really* stupid."

"Come," he said, leading her into the deli.

He sat her in the corner, away from the window, and, taking a handful of napkins out of the chalet holder, pressed them in her hand. She blew her nose and dried her eyes and Christian brought her a glass of water. Sitting down himself, squinting, he waited for her to speak.

"Mrs. Soloff has a number on her arm. A tattoo." When he nodded, Alison felt worse.

"You don't know what it means?" Christian asked. "She's Jewish. She's a Holocaust survivor. She was tattooed in a camp."

Alison covered her cringing face with both her hands. "I *am* stupid. I didn't know."

"It was a mistake."

"Now she hates me."

He pulled on a hand, took it off her burning face and patted it. "She doesn't hate you. She's just upset. In a few days you'll be her favourite little *shiksa* again."

"She hates me."

"Believe me. I have been *countless* times in Mrs. Soloff's position. People say things to me. Thoughtless things. 'Ever heard of plastic surgery?'"

"They don't say that," said Alison, appalled.

"They *do*. And *worse*."

"What do you say?"

"I say, 'I've *had* plastic surgery, but when are you getting your tact fixed.' There's nothing *to* do but cool off. People *are* stupid. I forgive them. If I didn't, I wouldn't have any clients. It's the ones that *mean* it who get to me."

She stared at him. "Who? Who would say something like that and mean it?"

"Sweetie." He chirred his sour laugh. "We have our enemies."

Who? Alison was about to ask. Who do you mean? But the deli man approached just then to ask if everything was okay. Christian turned to him. "Tell me. Could anyone hate *her*?"

He looked at Alison, dimple flashing. "I couldn't."

"See?" said Christian. "I have to get to work. Why don't you take the day off? I'll get your coat."

She waited on the sidewalk outside and through Vitae's window saw Christian coming up from the gallery with her coat over his arm, then stopping at the desk to use the phone. Opening the door, he handed Alison a ten-dollar bill along with the coat.

"Don't worry. We'll manage without you somehow." He kissed her cheek. "I just called you a cab."

She was still in bed when Billy got home from work. "What's the matter?" he asked. "Are you sick?"

"No. I'm stupid." She told him what had happened.

"Christ," he said and, sitting at the end of the bed, squeezed her foot through the covers and called her Shit-for-Brains.

"When was the war exactly?" Alison asked.

He rolled his eyes. "Which one?"

"You know."

"Nineteen thirty-nine to nineteen forty-five."

"Six years? So long?"

"The fight of the century," he said.

In high school she hadn't been much of a student. She hadn't really tried. But if she had known that the things they taught in social studies could have happened to someone she knew, someone *here*, maybe she would have paid attention. Maybe they would have seemed more real.

That evening Christian called to see how she was feeling. Billy handed her the phone, eyebrows converging in disapproval. "Some guy for you."

"I'm okay," she told Christian.

"Was that *Billy*?"

"Yes."

"I *like* his voice."

"I'll tell him."

"Do. Listen. I've written something and want you to hear it." A papery rustle, then Christian cleared his throat. "*'Mein lieber Herr.'*"

"What?"

"'Long have I sat gazing at your *Wurst* which dangles so comestibly. Across your groaning board, would I lay me down. Make me your *Vorspeise*, I do beg.'" A raspy pause, then he asked, "Well? What do you think?"

Alison giggled. Billy, lying on the couch, shot her another mono-browed look.

6

Alison wanted to tell Mrs. Soloff she was sorry, but worried it would only remind her of her mistake and cause her more pain, so she said nothing the next week when Mrs. Soloff came in. Instead, Mrs. Soloff initiated the reconciliation. As she was paying, she took Alison's hand and enclosed it in her tremoring own. "You're a good girl," she said and Alison, truly grateful, squeezed back an apology.

What Alison learned from the episode with Mrs. Soloff was that people had a past, but unless they told you, you could never guess what they had been through. She began to look with new eyes at the people in the salon, especially Malcolm's aging clients. Where had they come from, she wondered. What had they seen? Malcolm himself was an enigma, his clothes picked out of a dress-up trunk. And why was Roxanne starving herself? Who were the enemies Christian had mentioned? She saw her co-workers every day, yet only now did she realize that she actually knew very little about them.

She was quieter, more reflective. Everyone started asking her what the matter was. "Nothing," she told them.

"You seem sad," they said.

"Did you make up with Mrs. Soloff?" Christian asked.

"Yes. You were right."

"So what is wrong then?"

"Nothing's wrong."

Christian said, for everyone to hear, "I think Ali needs cheering up."

He brought her over to his station and opened the little lacquered box where he kept his combs and scissors. Inside was a letter and, on the flap, a heart crudely impressed in what looked like, and on closer examination proved to be, hardened Dubble Bubble.

"Who's it for?"

"Why, Karl-with-a-K. The Guy Who Should Be Gay. I was hoping you'd deliver it."

"Why don't you put it in the mail?"

"I can't. A *billet-doux* requires a seal. It will *bung up* Canada Post."

"You take it over," she said.

"It's a surprise. What if he sees me?"

"What if he sees *me*!" Alison retorted.

He narrowed his skewed eyes. "Oh, Ali. I thought *you*, of all people, would understand."

Instantaneous, her guilt. How many times had he been hurt in the past? Plenty, she could guess. His pursuit was hopeless—he was so ugly and the deli man so straight—but who was she to discourage him?

"All right." She took the letter and Christian, fluttering his hand in the direction of the door, commanded her with a squeal. "Go, my little Mercury! *Go!*"

She told him she would drop it off after work, but later that afternoon, when she peeked around the fake column into the window of the deli, the deli man was there talking to a customer. He spotted her and winked—exactly what she was afraid of. Mortified, she retreated, and if she hadn't already had to cross the street to catch the bus home, would have anyway, to avoid passing his window again.

By now it was clear that he thought Alison and Christian ate lunch there every day because *Alison* was enamoured of him. With increasing frequency he had taken to leaving the deli when there were no customers, stepping out on the sidewalk, hands on the hips of his white jacket, looking up and down the avenue. With an assumed nonchalance he would just happen to glance through Vitae's windows where Alison was sitting at the desk—glance in and smile. Alison, blushing hotly, would turn away.

That night in bed Billy woke and rolled over to see her wide awake and staring at the poster of the rat tacked to the ceiling. "Can't sleep?"

She was pondering the strange position she found herself in as Christian's go-between—a harbinger of unrequited love on either side. She was not about to share this with Billy. Instead she said, "I hate those pink eyes staring down."

"Really?" said Billy. "I find it comforting. It's sort of like believing there's a God."

The next morning, she dozed off on the bus, waking just before her stop, getting out and hurrying past the deli. All at once she halted. She had forgotten about the letter until she saw the deli empty. Retracing her steps, she tried the door. It opened; the deli man was probably in the kitchen. She had to squeeze in or the bells would betray her. In a dash, she made the counter.

She was wrangling with the coffee maker in Vitae's back room when Christian appeared in the doorway. "Well?"

"Well, what?"

"Did you deliver it?"

She nodded without looking at him. When he rushed over and tried to kiss her, she twisted around, showing him her back.

"You're mad at me," he said.

"I'm busy!" she told him, though she really was annoyed.

Later, towels folded, squared, put away, she came out to check the stock. Christian was just then exclaiming over a chalk-faced client, wrapping his arms around her neck. He nabbed Alison as she passed. "Barbara is pregnant!"

In the mirror, Barbara was staring dumbfoundedly at Christian. "How?" she stammered. "How did you know?"

"Congratulations," Alison said.

"Let's shampoo her," Christian said and Alison led Barbara to the sink. Still wearing a puzzled expression, shaking her head, Barbara laughed. "It figures that a gay guy would guess first."

"How did he know?" asked Alison.

She shrugged. "I'm only ten weeks. How does Christian know all the things he knows?"

"Lies! Lies! Who told you that? Oh, *your mother*. What *is* your mother? An old *wife*, I bet. Donna! Roxanne! Ali! Tell her a perm will hold. *It will hold!* Fumes? *Bah!* What have you picked for names? You're waiting to see? You want a name that suits? Ah. So, Sleepy should top the list. Drooly. I won't say *Pukey*, knowing how you're feeling. It won't do, Barbie. It sounds like Snow White's guest list." Comically, he burnished his bald spot. Out came an idea. "I *know*! We'll get the *Senator* on this!" The whole salon, party to Christian's conversation, rolled eyes in unison. "We'll take a *poll*! Ali, when you're finished there, cut some strips of paper and pass them around."

Then, with Barbara reluctant in piggy-back rods reeking of caustic, the timer in her expanding lap as if to measure her progress by the minute, Christian pushed the bust of the Senator around collecting suggestions in the trolley tray. "Remember *Christian* is a name that has fallen unjustly out of favour. The feminine form is *Christianne.*"

Alison was sweeping up when Thi called her from the front. "Someone's here to see you."

She turned and saw the deli man in his white coat standing between the columns, cap jaunty like a paper envelope on his head. Thi was mistaken, Alison thought. He was here for Christian, because of Christian's crazy letter. And suddenly, as if in so generously giving this moment to Christian, Alison was rewarded by becoming privy to his point of view. She saw what he would see—a sweet smirk, the divot hole of a single dimple mysteriously twice as cute as two, the potential for love that he seemed to offer in his outstretched hands, and no ordinary love, something perfect by virtue of its impossibility, and because of this impossibility—virtuous. Idealized, unchanging. It would be so simple.

Then she saw what was in the deli man's outstretched hands. She let go the broom.

His advance through the gallery of busts seemed almost ceremonious, the stylists turning, bemused, to watch, the clients baffled in the mirrors, Christian standing in the doorway to the back room, beaming over the successful climax of his joke. When Alison and the deli man were face to face, closer probably than Christian had ever been to him, she instinctively and reciprocally held out her arms so he might tip the sausage into them.

"Thank you." Alison dazedly drew it to her breast.

"Enjoy," the deli man said.

It was in the fridge when Billy got home. "Yikes!"

Alison, washing the dishes he never got around to doing, felt a thick prodding in the small of her back and turned to see him with it jammed between his legs.

"What a monster, eh?"

He leaned into her. It stabbed her belly and slid up, lewdly nudging her breast. They kissed and, laughing, fumbled with buttons. Billy tossed off his shirt. She pulled away, bowed, champed down. The casing wouldn't break. Worrying it, head tossing, at last she broke through and stumbled back, a chunk of pink in her teeth. She spit the casing in the sink.

When they reached the bedroom, the phone began to ring and a moment later Christian's grating laugh was amplified on the answering machine in the living room, as if he knew she was straddling Billy and mock-thwacking his bare back with the sausage. As if he were laughing with them. It gave her the creeps and at the same time made her sad. She wanted to do something nice for him.

"Lick it," she told Billy.

He rolled over and, wriggling on his back down the bed, started to pull at her panties. "No," said Alison, clamping her thighs around the sausage. "This."

"Uggh!" Billy fell back.

She took him by the hair. "Do it!"

Afterward, Alison took a shower to scrub the meaty smell off. She felt strangely dislocated from her other self, the sexual self—embarrassed, even sorry. Then, hair wrapped in a towel, she went to the living room and found Billy, still naked, scowling as he listened to Christian on the answering machine prattling on about the hair show on the weekend.

"I don't get how come he has to call every night when you see him every day."

"He doesn't call every night."

"Last night he called twice."

Alison, towelling her hair, said, "He wanted me to do something for him." She had in Christian, she realized, a

133

girlfriend. Since she'd met Billy, she hadn't really had time for one, so she'd forgotten how it could be: the confiding, the loyalty, then the punishing cold shoulder. She said, "He likes to keep in touch."

"You're turning into a fag hag," Billy said.

Alison winced. "I am not."

After the hair show, she went with Christian for a walk around the seawall, December waves lashing the concrete rampart, sometimes scaling it, tossing water across the path. Screeching, Christian swerved to save his suede shoes. It was as if the restlessness of the approaching Christmas season animated the water while the sky battened down with cloud.

As they rounded the bend, the Inuit stone man came into view, solitary on his own peninsula, elementary as a pictograph on a door. "Look," she said when they were closer.

Someone had cloned him in miniature. Stationed all along the rocky outcrop, perhaps fifty small rock-ribbed men, precarious on lithic thighs, puny heads saved from the slingshot. It occurred to Alison how many men they had passed on the seawall, how many walked in front and behind. The whole West End was the most beautiful gay club in the world and Christian lived somewhere in the middle of it, in one of these high-rises with a view over Vancouver Island all the way to Japan.

Three acquaintances of Christian's came along then, all so perfectly turned out they could have been models at the hair show. They stepped off the path to chat, more or less ignoring Alison. Christian put his arm around her shoulder, awkwardly, because he had to reach.

"Three hunks right there," said Alison after they had waved goodbye. "Aren't you interested?"

"In them? Ask if they're interested in *me*."

"Why wouldn't they be?"

He blinked at her. "I am *hideous*."

Stopping on the path, she took his arm, holding him back so they became an obstruction to the flow of strolling bodies. "That's not true!" Then, cringingly conscious of her own declaration, of strangers diverting around them and judging in a glance for themselves, their expressions reminded her that she was accustomed to the way he looked.

She let go of his arm. They walked on. It felt colder now and she turned up her collar. "What did you write in that letter?" she asked.

Smiling, he recited it. "'Pleased if you'd deliver one summer sausage a.s.a.p. next door. Payment enclosed.' I *forged* your signature."

"So it wasn't a love letter?"

"I did it to cheer you up."

"So you aren't in love with Karl?"

"Of course I am, but not seriously. He's not my way inclined."

Alison sighed. "*Can* you be serious?"

"About love? No."

"About anything?"

"Of course."

"Do you have parents?" she asked.

"Oh, God," he groaned. "I may *look* like Frankenstein, but I *assure* you, I was conceived by natural means."

She wished he would stop talking like that. When you look bad, you feel bad. He was making himself feel worse. "Brothers and sisters?" Alison asked.

"No. I was quite a shock to them. After me, they gave up reproducing."

"Where are they?"

"Who knows? They do not approve of me and I do not approve of them."

"Ah," said Alison, sensing it was better to drop the subject. This was the first time she'd ever seen him sad and she was sorry to have been the one to make him so. "I'm cold. How about a coffee?"

On Denman Street, she told him to go ahead and order her a latte. Farther down the block she found a grocery store fronted with plastic barrels of cut flowers, a bright frilled barricade. She bought him a bouquet.

"What's this for?" he asked when she got back to the café.

"Because you're nice."

A long moment with his face buried in the flowers.

"Are you okay?"

"Yes. Thanks. How's Billy?" he asked glumly.

Since he'd brought it up, she admitted it. "He's driving me crazy this week."

"Oh?" said Christian.

"He's jealous when anyone from the salon phones," she said. Christian, she meant.

"How sweet!"

"He calls me Shit-for-Brains."

Hooting, Christian slapped his hand on the table. "But he means it as an *endearment* surely?"

He did, she supposed. She sipped her coffee. "Another thing. He never cleans up."

Christian feigned a weary sigh. "Heterosexuals."

"Well, I'm not going to vacuum any more. I bet he won't even notice."

"Ah, *love*," said Christian, breaking off a flower. "It demands such *sacrifices*."

But why am I the only one making them? Alison wondered. Looking at her watch, she stood to go.

Christian stayed sitting, half smiling at the chrysanthemum.

"You're coming to the Christmas party?" Alison asked.

"I *am* the Christmas party," he said and Alison laughed.

Out on the street she watched him for a moment through the window. He twirled the flower coyly, then, fixing it behind his ear, frenetically scanned the café. From the corner of his veering eye he spotted her standing on the sidewalk. He grinned and blew a kiss.

7

"Look," Billy said, shaking out the dripping umbrella. "Here comes Santa and his paid companion."

It was Christian, dressed all in elfin green, rolling the Senator toward them through the columns, the Senator in a Santa cap and flossy beard. Laughing, Alison waved and called to him.

"*That's* the guy who bought you the sausage?" Billy whispered. "You should have told me."

"Told you what?"

"What he looked like."

"Then you wouldn't have minded?"

"No," said Billy. "Not with a face like that."

Christian plucked a pearl-berried sprig from behind his ear, dangled it and lunged for Alison, catching her on the lips. Quickly, Billy ducked behind Alison. "Billy," Christian said, leaning around her, "I know *everything* about you." Billy actually blushed. "And Ali, you look *radiant*." Undoing the topmost button on her blouse, Christian opened the metallic fabric a little more so the tops of her breasts showed, then sauntered off singing, *"Don we now our gay apparel ... ha-ha-ha, fa-la-la ...!"*

"What did you tell him?" Billy asked, holding Alison back.

"Nothing. Come on."

"How about I sit here next to—" He turned to the plaster Venus on her knees. "Yikes! She's topless! I'll definitely sit out here."

She wouldn't let him. They hung up their wet coats, then she steered him through the columns wound now with boughs and ribbon, to the gallery where every bust except the Senator was wreathed. She was leading him toward the sinks where Amanda stood with a punch ladle, but now Roxanne, standing close to Jamie, came to intercept them.

"Billy! It must be Billy! Christian's told us all about you!"

Roxanne and Alison kissed, then Roxanne kissed Billy. Jamie, his hair loose for the party, a mass of ragdoll spirals, kissed Alison.

"Billy. This is Jamie."

"You're not going to kiss me, are you?"

"Don't worry," said Jamie. "I'm not into that."

"Jamie's brought a date," Roxanne whispered plaintively to Alison.

"I'm going to get a drink," said Alison. She continued on, weaving through to the sinks, three black troughs, one filled with a creamy swill, the others with spoked discs of lime afloat in red wine. "Eggnog or sangria?" asked Amanda, grazing her lips against Alison's cheek.

Two glasses in hand, Alison peeked into the back room, found it on fire, brazenly taken over by smokers refusing to stand out in the rain. People she didn't know she guessed were dates and friends. "Hi, John!"

Robert's boyfriend looked up, his face gaunter than ever. The hollows in his cheeks had become caves. "Merry Christmas, Ali." He saluted her with a joint.

A guy called Spike, for obvious reasons, stood and announced he had something to show them all. To lewd cackling and cries of, "Take it all off!" he shimmied an arm out of his T-shirt sleeve and raised it up. Alison cringed. Crawling sleepily out of the dense nest in his armpit was a tarantula tattoo.

She found Billy by the hairdryers with an astringent-faced Donna and her hulking beau, the correct answer to the question: "Which of these is not like the others?" At least she had got him into a tie, though he'd been tugging on the knot so, loosened, it looked like a festive noose.

"Where were you?" he hissed.

"Getting you a drink." She handed him the sangria. "Have you introduced yourselves?"

Billy nodded. "Donna. Scott. Nice meeting you."

"Adrian," said Donna.

"What?"

"He's Adrian."

"Och," said Adrian. "He can call me Scott if he wants."

"Oh?" Donna raised her sculpted eyebrows. "Can I call you Jerk?"

Rumour was they were not getting along, not since Donna had learned he was having his hair cut somewhere else. Alison had not heard this from Donna, of course. Donna would never confide in her.

Billy was leading her away. Out of Donna's earshot, she asked, "So? Did you like her?"

"Who? The Ice Queen?"

The stations were cleared and lined between the busts with caterer's trays. Pine boughs and strings of Christmas lights, multicoloured and blinking, festooned the mirrors. Alison cut into a cheese ball and passed a cracker to Billy who had to yell to ask, "Are you actually enjoying this?"

"It's pretty much like this every day." She spotted Jamie in the corner; he *had* brought a date. She pointed them out to Billy. "He only goes out with redheads." This one was a veritable Rapunzel.

"And look at Christian," said Thi, coming over and greeting Alison with a kiss.

He was at the sink, kneeling on the chair, bowing to suck up the sangria; Amanda did not approve. She put on a collagen pout. Alison and Thi laughed and Thi introduced her husband.

"Nice to meet you," said Billy, shaking his hand. "You look normal."

"Yes," he said. "I'm an accountant."

Alison asked, "Where's Malcolm?" and Thi said, "I doubt he'll come. He didn't last year."

He was coming in the door, in fact, into the reception area, but just then the overhead lights went out in the gallery and the dancing started, so he stopped between the columns. Someone cranked up the music and bodies began spilling from the back. How had they all fit in? In the semi-darkness, he couldn't see their faces clearly, but knew they were mostly strangers. He didn't know that many young people.

He went over to the sofa and gave Venus's bare shoulder an affectionate pat as he sat. "You must be chilly, dear." In the gallery, they were moving as one tangled, orgiastic mass. Christian, he could make out swinging with the Senator.

A young man came through the columns, stopping short when he saw Malcolm. "I thought I'd cop a feel when no one was looking, but you got to her first."

"Pardon me?" said Malcolm.

Gesturing to Venus, he took a seat on the other couch. "Aren't you dancing?"

"Are you inviting me?"

He looked so utterly stricken that Malcolm apologized instead of laughing. "Who brought you?"

"My girlfriend. Ali."

Curious now, Malcolm looked at him more closely. He had a nice head of brown curls and was wearing the standard uniform of black jeans. In a confessional tone, Malcolm said, "Alison is a lovely girl."

He shrugged. "She's okay. What's *he* doing?"

Malcolm looked over to where the boy was pointing and saw that Christian had abandoned the Senator and was now standing alone on the floor, utterly still, arms above his head, wrists crossed, head tilted up—*à la* Saint Sebastian. He was imitating the pose of one of the nudes in the mock fresco on the back wall.

Shaking his curls, the boy said, "I study animal behaviour. That guy is weird."

"Are we animals?" asked Malcolm.

"I am," the boy said, getting up to leave. "I don't know about you."

Billy had given her his peevish permission to go off with Thi and her husband to dance. "Just two songs, then I'll be back," she had promised. Christian, having started a trend—a line to bow at the sinks—was first on the floor, but now he was at the other end of the room pretending to be nude. "Have a Holly, Jolly Christmas" segued into a disco version of "Little Drummer Boy" and Alison and Thi wound up for a hip collision—*pa rum pa pa PUM*! On the periphery of the crowd, Robert was guiding John to one of the chairs beneath the hairdryers, tenderly easing him down, then wrapping his arms around him from behind. He swivelled the chair back and forth so they were dancing, too.

Looking around for Billy, Alison was surprised to see Malcolm instead, coming back from the sinks with a glass in his hand. Malcolm saw her, too. She looked his way, and now she was coming over. All at once he felt exposed without a book, unshielded. He would not be able to pick and choose his conversations, or duck in and out of them as he pleased. Backing into the corner, he gave the glass in his hand a nervous little swirl.

"I asked about you earlier," the girl told him. "Thi said you never came." He could smell her perfumed hair when she leaned close to kiss his cheek. None of them had ever kissed him.

"Last year Christian called me Scrooge until July."

The girl laughed. "That's why you came? Are you alone?"

"Quite alone," he said and, without warning, tears sprang to his eyes. Then he told her. He had not planned to. The words simply issued forth. "My partner is in the hospital. 'A care facility,' they call it. He's been there for a month."

"Oh! I'm sorry!" She reached for his hand, "I had no idea!" and for a long, astonishing moment they stood together in the dark, a rap version of "Joy to the World" booming out. He felt the dry warmth of her hand around his icy and perspiring one and, looking down, noticed what odd fingers she had. Suddenly he was close to truly weeping, so he pulled his hand away.

"It's not the dread plague, if that's what you're thinking."

The girl blushed. "I wasn't thinking anything."

Miserably, he wiped his palm against his blazer, as if he could not tolerate a sympathetic touch. He could see it offended her. "I'll introduce you to Billy if I can find him," she said, but now she was avoiding looking at him.

"I believe I've met him."

"Oh! Where did he get to?"

Malcolm pointed to the reception area and watched her hurry off. Thi stopped her. "Ali," he heard her say, "Roxanne's crying in the bathroom. She wants you." Throwing her strange hands in the air, she went off with Thi instead.

"*Mal!* Where are you going?" Christian staggered, very drunk or stoned.

"I'm leaving," Malcolm said.

"Kiss me," Christian squealed, waving a sprig of mistletoe. "I *dare* you."

Malcolm came forward and, taking Christian's shoulders, not flinching or showing he was in any way repelled, he kissed his lips. Firmly. There. He had done one decent thing at least.

Christian stared, the mistletoe still raised up. He seemed in shock. Malcolm went to grab his coat. "Sister!" he heard Christian calling as he headed out the door. "Sister! Don't go!"

After Alison and Thi had put Roxanne in a cab, Alison found Billy up front. He was talking with, of all people, Christian, leaning back so far that if she'd gone and got the broom he'd have started them all on the limbo. For an expert in reading motives in body postures, he was no great shakes at concealing his own. Then, drawing near, she heard that they were, in fact, discussing this very subject.

"—what's called, ah, the resident-intruder paradigm. A non-resident is introduced into a resident's enclosure."

"Fascinating," said Christian.

"We study different pair groupings—male on female, female on female, male on, ah, *et cetera*—as well as looking at how factors such as pregnancy and sexual naivety influence agonistic behaviours."

Alison rolled her eyes. But she liked how Billy was the one squirming for a change, could see he was even sweating under Christian's baffling gaze. He had to look away. To his obvious relief, he saw Alison standing there laughing at him, Alison who wouldn't even feign an interest in rats any more. He suffered for it, she knew, like someone might suffer from lack of love or sleep. He simply yearned to impart what he knew.

Christian saw Alison, too, and slumped. Then, suddenly perking, he drew from the Senator's tray a bottle of Black Bush. "What a tantalizing paradigm! Go on!" He tempted with bottle, paused with it poised above Billy's empty glass.

Billy glanced at Alison. "Well ..." He cleared his throat. "Things usually get started with an exploration of the enclosure by the intruder—"

Smiling, Christian poured.

"—which involves locomotion, rearing, sniffing, marking—"

Christian nodded. "Checking out the art work, the titles on the bookshelf, lifting the lid off the pot, spilling the wine ..."

"Exactly. Cheers." He clinked his glass against the bottle. "Sometime during this exploration, the resident rat approaches the intruder."

Christian lit up. "So soon?"

"Circles him and when they're close enough, both rats usually exhibit what's called 'recognition sniffing.'"

"Ha-ha-ha!" trilled Christian. He leaned into Alison,

snuffling her neck until she playfully slapped him off.

"At this point dominance is usually established." He threw Alison a plotting smirk just in case she hadn't figured out who was dominant in this conversation now. "In most cases the resident is dominant and so exhibits certain characteristic behaviours. Standing over the intruder, for example. Walking over him."

"Not *chez moi*. They walk all over *me*."

"So long as the intruder stays in a submissive crouch, everything's cool."

"My *favourite* position."

"If he tries to assert himself, the resident will snap to what we call 'the aggressive upright posture.'"

Christian, clicking his heels together, saluted.

Billy looked at Alison again, wickedly. "This is usually accompanied by a piloerection," and Christian stepped back with a gasp. Quickly, Billy added, "In other words, his *fur* stands up."

Letting go of the Senator, Christian pushed up his green sleeve. "Look! *My* fur is standing up just listening to you."

Then Alison interrupted. "I think we've heard enough about Ratland," she said, uncomfortable with how Christian was acting in front of Billy. She would hear about it afterward, she was sure, and not like what Billy would have to say.

Billy protested, "But I haven't even got to genital sniffing!"

A delighted shriek from Christian, so, to change the subject, Alison asked what his plans for Christmas were. For a long moment he didn't answer, just stood staring at Billy with one eye, then, tilting his head slightly, the other. Billy squirmed. She had to wave her hand in front of Christian's stalled face before he came to. Leaning into her, he slurred, "Oh, Ali. I just *love* him. I really do."

"Me, too." She helped him position his hands on the Senator's plaster shoulders again, then sent him off through the columns.

"Can we go now?" asked Billy.

She took the whisky out of his hand and set it on the desk. "Can you drive all right?"

Robert helping John into his coat at the same time Alison and Billy were putting on theirs, Alison kissed them both and wished them a happy holiday. In the other room, Christian was singing to the tune of "Birdland," "Christmastime in—" She thought at first he'd said "Ratland," but no, he was singing about a land she would never know.

Outside, it was still raining. Billy put up the umbrella and walked with his arm around her, but as they approached the car, Billy opening the passenger door for her, he said something that made her bristle. "You guys swap too much spit."

She waited for him to get behind the wheel. "So?" she said.

"I don't like the thought of you kissing him, then kissing me. That's just one step removed from him kissing me."

"Who are you talking about? John?"

"Christian." He started the car.

"Ha! I'm sure Christian would *love* to kiss you."

"Ali!" He beat the steering wheel. "It's Christmas, for Christ sake!"

"The season of *brotherly love. You're* one to talk."

Billy was aghast, but what could he say? He knew what she was referring to. They'd had a great time with the sausage, she not really even goading while he took it in his mouth, so it must be true what they say. That it's in everyone after all—the potential to love anyone.

They drove on in silence, Alison staring out the window, thinking how hardly anyone put up Christmas lights any more. There seemed to be, year by year, measurably less light in the world.

Christmas already: the strain of the why-aren't-you-married innuendo from Billy's parents, then the annual taking of the turkey to the mission with her mother and all the guilty memories that brought. Then she thought of Malcolm and the feeling she'd had when he told her about his friend. She hadn't even known he had a lover, let alone that he was sick.

Awful. She'd felt awful.

Billy was looking at her now like he wanted to make up in his usual fashion—with a bad joke.

He ho-ho-hoed in a Santa bass. "On, Prancer, on, Mincer!"

Wearily, Alison leaned her head into the window. "Oh, shut up."

8

In November Denis had finally been placed in care. November, a sodden month, that synonym for grey. Malcolm left him on the ward, Denis oblivious to his parting, and went back home alone. That very day his centre disappeared. The core of him went and he knew himself to be drifting, as if he were made of smoke or vapour or some other intangible material. He couldn't act; he had no substance. Anything he touched, surely his hand would go right through. Yet when he arrived back at the apartment, he was somehow able to get in, and lock the door behind himself, too. He locked it and fastened the chain, then went around to all the rooms and made sure the windows were shut up tight, the curtains drawn, the blinds lowered. He was sealing the apartment up, with himself inside, and the dog. From now on he would roll the stone away only to go to work or walk Grace or visit Denis. Until the end of the year, when the lease was up and he had to vacate, the apartment, dim and airless, was going to be his tomb.

He went out with Grace, not for the dog's sake, but for the sake of Mrs. Parker, Mrs. Rodeck and Miss Velve, whom he would not let down. Apart from each afternoon's brief hyper-animated walk, and his one unfortunate excursion into society—the Vitae Christmas party—he sank quickly into dormancy. Amazing how easy it was to shut his mind off. Hours he spent sleeping or sitting in the dark. If he had a thought it was this: that maybe he wasn't suffering because of Denis, maybe he was suffering because he was thinking about Denis. In the blank moments, he felt at peace. He felt this was the blissful nothingness that death promised.

One morning just before Christmas the buzzer rang and ruined everything. When he had ascertained what day it was, Sunday, and seen the time, just past ten, he sat up, bewildered. On the second buzz, he got up. Grace was in paroxysms, leaking everywhere, so he put on Albert Parker's dressing gown and headed down the hall. Who was at the door? Yvette? No, she always rang with her signature three blasts and, besides, she was no longer in his life. It had to be a client—Mrs. Rodeck, perhaps? She had hinted during walkies yesterday about a spare opera ticket, but surely she would bring it to him that afternoon, at the park, not here.

In a flash it came to him that Denis was at the door. Denis had come back. Somehow he had gotten out, escaped and found his way, but how could it have happened? Malcolm was the one entombed here. Malcolm was the ghost, yet Denis, so offensively alive, so maniacal with vigour, *he* had come to haunt. Now he was buzzing like a trapped wasp, demanding to be let up. Furious. He was furious with Malcolm and there was going to be a scene: objects, priceless in sentiment, hurled, fisticuffs, the shriek of ugly names. The names were the worst. It was as if the cap on his unconscious had been eaten through by its acid contents. Give me sticks and stones, thought Malcolm, pressing the intercom button with trepidation.

"*Âllo?*"

"I've got the croissants. You supply the coffee."

It was a familiar voice, cocky and nasal, the pause filled with noisy breath, yet Malcolm, stunned, drew a blank.

"It's me, Christian. The *homunculus* you work with."

At first he was relieved. Then he was annoyed. "I'm not dressed. You got me out of bed."

"I'm not dressed either. I'm standing down here *stark naked*. Quick! Buzz me up!"

Malcolm didn't think so. Christian was a madman and this only confirmed it.

"Never mind," said Christian. "Your kind neighbour has just arrived."

Malcolm heard Christian introduce himself and the startled woman agree to admit him. The door slammed closed behind them. In the time it took Christian to climb the stairs and find the apartment, Malcolm seemed unable to move except to knock his head a few times against the wall. When Christian rapped his arpeggio out on the door, Grace joined in the racket, scratching where she'd already taken off a patch of paint. "Stop that," Malcolm told her, hooking her with his foot. "Haven't I lectured you enough about our damage deposit?"

He opened the door. There, grinning in the hall, was Christian, one eye rolling back and to the side, a manikin. He wore an outrageous get-up, as usual, and held out a paper bag. "A dog!" he exclaimed as Grace lunged for him. "Can I pick her up?"

"At your peril."

Instead he squatted. Amazing he could get down that low. His jeans were very tight and very torn and for a belt he wore a length of chain padlocked at his fly, the key hanging on a string at his throat. Grace, rapturous, washed his unfortunate face, hoping to be rescued, but Christian didn't know that. "I *knew* you had a secret love," he said.

Since Christian was there and could not politely be made to go, Malcolm went to the kitchen to make coffee, leaving the two of them alone.

"Where did you get all these *things?*" Christian exclaimed from the living room.

"In the nineteenth century," Malcolm called back, adding wryly, "Make yourself at home." Numbly, he knocked yesterday's grounds out of the espresso maker. He was fumbling through the motions.

"So many *books!*"

The croissants he took out of the bag and set on a plate, and when the coffee was ready, brought it all to the living room on a tray. Christian was wandering the room examining the *objets d'art* and the paintings, Grace at his heel, her tongue out, smiling, confident she was going to be delivered. Stopping at the sideboard,

Christian opened the middle cupboard, gasping when the panel on the top slid back. "*Nifty!*" The open door made a shelf to mix drinks on. He stooped and looked past all the near-empty bottles at his own image in the discoloured mirror at the back of the cupboard, the only undraped mirror in the apartment. He straightened with his tongue out, too, and casually picked up the picture of Denis that was sitting there on the sideboard in an old ecclesiastical frame.

"Here's your coffee," Malcolm said.

He set the picture down, thankfully without comment, and sashayed over to the sofa. Helping himself to one of the little cups, spooning in sugar from the bowl, he said, "It's dark in here. Can we open the curtains?"

"I'd rather not." Malcolm tugged the dressing gown over his bare knee. "So what brings you on this unexpected visit?" he asked, hoping to speed it along.

Christian sipped the coffee, his little finger jutting, affecting the stereotype. "We *kissed*. Don't tell me you've forgotten."

"We what?" said a flabbergasted Malcolm.

"At the Christmas party. Only a week ago."

"Oh, *that*. As far as I could tell, you kissed everyone."

"After *we* kissed, I assure you, I *abstained*." Setting the coffee cup down, he looked at Malcolm with that peculiar gaze of his. "Malcolm! I have been trying unsuccessfully to corner you all week. Here we've worked together for over a year, but until now you have steadfastly resisted my charms. That kiss could be the start of a beautiful friendship. What do you say?"

Malcolm didn't know what to say. Was Christian just having him on, or was he in earnest? He couldn't tell, just as he couldn't tell which of Christian's eyes to look back into. Then Christian helped himself to a croissant and, biting into it, showed Malcolm the chocolate filling. "*Poo!*" High-pitched, his laugh. He expelled a gust of pastry flakes.

Malcolm stared at him, unamused.

"Tell me about Paris," Christian said.

Malcolm frowned. "I never liked it," and when Christian looked incredulous, he asked, "Have you ever been there?"

"In my dreams."

"I always felt out of place, particularly in the language. They are very fussy. Even after I had learned French, perfect strangers would correct me or snicker at my accent. Certain national pastimes I abhorred—the affairs and the endless talk of them, and how everyone seemed to own a revolting little dog—" They both glanced at Grace licking pastry flakes off the carpet and Christian trilled a laugh again.

"And speaking of poo," Malcolm added. "It is everywhere on the sidewalks."

Over the years the streets had come to oppress him more and more, and it was not just the excrement. In their own neighbourhood heretics had been burned during the Inquisition, the Bastille stormed, guillotines erected in hotel courtyards; Jews had been rounded up there during the war and, in the eighties, bombed in delicatessens. Lately, this last bit of history had begun to weigh on him particularly. Home, meanwhile, became burnished in his memory. Except for the separatist movement, Canada was rarely mentioned in the papers. Nothing ever happened there, and he saw that as idyllic.

Once, he had almost returned, had gone so far as to get Denis his landing papers, ship the furniture over and close the sale on the salon. The compromise had been Montreal, but in the weeks before their departure Denis kept on withering until, virtually catatonic, he lay on a pallet on the floor. "Come, come. This is not a Faulkner novel," Malcolm had said, in reference to the pallet. The bed had long since gone. He wrung his hands over Denis's prone body. "Do you realize what this will cost us, dear?" There had been oily lawyers to hire and damages to pay. Two months later their furniture came back. It was better travelled than they were. As for Denis's papers, Malcolm filed them in a drawer, but after that debacle, he stopped asking to go home.

"*Affairs* a national pastime? That sounds swell," said Christian.

"And the desecrated Jewish cemeteries? The little Muslim girls barred from school for wearing headscarves? The Algerians bound and thrown into the Seine? You are familiar with the increasingly popular Front National of M. Le Pen? How about the government minister, Jewish, whose name Le Pen made to rhyme with *crématoire*? Or how '*sidiques*'—persons with AIDS—strangely echoes '*judaïques*'?"

Christian turned his head, seemingly to look at Malcolm with the straying eye. "I'm not political."

"Neither am I," said Malcolm sternly.

It was France that had corrupted Denis. Malcolm blamed France. The country was full of anti-Semites and racists of all denominations such as you would never find here. Denis had been an adolescent during the war and seen his country collaborate. No wonder, Malcolm thought. No wonder! Then: *Christ! He was thinking again.* He had opened the apartment door and the next thing he knew he was exonerating Denis.

Christian wiped the corners of his mouth and, to change the subject, pointed to the Egyptian head on the coffee table. "Who is *she*?"

Malcolm shrugged, irritable now, sarcastic. "Nefertiti."

"You have *connections.*" He gestured across the room. "Is that a *hi-fi?* Are those *records?*"

"It's a veritable museum, isn't it?"

"Is that your *lover?*" Christian asked.

In the picture on the sideboard, he meant. Instantly, Malcolm's eyes teared up, but he pressed them quickly and turned away. "Yes," he answered in what he hoped was a steady voice. It was no lie. That picture had been taken twenty years before.

When he turned back, he saw that Christian himself had deflated. He had been sprawling on the sofa, legs splayed, fingering the key around his neck that would unlock the padlock at his waist. Now he sat up straighter, knees together, which made him seem all the more diminutive; his feet didn't touch the floor. He stared off vacantly and in two different directions and his face, despite all the chaos on it, registered disappointment.

"I'm *jealous,*" he said. "He's very handsome."

"But that is the least of why I loved him," said Malcolm, impatiently and immediately regretting the past tense usage. He made a dismissive gesture. "You are all unnaturally obsessed with appearances."

"But appearance is our occupation," Christian argued.

"Not at all," Malcolm countered. "Service is."

Christian pondered for a moment. "Why do you love him then?"

Malcolm flinched a little to say it: "He is kind." Then it occurred to him that, after "madman," "kind" was how he would describe Christian, too. His pranks and gossip, his stream-of-consciousness patter aside, the little man had the ethos of a saint. He spoon-fed their in-house anorexic and charged his clients on a sliding scale. And here he was now, paying this mercy call to Malcolm. "Like you," Malcolm told him. "Like you."

Immediately Christian brightened. "Then there's *hope* for me yet?"

Do not hope for love, Malcolm advised him in his mind.

Christian, looking vaguely over his shoulder to the hall, asked, "Is he here?"

"No. He's—away."

"In Paris?"

Malcolm said, "Yes." And Denis was, in an manner of speaking. Then he stood and Christian, taking the hint, rose as well, though clearly he would have liked to stay.

At the door, he fawned over Grace again. "What's your lover's name?" he asked.

"Denis."

"Denis. I like what you said about him." Misunderstanding Malcolm's wince, he said, "No, I'm serious. I meant what I said, too, about being friends. Do you and Denis have plans for Christmas?"

"Yes," said Malcolm.

"Then how about Tuesday? Do you want to have dinner or a drink?"

"A drink would be nice."

"Good," said Christian. "I'll be in touch. In the meantime, decide where you want to go." Stepping away, he cried, "*Au revoir!*"

Strange how this impromptu visit jump-started Malcolm. The very next day he began to do something about packing, taking several trips to the liquor store for cardboard boxes, even treating himself to a litre bottle of plonk.

When Christian didn't call as promised, Malcolm

withdrew once again. Of course, there was a chance that Christian would still be in touch—he was notoriously unpunctual—but on Christmas Eve Malcolm gave up. He unscrewed the cap on the bottle, poured himself a glass and, looking on the bright side, comforted himself with the realization that he was still a sentient being: it actually stung to be stood up. Then he set to obliterating his newly recovered senses. The wine was blood-thick and tart.

In the living room, he went over to his obsolete hi-fi, where he began looking through his obsolete records. Bach, he thought, would soothe his wounded pride. A cantata would succour him. He placed the record on the turntable, lowered the needle and took the album cover over to the armchair. What would Christian tell the others, he wondered. Would he say that he had gone into Malcolm's apartment and found that time had stopped?

From the old leather armchair he listened, in the dim room, air stale, uncirculating, hermetic, the glass of sour wine in hand. "*Die Schätzbarkeit der weiten Erden*," sang the soprano, the organ a jolly fairground piping under her lilting voice, the violin a joyful line above. "*Lass meine Seele ruhig sein*." Jamie at work suddenly came to mind, his forearms through the copper sheen of hair tattooed with song lyrics. Maybe Malcolm, too, could modernize himself to fit in better. He could advertise his motto on his flaccid upper arm. On the inside sheath of the album, he found the title of the cantata in translation, pictured it written under his skin in Gothic script: *Let What the Wide World Values Leave My Soul in Peace.*

9

Stepping out of the elevator on Christmas Day, he was greeted by a nurse, Nurse Hygiene or Nurse Health. He had to look twice; both of them were statuesque and broad-hipped, with pillar thighs and mannish faces, dressed in the inevitable pastel hues. Once again, he couldn't help wishing that the nursing profession would re-adopt a standard uniform. The caps were smart, the white dresses antiseptic. In running shoes and pant suits, they looked so cheap.

Malcolm liked Nurse Health better. She was a lesbian, he was almost certain, and naturally more sympathetic, but it was the primmer Nurse Hygiene, all in peach, telling him, "I'm glad you came early, Mr. Firth. I'd like to talk to you."

He set down the poinsettia and the box of chocolates on the tinselled counter of the nursing station. "For you and the rest of the staff."

She thanked him and, as he followed her to the cubbyhole that was her office, asked, "You didn't bring the dog?"

"Oh, no. The festivities would overwhelm her."

Taking her own place behind the too-small desk, she gestured for him to sit. "We had a little problem this morning."

Denis, she meant, and Malcolm felt something he had thought he would never feel in his life: like a father, a chagrined father facing the headmistress of a reformatory, though in the last six years he had been assailed by so many unlikely emotions, he should have been used to it.

"Mr. Firth," she began in a solemn tone, "Denis had a bowel movement in Mr. Stavros's dresser drawer."

For a moment he only stared, then the images flooded in: Mr. Stavros sleeping gape-mouthed in his recliner while Denis maliciously crept in. Mr. Stavros's bottom drawer open, his socks inside, neatly balled and clean. Christ, he thought with a shudder and Nurse Hygiene nodded, approving of his mortification. She pursed her mouth, waiting. Did she expect an apology as well? He wasn't going to give it. He was going to separate himself from Denis's actions and opinions; he had to. The guilt was killing him.

Compare this to what had happened with Yvette when he gave her her last cheque. "You'll miss Denis, I suppose," he had said, but to his surprise she had replied, "No, not really. He got so mean there at the end."

They had never spoken about it so he had assumed that Denis had only showed his darker side to him. "I'm sorry," he told her.

Yvette hefted her shoulders. "Why? It has nothing to do with you." But he felt it did. He felt anything to do with Denis reflected back on him.

In Nurse Hygiene's little office, he stood. "I'll go and see him now."

"I thought you should know, that's all."

"I understand." He hesitated. "Did he do it on purpose?"

"They get confused. It's happened before with other patients."

"Oh," said Malcolm, "the high jinks around here."

"With Denis, mind you, you just don't know!" She laughed and he was suddenly embarrassed again. He almost asked her to spare him in the future.

The ward had been decorated for weeks with streamers and Christmas cut-out ornaments. On every door, a more permanent display: photographs behind a plexiglass plate showing at different ages the patient who resided in each room. Walking along the hall, Malcolm liked to stop and look at who these people had been in their childhood and their youth. There were graduation pictures, wedding pictures, pictures of spouses and children and long-dead parents now called upon and talked to by people who were themselves grandparents.

Next to Denis's door, three photos: one in colour taken when Denis had been admitted, another in black and white of Denis as a child in short pants and suspenders, his hair an incandescent blond, head cocked, mouth pouting. He was so clearly that cross little boy again, taking that very pose, putting on that same expression, his hair an incandescent silver, that Malcolm felt a chill every time he saw it. Don't we change at all, it made him wonder. Are we the same from birth to death, only pretending in the middle years to be someone we're not?

The third was taken in Paris in 1963. Also in black and white, it showed a much younger Denis and Malcolm flanking Denis's saintly namesake in stone. A halo illuminating the stump of his neck, the statue stood with his own crowned head in his hands.

From behind the closed door came the sound of a trapped bird colliding softly with the furniture and walls. It was only Denis making his rounds. About to walk in on his hallucination, Malcolm looked up and saw Mr. Stavros coming down the hall. Reddening, he waited until Mr. Stavros had passed in case he should glimpse Denis when the door was opened. Mr. Stavros showed no sign of recognition, did not link Malcolm with the outrage that had been perpetrated against him. He did not remember the outrage. He was carrying a pillow in a pink crocheted case, looking utterly blank, mouth open, jaw unhinged. His eyebrows under his wing of salt-and-pepper hair were black and long as insect parts.

When he had passed, Malcolm opened the door on the room, small and monkishly spare without anything to decorate or personalize it. There stood Denis, berating the air. "Who are you talking to?" Malcolm asked.

Denis swung around. "*Qui-êtes vous?*"

Malcolm still used the cheap black rinse every time he washed his hair, even through this, their long Absurdist period. He knew he should give it up, but somehow he couldn't. "The love of your life," he answered.

Denis scoffed. "You're not my type," and Malcolm tried to act bemused. He had long ago learned never, never to contradict.

"What's your type, dear?"

"*Plus jeune.*" He looked Malcolm critically up and down. "*Beaucoup plus jeune!*" Suddenly agitated again, he began to wander the room making his tactile inventory, touching everything with tentative patting gestures. He picked something up and put it in his already bulging pocket. Malcolm, following along behind, pulled a catheter tube out of the pocket, hand over hand.

"Did you have a good day?" A spoon clattered to the floor.

"Good day to you, too," Denis replied, hotly.

"How was it?"

"I wouldn't know!"

Malcolm sighed. "Aren't we especially *Pinteresque* today?"

Balls and balls of tissue, a broken cookie. From the other pocket he pulled an enormous pair of cotton incontinence pants and, in a flash, saw his future as a series of slapstick attempts to return stolen undergarments and prevent Denis from moving his bowels where he shouldn't.

"Bad boy! Bad! Where did you get them?"

"*Quoi?*"

"These!" He waved them like a toreador.

"*Je ne les ai jamais vus!*" All at once, he let loose a childish wail. It was the accusation that offended him. He had to be led over to the bed where Malcolm wiped his face with the panties. Malcolm, for his part, worried that the staff passing in the hall might overhear and perceive an unkind edge in his voice. If Denis had spoken English, they would have heard for themselves just who was unkind and who was coping with unkindness. Malcolm had even thought to translate some of the remarks Denis made, but decided he would only look childish himself. "Madam? Denis considers your perm a scandal. In his opinion the standard of grooming in this establishment leaves much to be desired."

The panties were forgotten before Denis's eyes were dried. "I'd like some pudding."

Malcolm looked at his watch. "It's nearly five. We'll be having Christmas dinner in half an hour."

"Pudding!" Denis demanded.

Through the half-open door, Malcolm glimpsed a shuffling migration to the dining area, everyone waking, even the seemingly catatonic in the row of armchairs he had passed in the corridor. "Let's go and see if there's any in the fridge."

Outside the door, Mrs. Mikaluk stood clutching the handrail and bobbing. Stout, she seemed to be constructed entirely out of spheres—head, belly, breast, the left one missing due to a long-ago mastectomy. Brightening when she saw Malcolm, she did not so much reply to his "Merry Christmas!" as continue her low, incoherent murmur. Her smile was beatific.

"You look lovely. These are very pretty." He pointed to the heavy gold rings in her ears. One warm ball of a hand clutched his. The other, in slow motion, reached up to where she thought he was pointing, but instead of an earring, her fingers landed on her cheek. Feeling around, she found two warts and began fiddling with them.

Denis walked on, brisker than ever; the apartment could never have contained him now. He needed these broad corridors to stalk his fury through. Malcolm and Mrs. Mikaluk moved along much more slowly. Halfway to the dining area, they came upon a woman transfixed before what appeared to be a blank wall, very solemnly running a finger down it. She was tracing a faint hairline crack, Malcolm observed as they drew near. She was feeling the fault where the eggshell world was bound to split apart.

"Hello," said Malcolm.

She swung around and, as if she had been caught at something naughty, giggled. "It's a jumbled roth!"

"Is it? I don't think we've met. I'm Malcolm."

"It doesn't cart!"

"What's your name, dear?"

Blank and pained, her expression. A skin condition had ruined her face; it was raw and tagged with scales, and her hair, overpermed, had taken on a slightly green-ish tint. Just then an East Indian nursing aide passed by. The woman reached out and gripped her braceleted arm. "Congratulations, dear!"

"This woman has only got one shoe," Malcolm said, noticing just now.

"Where's your other shoe, Midge?" asked the aide. "Where's your shoe?"

"I left it in Chicago."

"I'll go get it for her," the aide told Malcolm as Midge slipped an arm around Malcolm's waist and began a tender exploration of his face. The aide chimed a laugh. "She thinks you're her husband! Everybody is Midge's husband!"

Her fingers against Malcolm's cheek felt like sandpaper.

Two women hanging off him now, he felt more popular than ever. Would any of his old dears from the salon end up here, he wondered. Mrs. Mikaluk burbled in tongues. Midge whispered, "Will you phone the campfire girls?"

Denis was standing in the wide doorway to the dining area, hands on his hips. "Who are these people?" he demanded when Malcolm and the women had finally caught up.

"Friends."

"Yours, I'm sure."

In an attempt to placate him, Malcolm said, "I agree, it's quite a scene." A long banquet table draped in plastic, wheelchairs wheeled up, everyone in his or her best bib. In the corner, the artificial tree kept on winking at the joke while carols played in a loop on a stretched and warbling tape. Most of the more cogent patients had been taken home for Christmas, so they were outnumbered by the unloved and the living dead.

Mr. Stavros was already at the table, staring from under his feeler-like eyebrows, the crochet-covered pillow before him. At the other end was a tiny man in a wheelchair, doubly afflicted with Parkinsonian tremors. Next to him was an old lady, Buddha-like in her tranquillity and obesity, the likely owner of the incontinence pants.

An aide came over with a bib. "*Qu'est-ce que vous voulez?*" Denis hissed. "You are so *beau*, Denis," she cooed. "*Beau.*" She pinched his beautiful cheek to distract him. He knocked her hand away, but by then she had skilfully pressed closed the Velcro tab and got the bib on without his noticing.

Leading his lady admirers over to the table, Malcolm seated Mrs. Mikaluk next to Mr. Stavros. Mrs. Paxton and Mrs. Ross were talking nearby.

"What do you think it is?" asked Mrs. Paxton, who was heavily wattled.

"I have no idea. It's probably a trick."

Mrs. Paxton raised a startled eyebrow and, glancing sidelong at Mr. Stavros as she approached the table, picked the pillow up and began turning it over in her hands. Every inch of it, she examined, plucking in bafflement at the cover.

"It's a perfect crean!" Midge told them jubilantly. They ignored her. Mrs. Paxton said, "They'll be asking for it."

"I don't give a fig," said Mrs. Ross. "I'm leaving anyway."

"But what about the boys? Aren't you going to see them off?"

"I don't have time for that!"

"Well, there's no need to get huffy," Mrs. Paxton told Mrs. Ross. "I only said—" Midge, still holding Malcolm's waist, interrupted with a "Hello, dear!" that flustered Mrs. Paxton. "Now I forgot what I was saying!" She chuckled. "Anyway, I'd better hop to it."

"This is my husband," said Midge, referring to Mr. Stavros.

"Where's mine?" Mrs. Ross asked, looking around the room.

"Now that's a good question," said Mrs. Paxton. She

turned to Malcolm who was attempting to unpry Midge's scaly grip. "You don't know where you are half the time, I'll bet."

"You're right," Malcolm laughed.

The Indian aide appeared, pushing another patient in a wheelchair and bearing Midge's shoe. It was the wrong shoe, but the right foot, so she put it on her anyway. "Where are you going?" she asked Mrs. Paxton and Mrs. Ross.

"We're getting out of here," said Mrs. Ross, grabbing Mrs. Paxton's arm.

"We're going to have singing in a minute."

Suddenly, Mr. Stavros came to life. A gale-force sneeze reanimated him. "*Fermez la gueule!*" Denis catcalled from the door.

Mr. Stavros was known for his resounding bodily disturbances: thunderously, he cleared his throat.

"*Ô, mon Dieu!*"

Was he actually going to speak? Slowly, he turned his feelers towards Mrs. Mikaluk, who sat lopsided and muttering next to him. Miraculously, a human sentence was produced. It was in Greek and Mrs. Mikaluk, in continuous reply, streamed her under-the-breath Ukrainian. At one time, they had spoken fluent English, but both had forgotten it. For a minute, though, they seemed to converse, then Mr. Stavros clapped his hands, once, summoning the genie of catalepsy. Mrs. Mikaluk imitated him, clapping again and again.

"*Arrêtez!*" Denis shouted. "You silly little bitch!"

Malcolm hurried back to Denis. "Why don't we sit down?"

"*Pourquoi?* Let's get out of here. *Allons-y.* Take me home."

"You're home," said Malcolm, leading him to the table.

"I'm not home yet. I only stopped here for the night."

"Where's here?" asked Malcolm, curious.

"L'enfer, bien sûr!"

As if on cue, Nurse Hygiene came silently into the room on crêpe soles, a sheaf of sheet music under her arm, booming hello. "Who's the fat cow?" Denis asked as she sat down at the piano, Malcolm ever-grateful that this was a ward in Babel.

"Silent Night." At once everyone began to sing. In whatever language they remembered, they sang—even Denis. The logy and the stuporous, the tremoring and inert, their lips began to move, their voices stirred. Midge raised her sore face heavenward and sang gorgeously. *"All is calm, all is bright ..."* One by one, the staff trickled in, the orderlies and the aides, the other nurse on duty, adding to the choir.

In the corridor, Mrs. Ross asked Mrs. Paxton, "Will you close the door behind me, at least?"

"I'm not getting into any trouble."

"I'll pay you."

"I don't want your money!" cried the offended Mrs. Paxton.

The music drew them back into the room.

"Sleep in heavenly peace, sleep in heavenly peace."

In the middle of "O, Little Town of Bethlehem" they heard the elevator bell, then the tinkling of the dinner carts as they were wheeled down the hall. This was the moment Malcolm had been dreading since the Christmas decorations went up: when they would have to sit down together in a spirit of peace and love. But listening to their soaring voices, voices that seemed independent of the lost souls who were singing, he thought that maybe it would be all right. He sat down with Denis on his left and Mrs. Paxton on his right. Nurse Hygiene stood at the head of the table and, once the trays were distributed, raised her glass of apple juice. "Merry Christmas, everyone." She turned to Malcolm. "And a special welcome to Mr. Firth."

It was the traditional Christmas dinner, cranberry sauce spooned out thick over their plates like a fresh kill. Denis demanded his pudding right away. "That's dessert," Malcolm told him and Denis slammed a fist on the table.

"What does he want?" asked Nurse Hygiene.

"His pudding."

"Oh, let him have it," she laughed. "It's Christmas."

Malcolm cut up the rubbery turkey; when the orderly had passed him the pudding, he doused the turkey with it.

Denis glared down at his plate. "Is it butterscotch?"

"*Oui!*"

Surprising how many could feed themselves. Midge worked the knife and fork with dainty gestures, keeping her elbows close to her sides. They gave Mrs. Mikaluk a spoon, which she could raise, but not always get in her mouth the first time. Even Mr. Stavros recalled the motions. Denis was among the worst, plunging his thumb and forefinger into the cold pudding and feeling around for a piece of meat. He popped it in his mouth, sucked noisily, then ejected it clean through puckered lips. The lady Buddha had to be fed. Like an outsize infant, she merely opened her mouth to the proddings of the spoon.

Mrs. Ross, across from Denis, wasn't eating. "I thought I was going home," she said, pushing the tray away.

"Aren't you staying for dinner?" Nurse Hygiene asked her.

"No. I'm going to make a call. Someone's supposed to pick me up." The Indian aide followed as Mrs. Ross got up and wandered off.

"Where is her husband?" Malcolm asked. She was a handsome woman, after all, and well dressed, as though someone still cared.

"I believe he has a lady friend," Nurse Hygiene said.

Mrs. Paxton turned to Malcolm, "And where are you from, dear?"

"Vancouver."

"Vancouver! You must be homesick! Are you coming to see the boys off, too?"

There must have been an army base close to where Mrs. Paxton had lived. "I'll be there," he assured her, sighing. That damned war. He wished it had never happened.

Mrs. Ross came back, led by the Indian carrying the phone book. She settled Mrs. Ross back in her chair and set the phone book in her lap. "Why is that man looking at me like that?" Mrs. Ross asked.

She meant Denis, who was shooting daggers at her as he gingerly placed a sucked morsel of meat on the edge of his plate.

"Never mind him, dear," Malcolm said, growing alarmed himself.

She opened the phone book at random and, looking over the top of her glasses, used a finger to scan a column.

"Who are you going to phone?" asked Nurse Hygiene.

"My mother. She's going to come and pick me up."

Malcolm was glad she'd forgotten her husband: tit for tat, he thought. Then Mrs. Paxton nudged him. "Her mother's dead." She nodded knowingly and Malcolm found it hard to suppress a laugh. "I wouldn't want to be that old," said Mrs. Paxton, who had at least fifteen years on Mrs. Ross. "You don't get anything done."

"Tell me the truth," Denis piped up. "Isn't she a Jew?"

"She's not," said Malcolm curtly, hoping to cut him off. He pressed his eyes and would not look at Denis. "Definitely not."

"Ha!" He set down the bit of shredding meat. "For all I know, you could be one, too."

He suspected everyone now. The man who owned the café on the corner—that is, their corner in Paris. Politicians. Their clients and neighbours, the man who sharpened their scissors—well, he *was* a Jew. All these people he still met daily and when Malcolm visited, Denis would at some point detail their common offence: they were Jewish *and Malcolm knew what that meant*. This from a man who, for the previous thirty years, had not uttered a word against anyone within Malcolm's hearing.

Malcolm said he had no problem whatsoever with Jews.

"You are astonishingly naïve."

"Naïve!" the delighted Malcolm would exclaim. "How refreshing!"

"Jews are everywhere," Denis declared now.

Malcolm raised a finger, concurring. "Particularly in the synagogues and delicatessens."

"Why is he looking at me?" shrilled Mrs. Ross and the phone book slid out of her lap. As it thudded on the floor, everyone looked up with a start.

"What is he saying?" Nurse Hygiene asked Malcolm.

"He is wishing you all a Merry Christmas."

Raising in unison their plastic glasses, the staff echoed, "Merry Christmas, Denis!"

Mrs. Ross began to scream. So much fear and confusion in her voice, the other patients panicked, too. Mr. Stavros swept his tray onto the floor, startling Midge who put both hands to her face and began to rock. "Oh, dear! Oh, dear! It's a broken coop!" When an aide got her to her feet in their sorry mismatched shoes, Malcolm saw she'd wet herself. Mrs. Mikaluk's whispery prayer grew tremulous and shrieky, but was drowned out by Mr. Stavros's animal bellow. His arms swam as he roared. With all the orderlies trying to subdue him, Mrs. Ross was left standing in the middle of the room, Denis pointing his finger at her as he accused.

"Jew! Jew!"

She stared in horror. She had no idea what he was saying, but anyone could understand his tone. Malcolm, shaking with rage, clamped a hand over Denis's mouth. Denis bit him. "Look what you've done, you twit!" he roared, showing Denis the blood.

Denis fixed a blue eye on Malcolm and countered coldly with, "*Tapette.*"

Tapette? Faggot? Malcolm recoiled, wincing.

Nurse Hygiene sat down at the piano and struck up "Hark, the Herald Angels" just as reinforcements arrived via the elevator to shut down the apocalypse. Mr. Stavros was led away flailing. *Fa-la-la, la-la-la, la-la-la!* They took Denis, too, but Malcolm did not assist, or even look up to watch him go. He sat at the table with his face in his hands, blood from Denis's bite running down his cheek, only lifting his head when it occurred to him that they might come to fetch him next.

He and Mrs. Paxton were left, and Nurse Hygiene still hammering the piano keys. Mrs. Paxton daubed at the corners of her mouth with her bib. Her wattle swayed. Calmly, she rose to her feet and, turning to

Malcolm, said, "I'd better do some packing myself, by the sounds of it."

10

That Christmas, Alison and Billy had agreed not to exchange presents so that they could save their money and maybe take a real trip next year, not just to Vancouver Island, but to Mexico or the Caribbean. But on Christmas Eve, which they spent with Billy's parents, he surprised her with a gift.

"William," said his mother, leaning forward in her chair. "That looks like a ring box!"

"Maybe you'd like to open it, Mom."

"No, no," she said. "Let Ali."

All Billy's mother wanted was for them to get married, that or for them to stop living in sin. Alison thought she'd probably prefer the latter. Though she seemed to like Alison, and was certainly nice to her, she continually made reference to Billy's having a M.Sc. and how he would surely go on to get his Ph.D. Nothing so important as education! Clearly, she didn't think Alison, a future hairdresser, and Billy, a future scientist, were a great match, but if they were determined, at least they should marry and save themselves and Billy's mother from disgrace, especially at parish functions. Billy, as lapsed a Catholic as any, loved to torment her with irreverence.

Alison tore off the paper; inside, a blue velvet box. The hinges creaked as she opened it.

"Let me see!" said his mother. "Let me see!"

"Do you like it?" Billy asked. "It's *zircon*. I got it off the TV."

"You did not," said Alison. "It's glass." A chunk of beach glass rendered opaque by sand and waves, it looked like rock salt mounted by crude steel claws on a steel ring. Billy got down on one knee and, slipping it on her finger, asked, "Will you continue to shack up with me?"

"Only if you start vacuuming."

Ignoring her request, he held her hand out for his mother to see. "What do you think, Ma?"

She fell back flustered in her chair. "Oh, you are a brat, Billy."

Christmas Day they celebrated with Alison's family. Taking the ring off to stuff the turkeys, Alison dropped it in an empty jar by the sink where it looked like some kind of geological specimen. "He wanted his mom to think we were engaged," she explained.

Her mother asked, "Are you then?"

"Engaged?" Alison laughed. "No. But I like the ring. It's cool. It's made of completely recycled materials."

Her mother sighed. "You're getting tired of my sweaters. I should think of something else one year."

Billy always said Alison didn't have a closet problem, but a shoe problem. Not a drawer space problem, but a sweater problem. Billy said that unravelled and tied end to end, her sweaters would stretch, a multicoloured acrylic lifeline, all the way to Hope. In her parents' living room the electric fire crackled, and the Christmas tree in the corner was adangle with its mortifying ornaments of nostalgia—egg-carton angels and pipe-cleaner stars made by Alison and Jeffy as long ago as kindergarten. To walk anywhere near it was to porcupine your socks with dry dead needles. This year, like every other year, they all got matching sweaters.

Alison looked at her mother and for the first time in ages didn't think to nag her about her provisional-looking hair. For her part, her mother hadn't mentioned the nursing profession once, so despite all Alison's fears Christmas seemed to be working out. She should have wrapped up all her dread in coloured paper and tied it with a bow.

"Oh, Mommy," she said, "I love your sweaters."

"Mommy? You haven't called me Mommy for years." Smiling, she took another handful of stuffing from the bowl. "Do you remember what you used to call Santa?"

"No."

"Santa Because."

In the living room, her father and Billy were watching *A Christmas Carol* on TV. Alison joined them when she and her mother had finished with the turkeys.

"Where's Jeffy?"

"In his room," said her father. "He's not feeling too good."

She didn't ask what was the matter with him; she knew. He was sick of his family. She remembered her sullen self at thirteen, hair sticking to her face, wearing those big owly glasses that were always slipping because she had what the magazines called "combination skin": the letter T slicked across her forehead and down her nose and chin, the greasy brand of a Teen.

Christmas cards lined the mantel and the sideboard in the dining room. She went around reading what was written in them under the Hallmark greeting. "I don't know what I'd do without you, Ruth." "May you get back in '95 all you gave in '94!" "Thanks tons, Ruthie."

"Come on in, sport," her father said, and Alison turned and saw Jeffy in the doorway.

"What happened?" she blurted.

He dove onto the floor, their father hurling him a cushion which Jeffy slipped under his chest, propping himself up on his elbows too close to the TV. At the back of his head, a twist of hair stood up on the pivot point of his scalp, but it was his eye that had made her cry out, the grape stain of the bruise.

"Jeffy?" She was going to ask again, but Billy signalled to her and shook his head.

The matter went undiscussed until the turkeys were done and she and her mother left to take one of them down to the Mission. They drove off, Alison waiting for her mother to volunteer the story. She had to keep wiping a circle on the window to see the Christmas lights on the houses, the turkey's warmth and their breath condensing on the cold glass. The closer they got to downtown, the fewer lights there were.

"Why don't they put lights up at the Mission?"

"They used to," said her mother, "but the men wrapped themselves up in them while they were waiting to get in. You know, to keep warm."

She pictured a scene less forlorn than usual: tattered figures lit up like trees. "That would look nice."

"They wrapped them under their coats."

"Oh." They drove in silence. "So," Alison said finally, "what happened to Jeffy?"

"He's had some trouble at school."

"He's been fighting?" She was surprised. He was too small for that pursuit.

"He says he didn't start it. They were calling him names, he says."

"What names?"

Her mother's lips made a tight line. "He wouldn't tell me. The principal told me."

"What did he say?"

They stopped at a red light and her mother turned to her. "Don't tell Billy."

"I won't."

"Don't tell your father either."

"What names?"

The light changed and her mother sighed and drove on for a few more blocks. "I'll put it this way. There might be more than one hairdresser in this family."

Alison stared, then Jeffy's out-of-bounds room came to mind, the door and desk marred by stickers, the cast-off clothes a strewn layer across the floor. There was no scheme to his rock star posters or his mess. Also, his ears were always filthy and his nails gnawed down. His hair stuck up. She laughed.

"That's funny?"

No way was Jeffy gay. Not unless there were messy gays as well as neat gays, just like there were neat and messy Virgos. "Do you think it's true, or are they just being mean?"

"I found eyeliner," said her mother tersely.

"Eyeliner? Where?"

"In his room."

You went in his room? Anyway, eyeliner means nothing. Kurt Cobain wore eyeliner."

"Who's Kurt Cobain?"

"The guy in the poster above Jeffy's dresser."

"That's eyeliner?"

"What did you think?" asked Alison.

"I thought it was dirt."

They found a parking spot not far away, then each took a handle and together they toted King Butterball in his aluminum litter out into the rain. Along the edge of the syringe-strewn park, the gutter was awash with bilgy run-off and condoms like the shed skins of water snakes. They passed an alley where the sodden contents of the dumpster had been turned out, picked through and left to dissolve. Alison shrieked "P.U.!" A mattress unsprung, a sandwich bag filled with—she looked twice—blood? The reek was rot and urine.

"Who was that kid over for dinner that time? When Billy and I were there."

"Kevin Milligan?"

"It was him, wasn't it? He started calling Jeffy names."

"I don't know who it was," said her mother.

She remembered now: they had been grappling on the bed. Alison said, "It was him. You know what makes me mad? How people still say 'faggot.' I mean, nobody would dare say 'nigger' any more or 'chink' or—what's that word?"

"What word?"

"That ugly word for somebody Jewish?"

"I don't know."

"It's on the tip of my tongue. You know."

Her mother shook her head. "I have no idea."

The worst thing about the Mission was that it smelled of what she and Jeffy used to call "Wet Bums." How sincere did "Merry Christmas" sound pronounced while breathing through the mouth? Alison pushed open the door and threw back her hood, keeping her eyes off the garish beacon of the cross; into the dining hall they trooped. The ones who had volunteered to lay the tables in order to get in early were listlessly unfolding paper tablecloths. Because all the years blended as one memory, Alison couldn't recall if last year they had looked so young. Probably in childhood her mind had taken, as the template of the Wet Bum, Alastair Sim in fingerless gloves and a seedy muffler, then replicated and filled the hall with him; but now she saw it was not so. She saw an Iroquois cut dyed neon green and army boots and a man of maybe thirty conversing with himself in two distinct voices and what he was saying was the farthest thing from, "I wish you a Merry Christmas!—No, *I* wish *you* a Merry Christmas!" No one said "Merry Christmas" at all except the kitchen help who had been born again and didn't have to sleep there.

Her mother took the turkey into the kitchen while Alison waited, reappearing a few minutes later with the empty roasting pan. "Mission accomplished." They went back out into the rain.

"Pretty depressing," said Alison.

"I know. I always have a little cry on Christmas night. Your father thinks I'm crazy."

"Why do you do it then?" She and Jeffy had been raised agnostic. "Do you believe in God after all?"

"No. I just add that extra letter," said her mother. "I believe in Good."

They got into the car and her mother found her keys, but before she turned on the ignition, Alison reached out and stopped her hand. "What about Jeffy?"

"What about him?"

"Would you mind if he was?"

"Gay?" Instantly, she cheered up. "They're very good to their mothers, I hear."

As soon as they got back, everyone sat down at the table and popped their crackers. Her father rose to his feet, but instead of bellowing his usual crass grace, paused with a big hand on his swell where the new cardigan did not come together between the buttons—a gesture that really betrayed him as most other men would have made a declaration from the heart. "Now in his youth a man finds a gal and head over heels, as they say. At least, with your mother, she was able to coax me, ha ha. Time goes by, as everybody knows. It was all very satisfying in hindsight.

I remember when Alison was born in the middle of the night, I'm not ashamed to say how I felt. Then Jeffrey. You think it's going to be one way, but not at all. Not at all ..." On and on and with the paper crown on his head, he looked the Shriner that he was. "Now Ali seems to have pulled herself together, to her parents' great relief. We're sorry she's not a pianist, but she has a job she likes. Jeffy, on the other hand, has become exactly what his parents always feared: a teen. We can all take some comfort in the fact that Ali survived those years."

Billy dropped his chin to his chest and began a mock snoring. Taking his cue, Alison clinked her knife against her glass. And her father, words like the yarn of an unravelled sweater tangling all about him, seemed relieved to get out of the snarl. "Who gives a damn? Everything works out in the end." He patted his stomach. "Thank God supper's ready!"

"Anybody make any sense of that?" asked their mother, filling the wine glasses from the litre bottle.

"Who's a Catholic? Who wants the Pope's nose?" their father brayed and Billy held out his plate.

Then Billy made a speech, a chumming overture to Jeffy. "When I was a kid, I had three gerbils, Chico, Guy and Goober. One day Chico and Goober ganged up on Guy and chewed his tail off." He began acting out with skittering hands across the tablecloth the part of Guy on the run, forcing air out of his cheeks in a series of long shrill squeaks. Everyone laughed, even Jeffy, their mother till her eyes filled with tears. "I was deeply affected," he said. "Poor Guy, rathood reduced to a stub. There were parallels in my own life, see? I was the kid who got trounced every day at recess for being small and brainy."

Alison, who had never heard this story, wondered what names they had taunted Billy with.

Nudging Jeffy, Billy winked. "They don't call me Stub any more. No, sir. Ask your sister."

The next day Alison and Billy were on a ferry to Vancouver Island in a steady drizzle. Alison stood out on the deck in her raincoat, looking up, wetting her face. "Please stop raining. Please let the sun come out." The closest she ever came to praying was talking to the sky.

The white of the beach astonished her, a recompense for snow. They looked behind at their footprints, then Alison fell flat on her back and ploughed an angel with her limbs through the wet sand. The second day it was no longer drizzling, though a flannel cloth of cloud was still draped over the island. Come afternoon, her skyward entreaty was accepted, twice.

At her feet, it was bigger than a dinner plate and burning orange. "A sun star," said Billy.

No spots on the ten long rays, sun *stripes*, greyish purple. She crouched, put a finger on its gritty centre; it was cold. The tide had left it stranded. "Shouldn't we throw it back in?" she asked, but was afraid to pick it up herself. Billy carried it out in the shifting water to the limit of his boot tops, then tossed it. Going down, it ought to have blazed a fiery emanation, but it didn't, or even really splash. A wave tilted it and towed it under.

Minutes later, in a fairy-tale causality, the real sun came out. Alison shielded her eyes from the surprise. Everything seemed so perfect.

That night, making love, she opened her eyes to watch Billy. With so little light, just what streamed off the lamp above the motel office door outside, it took a minute for her eyes to adjust. As all white objects emerging from darkness seem to glow, his face was luminous, peaceful as in sleep, but also inspirited, though not in expression—underneath. Beautiful. He looked beautiful. Then she heard his accelerating breathing, saw how he grimaced nearing climax. Lips curling back, he showed his teeth.

Abruptly, she pulled herself off him. He opened his eyes, staring in a way she'd never seen—wildly, animal-like. "What are you doing!" he hissed. "Don't stop!" Then he came anyway with her sitting on his thighs, hugging herself.

"I thought you were mad at me!" said Alison.

Quaking all over, he turned his head on the shining pillow, beautiful again. "I was," he whispered. "Mad knowing in a second it was going to end."

She could sort of understand. When she was most blissful with Billy, those were the times she was also most vulnerable to thoughts of his dying or leaving. If she thought of her life before they were together, it seemed so bereft, though it hadn't at the time. She hadn't known she lacked for anything. Now though, now she would know. This fear of losing him almost made her wish she'd never met him.

Billy pulled her down on top of him, the warm puddle of his satisfaction squishing out between them. "Oh, no! Crazy cum! Now we're joined forever at the belly!"

Alison was crying.

"Shh," he said. "We'll manage somehow. We'll stay in bed forever."

And when she had calmed, she slid off him and lay with the ball-joint of his shoulder in her cheek. He used her hair to wipe her face then, tenderly, raised her arm and bent her fingers back so the piece of glass on the ring hovered above them like an extinguished meteor.

"What about this rock, eh?"

"Your mom was disappointed."

"You're not, are you?"

"What?"

"Did you want to get married?"

"Do you?" she asked, surprised.

"No, but I want you to be happy."

"I'm happy!" she cried, throwing her arms around him. "I'm happy!"

Outside the cabin, water dripped and the ocean, in the distance, kept rolling over with a hollow, muffled crash. Before long, they were both lulled into sleep.

It was the middle of the night when she finally remembered the word. It came to her from her unconscious, though she had no recollection of dreaming anything. She simply sat up in the dark and said it. "*Kike*."

"Ali," Billy muttered. "That isn't very nice."

VOUS VOUS TROUVEZ AU LIEU DE
L'HORREUR ET DE LA TRAGÉDIE
EXCEPTIONNELLE. COMPORTEZ-VOUS AVEC
LA DIGNITÉ POUR RENDRE HOMMAGE À
CEUX QUI ONT SOUFFERT ET ONT PÉRI ICI.

Shut off the engine and sit a moment in the dark. Before you, the rusted chain-link fence and sagging wires, the wasp-sharp barbs meant to keep you off the tracks, four straight tracks running east and west. In the distance, a sound reverberant and loud enough to feel—railway cars coupling violently.

The time is 12:53, you know because you can see in reverse in the rectangle of the rear-view mirror the sign for Maple Leaf Self Storage, 251-1200, which alternates time and temperature on a partially extinguished pix-elite grid.

Driving by, you passed another sign, red-lettered—

WARNING—DANGER
INDUSTRIAL AREA
ENTER AT OWN RISK

—then noticed this parking lot from the street, a car just leaving, one arriving—telltale—so, without think-ing, almost instinctively, you circled back. Only now, stopped in the dark, in a parking lot sprinkled with granular glass from car windows shattered, are you afraid. Anticipation sweetened by this sugary dread. The longer you wait, the sweeter.

What a guy has to go through just to cheer up a little!

On the other side of the tracks, naked trees line up behind a wire fence, staring out. The foreshortened green beyond, unlit, appears now as a void, but the inlet glows, reflecting back the dockyard on the far shore. Street lamps spark in bands above tankers being loaded. At the top of the mountain the Christmas lights have come unstrung, or so the ski hill looks at this distance. This is limbo week, the interval between Christmas and New Year's—when happy people are dazed with glut and everyone else just numb. There, dangling on the wire, a limp condom, and for tinsel, dried strands of bindweed. No festive lights here, no lights at all except those with bowed backs turned to shine on the six lanes of asphalt rising to the Y that shunts traffic to the bridge across the inlet or the highway connector that leads to Hope and beyond, but their glow is residual. Here, then, is a physical limbo to match the temporal one: bounded by twinkling coliformic waters, an illuminated sand pit, train tracks and the monolithic Alberta Wheat Pool terminal—a space unindustrial and unlit.

The trains smash together again, seismically, a crash and shudder that jump-starts your heart. It's 1:02. Get out of the car.

Wait. First look around the lot again. Here is a tidy Accord, gleaming, and at the far end a Land Rover parked without regard to the lines, window shattered or left down. Two degrees, the sign reads. You begin to shiver. What are you waiting for? Go heat yourself up.

In your mind now, get out of the car.

And watch yourself as, feigning nonchalance, you cross the darkened lot without glancing back at the Accord. This is how you have seen others go, how they see you from wherever they watch. Hands in pockets, you saunter past the Land Rover embossed with rain. To cross the tracks, go under, through a concrete tunnel at the end of which the lights from the dockyard across the inlet illuminate the arch. Emerge on the other side, on the darkened green. Ahead of you the tires and plastic cylinders and metal bars of the climbing apparatus seem an art installation set against the backdrop of Alberta Wheat Pool's massive chute and the cross-hatched steel girders of the bridge. Walk around it, past the swing set and the drained wading pool, then, saturated to the ankles by wet grass, continue on towards the park's one building.

Stand before the door. Dimly, make out the little man, absurd in his simplicity, standing for matters too complex to voice. Clear your throat. Push against the door.

And readjust your idea of darkness. Outside was not half so black. This is a void. Raise your hand before your face and you can't see it; neither would you see a hand reaching out for you. Water echoes like your own sweat would, dripping on the floor. A shoe scrapes resoundingly on concrete. Your heart signals in dull thumps an S.O.S.

Flick.

In the blackness the flame magnifies to torchlight so in one take you perceive the room around you, a negative enlightenment—three stalls with closed graffiti-scarred doors, a trough of sinks, the urinals, walls blotched with damp—all of it thrown back in the mirror. Behind the door of the disabled cubicle, a cigarette lighter burns for you.

To a touch, the door swings open, but in the same instant he lets go the flame. Briefly, though, you glimpsed him sitting there, face lit from below, features distorted by shadows and light. He could be anyone.

Let the door close. Wait. For a long time your only contact is breathing—your sharing of the air. The tap keeps on dripping, a water torture, then he moves. You hear him rise and come towards you, and his hand, grazing your shoulder, makes you start. This close, you can smell him over the mildew and spunk. He smells good.

Always it begins this way, with a small gesture, a touch so tentative in the dark it seems to ask, "Are you there?" On occasion, there has even been a kiss. Lean toward him now. Offer him your lips.

Train cars colliding jerk you out of reverie. Look around again. The time is 1:13 and it's one degree. The parking lot is filled with broken glass.

Open the door now and get out of the car.

And see that the night sky, no longer obscured by cloud, is darker for it. Damp air pimples you beneath your clothes. Why lock the car when the ground beneath your feet crunches? Lock it anyway if it makes you feel safe.

The Land Rover, when you reach it, is not as you imagined; in the dark you can't distinguish beads of rain from blistered paint. Inside, no back seat, just a bare metal repository for crushed beer cans. You didn't even look at the Accord.

Go. Keep moving or you'll lose nerve, the filament that pulls you on, forward and through the tunnel beneath the tracks where, on the walls, graffiti luminesces faintly, paleolithic-seeming and obscene.

At the other end, a sign:

No Person Permitted
In This Park
10 p.m. to 6 a.m.

But what overwhelms is the massive floodlit edifice of the Alberta Wheat Pool terminal with its columnar storage tanks ten storeys high, its Eagle's Nest. Just ahead of you, the tennis courts, bereft of nets, seem part of the complex. They seem a prison compound. Rail cars smash and quake the ground again. The terminal is that very building.

Turn and start walking. Pass by the climbing apparatus, the wading pool, under the gallows of the swings. Lit-up in the distance, piled sand in the quarry leached to the colour of ash and a bulldozer stopped in zippered tracks. In the foreground, silhouetted: the toilets.

Stop. You hear laughter. At least you think it's laughter—a shrill ascent of the scale, a sour plummet. Continue on, but keep your distance, rounding the building until the door is in view. Again the laugh, amplified in the echo chamber of the toilet, the door open, the light on. At once the desire for the jeopardy of an unseen partner is replaced by the titillation of the voyeur. *You* have become the unseen factor. *You.* Advance now until you hear without distinguishing actual words a fey babble alternating with the queer, quavering laugh. A figure blocking the doorway, his back to you, abruptly lunges forward while someone else bursts through, propelled by a resounding metallic CRACK!

A boy shrieking, then two figures giving chase. All three barrel across the wet grass, the boy pumping limbs, the other two gaining, one holding out a stick to trip him up. You don't move, either to help him or to retreat. You are frozen where you stand.

From the corner of your eye, a fourth figure. See him moving in the same direction, but in no kind of hurry, stiffly, almost regimental, in the manner of police.

No person permitted in this park.

The boy is still running, then, hooked at the ankle, he goes down—face first, almost comically. A hysterical, half-nauseated little laugh slips out of you. And then the joyless robotic kicking, the grunting—their exertion or the boy absorbing blows. *Fucking, fucking, faggot* they chant. When the fourth reaches them, he takes the stick, raises it and, in the air, it glints. Savagely, he brings it down just as two trains smash together. The ground shakes.

Faggot, faggot, faggot!

Bright, the metallic arc—the stick coming down again, again.

THINGS GET VICIOUS

1

Late getting to Vitae the first day after the holiday, Alison hurried through the gallery, past the glowering Senator. In the back room, Thi had already started on the coffee.

"Sorry," Alison told her. "I slept in and missed the bus. Here, I'll do that."

"The problem with holidays," said Thi, passing her the pouch of coffee, "is coming back to work."

"Did you have a good one?"

"Mmm. You?"

Roxanne appeared just as Alison flicked on the coffee maker. "Well? What do you think?"

After the Christmas party Billy had made the comment that Roxanne would not be going to any far-flung destination for her holiday since she could never have gotten through the metal detector at the airport. Now, in addition to her nipple and navel rings, her grommeted ears and studded tongue, a steel ring was wedded to her bottom lip.

"Very pretty," said Alison, deciding not to show her own ring as she had planned. It was in her purse. The claws would catch in the hair if she wore it while shampooing. At lunch, she would take it out and show Christian and re-enact Billy's mock proposal.

"Can you shampoo my client?" Roxanne asked.

Up front, a young man was waiting. "You belong to Roxanne, right? Come with me." Alison led him through the columns to the changing room and, drawing back the curtain, handed him a smock. Then Malcolm came in wearing, of all things, an ascot, and Alison bit her tongue so as not to laugh.

"Hi, Malcolm. Did you have a good holiday?"

"I didn't have a holiday," he said. "I moved." But he had celebrated the New Year in his own way—reviewing his bank statements over the remains of the bottle of plonk, then vomiting purple and crawling into bed by ten. *Should auld acquaintance be forgot.* The morbid effects of this indulgence he continued to feel even now; he was still queasy from the bank statements.

"Did you do anything for fun?"

He hung up his raincoat and began fussing with his cuffs. "I took the dog out," he said at last, "if that's what you'd call fun."

"I didn't know you had a dog. What's his name?"

"Her name. Her name is Grace."

"What kind of dog is she?"

"Grace defies description."

For the first time, it occurred to Alison that Malcolm might actually be a very funny man. She laughed, then asked, "How's your friend?" and by the startled way he looked at her, she guessed he'd forgotten what he told her at the Christmas party.

"Worse," he said, turning quickly away. "And worse."

Roxanne's client stepped out from behind the curtain, so Alison only had time to say, "I'm sorry, Malcolm."

Shampooing, she found the music getting on her nerves. They'd only got back last night on the late ferry, so she was unaccustomed to that kind of noise. Not that it had been quiet on the island. The glottal glugging of the ravens had woken them, the surf boomed and fizzed, rain fell in an ambient shush, then stopped, and for the rest of the day dripped off the trees.

After the shampoo, she escorted Roxanne's client, wet-headed, to Roxanne's station, then went to the back room to get him a pot of tea. Crowded because Donna and Jamie had arrived and it was too cold to open the parking lot extension, she felt as if she'd walked in on a group-therapy session, even Malcolm present, though in the corner he looked more trapped than participating.

Donna was venting. "I mean, we had plans! I waited till, I don't know, seven. Seven! We're talking *New Year's Eve* here, and still he didn't call!"

"He's ready," Alison whispered to Roxanne who was drinking black coffee through a straw. She put the teapot of water in the microwave and, while it heated, leaned against the counter to listen, too.

"It was humiliating waiting by the phone!"

"Fucker," said Jamie. "What a fucker."

"That's what I called him when finally he phoned."

"When was that?" Thi asked.

"New Year's Day!"

Everybody groaned.

"So you stayed home?" asked Roxanne. The pained sound in her voice, Alison realized, was more than sympathy; the straw was because her lip hurt. She shuddered at the same time the microwave started beeping.

"Of course not. I had an alternate. My point is the humiliation!"

She brought Roxanne's client his tea just as the phone up front began to ring. When she got there to answer it, she found three clients waiting. "Vitae. Can you hold, please?" She covered the receiver, apologized to those there in body, then got back on the line and booked a cut.

"Mrs. Leonard is here for Malcolm. Who are you waiting for?" she asked the other two.

"Christian," they chorused.

Alison sighed. "Not again."

What Malcolm thought was that Christian was too embarrassed to face him after he had stood him up, that that was why he didn't show up for work. It was a ludicrous notion, of course. Christian was no blusher.

By mid-morning Thi and the girl began to call him. They left a series of messages that, even in their hello, betrayed a vibrato of concern. Then came a flurry of rescheduling: "He isn't in today. Can you change your afternoon appointment?" Again and again, Malcolm overheard, "I don't know. I don't know where he is."

Jamie, on his lunch break, drove downtown with Thi to knock on his door, just in case he simply wasn't answering the phone.

"He's not there," he said when they got back. "We got the super to let us in."

"Did it look like he'd gone away? Like he'd packed or anything?" asked Donna.

"No," said Thi. "Everything looked normal and, you know, neat as a pin."

They were in the back room. Alison sank down on the bench beside Malcolm and, with her face in her hands, asked, "Do you think we should—?"

"What?" asked Malcolm.

She whispered it. "Call the police?"

As soon as she said it, it was understood that something had happened to him, almost as if her question had evoked a spell. Her question *caused* something to happen to him, retroactively.

"No," said Roxanne, and she teetered angrily out of the room, back to her client.

"Did anyone check the deli?" Robert asked, trying to make a joke.

Who finally called, or when, Malcolm didn't know, but the next morning there they were. Normally no one would have noticed their entrance, people came and went all the time, but Alison shut off the music so they all looked up and, seeing the two in blue, froze—all but Malcolm, who had closed his eyes. What a relief not to hear that beat pounding out like a pneumatic drill! Savouring the silence, he lowered the dryer onto Mrs. Creighton's curler-armoured head, loath to turn it on and spoil the moment. Then, catching sight of them in the mirror, he abruptly swung around. Everyone was looking at him. The police saw everyone looking at him, so toward Malcolm they came—slowly, the long length of the gallery, their leather creaking. Had Christian been there, he would have squealed with delight.

It seemed to take a week for them to reach him. All that time Malcolm wondered why. Why were they coming for him? What did they think? That he was the owner?

"Sir," one of them said. "May we have a word with you?"

They stepped into the back room. Strangely, Malcolm couldn't seem to hear a word they said. It was as if he were holding a seashell to both ears; a muted roar, the surge of his own blood in his skull. It's not fair, he was thinking. They had not drawn straws or, from the top tray of the Senator's trolley, names on paper slips. The fair-haired one, he noticed, was in need of a moustache trim.

From their gestures, he understood that he was going to leave with them. He led the way, stopping briefly where Mrs. Creighton was still waiting under the dryer. "I'm sorry," he told her. "Alison will have to finish you today."

She grabbed his hand. "But Malcolm, tell me what you've done!"

In the police car, the radio issued intermittent bursts of static and cryptic dispatches. Mostly they did not speak; now and then the two officers exchanged a comment in low tones. Then the one not driving turned and asked Malcolm, "How long did you know him for?"

"About a year and a half." It was a brilliantly sunny day and they were driving along parallel to the railway track. "Where are we going?"

"To the morgue."

"Oh, the morgue." He pressed his eyes and for no reason said, "It's the same word in French."

The one driving said, "I guess a lot of words are the same."

"The pronunciation's different," the other added sagely.

Then Malcolm found himself being ushered into a cold room where, on a gurney, a curiously shaped object lay under a sheet. He had understood that they were going to show him Christian's body, but whatever was under the sheet was much too flat. A sudden battering headache—from the chemicals, Malcolm thought. As he pressed his fingers to his eyes again, it occurred to him that he was dreaming. That was what he had been telling himself the last six years. And when the sheet was drawn back, though he didn't recognize Christian, he didn't say, "I don't know this person." He asked instead, "Is this a person?"

Why had they picked him? It seemed especially cruel after all that he had been through. Now, along with the memory of Denis's disease, there would be the memory of looking down on this obliterated face.

"May I touch him?" he asked. "I can't tell unless I do. He'll have a certain callus." He showed them his own on his thumb and finger. "From the scissors."

The sheet was lifted at one side to expose a lifeless hand, but Malcolm didn't have to touch him after all. "Yes, it's him," he told them. He knew by how small a hand it was.

They were kind enough to drive him home. Again, no one really spoke. Malcolm, for his part, was thinking about how trivial his complaints had actually been before today. Visiting Denis, he sometimes met spouses of the other patients, people whom he would spend a few moments commiserating with. A retired roofer, a retired lawyer, a housewife, a retired poofter, they made an unlikely group, but Malcolm nonetheless considered them his peers. All of them had seen their loved ones become different people. Denis had become demanding and unlikeable, hate-filled, a person who had to have butterscotch pudding thick over everything he ate. It tormented Malcolm wondering which Denis was real, the gentle man he had seemed to be up until his illness, or who he was now. Yet his situation was hardly unique. The roofer and the lawyer and the housewife, they wondered the same thing. In essence, their pain was even commonplace: their lovers had abandoned them and so they grieved. Who, after all, had that not happened to?

He had seen Christian lying on a morgue gurney. Nothing would ever be as bad as what his face had looked like under the sheet.

And now he noticed that a peculiar odour had followed them into the car. Smelling it, Malcolm hoped he would not start to weep. When they dropped him off, they said that they would be in touch. Malcolm thanked them with a wince.

He didn't come back to the salon. They were all waiting, expecting him, growing more and more edgy by the hour. Before closing, Alison finally phoned. She saw the crossed-out address in the Rolodex and the same number as before. It took a long time for him to answer, and when he did, he sounded as if he'd been asleep. "What?" he asked. "What do you want?"

"We have to know what happened!" she cried.

"If you're all so curious, why didn't one of you go instead?"

She had nothing to say to that. She simply sat there clinging to the receiver, not looking at the drawn faces of the rest of them gathered in the reception area. After a long pause, Malcolm exhaled and said, "He's dead."

"No," said Alison.

"*I saw him!*" he fairly screamed.

Amanda closed the salon for three days, but even then Alison didn't completely believe that Christian wasn't going to come back with the rest of them. They were hairdressers, after all. What did death have to do with them? The only other person Alison had known who'd died was her grandmother, back when Alison was twelve. But she'd been old, white barbs of whiskers on her chin. After a series of strokes leading up to the one that finally killed her, she hadn't known who Alison was, or even Alison's mother, her own daughter. It was natural that she died. Christian had been thirty.

Three strange, suspended days. "My friend is dead," she told everyone she met. "My friend was killed." Then she would begin to cry hearing herself say it, but if she didn't say it, she didn't feel a thing.

The telephone was partly to blame. When she called him, this was what she heard: "Greetings, *loved one,* you have reached three-three-one, zero-two-four-nine ..."

It sounded like Christian alive and braying.

"... Though I can never *truly* express my deep regret at being unable to take *this,* your *treasured call,* I *pray* that at the sound of the tone you'll let me know I missed you."

And in the pause she heard him, too—heavy in-breaths through his mouth. *He's there,* she thought. *He's there.*

"Dear friend, as you make your way through this *long day,* be it *blissful* or a *trial,* rest assured that I do, with all my heart, miss *you.*"

"It's like that when a friend goes," was her mother's opinion. "If it's not someone you lived with, someone you saw every day, it takes a long time to sink in. When you get back to work, it will seem more real. Is there going to be a funeral?"

"I don't know."

"There ought to be. You'll need one, especially in circumstances like those."

On the third night she dreamed she met him. They were in front of Vitae after hours, the salon darkened, Christian searching his pockets for the key. People walking past were slowing to look at them and, whereas in waking life they would have stared at Christian, now they looked at Alison suspiciously. It made her nervous and she wished Christian would hurry and unlock the door. When they finally stepped inside, she heard someone shout, "What do you think you're doing?" All at once she understood that no one could see Christian but her. Somehow, too, in that logic peculiar to dreams, they knew that she didn't have, was not supposed to have, a key.

In the dream, she worried that someone would call the police. If the police came, they would ask what she was doing there and how she had got in. If she told them she'd come with Christian and they couldn't see him there, what would they say? That it was impossible? That he was dead?

He had gone ahead into the gallery where he stood waiting for her, looking just like Christian in his chains and jeans strategically ripped. His skin, as always, was wet and shiny around his nose and upper lip. But he wasn't speaking and that, so out of character, began to make her feel afraid. Slowly, she walked toward him, Christian watching out of one eye, then the other, and when she was almost in front of him, when she could hear his clotted breathing, she reached out her hand for his.

Warm. Though nothing else in the dream was hot or cold, his hand in hers gave off a palpable heat. He was alive, she understood. Alive, and she the only one who knew it.

They set to doing what they had come for. In the gallery, the floor was strewn with hair. No one had remembered to sweep up, not for weeks, it looked like. Without speaking, Alison and Christian began gathering up the hair, scooping it up in handfuls, filling their arms with it. And when she woke in the middle of the night, she lay there smiling in the dark. For the first time in her life she had dreamed a temperature. The dream felt more than real.

When they came back, it was to a macabre barber shop, black ribbons wound around the outside columns— Amanda's idea. Too ostentatious, none of them liked it; it smacked of a business opportunity.

Thi brought two newspaper clippings. One article her husband had found when he had gone through their recycling box. The headline none of them had noticed during the holidays: SLAYING SIGNALS INTOLERANCE. "A victim as yet unidentified ..." it began.

The second, from two days before, named Christian. Alison never read the paper, but she believed if something were reported in it, it had to be in essence true. They would not, in other words, say Christian was dead if he wasn't, though contrary to what her mother had said she still expected that he would walk in at any minute. He was going to walk right in and she, she would run to greet him and, laughing, say it had been his best joke yet.

What she had not expected was there to be so much anger, or that half the talk would be, not about Christian, but the nameless, faceless person who had killed him. She had not herself thought about revenge. But listening to Robert list off his friends and acquaintances who had been beaten up or threatened, she understood at last what Christian had meant by enemies. The gentlest person she knew was Robert. Now he sat fingering the ring in his eyebrow and talking about hate.

A week with no dance track, just sibilance and hush—whispers, scissors snipping. Alison sweeping up the hair. Pushing the broom against the little door, she remembered her dream.

"Can somebody please tell me where the hair goes?"

In the back room, her question went unanswered because it immediately prompted that other proverbial one: does hair continue growing after death?

"No," said Malcolm.

Roxanne said she thought it did. "They know from when they unwrapped the mummies."

Beautiful to believe in something tangible and continuous, something to run the fingers through and catch hold of when everything else seemed so unreal. That first week, if someone called for an appointment with Christian, and Thi was there, Alison would hand the phone to her, then duck outside and only come back when she saw through the window that Thi had hung up. It got so she didn't want to be alone up front.

"I don't remember his name, but he permed me once and it lasted and looked good right to the end."

"Jamie?" she hoped. "Robert?"

"He's kind of dwarfish."

"Oh. He's not here any more. Would you like to book another stylist?"

"He was brilliant. Do you know where he is now?"

Good question, Alison thought. What it seemed like: that Christian had simply stepped away from their little circle so the rest of them had to draw in tighter to close the gap. No one complained about the back room being cramped any more; they huddled there between appointments and on breaks, ordering sandwiches from the deli to share. They gave each other back rubs and dried each other's tears. Except for Malcolm. They found it hard to look at him.

Donna told Alison she was sorry for all the times she'd been unkind. "Christian told me I was a bitch to you. I am a bitch. I just am. I'm sorry." They hugged, Donna murmuring that life was too short to be mean. "Let's be friends."

"Friends," Alison agreed.

The next week the memorial service was held in a packed chapel. Though Alison didn't see anyone who looked like family, his regular clients were all there paying the greatest tribute possible to a hairdresser: all of them, without exception, looked fantastic. Barbara, the pregnant one, told Alison as she offered tissue from a box, "You know, I'm seriously thinking of Christian for a name." The deli man was there, too, but without his coat and cap Alison didn't recognize him until she saw the dimple. On the chapel steps, she threw her arms around his neck and sobbed.

What struck her, listening to the testimonies, was how loved Christian had been. All the stories people got up to tell were about Christian the clown and how much trouble and expense he would go to for a joke. In his own zany way, he had devoted himself to making the world a better place—by helping people feel good about how they looked, by making them laugh. And no one failed to point out that the brutality of Christian's death showed just how badly the world needed him.

After the service, they went back to Vitae where Roxanne announced she was going to shave her head.

Alison stopped kneading Donna's shoulders. "Why?"

"Because I'm mourning. Jews do that."

"They do not," said Malcolm, who had surprised them all by coming back with them.

"Somebody does. Is it Buddhists?"

"I think you should do what Christian would have wanted," said Alison. "He wouldn't have wanted you to shave your head." He would have wanted for Roxanne to eat a square meal, Alison knew.

Her ribs like slats on a cradle, she hugged herself and began to rock. Jamie, taking Roxanne's arms, lifted her off the bench, slid in under her and resettled her in his lap with his scribbled arms around her. She looked like she was faring the worst of all of them, but maybe that was because black didn't become her and her lip was still swollen and her face full of metal.

"He used to drive me crazy phoning all the time. Sometimes I'd swear at him, you know, 'cause he'd wake me up."

"When did he call?" asked Alison, thinking she meant the middle of the night, which would be when he wasn't on the phone with her.

"I don't know. Nine or ten. I go to bed early. I like to turn out all the lights and curl up and not think. Now nobody calls."

Alison had noticed this herself. It was as if death had turned the ringer off the phone at home.

"He even called me," said Thi, blowing her nose.

"He came over to see me," said Malcolm, "unannounced, of course."

"He had this uncanny habit of calling me when I was in bed with someone," said Donna.

Jamie laughed. "Me, too!"

"Babbling away on the machine right there. Like he was watching."

"I've been calling him just to listen to his voice," said Alison. "It's so clear. It sounds just like he's there."

Everyone looked at her, surprised, and Donna said, "Aren't you smart?"

Silently, they filed to the front, Alison, Jamie, Roxanne, Donna, Thi. "Greetings, *loved one* ..." The receiver passed from hand to hand. "... You have reached three-three-one, zero-two-four-nine." Robert and Malcolm came up last and Alison, handing Malcolm the phone, said something she immediately regretted. "I didn't think you even liked him."

"... rest assured," said Christian, "that I do, with all my heart, miss *you*."

At home that night, Alison called one last time before she went to bed. Billy, lying on the couch waiting for her, said nothing. He'd been so sweet and tender with her these last few weeks.

When the recording started, she suddenly remembered a moment during the holidays: standing on the white beach and watching it rain. Where she had stood it was sunny, but far out over the ocean a dark curtain was being pulled across at a slant. Hours later, at dusk, they walked back together to see the sunset. She'd expected as clear a distinction between day and night as raining and not raining, but even after the sun had sunk below the water, the sky shone yellow between where the clouds had broken up. It lasted a long time, fifteen or twenty pinkening minutes, the moon right behind them—the two halves of the day overlapping.

Rare, actually, to catch that earlier moment, to know precisely when something ends.

She had just caught it again.

"*I'm sorry. The number you have dialled is no longer in service. Please hang up and try your call again.*"

2

The day after the memorial service, one of the police officers phoned Malcolm with some information for him to pass along. Malcolm took it to work with him, walked in announcing, "They have been caught."

All of them stared, aghast. "*They?*"

"Yes. Three strapping lads. They'll be making a court appearance tomorrow. I do not intend to go."

Ever since his trip to the morgue, he had found himself continually battling a public display of weeping while, alone, in private, when crying might have restored him, he dried up completely. At Vitae, he watched them shed their tears unselfconsciously, comforting one another through their little cathartic moments, even sitting on each other, yet flinching when Malcolm came near, as if by taking on the dirty work he was in some way tainted or complicit. Hurt, indignant, he was not going to have anything more to do with it.

Who would go then if not Malcolm? He heard them talking about it all day. Finally, the girl approached him. "I'm going to go," she said. "Can you tell me where it is?"

He stared at her. He did not believe she was serious. All along she'd worn such a look of wide-eyed bafflement that he couldn't help but think she had not completely grasped what had happened to Christian. He kept wanting to take her hand and, patting it, tell her, "He's gone to heaven. Do you understand that, dear?"

Tomorrow she would understand. Tomorrow it would become quite clear.

Through the glass doors of the court house stood the second portal of a metal detector. Two giants in tan uniforms, sheriffs, she read on their shirtsleeves, were there to tell her what to do, one motioning to search her handbag, the other mechanically beckoning her through.

The courtroom was to the right, at the end of the lobby. Entering, she found herself teetering at the top of a large auditorium-like space, looking dizzily down the aisle of stairs between the rows of seating to a judge in the topmost tier of a platformed bench, God-like in his robes. On the wall above him hung a crest in gaudy colours and gilt. Below him, in the middle tier, were two young women, angel stenographers, and below them, two lawyers faced the judge with their sombre-suited backs to the room.

She took a seat close to the door and tried to make sense of what was going on. The lawyer on his feet was reading an account to the judge in a matter-of-fact voice. "Mr. Mitchell then seizes the complainant by the back of the neck and squeezes. The complainant tells Mr. Mitchell that it is impossible to drive safely under such conditions."

Mr. Mitchell, Alison guessed, was the man in the dirty blue ski jacket standing in the box to the left of the bench. He kept his head lowered, moving only to brush the lank hair off his face and, as he did, Alison saw that his cheekbones and forehead were oddly protuberant and that he could not seem to close his mouth. Meanwhile, there were constant comings and goings. At the far right of the bench was a door; another was just beside the box on the left. People criss-crossed the room, in one door and out the other, bearing briefcases and file folders and each time they passed in front of the judge, they bobbed perfunctorily.

"Having pressed the distress alarm," continued the lawyer, "the complainant notices he is being followed by two other Yellow cabs. Past Boundary Road he is able to pull over and run from his vehicle, at which point Mr. Mitchell gets out as well, walks off, and is apprehended several minutes later."

She looked at her watch, then around at the scattering of people in the public seating. Across the aisle and a few rows ahead a young man and woman were whispering together. In front of them a middle-aged woman was taking notes. Alison was alone in her bank of seats except for a man with very dark hair directly ahead of her and closer to the front.

The lawyer concluded by recommending Mr. Mitchell's continued detention, then the second lawyer rose and began to speak on behalf of Mr. Mitchell, giving his address and record of employment and extolling his willingness to continue alcohol counselling. Then a gesture made by the dark-haired man in front caught Alison's eye; she saw his head bow and his hand reach for his face, so that even though she was looking at him from behind, she knew he was pressing his fingers to the corners of his eyes. Immediately she got up and clumped down the stairs to where he sat.

"Malcolm," she whispered, making him start. "*You're here.*"

"I am," he said, as if he regretted it.

"Thank you," she told him, taking the seat next to him and smelling the familiar mothball odour coming off him, strangely comforting now. "Thank you for being here."

"Calling number 17 on the list, Vorst, in custody."

The sheriff in the box opened the heavy metal door, glancing in a room they could not see into, then letting the door go with a slam.

"Where's number 17?" asked the judge.

"They're pulling him," said the sheriff.

In the pause, as they waited, Alison began to feel cold. She had just taken off her coat, but now she put it on again. For the first time since she came in, all the back-and-forth bustle ceased. It seemed that everyone was waiting, everyone suddenly interested, everyone looking at the box where the sheriff opened the big metal door once more.

He entered so rapidly, darted in and came up against the wall so fast, that he gave the impression of being about to vault right out of the box. With the startling vitality of an animal released from a cage, he was suddenly there, a chill coming up behind him.

"Your Honour," said the lawyer for the Crown, "this is Mr. Vorst."

Despite his disarming attire, dull green pyjama-like prison shirt and pants over a white sweatshirt, he did not seem like a Mr. or even a person with the pleasantry of a first name. He seemed like a Vorst. He was tall and, through the two loose layers of shirt, Malcolm could see the contours of a sculpted torso and arms hard-packed with muscle. Above his shirt collar, the Adam's apple could have been a fist. The chords of his neck emerged like rebar, supporting a blocky head and a face sullen and appallingly young and irredeemable. Then Vorst turned his blond close-cropped head to look back at his judge. The girl gasped and grabbed Malcolm's arm; Malcolm, too, was shaken. In his long career he had seen his share of scalp afflictions—scales and shingles, baldness in patches, unhealed sores—but here, on this teenagers' square skull, was a disease of an entirely different magnitude marked out in right angles with a razor. The last time he'd seen a swastika was on a wall in the Paris Metro.

"The Crown is seeking Mr. Vorst's continued detention," the Crown's lawyer said. He began his present-tense recitation. "On December 27th, 1994, at approximately 12:10 a.m., Mr. Vorst, in the company of his two co-accused, both minors, leaves the bar of the Princeton

Hotel, 1901 Powell Street East, with a prostitute. They drive her to the parking lot of New Brighton Park, 3000-block Wall Street, where they avail themselves of her services, then refuse to drive her back to the Princeton. A dispute ensues, at which point a second car enters the parking lot. The prostitute gets out of Mr. Vorst's vehicle and proceeds toward the one that has just arrived. The prostitute, who is serving here as a Crown witness, reports seeing a diminutive blond man in the car and, immediately recognizing that he is unlikely to be a client, instead returns on foot to Wall Street where she hitches a ride.

"At approximately 1:00 a.m., a second witness arrives on the scene to find two empty vehicles in the parking lot, the one belonging to Mr. Vorst and the other to the deceased. This witness then leaves his car, enters the park and proceeds toward the public toilets. Nearing them, he becomes aware of a disturbance within. Disputing voices are heard, then a man, identified now as the deceased, Mr. Christian Weber of 1271 Nicola Street, is seen running from the toilets, followed by two assailants. The assailants catch Mr. Weber and commence their assault. Mr. Vorst then joins his two co-accused. Their weapon is later determined to be a golf club.

"The witness particularly notes the savagery of the attack, its length, and how anti-homosexual epithets are chanted during it. At this point, fearing for himself, the witness leaves the scene. Mr. Vorst and his two co-accused, having assaulted Mr. Weber to the point of unconsciousness or beyond, take both his wallet and his car keys. They then leave, Mr. Vorst and a co-accused in Mr. Weber's car.

"At approximately 8:30 a.m. of the same day, a third

witness, walking her dog on the scene, discovers Mr. Weber's body. She reports that she is, at first glance, unable to determine Mr. Weber's sex from the features of his face, so badly was he beaten."

Alison, shivering in her fake fur coat, was crying now, noisily, for the sheriff at the desk looked back at her, as did the lawyer for Mr. Vorst. Then Mr. Vorst himself raised his eyes, not so much looking at her as through her. She was, she realized, nearly convulsing with sobs.

"Indeed, it was difficult to establish the identity of Mr. Weber's remains due to their brutalized state. When Mr. Weber's car was recovered, traces of Mr. Weber's blood and fingerprints belonging to Mr. Vorst and his co-accused were discovered.

"Those are the circumstances of the charges, your Honour. Mr. Vorst does have a criminal record which includes several previous assault convictions and a charge of vandalism against a Sikh Temple in Surrey for which he is scheduled to be tried in April. I'll show these to my friend. Needless to say, the Crown considers Mr. Vorst a danger and not likely to abide by parole conditions."

He located a sheet in the file before him and carried it to the other lawyer who rose and showed the paper to Mr. Vorst. Mr. Vorst barely glanced at it before stepping back and, making a jerky, tic-like movement with his head, audibly cracked his neck.

The judge took the sheet, read it without expression, then looked up at the second lawyer.

"We are seeking," said the second lawyer, still on his feet, "Mr. Vorst's release." His deposition was much shorter. He gave the boy's address, a suburban series of numerals that could almost be mistaken for a phone number, and the name of his employer. "All Mr. Vorst's convictions date from when he was a juvenile. He has been law-abiding for the last eleven months and in this time has even managed to complete his high-school equivalence. We recommend that he be released upon conditions."

The judge frowned for a contemplative moment before asking the Crown's lawyer, "Is this park a frequent meeting place for homosexuals?"

"Not by reputation. The second witness claims he had never been there for that purpose. Mr. Weber seems to have been taking a bit of a chance."

Malcolm lifted his face and looked at the judge, wondering what he was getting at. The girl was still crumpled up beside him, but when the judge began to speak, she managed to calm herself enough to hear him.

"I'm not impressed with Mr. Vorst's hairdo," was his first remark and Malcolm almost laughed out loud. "I am not impressed with Mr. Vorst at all. He may not have originally set out to 'bash a gay,' as they say, but he seems ready for anything. What were you doing running around with a golf club, Mr. Vorst? You're not a golfer, I presume."

In the box, Mr. Vorst smiled and this, the ability to recognize an ironic statement, evidence of an intelligence at work, distressed Malcolm all the more. Until that moment, he had taken him for a stupid brute.

"You're detained. You're locked up," said the judge. "We'll break for lunch, though Mr. Vorst has ruined my appetite."

"Clear the court," the sheriff called from the bottom of the stairs, then climbed, making sweeping gestures with his hands. Mr. Vorst, too, gestured. When the metal door was opened, he turned back to face the room, raising his right arm rigidly in the air, straight at the elbow.

In the lobby, the girl rushed for the washroom. Malcolm waited, intended to wait, but after a minute he realized he'd seen all that he could bear marked out in stubble on the back of Vorst's head. Still he stood there, willing the girl to come out so he could at least tell her he was leaving. Almost uncontrollable, his urge to pound his head against the walls of justice.

He tried the door again, but the unsteadiness in his hands seemed to prevent him from fitting in the key. Desperate to get in off the street, he fumbled and dropped the key ring. Only when he stooped to pick it up did it occur to him that he didn't live there any more. He'd come to the wrong building, the one he'd lived in with Denis.

The cab had long gone. Numbly, he began the eight-block hike back to the avenue, to the glass door that stood between the bookstore and the Oriental carpet boutique. It opened onto a heap of unread flyers and a brown-carpeted stair. Even before he had reached the top, he could hear the dog. Did she yodel like this all day or were her hairy ears acute enough to pick up the sound of someone entering one floor below? Then, as he neared the end of the hall, her whimpering ceased. Either she recognized the tread of her master-by-proxy, or she smelled him. Malcolm thought she smelled him.

He, he could smell himself.

She was waiting there as usual when he opened the door, putting on that hopefully, gooey look. Malcolm sniffed the air, then pulled his cuff back and sniffed his wrist. Immediately, his head began to ache. It was the same smell that had been coming off Christian's body, the smell of what they had done to him, all over

Malcolm again, all over his clothes and skin. Stepping right over the dog, he undressed and put in a garbage bag the clothes belonging once to a brother of Miss Velve. Knotting it tight, he left it by the door to throw away next time he went out.

Perhaps he only imagined the odour. It seemed impossible that it could be clinging to him still. Yet what other explanation was there for why, at Vitae, they all instinctively kept away?

He *was* tainted.

Disinfectingly hot, the shower. Afterward, rubbing a circle on the mirror, thinking about what he had heard in court, he saw narrowed eyes and—Oh, the rejuvenating properties of hatred!—could actually make out through the jowls the line of a clenched jaw. Denis had had a lot of trouble with these nasty mirrors. What Yvette had told Malcolm: that Denis no longer recognized himself. Now another explanation occurred to Malcolm: that Denis just didn't like what he saw. It was not a pretty picture, after all, a person who would soon be screaming, "Jew!" at an old lady.

Condensation reformed on the glass. His hardened face grew dewy in the circle, like a starlet seen through the filtered lens. What he was beginning to understand as connected in a continuum: Denis's illness and Christian's death. To stop himself from also hurling something at the mirror, Malcolm draped a towel over it.

He found Grace by the bag of clothes, torn open now at the corner. She had pulled out a tuft of fabric and was sucking on it, looking guiltily at him, but not quitting her pleasure until he came over and kicked her in the ribs. Yelping once, she backed away, her dishevelled little head cocked, eyes runny and pleading. Malcolm felt awful. How could he have been such a brute? At the same time his gorge rose and he tasted a stinging residue of bile. Just looking at her made him sick.

Squatting to her level, he extended an apologetic hand. Immediately, her stump began to twitch and she turned a fawning circle, licking around her thin black lips. She kept her head down as she approached, submissive, dribbling, and when she was near enough for him to touch her, she paused to whine below his outstretched hand. She raised her snout thankfully—those were tears of joy in her eyes, not glandular secretions—and her damp nose touched his fingers.

Abruptly, he stood up and walked off, leaving her there obsequious and squirming. He could have given her away, he realized then, but she was Denis's dog and he decided that he didn't want her to be happy.

Alison thought she was sick, that she was coming down with something. When the cab dropped her off, she hurried up the walk, came straight in without removing her shoes or coat and, in the bathroom, sank to her knees and vomited. She had not eaten all day so had to labour to bring something up. All at once she began to shiver, like she had in court. Icy, her trembling fingers. In the mirror, her lips were blue. She ran a hot tub and for a long time soaked herself, but as soon as she got out, she felt the same numbing chill.

At the courthouse that morning she hadn't been able to stop sobbing. Malcolm was waiting in the lobby for her but she hadn't been able to come out of the washroom. Several women came in and a few knocked on the door of the cubicle she was sitting in and asked if she was okay. "Leave me alone," she had told them between gasps.

Billy came home from work and found her still

curled up in bed. She hadn't slept, had just lain there as the room grew dark. All afternoon the phone kept ringing, but she had not got up to answer it. Neither had she imagined it might be Christian calling; that fantasy was finished. They were phoning from Vitae to find out what she'd seen.

"Was it bad?" Billy asked, turning on the light.

She winced in the sudden, interrogating glare.

"You shouldn't have gone alone. I would have gone with you."

"What was he doing there?" she asked.

"Who?"

"Christian. In that park so late at night."

"He was having an assignation, I suppose."

"I know, but why? Everybody loved him. Why did he have to do it?"

"It's different for men. Men need sex." Sitting on the edge of the bed, he started to explain—instincts and impulses, aggression. Rat talk again. The pink-eyed rat in the poster stared unblinking from the ceiling, the glow off its domed eyes and the pink transparent skin of its paws and ears making it look as if it were lit from within by a miniature furnace. Even when Alison closed her eyes, she still felt its stare—dispassionate, amoral, omniscient. Nothing more dangerous, Billy was telling her now, than a male of any species in its sexual prime. "Except a lactating female protecting her young."

"In other words," said Alison, remembering their love-making on the Island and the hideous face she'd seen him make, "nothing is more dangerous than love."

"Why are you blaming him, Ali? He should have stayed home and locked his doors?"

"I just don't want him to be dead!" she cried.

"I'm sure," said Billy, "that he doesn't want to be dead

213

either." He put his hand on her forehead. "You're hot."

"No, I'm freezing."

He shrugged. "What do you want for dinner?"

She said she couldn't eat.

"I'll order myself a pizza then," he said and left her on her own.

Was she blaming Christian? She gagged on the thought, but the truth was that was how she had finally got herself out of the courthouse washroom: by remembering the lawyer saying that Christian had been taking a chance. All at once she had been angry at him and, as abruptly, her tears had stopped. Malcolm had long gone, of course, but she didn't blame him. She only blamed Christian and, steeled by it, was able then to sit alone through the afternoon hearings of the other two boys.

Now, throwing off the covers, she got up and staggered down the hall. It was there, in the bathroom, after retching into sink, the muscles around her ribs and stomach straining as she heaved, that she raised her eyes and, in the mirror, saw herself as selfish. Her face was crimson, eyes and nose streaming—an ugly sight. In the white of the sink, a green worm dribbled.

"Are you okay?" Billy asked, appearing in the doorway.

"No," she told him. "I'm not okay at all."

3

She hurried in, head down, hair like blinders, her wordless passing through the gallery leaving them all blanched and looking like the busts. Everyone followed, crowding in the back room. "Well?" asked Donna. "Well?" She took Alison by the shoulders as if to shake an answer out.

"He was in a park," Alison began dully. "Late. There were three of them, like Malcolm said. They've moved them all to adult court. One was nineteen, but the other two were, like, fourteen and fifteen."

"What did they look like?" Thi asked.

The second boy, the fifteen-year-old, had reminded her at once of Kevin Milligan, not in appearance, but by his edginess, his downcast darting eyes. Though he didn't say a word, she could hear him taunting. The third, only fourteen, was slightly overweight, the very picture of cherubic sweetness with his apple cheeks and curls. The lawyer pleading for his release had said that this was his first dealing with the law, that he was a B student, particularly good at science, though this same boy, the Crown had noted, had been suspended from school for repeatedly using the Nazi salute.

"One," Alison told them, "had that thing shaved on the back of his head."

"What thing?"

Maybe it was the first time she had actually said the word. She swallowed and felt its blades sticking in her throat. "A swastika."

They recoiled, recoiled and gaped. It was a sacrilege. "Who would do that?" Robert asked, looking like he would spit. All of a sudden they seemed angry, angry at her, though what had she done but volunteer to do what no one else had dared? Nevertheless, she felt guilty, as if by talking about them here, at Vitae, she had let them in. As if they had booted their way in so a lightning crack forked down the glass door.

"Where did they come from?" they wanted to know.

The suburbs. "Surrey," Alison said, but even as she told them, she knew, in fact, that they had come straight out of the past. She remembered the time last fall she had offended Mrs. Soloff with her stupidity. Before that, she had never given a thought to such things happening. Now, now she knew they might happen still.

An awful day. No one spoke. Over the last few weeks, they had grown as close as a family, but in one day they fractured and each of them stood alone on her little shard of shock and grief.

Alison had not been to the public library since she was a girl. Going in after work, she felt unaccountably self-conscious, though it was hardly an imposing place—a single large room crowded with metal shelves in the basement of the community centre. Where to begin to look? She went over to a computer and tentatively pressed a button, but the machine only bleeped with irritation, yielding nothing.

The librarian was busy at her desk. At last she noticed Alison standing there, and took off her glasses, letting them hang on her chest from the beaded chain. "I'm looking for a book," Alison told her.

"Any particular subject?"

"Nazis," she said.

The librarian's expression remained neutral, though Alison expected her to be shocked, expected her at least to ask the reason for her search. All she did was rise from her desk and somewhat ominously say, "I'll show you where to find History."

There were books about the different battles, about Hitler and Stalin. A book about the Holocaust and another on Vichy France. The librarian pulled down *The Rise and Fall of the Third Reich*.

"This is a good overview."

Alison opened it. The pages were black with text.

Instead she picked a big picture book: *A Photographic History of the Third Reich*. She didn't look at it on the bus. It didn't seem appropriate. She sat with the burden of the book in her lap and her hands spread open to conceal the cover. Once home, she brought it to the couch and began flipping at random through the pages.

Though all the photographs in the book were in black and white, the first image her eye landed on was a colour legend. It showed, sewn on the breast of a striped prison uniform, a simple triangle. The caption underneath explained how the triangles were different colours, according to each prisoner's "offence." She read the words "Jew" and "homosexual" and quickly turned the page.

And found herself staring at a pair of half-shadowed naked buttocks, the same striped shirt lifted to the waist. Across the one buttock not obscured were more stripes, diagonal from the lash, the black lips of the welts raised between the weeping lacerations.

How to respond to such an image? Alison, so accustomed to looking at photographs of beauty—of couture and models—tried not to shrink, but she thought of Christian and how he had been beaten. Unimaginable, his wounds.

She skipped ahead to a dump or midden full of eggshell fragments and black molten lumps. In the middle was a bald head of indeterminate sex, face fixed in a grimace—the charred head of a mannequin, her first thought. But no. Here was a foot, too, lying half-carbonized in the ash. The shells were shards of bone. It was an open-air crematorium.

She had her face partly turned away, the end of her recoil. She thought she would be sick and hurriedly flipped the pages again, closer to the front.

A bloated dandy in a feathered cap. Hermann, she

read. Hermann Goering, "master of the hunt," a falcon perched on his puffy forearm. In the sky above him, someone had written something in blue ink.

He was a good man.

Alison blinked. Someone in this very city thought and had written here with a ballpoint pen that this Nazi Hermann Goering was *good.*

Cringing, she tore the page out, tore it into an impossible jigsaw, into ugly confetti, then scooped up the tiny pieces in both hands and carried them to the kitchen to dispose of. Some pieces had escaped, she noticed on her way back to the living room. Crouching to collect them, she saw the carpet packed with crumbs and dirt.

Alison had been waiting Billy out. For almost two months the vacuum cleaner had stood in the bedroom closet, silenced. She went and got it now, hauled it out, wrangled it on unaligned wheels down the hall. Intractable, it tripped her with its nozzle. She lashed at it with the cord. When she plugged it in, to her surprise, it sparked and shocked her, then backfired, spewing dust. There she sat, on the floor, staring up in horror as the dust descended. Uniformly grey, it was the very colour of ash and, because her mouth was open and astonished, she could taste it.

Billy home by the time she got out of the shower, she began to cry explaining the mess. "I'll deal with it," he promised and, sure enough, ten minutes later, when she tentatively poked her head out the bedroom door, the rabid thing had been disposed of, though the carpet was still grey.

Dust, Billy told her, was mostly flakes of human skin. Alison shuddered. It had tasted sweet.

After dinner, Billy stretched out to watch a hockey

game with Alison cross-legged at the other end of the couch, the book weighing down her lap. She opened it close to where she had torn the page out, saw three peasant girls in a field, their blond braids pinned in a halo; in the background, a boy on an archaic tractor beamed. The facing photograph showed the same beautiful people wearing gowns and tuxedoes, dancing in a ballroom. She bent closer. Not the same people, it was just that the fair-haired and gorgeous looked so much alike.

"The Aryan Ideal" read the caption.

"Yes!" cried Billy. "Yes!"

She glanced at the TV just as a player lurched unimpeded toward the net and scored. "*Et le but!*" cried the commentator. The game was in French, an excited gibberish over the crowd ecstasizing.

A throng rallying in a square. On every flagpole, the bloody rectangle of sky, a crook-legged spider squashed against the moon. Staring down at the photo, she heard them roar.

Billy muted the set for the commercial and, standing over her, asked if she wanted a beer.

"No, thanks."

He clicked sock heels together, his right arm swinging upward stiffly. Intense, fierce with concentration, he held the pose. Such a cold, hard look on his face. He looked like Mr. Vorst.

"Billy," she said. "Don't."

Slowly, very slowly, he turned his head and sniffed his armpit.

Alison was not amused. She left him to his game and went to the bedroom with the book.

Kristallnacht—all the windows of the pretty shops smashed. On a brick wall someone had painted "Jude."

Then the stars sewn on coats, the trains, the bewildered assembly on the platform, the boxcars crammed with human cargo. She closed the book and held it to her chest a moment, breathing hard, thinking. Sombre with intent, all her previously scattered powers of attention focused, Alison opened the book again but, this time, she began to read it.

Anyone with a television has seen a thousand Nazis. All Alison's life, they had jackbooted across the screen. Strangely though, their omnipresence only made them seem less real. Cartoons to her, they had long ago ceased to inspire shock or dread. The imagery of terror had become mundane and commonplace.

Now, reading, she understood something about television that had not occurred to her before: that it pushed you only so far, lest you turn it off. She had never seen a mobile gas chamber in a movie-of-the-week, or a baby picked up by the heels and smashed against the white trunk of a tree. No beards set aflame or gleeful rapes, no eager complicity of locals. No woman tied by the hair to the tail of a horse and dragged to death.

How had she not known about these things, she wondered. Had she learned it in school and then forgotten?

At the beginning and the end of the book was a tableau of prisoner identification photos, each person shorn, in profile, straight on and turned three-quarters—women and men, young and old, staring out, but holding back so much. She studied each one carefully, searched eyes, pondered over profiles, the angles of facial bones. At first she didn't realize that she was looking for a resemblance, that she was looking for someone she knew. Alison was searching for Mrs. Soloff and when she thought she had found her in a young woman with bright and fearless eyes, she continued looking, looking for Christian, too.

Relocated to ghettos or holding camps, Alison read, *their property confiscated for the Reich, auctioned off to Aryan neighbours, or stolen, now the Jews were told they were being transported to work camps.* On the measled map of Europe, each red dot was a camp—a prison camp, a detention centre, a concentration camp. Sixty or a hundred people locked into boxcars for as long as ten days while the trains travelled along inconspicuous routes, avoiding population centres. There was no sanitation, no food, no fresh air. Many died. The ones who survived might have been glad to arrive.

Leaving their luggage on the platform, they were made to parade with the others past a camp doctor or SS officer who then signalled left or right. Those directed right went to work in munitions factories, mines, farms or rubber works, twelve hours a day on starvation rations. On average, they lasted three months. Those sent left, ninety percent of every trainload, were gassed within an hour. If the barracks happened to be full, then everyone was gassed.

Mrs. Soloff went right and stood in line to be tattooed. Christian, small, deformed, marked for death, went left.

They undressed for the "showers," two thousand at a time, while an orchestra played selections from light opera. "Don't forget your soap and towel" read a sign. Only if someone panicked, noticing the lack of drains, were clubs and whips used to get them in the gas chambers. The door was bolted. Zyklon B poured in. A single consignment of Zyklon B filled as many as twenty trucks. At Birkenau the gas chambers had the capacity to "process" five thousand corpses an hour.

Afterward, special commandos entered the chamber bearing the hooked poles used to pry apart the bodies. With ice tongs, they dragged out Christian by the head. His jewellery was removed, his gold teeth extracted with pliers. And his luggage, left on the platform with Mrs. Soloff's, was sorted, catalogued, distributed. Gold, precious stones, currency, if they had any left, went to a special account at the Reichsbank, to pawn shops, the Swiss jewellery market, or into someone's pocket. Mrs. Soloff's silk underwear was sent as a wedding present to a blushing SS bride and Christian's corpse to the crematorium where, frequently, a foot or more of human fat had to be scraped off the chimney walls.

The next day, when she came into the back room for her break, it occurred to her that for the first time she and Malcolm had something in common. "What are you reading?" she asked.

He continued to the end of the line before closing the book around his finger. "Dante's *Inferno*."

She took her own book from her bag and opened it. "Ah," he said, "Vorst has inspired you as well."

"I guess so," she said and resumed reading where she had left off the night before.

"Why did you think I didn't like Christian?" Malcolm asked.

She looked up at him, surprised, and, remembering the moment, reddened. "I shouldn't have said that."

"But you did." It still bothered him immensely.

She had never noticed Malcolm's eyes before, dark with dark shadows underneath, and found now that she had to look away from them. The truth was he didn't seem to like any of them, but it would have been unkind to say that, so she said nothing, just bit her lip. Then Donna stuck her head in the door and asked her to shampoo her client. "And This wondering what you're doing. She says your break is over and you should be up front."

Alison hurried off without answering Malcolm.

At the sink, she found a young man as agitated as she. "I think my hair is falling out," he said, his voice a petulant whine. "I think I'm going bald."

She wrapped a towel round his neck. "There's not much you can do about it."

"I can't accept that. I have a very unattractive head."

"If you adapt your hairstyle—"

He grabbed her hand and forced it down on his crown. "Feel that?"

"I feel, like, an indentation."

"It's a cleft! It's a crack! I've got butt-head!"

Alison rolled her eyes.

"You don't get it, do you? If my hair falls out, when I bend over people will see it. They'll think I'm mooning them every time I tie my shoes."

"There are worse things than going bald."

"Name one," he said. "Go on. Name one."

"Being in a concentration camp."

"I'd rather be in a concentration camp," he said.

Didn't he know they'd shave his head anyway? Had Alison herself known that? She eased him back in the chair and turned on the water, directing the nozzle over his crown. "I see what you mean," she said after she had shut off the tap. "It's very thin on top."

"Oh, Jesus," he whimpered and shut up to brood while Alison shampooed.

Donna, Alison found a few minutes later in the back room, alone, gaping at the pictures in her book. "He's ready," Alison told her.

"Is this yours?" Donna asked.

"You know," said Alison, "it's really scary how it happened. There was a lot of unemployment and disillusioned youth because after the war—"

Passing in the doorway, Donna shook her gleaming head. "I've had enough already. I had to get a prescription."

"What kind of prescription?"

"Tranqs. If I hear another word about death I'm going to take them all at once. And Thi is still waiting for you. Are you going to leave her there all day?"

Alison, hurrying to the front, wondered what had happened to Donna's resolution to be nice.

"Finally," said Thi. "I deserve a break, too, you know."

"I'm sorry!" Truly mortified, because Thi was so sweet and had never chided her before, Alison watched her put on her child-sized coat and leave without a word. "Take your time!" she called, but ten minutes later Thi was back, drawing a newspaper from her bag and laying it on the desk in front of Alison. There was Christian's face and name, his abruptly terminated story in black and white, and a picture of Mr. Vorst. What struck her immediately was how, at a glance, a skinhead seemed a victim. Mr. Vorst's hair was shorn like Christian's, like the prisoners' in the tableaux, and he wore the same expressionless stare as all the prisoners. Mr. Vorst was posing as an innocent. It made him all the more obscene.

She looked at Thi rubbing circles on her temples, then past her, through the window to the sidewalk where Amanda was gambolling in a long dark coat. It was raining and she was holding a purple umbrella and stretching her free hand in the air as she leapt. Not a frisky person even in happier times, Alison couldn't believe her now as Mary Poppins. She pointed, but Thi didn't seem to think it an odd scene. Because she had met Amanda outside, she knew already what it took Alison a moment to figure out: that Amanda was trying to untie the knot halfway up the column. Succeeding, she pulled free the black tail of sodden ribbon, unwinding it from the column, a funereal maypole. Their mourning officially over, now they would have to get on with it—life.

Billy asked her, "Are you still reading that book?"

"I renewed it."

"You're applying for a job at the Simon Wiesenthal Centre?"

"What?"

Moving closer, he began a ticklish sniffing at her neck. She shut the book and rolled over to face him; it slid off her chest and down between them like a wall. For a minute they kissed over top of it, then Billy took it and dropped it on the floor.

"Just today I read in *Physiology and Behavior*, volume forty-five, number two, a study by Albert and Petrovic. They found that female Wistar rats become aggressive when cohabiting with sexually non-performing males. It's definitive. Naturally, I'm concerned now that if I don't put out soon, you'll get ugly on me."

Alison rolled onto her back again. "I'm not a rat," she said.

At her request, he had taken down the poster, so now she stared up at what had been under it—a clean white rectangle on the yellowed ceiling. The problem was, it seemed so like a screen now that the images she had been staring at in the book projected out of her stunned retina and shone horribly back down on her.

"I hate to beg," said Billy, "but—*please, please, please.*"

She put her hand over her eyes to block them out: the open pit, the naked bodies jumbled in it, the limbs like sticks. Oh, Christian, she thought. Oh, all the people who had perished.

"May I cop a feel?" asked Billy, trying to be funny. "Or rub myself against your thigh at least?"

"No." She curled up, hugging her knees. "Don't touch me. Please."

He rolled over, his aggrieved back against hers, and turned out the light without telling her good night. Five weeks ago, when Christian was killed, Billy was as horrified as any of them, but now he was tired of hearing about it. He wanted Alison to get over it, and why wouldn't he? He had only met Christian once. How could she expect him to feel for a person he barely knew? Yet, as she lay there with her face turned to the wall, she knew it was possible to care, even for a total stranger. That was one of the things she hoped to learn herself.

4

The moment Alison opened the door, she smelled cinnamon. Mrs. Branz, their landlady, was in the vestibule, her back to Alison, snooping on the other side of the staircase where the couple they shared this floor with kept their bicycles.

"Hi," said Alison, cautiously.

Mrs. Branz swung around, but her grey hair didn't move so Alison couldn't help but picture her before the bathroom mirror wielding Final Net with the same ferocity as a can of Raid. "Are these your bicycles?"

"No. They belong to—" Alison pointed to the facing door. She didn't know their neighbours' names.

"They are marking the walls. Tell them when you see them."

"I never see them," said Alison.

"Knock on their door and tell them, yes? I have come about your refrigerator."

She meant Lake Superior. Last year, when the puddle stayed around the fridge door for days before migrating across the floor, they had not really bothered to press her on the problem. Now it reached near-flood proportions almost every day and Billy was annoyed.

"You're supposed to call first," Alison said.

Already, Mrs. Branz was marching in. Removing her shoes, she didn't just stoop, she swooped as in an exercise regime. Quickly, Alison closed the closet door so Mrs. Branz wouldn't see the heap of shoes there. Even as she reiterated, "You should have called," she got behind Mrs. Branz and began shepherding her down the hall before she saw *A Photographic History of the Third Reich* open on the couch.

"Your husband called me," she said as they reached the kitchen.

"Did he?" Alison grabbed her arm to prevent her from stepping in the puddle, Mrs. Branz surprisingly muscular for an old lady. "He didn't tell me. And he's not my husband."

"Whatever." She opened the fridge.

Alison blushed. Not much in there and what there was was either decidedly unfresh or in a Styrofoam container. She had no appetite these days and Billy was too lazy to cook. Mrs. Branz waved her sinewy hand around inside. "It is working. It is cold."

"But it leaks. There's always water on the floor."

"You have a mop, yes?"

"We'd have to mop, like, every day."

"Every day I wash my kitchen floor."

"We might slip and fall."

"Ach," she said, dismissively. "This is the problem. If I have to buy a new fridge, I have to raise the rent and then you will complain even louder."

"Can't you just fix it?"

"I will phone. I will find out how much it costs." She closed the fridge, the jars in the door rack chattering like teeth.

Back down the hall, Mrs. Branz, her arms stiffly swinging, reminded Alison of a mechanical toy soldier. Maybe this was the source of her vigour. Maybe she wound herself up. Halfway to the living room, she came to a martial halt and stared down at the carpet.

"The vacuum cleaner is broken," Alison hastily explained.

"I see. You won't fix your vacuum and so my carpet is filthy and becoming ruined, yet I must fix the fridge."

Alison felt herself reddening again.

"Yes. Life is not fair," Mrs. Branz said, her eyes crinkling in advance of her chuckle. "You are young. You don't know this yet."

What I don't know, thought Alison, *fills a book, but now I am reading it.*

"I have a nice strudel in the oven," she told Alison as she put on her shoes. "I will phone you when it is ready. Come over and get some, yes? I saw what is in your refrigerator. Your husband will like it. It will be for him a treat."

After Mrs. Branz had left, Alison went to the window to watch her brisking across the street. "He's not my husband," she said. She wanted to thumb her nose, too, but what if Mrs. Branz turned and saw?

Coward.

So much a coward that a half an hour later, when Mrs. Branz called, Alison put on a sweater and went.

She lived on the fourth floor, in the penthouse. Alison buzzed and Mrs. Branz let her into the mirrored lobby, spotless and jungled with plants. The elevator opened directly across from her door. "Come in!" sang Mrs. Branz.

In the apartment, redolent of cinnamon and apples, Alison slipped off her shoes and followed the parquet hallway to the kitchen where Mrs. Branz was holding the strudel on a baking sheet, crinkling her eyes again in self-satisfaction.

"I will cut you a nice big piece."

Waiting in the kitchen doorway, Alison could see into the living room where, above the couch, hung a painting of the Alps and Dresden figurines posed here and there. Everything was in its proper place and free of dust. The untracked carpet looked like it had been brushed.

"Here you are!" Half the strudel on a blue plate. Mrs. Branz led the way to the door bearing it proudly. Passing the desk in the hall, Alison noticed a black and white photograph of a fair-haired young man and woman in a standing frame.

"Is that you?"

"I and my husband. *He was a good man.*"

Alison winced.

"Unfortunately, we did not have time enough. We did not have children. After losing him, that is the great woe of my life. Now, all the young people, I make my children." She cocked her head and winked.

Thanks, but I already have a mother, Alison thought.

Then she thanked Mrs. Branz for the strudel though she knew she wouldn't eat it because the pastry looked like dried skin.

In her mind, as she left, she christened Mrs. Branz's husband "Hermann."

At Billy's insistence she went to see the doctor, who listened patiently to her story, then sent her to the lab for tests. By nightfall, a huge purple macula appeared on her arm where the needle had gone in, the smeared tattoo of a rose. It worried her, this stain under her skin, but when she went back to the doctor, all he did was tell her her blood test was normal—no anemia, no hormonal irregularities. He asked if she wanted an antidepressant.

"Why—?"

She was asking about the bruise, but with the waiting room crowded with the unwell, he interrupted. Not that he was unkind or negligent. He made time to wax philosophic about the vicissitudes of life and how the body, naturally, felt these too. After what had happened to her friend, of course she felt depressed.

"Those are legitimate feelings of grief, but aren't they dragging you off to a different place now? You can go there if you want, but these days, it's not necessary."

Alison wondered if all of them at Vitae had seen the same doctor; one by one they had each brought in their pills. The doctor, reading her mind, laughed. "Look at it this way. Feelings are chemicals, too. They're just chemicals in the brain."

"Oh?" said Alison, dubiously. "Are they really?"

She dropped the prescription off at Shoppers Drug Mart and went back to work. Mrs. Soloff was in the waiting area when Alison arrived. They greeted each other warmly, as if there had never been any tension between them. Mrs. Soloff was, after all, a great and gracious lady of immense fortitude. Mrs. Soloff had come back from the dead.

Alison led her to the dressing room. She had always been respectful; now she was reverential. "How are you doing? Would you like my help?"

"Yes, dear."

She stepped inside and slipped Mrs. Soloff's blouse off her bowed shoulders, averting her eyes so as not to see the numbers. Close to her like this, she was again aware of the paradox of the old lady's tremendous frailty and inner strength. She couldn't help comparing it to their landlady's brusque stamina and attitude. She tied the ties, pressed the Velcro, then offered her arm again. Counted out in her head, as she led Mrs. Soloff to the sink, how old Mrs. Branz would have been fifty years ago.

After work, she collected her prescription and took it home. As soon as Billy got in, he wanted to know what the doctor had said to her.

"I'm depressed."

He laughed. "You needed a doctor to tell you that?"

"I didn't think I needed a doctor," she reminded him, going over to the window.

"What are you doing?"

She was standing there peeking between the drawn curtains at Mrs. Branz's little fortress penthouse, its ramparted balcony—her Eagle's Nest across the street.

"Did he give you anything?"

She nodded, still staring out. The prescription was lying on the coffee table. Billy put down the papers he had brought home and opened the bag. "Great. How long do they take to work?" Then he asked if the repairman had come and went off to the kitchen to see for himself.

He came back railing. "What does she think? That apple pie makes up for a piece-of-shit fridge?"

What Alison was thinking: that she wasn't going to take those pills. There wasn't anything the matter with her.

"You mind if I go over there and punch her lights out?"

"Oh, Billy." She put her hands over her ears.

"Come here," he said, patting the place next to him on the couch.

She came and sat. Across the coffee table, he had spread a half-dozen travel brochures, glossy, in blinding colours. "What's this?" she asked.

"We talked about a holiday."

"Next Christmas."

"I thought we could go sooner. You know, get away and dry off." It was a lot cheaper in the spring with all the package deals. They could afford it. "Look." He put a brochure in her hands and drummed his tongue. "*¡Viva la Revolución!*"

Flipping through the smooth pages, she saw all the photographs of fun: bikini-clad women dancing on the Cuban sand, hibiscus flowers, foot-long cigars. Such easy pictures to look at.

He made her promise to go through all brochures; Mexico, Hawaii, Costa Rica, the Caribbean. She agreed. Of course she would.

"Do you have a passport?" he asked.

"No."

"We'll have to get you one."

When they got into bed that night, she wanted him to look at pictures, too. First she showed him the photograph in the book of the shoes. They were collected together in a very large high-ceiled room. It could have been, in fact, not a single room, but several amalgamated by the knocking down of walls; there were posts that might once have been doorways, but they led only to more shoes. In the background, someone had propped a ladder up against where the shoes were piled the highest, to the ceiling, but now the ladder, too, was engulfed by shoes. Shoes flattened and stacked like cordwood, shoes avalanching into the foreground, shoes and shoes and shoes.

"I keep telling you," said Billy. "That hall closet? One day the door is gonna give and the whole apartment will look like this."

Then he asked her if there was a picture of her sweaters. He meant to make her laugh, and did, proving to her something she had been gradually comprehending—the duality of all, even ordinary things. Every person, every action, every object invested with equal potential for love or malice. In a picture of a room full of shoes, she saw horror; he saw too many shoes.

In the middle of the night Alison, sleeping fitfully as usual, got up and went to the kitchen for a drink. She lost her balance when her bare feet hit the puddle, grabbed the counter, dropped the glass. The sound it made shattering in the dark frightened her.

Turning on the shower the next morning, she paused before stepping in. She would never be able to take a mindless shower again. Never, she thought. Afterward, she dressed, throwing on anything and a sweater, and said goodbye to Billy. On the way to catch the bus, she stopped on the railway tracks and looked down the gradually converging rails to the vanishing point, so ironic. So aptly named. The bench where she sat in the sunshine waiting for the bus had a view north to mountains two-toned with snow. Ten minutes west lay the ocean, that plated sheet. Her own country she had barely discovered; it was beautiful and wild. Safe, peaceful, affluent was how she had heard it described all her life.

Shoes were just some of the plunderings. They took everything—prayer shawls and eyeglasses, jewellery, teeth, everything—and stored it in a warehouse, and when that warehouse had filled, they built another and crammed it, too, with booty.

Warehouses named *Kanada I* and *II*.

5

At Vitae, Malcolm marvelled to see how they put the tragedy behind them—so soon, when he was still sniffing his wrist and cringing. Of course things were not as before: tempers flared, and here and there a shaved head appeared, but there was a consensus among them, most of them, to recover. They even brought their recovery in and passed it around in the form of pills.

That the girl was in disagreement was soon apparent. Alison had used to do any task you asked of her, promptly, enthusiastically, grateful for the opportunity to do the very things you shirked. But now she had slowed down and there was instead a listlessness about her. She seemed suspended in distraction. Whereas before, if she displayed the ability to read it would be the back of a shampoo bottle or a magazine, now she began to show up with a book.

"Oversized" read the label on the spine, the damn thing so big it had to be toted in and out each day in a canvas bag possibly purchased to bear this very burden.

Immediately after putting on the coffee, she would heft it from the bag; she needed both hands to do it. Open in her lap, it seemed to hold her there, preventing her from getting on with the day. She would stare at a page, sometimes not even reading, just looking at a photograph and twisting her dark hair around a finger. Eventually Thi would have to send someone to tell her it was time to get to work.

Their reactions to the book he observed with black amusement. At first everyone recoiled to see it there, juxtaposed with *Chatelaine, Hair Flair* and *Vogue.* Cautiously, they approached—there was barbed wire on the cover. The first plate, a blurred sepia-toned enlargement of a crowd, Malcolm himself had to look at twice to figure out. It was a crowd of children mostly dressed in stripes, each extending a bare arm. In the centre of the photograph, one child was frozen in the act of pulling up her sleeve. All of them holding out their left arms to show their tattooed numbers to the camera.

Roxanne's reaction was to shut the book quickly; with her every edgy movement, jewellery rattled, or was it her bones? Thi turned a few pages pensively. When Malcolm asked if she had been born in Vietnam, she answered, "Yes. We came here when I was a child." Her doll's face darkened; at some point, she had likely been in a camp of sorts herself.

Robert actually studied the book for the length of a coffee break. He'd always seemed to Malcolm the most reflective, brooding and serious, like a missionary trying with his pierced eyebrow to insinuate himself among the natives. Jamie dismissed the book entirely. Amanda stood with her hands on her hips and said, "Can't we do something about this clutter?"

The whispering started between Roxanne and

Donna. All Malcolm heard was, "The book, the book, the book ..." Then Thi added her discontented voice and it became The Book.

The appointment book was on the desk before Alison, unadorned black leather with a spine that made a cracking sound every time she opened it. She found the name she was looking for and started to read it out, but her voice cracked. She had seen a photograph of one of the leather books they had recorded the prisoners' names in at Auschwitz. Covering the page with the strange shape of her own hand, she asked the woman there, "Are you next?"

She led her to the dressing room, then continued on to the back to get her tea. Amanda and Thi were there having their weekly conference, this time with Donna. Thi asked, "How many heads have you done so far, Ali?"

"Yours, Jamie's and Roxanne's." She filled the teapot with water.

Amanda hooted. "Roxanne looks fabulous!"

"Roxanne did that after," said Thi, grumpily. "Ali's cut was great."

"How about Ali doing Donna's client's highlights, with Donna supervising?" Amanda suggested.

Donna said, "She's not ready."

Thi threw up her hands. "Of course she is!"

Alison took the steaming teapot from the microwave, assembled the tray and carried it out with Donna trailing.

"Where is she?" Donna asked.

"Up front."

"I thought you said she was ready."

She set the tray down at Donna's station. "You said I'm not ready. She's changing."

"Snarky, snarky. Where are you going?"

"Don't you have to cut her first?"

"I cut her yesterday! We didn't have the time for the highlights!" Harrumphing, Donna went to collect her client. She came back a different, gushing person. "Oooh, I still like it. It defines you. The highlights will give it texture. I was thinking red might be nice." Her fingers, under the woman's hair, tilted her head at different angles.

"Red?" she asked, dubiously.

"Well, reddish. Alison, bring the colour samples. Alison is going to help today."

Recapping bottles, Alison happened to be right next to the sample board, so she brought it over to Donna—hair fixed in rows, all colours, the whole human spectrum bound into single locks by plastic tabs. Donna moved her open hand around the board, as if choosing by aura, then disengaged two locks, one blond and one copper. "If we blend them. They look bright against my hand, but—" She ruffled them into her client's hair. "Oh, I *like* this one." Laying the copper lock against her own bleached head, she shifted her weight to jut a teasing hip.

"You'd go from that to that?" asked the client. "How daring."

"Listen. If I wanted to know what colour I really am, I'd have to see a baby picture. You like this combination? Good. Maybe Alison, since she's just standing there staring, wouldn't mind getting the cap and hook."

Alison went to the back room and took the cap out of the box. It was made of a waxy-looking rubber, semi-transparent, perforated. She dusted the inside with talc and brought it to Donna's station. With the client holding the rim tight against her forehead, Donna pulled it down with a jerk, talc puffing out the perforations, as if the woman's head were smouldering inside it.

"Where's the hook?"

She passed it to Donna who poked it into a hole and drew out a tuft. Across the room, a shaver came on with a buzz, Robert's client just then bowing his head, meekly presenting the back of his neck. Through the fresco window on the back wall, she saw the nudes in their distorted poses. *First they were stripped naked, then they were shorn.* Donna, moving her wrist in expert flicks, pulled hair through the cap in a patch until the client looked almost, but not quite, shorn. She looked as if she had escaped just before the shearing was finished.

"Here." Donna handed the hook back to Alison. "Like I just did."

It seemed absurdly the opposite of plucking a chicken. When she finished, Alison stepped back. Ghastly, the tufts poking straight out or drooping. "I look like I just had chemo," said the client. "You know, it always amazes me how ugly I am when I'm sitting in this chair. My hair's parted in the middle and pasted down. Under these lights I'm yellow. My moustache shows. But by the time I go, I'm beautiful."

It was something Alison had used to marvel over herself, but now she wondered if it really mattered how we wear our hair.

Donna reappeared in rubber gloves, a plastic bowl in each hand, paintbrush held in her mouth like the stem of a rose. "Take these," she told Alison through bared teeth. Immediately, Alison recoiled from the fumes, stood holding the bowls away from her body, head tilted back, mouth-breathing while Donna dipped into the yellow paste and began painting a broad vertical stripe on her client's head. It was not so much the actual fumes coming off the paste that bothered Alison as the idea of fumes, of chemicals, of gas.

"Excuse me," she said, abruptly setting the bowls down. She bolted for the bathroom where the door was ajar, went in without knocking, burst in, then gasped and turned away—but would never unsee it because already it was in her portfolio of horror: Roxanne in the mirror squeezing pus from her bottom lip. With her mass of fecund and trailing hair, she had used to look like a hanging plant on a pole; now that she had shaved her head, she looked just like the pole. Mouth open as she prodded, her cheeks sunk in. Her eyes shifting listlessly toward Alison seemed over-large now in their shaded sockets. She seemed to see Alison from the bottom of a pit.

"You should go to the hospital," Alison said.

"I know," Roxanne replied dully, poking at the lip. "It won't heal up no matter what I do."

Alison backed out of the room. She turned and headed through the gallery to phone Jamie at home, because after Christian he was the closest to Roxanne. They were supposed to love each other. Donna was just then lowering the hairdryer onto her client's head. What could possibly have been the harm in that, but how it descended upon the head, how the head fit it as it would fit a light socket, and knowing, too, that a current ran through, made Alison shudder. In the dance track, she heard whips. Robert was raising the scissors momentarily in the air, tips ceilingward, to free his wrist from a constricting cuff. Scissor points and blades, straight razors, different kinds of clips: oh, the things in that room that cut and pinched. Also, Malcolm must have been working with the curling iron because Alison thought she could smell burning hair. There was hair all over the floor. This was how it started. Then it filled the room.

She about-faced and went to get the broom.

On the way she noticed that Robert was wearing a pin against the blue and white stripes of his shirt, a pink enamel triangle. They didn't like to be interrupted when they were working so when he asked, "What are you staring at?" he sounded annoyed. She was going tell him what the pink triangle stood for, but probably he knew.

"Nothing," she answered.

Maybe nothing was the matter with Roxanne, either. Nobody else had mentioned they were worried. Maybe she was just skinny and Alison perverse. She had been on her way to phone Jamie when she got distracted, but now she decided not to call him.

She went to the back room where Malcolm sat with her book open in his lap. "Where did you find it?" she asked. "I was looking for it earlier."

"In the dryer."

"The dryer? How did it get there?"

Without replying, he turned a page and looked down unflinching. Then Thi came in and told Alison, "Pour me a coffee, too." She'd been in an erratically bad mood for a long time—either up and down throughout the day or fixing on one particular person, seemingly at random, to be angry with. Last week Donna had told Alison that Thi was trying to decide whether or not to quit. It was painful news to Alison, first because Thi had not confided in her and, second, because Alison did not think she could stay herself if they lost Thi, too.

She handed Thi the mug, Thi immediately slamming it down on the counter, sloshing coffee. It must have been too hot, Alison thought. Then she saw Thi glaring at Malcolm. Thi rushing at him. Malcolm raised the book as a shield, but Thi took hold of it, wrenching it away. Cowering, Malcolm brought his hands up to stop the book from coming down on his head.

Instead, Thi swung around to Alison and told her in a near-shriek, "Why do you keep bringing this here? We feel bad enough already without having to look at these awful pictures!" She marched to the door, opened it and hurled the book. From where Alison was standing, she could see the pages flapping, the book a huge bird with nightmare plumage dropping from the sky, then landing with a hollow foreboding thud on the hood of Jamie's car. She saw the licence plate beginning ADD. A vanity plate, Christian had called it. Attention Deficit Disorder 368.

Thi slammed the door and, locking it, jabbed a ringed finger at Alison. "Don't you dare go and get it. Do you hear me? Don't you bring it here any more."

She left the room in a flurry, Alison staring after her and hoping this incident wouldn't be the one to finally incite Thi to quit. Strangely, Alison herself was momentarily relieved to have the oppressive book off the premises. Without that reminder, perhaps she, too, could start to get on with life. Of course, she didn't really believe anything would be different, any more than she believed the book was to blame. Once again, she found herself in tears. "Why are we turning against each other?" she asked. "When Christian was here, we were so happy. He made us happy. Now everything's different."

A hand on her arm, Malcolm guided her over to the bench. She sat and he brought a box of tissue and placed it carefully in her lap.

"Thank you." She sniffed, surprised he hadn't fled. Instead, he stood there, mothball-scented and visibly distressed, clasping his hands, wringing them. Very tentatively, he reached out to pat her head.

In Malcolm's apartment, the phone kept ringing. Every day, morning and evening, it shrilled at him, but he would not pick it up in case it was the police with some new horror to communicate. When it rang that afternoon, he only answered because he thought it was going to be the girl. She had seemed so upset earlier at work and he had comforted her.

"Mr. Firth?" It was a woman's voice, middle-aged, so not the girl. "I've been trying to get a hold of you."

"Who is this?" he asked, suspiciously.

She said a name entirely unfamiliar to Malcolm. Just as he was about to hang up, she added, "from Denis's ward." Nurse Health. Nurse Health was calling him. Immediately, he pictured her standing high on the ledge of the medical arts building, holding a telephone.

Nurse Health was the kind and probably Sapphic one, the one always encouraging him to join their little support group. She wanted him to sit in a circle with family of the other patients and share his pain while everyone squirmed and looked away. Nonetheless, he appreciated her concern.

"Were you away?" she asked.

"Pardon me?"

"Away. You haven't been in since Christmas and we've been trying to get in touch with you."

Oh, Christ. Malcolm closed his eyes. *What now?*

"Mr. Firth? Are you there?"

"Yes," he choked.

"Is someone at your door?"

"What?"

"I hear knocking."

He was thudding his head against the wall. He

stopped. "No one's knocking."

"Are you all right, Mr. Firth? You used to come every day. We haven't seen you in such a long time."

"How is everyone?" he asked in a faltering voice.

"You mean Denis?"

"How are Mrs. Mikaluk and Mrs. Paxton? How is Mrs. Ross?"

"Mrs. Ross passed away."

Stunned at first, then he began silently to weep. He saw her standing there, accused, confused, while Denis screeched. Probably she was an Anglican, but no one screamed "Anglican!" with such venom. Oh, Christ. Was that what had killed her?

"Mr. Stavros, too. Denis—"

"I don't want to hear what he's done!"

"He hasn't done anything, Mr. Firth. He's ill with this flu that's going around. It hits them hard when they're old. Denis's in the hospital. Do you want to see him?"

"I can't." At last the dam had broken. He came unstuck. He was sobbing. "I can't. I can't. I must hang up."

"I'm going to call tomorrow, Mr. Firth," he heard as he lowered the receiver.

He had to negotiate the maze of furniture to get over to the bed. Lying there, curled up, he wept—not like a baby, like a beast. Bellowing, he tore at the sheets, pounded his head against the headboard, roared. He heard himself and knew they could probably hear him, too, in the bookstore underneath. Paging through their bestsellers, they would be looking up in consternation at the ceiling.

Mercifully, he fell asleep. The room dark when he woke, he sensed first by the air, hot and offensive gusts of it, that he was not alone in the destroyed bedclothes. Grace had come to comfort him. For a second Malcolm stared at her tucked up in his arms, blinking back at him with sympathy and goo. He marvelled, considering all he had put her through.

It was his habit now during walkies, when the ladies had gone home, to have a little sport with Grace and the doggie biscuit. He'd whistle and, seeing the bone-shaped treat in his hand, she'd scurry over and begin prancing at his feet, as if she could not remember what had happened yesterday or the day before, or was she that optimistic? He would pretend to throw it, but really slide it down his sleeve. Off she'd dash, searching, searching, and coming back just as eager. After three or four rounds of this, Malcolm would grow bored. He'd call her over and, to her delight, lift her and carry her over to the garbage can. Usually he wouldn't deign to touch her except to fasten her leash or tie up her hairs, but under his arm she could better see him toss the biscuit into the garbage along with the plastic bag of shit.

Now, in the dark room, he asked, "So you forgive me?" His head ached and his tone was sarcastic. She got up with a lurch and backed to the end of the bed.

"I don't know how you do it, darling. You are a superior being."

Her little knees began to shake, if she had knees, that was.

"Get down," he commanded.

Suicide-like, she leapt off the bed.

6

The eye on the answering machine, red and domed, was winking. Alison rewound the tape.

"Ali, it's Mom. I'm just wondering how you're feeling."

"Bad," Alison answered.

The second beep sounded. "Yes, it is five April and I do not have the cheque from you. Please bring it or, if it is better, I will drop by later to get it. Call me, yes, to tell me what you will do."

Billy had already spoken to Mrs. Branz, told her in no uncertain terms that they would not pay the rent until the fridge was fixed. Going over to the window, Alison looked out between the drapes she always kept drawn now so Mrs. Branz couldn't see in. Along the walk leading up to the house the tulip shoots were the tips of bright green bayonets. And there she was, Mrs. Hermann Branz herself, tootling out of her building, wicker basket of gardening tools on her arm, her ridiculous athletic knee pads outside her trousers.

Alison found the number and dialled. She planned to repeat exactly what Billy had already told her, but when she heard the message on Mrs. Branz's machine, guttural and pushy, she thought of something else. To disguise her voice, she dropped it down an octave, let it fall far back in her throat. "Nazi," she croaked, then hung up quickly. With a shaking hand, she dialled her parents' number.

"How's Jeffy?" she asked when her mother answered.

"He's in his room blowing people away on the computer. How are you?"

"Okay."

"When's your day off this week?"

"Thursday," said Alison.

"I was planning to go over to North Van and tidy things up. Do you want to keep me company?" She meant the cemetery where Alison's grandparents were buried. Alison, who didn't care what she did any more so long as she didn't have to pretend to enjoy it, said, "Sure. Okay."

"Really?" said her surprised mother. "Oh, thank you.

No one else will go."

From her parents' house they drove over the Second Narrows Bridge toward the mountains standing shoulder-deep in cloud. Below, Indian Arm reached crookedly up the inlet. The water, completely flat, was the colour of aluminum. Again her mother asked how she was, and when Alison shrugged she simply nodded. What a relief not to have to explain herself, Alison thought. She looked fondly at her mother, saw her completely grey at the temples now, the skin around her eyes spoked with lines. Yet she wasn't even fifty. Anyone looking at Alison's mother would see a woman whom age had not been as kind to, as she herself had been kind.

"Billy's driving me crazy," she admitted.

"Why is that?"

"He wants to go to Mexico."

"Mexico? When?"

"At the end of the month. What he really wants is for me to cheer up."

Her mother said, "He wants you to be happy. Are you going to go?"

"I think I have to," she said. "Every day he asks me if I got my passport pictures. If we've stocked up on Imodium."

Her mother laughed.

"He booked the tickets, but I don't feel like it, Ma. I just don't."

"You're going to have to tell him."

Alison sighed. "I hate a fight."

After the bridge, they exited the highway and looped onto an ascending, tree-lined road. This part of the city was built in deference to the rainforest; in every yard, on

246

every street, shaggy giants towered. When they turned onto the drive that led to the cemetery, it was as if they were driving into a forest clearing. Past the office and the chapel, they parked. Out of the trunk, Alison's mother took a flat of bedding plants.

Alison followed carrying the cardboard box with the tools and watering can. As they made their way along the path, her mother stopped now and then to point out a headstone. "Look. This old gal lived to be a hundred and three. But here. See? This one was a baby."

Her grandparents' grave had a single headstone with both their names carved in it. It was a simple black granite rectangle surrounded by drooping blade-like leaves of something past flowering. "What do you want me to do?" Alison asked, putting down the box.

"How about filling the watering can? There's a tap behind the office."

She took the can and started back along the path. Paved and meticulously edged, it was the main street through this necro-suburb, this North Vancouver for the dead. None of the graves were old. They were the same modest granite markers as her grandparents had, upright or laid flat—the cemetery equivalent of ranchers and bungalows. Everywhere, the sweet smell of cedar and the calls of unseen birds. She was not afraid. There was nothing remotely frightening here. It struck her then that the usual experience of death was actually quite banal. Her grandfather had died before Alison could know him. She remembered her grandmother's dying as her father coming in her bedroom and saying he was going to get take-out for her and Jeffy. Their mother would not be eating. A very sad thing had happened. Ever after, if take-out was offered on a school night, Alison's first thought was that someone had passed away.

The path veered toward the A-framed chapel, a structure half made of glass with a single-storey wing that was the office. The tap was under a window. As she stood filling the can, she could see inside to a small kitchen where a heavy-set woman sat at a table reading *Maclean's* and drinking coffee. A man in a dark suit came in and said something to the woman to make her laugh. These were the jolly, guiltless people who ministered to the dead.

Her mother had cleared out the bed by the time Alison got back. Now a bright border of primula replaced the lank overgrowth. From a bread bag, she was sifting dirt around the new plants.

"What's that?" Alison asked.

"Compost." She pressed the soil down with her gloved hand.

"This grave looks the nicest," Alison commented. Very few were decorated with flowers. A faded plastic bouquet stood stiffly in a granite vase not far away, but mostly there was just the green blanket of grass.

"I like to come here and have a chat. The plants are my excuse."

"Oh," said Alison. "Should I go away again?"

"It's all right. I've said what I came to say already."

"Are you and dad going to be buried here?"

"We're not going to be buried. We're going to be cremated and scattered."

Alison, who had not previously given any thought to her parents' eventual dying, suddenly felt hurt. Seeing her expression, her mother said, "It's better for the environment, isn't it?" She straightened and took the watering can from Alison. "Just add me to the compost."

"What if I want to come and have a talk with you?"

"It's silly, really," said her mother.

"I don't think so."

"I'll tell you what. When your father goes, you can have his La-Z-Boy. You can sit in it and commune with him."

"Ugh," said Alison, turning away. "It takes up half the living room."

Christian didn't have a grave. Alison thought of this as they were driving back over the bridge. At the memorial service, there wasn't even a casket. She wondered what had happened to his body. And what of all the others, the millions turned to ash in ovens or thrown into unprivate, unmarked pits? Where to bring the gardens and gardens of their flowers? Once again, she felt overwhelmed by the seeming ceaselessness of grief.

They had reached the crest of the bridge. Alison, looking down on the inlet's opposite shore, saw along the metallic water the green spread of a park. Between it and the bridge was an enormous structure, like a prison or a factory, painted white. They were driving past it now, looking down on, but somehow not dwarfing it. ALBERTA WHEAT POOL, read the logo on the tower.

The exit ramp brought them down next to a junction of railway tracks, rows and rows of boxcars standing. A moment later they passed the park she had just seen from the bridge. Almost blurred, the sign, she couldn't really read it, but still it snagged her eye. Quickly, she swung around, then stayed like that, frozen backward in the seat, the hair on her arms, on the back of her neck, rising up.

At first Billy didn't want to go with her. "Call one of your buddies from work."

"No one will want to go."

"Why do you want to?" he asked.

"I want to see where he died."

"Right," said Billy. "But why?"

She didn't want to say that it was because he had no grave. Billy would only reply, "So what?" Turning, she walked out of the bedroom. She would find her way on the bus. To her surprise, Billy followed, so she knew he'd changed his mind.

In the car, she directed from the map in her lap. She picked the route the bus would take, the busiest, which led them straight into Chinatown. Billy, hoping to extricate them, tried a side street, but it was even more congested, trucks in the middle of the road disgorging their arsenal of fruit, alleys blocked with wooden crates, pedestrians shuttling between the stand-still cars and spitting.

"Billy!"

He steered up the wrong side of the street, then had her get out of the car to press the pedestrian light so they could cross Hastings. They tore across and, all at once, Alison recognized the place. They were driving past a block-square park where the men lay collapsed under the trees with their shopping carts filled with scavengings. She pointed out the building. "That's the Mission." She'd never been there except on dripping Christmas days, but was somehow unsurprised that neither springtime nor sunshine cheered the place.

Billy drove on, too fast, determinedly cranky, past listing wooden houses and old warehouses. She wanted to tell him where to turn, but knew better than to offer a suggestion now, no matter how correct. They missed the exit, which put them back ten minutes while they looped around the empty Pacific National Exhibition fairground. Finally, they pulled into the parking lot where the sign for the storage company next door told them it was thirteen minutes past noon.

They got out and walked. To get into the park, they had to enter a tunnel under the railway track. When Christian had walked through it that night just after Christmas, it must have been like entering a void. Now light reached in almost all the way to where the light coming from the far side ended. At no point was it even dark.

"Look," she said. It was wheeling above the other more cryptic graffiti—a sinister windmill, an evil insect. Billy only grunted. Then they heard a scream and Alison clutched his arm. A child in a pink peak-hooded jacket appeared in the bright arch of the opening, but stopped because someone called her back. She squealed again, gleefully stamping rubber boots, turned and galloped off.

Emerging from the tunnel, Alison saw the children playing on a jungle gym. Three young mothers were watching from a nearby bench, drinking out of thermos cups. Before the bridge stood the massive Alberta Wheat Pool building she had seen a few days ago. On the tennis courts a man was lobbing against the practice board a cheerfully percussing ball.

She started in the direction of the toilets, Billy in tow, and when they reached the building, she asked him to go in. Wordlessly, he complied, coming out a moment later. "What's it like?" she asked.

"It's a can. It stinks."

"Is anybody in there?"

"Just a couple of guys going at it. Ha ha."

"You keep watch," Alison said, stepping inside herself.

Immediately, she began breathing through her mouth. It did stink—of new paint. Each of the shiny cubicle doors she pushed open. Nobody, nobody. The last, larger and wheelchair-accessible, she entered. This was where he had been waiting, here, she was sure. Behind these very metal partitions Christian had stood. For minutes, she concentrated, but in the end sensed no presence, felt nothing, no recoiling of her soul. Beneath her feet, the concrete trembled not at all.

"Christian?" she whispered. "Christian?"

When she opened her eyes again, it was to a banal white toilet and chrome handrails.

Outside, Billy was waiting with hands in his pockets. In silence they began walking back, Alison slowly, keeping her eyes to the ground, tracking. She was searching for some mark, a sign of where the golf club had come down. But that was months ago. Weeks and weeks of rain had washed his blood into the grass. Past where the children had clambered down from the jungle gym, they were tearing after one another, screeching. For a moment, Alison stopped to watch the little girl in pink running for her life, then falling.

Back at the car, Billy unlocked her door. Curls edged his cap and poked through the arch above the sizing band. "You need a haircut," she said.

They stopped for groceries and beer on the way back. Billy chose his own route, so was less irritable when they got in. He made himself a sandwich, and after he had eaten Alison went to fetch the comb and scissors.

"So?" he said. "Did you see what you wanted?"

She shrugged. All she had seen of any significance was spray-painted in the tunnel, but swastikas she saw everywhere now—on stop signs and garage doors, carved into trees, on newspaper boxes, in the dirt on parked cars, on bus seats.

"Could it happen again?" She asked him because, after all, Billy was the most intelligent person she knew.

"Of course," said Billy. "Gays get it all the time."

That was not what she meant, of course, but she did not correct him. Coldly, she said, "You say that so matter-of-factly."

"It is a fact," said Billy.

"My friend died," she reminded him.

"I know."

The towel in her hands, she stared at him.

"You hardly knew the guy, Ali. Not really. I mean, you worked with him for four or five months. If he'd quit and moved away, you wouldn't still be thinking about him."

"He didn't move away," said Alison. "He was killed."

Billy sighed and looked up at an ancient curlicue of spaghetti stuck on the ceiling. "Are you going to cut my hair or not?"

She draped the towel around his shoulders, though she didn't feel like cutting his hair any more. She didn't feel like touching him, but his head was bowed, waiting, the furrow between the tendons on his nape showing.

"Remember Mrs. Soloff?" she asked, raining mist all around him with the spray bottle.

"Who?"

"At the salon. The old woman who was in Auschwitz." On his head, she marked the sections with the comb, starting at his crown. "When I asked you if it could happen again, that's what I meant."

"Auschwitz?"

"Yeah."

"No way."

She marvelled at his confidence. "How do you know?"

"I just don't think people would fall for that again."

"Those kids who killed Christian, they fell for it."

He looked over his shoulder, frowning. "I thought you took that book back."

She reddened. She didn't know what had happened to it. The day Thi threw it out the door, Alison had snuck around after work to retrieve it. She'd even scaled the blue steel wall of the dumpster and peered under all the cars, but it was gone. Vanished.

"I've been thinking," Billy said in a gentler tone. "Maybe you should see someone."

"Who?"

"A counsellor."

"There's nothing wrong with me." There was, Alison was convinced, something wrong with everyone else. They were all blind, or wearing blinkers, remarkably unperceptive or just naïve. As she had been, not long ago. She marked out another section to cut. In Billy's lap, smiles of curls.

"Well, those pills aren't helping much. If things go on like this, you'll be a virgin again before too long." He glanced back at her to see if he had made her smile and, while he was still looking at her, his expression changed. His face lit up, eureka-like. "Are you *taking* the pills?" he asked.

She started to stammer something. He stood, scattering the hair. Straight through Lake Superior he walked, and out of the kitchen. "That explains a thing or two," he said.

She heard him rifling through the bathroom drawers, slamming cupboards. He reappeared a moment later, uncapping the bottle. The cotton stopper was still in place. "Why?" he asked. "Why aren't you taking them?"

"Because I don't want to feel nothing!"

"You won't feel nothing. You'll feel better, Shit-for-Brains."

"Don't call me that!" she cried, flashing the scissors at him.

He came toward her and fearlessly disarmed her, taking the scissors right out of her hand and dropping them on the table.

"I don't want you to call me that any more!"

"All right. I won't. Now open up." His arm around her, he held a pill close to her face. "Come on, Ali. Open up." She took it her mouth. "Atta girl," said Billy and, with his arm still around her, he led her off down the hall.

In the living room, he sat her down and began to stroke her hair. "I love you," he said, "don't you know that?" She nodded, but did not look at him, so he pressed his forehead to hers, forcing on her his earnest gaze.

"Do you love me?"

She didn't want to answer, didn't want to speak at all because the pill was stuck up under her lip against her teeth—a little trick she'd learned from watching Roxanne pretend to take Christian's vitamins. He kissed her face, murmuring—did she love him? She did. Of course, she did. She just wasn't sure if she liked him any more.

Her luck Monday morning to flee the apartment and run straight into Mrs. Hermann Branz on her knees at the bottom of the walk. "I have called! He is coming! Now you must give to me my cheque!" She stood and with muddy gloves made a motion to shoo Alison back into the house.

"No," said Alison, boldly. She told her no, and more. "This isn't Germany, you know. Not yet. And another thing, you are the rudest person I've ever met!" She even mentioned Mrs. Branz's husband. "Where is Hermann, anyway? Hiding? Is he hiding?"

Mrs. Branz, struck mute, stared at Alison with her gloved hand over her face, mud streaked across her cheek. It didn't make Alison feel very good to have finally stood up for herself. Watching the landlady's tearful retreat across the street, she actually felt worse.

Arriving at Vitae, she went straight to the back room, but instead of starting on the coffee, she sank down on the bench. "Oh, God," she said, "I just did something really mean."

"There is no God," said Malcolm, standing there in a tweed jacket too long in the sleeves.

No God, Alison thought. Just a rustle overhead, the clicking of little claws. There was a rat in the sky telling them all what to do.

7

"Very peaceful," the photographer told her. "You look like you are dead."

Alison stared at him, unflattered, though from his accent, she guessed he was unaware how rude his comment sounded.

"I will retake it again."

"No, no. It's fine," she said. The first hurt enough— the put-your-eye-out flash, then his jerking the picture out of the camera, flailing the air with it to dry it, ripping away the plastic coating. Apparently, though, the law prescribed that eyes had to be open in a passport photo, just as the law prescribed that a dead person could not be issued a passport. The photographer intimated that these two statutes were somehow connected as he raised her chin a second time. He ducked behind the camera and, after letting her cringe a long anticipatory moment, asked, "You never learn to smile?"

As with the first, this picture developed mysteriously in double behind the black coating. Alison hardly recognized herself as happy. The photographer, however, saw a satisfactory likeness. He wandered over to the counter, dropping the failed picture to one side as he raised the arm of the paper cutter. "Where are you going?" he asked, bending to align the good picture on the cutter's grid. "On a trip?" His scalp through lank thinning hair was red and embarrassed to be seen.

"Yeah. Mexico, I guess."

She looked away, to the walls crammed with wedding photos, stiff-gowned and tuxedoed groupings under arbours, poof-sleeved brides with bad perms, circa 1980, which could have been the last time he worked judging from the dinge of the place. She imagined his reputation souring after a few too many comments like, "It is your wedding day and you look like death."

Her own twin photos were lying there, she went over to look at them again. "What do you do with the pictures that don't turn out?"

"I discard them away."

She picked up the picture at the same moment he brought the cutter's arm down. "You can't have it!" he said as sharply as the blade.

"I was just—" Nothing. Just looking at herself. She saw the wastebasket behind the counter, was about to tear the picture up when he snatched it from her and stuffed it in his shirt pocket.

Now everything about him was jerky and furtive. Avoiding her eye, he opened a drawer and fumbled in it, took out an ink pad and stamped the back of the two good photos. Furiously. "Twelve dollars plus tax. Thirteen sixty-eight." He slid them in an envelope across the counter to her.

"What are you going to do with my picture?" she asked.

He twitched, then for a long moment neither of them budged until, finally, the photographer backed down. He took the picture from his pocket and, pausing first to determine if it was damaged, disappeared through the curtained doorway behind him.

She just stood there. Maybe he was hoping this was some kind of deal, that she would take her smiling picture away for free. But after a minute he pulled the curtain back and, glaring, motioned to her.

"I am an artist. I am making an installation."

Storage room close, dim, vinegar-smelling, it was lined with shelves of darkroom chemicals and supplies made inaccessible by four large panels leaning up against them. On the panels, glued in perfect even rows, were doubled passport images, hundreds of them, rejects due to blurring or a grimace or closed eyes. The photographer was brushing the back of her picture with rubber cement as he explained what he would do with the panels when he had filled them, but she wasn't listening. She was looking at the children, the old, the people of all ages in between. For once they looked afraid.

"Here. I put you here." At the end of a row. He pounded the picture to make it stick. "What is the matter? Are you sick?"

Her voice wouldn't come. She had both hands on her chest where her heart was beating out its panic. It sounded in her ears like pounding fists.

"Come," he said, taking her arm and leading her back

through the curtain and over to the stool. "Sit."

Then she cried out. The pain almost knocked her flat. Surely, she would faint. A thousand fists hammering, fingers clawing, trying desperately to pry apart her ribs. The whole of her breast was being wrenched open from the inside and she couldn't even weep. She just sat there, bowed over, paralysed and shuddering.

"What is wrong?" asked the photographer. "Should I call an ambulance?"

"All those people," she whispered. "Those poor people."

And there she was, herself among them. Now she understood what he meant by dead.

Her chest still ached. It would hurt her the whole day. On her way through the gallery to get the broom, Alison paused to watch Malcolm pump the chair. Mrs. Soloff ascended, a towel over her head. When he lifted it off, the fine white floss that was her hair seemed to have all but disappeared. In two broad hands, he enclosed her skull, moved it very slightly, as he would move something exceedingly precious. A finger steadying her forehead, he took up the comb and in one smooth gesture drew it over her crown so the hair showed again, silvery. Alison wondered how long it had been that colour and if it had turned white in the camp.

"How are the grandchildren?" asked Malcolm.

"Oh, marvellous. They can do no wrong."

"And how's your niece?"

"Elaine?" A weary sigh. "Still single. How is Grace?"

"Irrelevant."

Mrs. Soloff laughed.

He was not the sort to leave his client unattended even for a moment while he rooted around at another station; neither was he one to make off with another stylist's clips. His were fixed to his jacket cuff. All the tools he needed were close by and he needed only the essential: scissors, comb, end papers, rollers, clips. Mrs. Soloff's hair fixed at her nape with the ibis beak of a do-all, he began to trim—less than a half a centimetre, in a perfect line.

"Did you try that concoction?"

"What, dear?"

He removed the clip and returned it to his cuff while he marked out the next section with the comb. "The Chinese liniment I recommended."

"Oh, yes! I meant to thank you! It helps a little."

Alison got the broom and started sweeping her way back through the gallery. When she neared Malcolm's station again, she saw the cut was finished and he was pausing to change Mrs. Soloff's towel. He brushed clean her neck, placed a fresh towel around her bent shoulders and pulled the curler trolley close.

"Now, Mrs. Soloff, you will tell me if I roll too tightly?"

"Yes."

"I think you don't, though. I see it on your face."

She sighed. "Malcolm, it is like this. For me, everything hurts."

All at once Alison realized why she could not get over what had happened to Christian. It had only really been about him at the start. Then it was about Mrs. Soloff, and not just Mrs. Soloff now. She looked down at her feet and saw the hair, all colours, gathered by the broom.

Malcolm's fingers folded the end paper, then deftly rolled the curler and snapped it shut. In the mirror, Alison saw Mrs. Soloff's head tip back. With closed eyes, all the lines dropped from her face and she looked to be at peace. Malcolm didn't move, just stood there, very still, trying not wake her. With Mrs. Soloff's sleeping head against his chest, he closed his eyes and bore her weight.

At the end of the day, she sat at the desk watching him put on his trench coat and wind the monogrammed scarf around his neck. "Those aren't your initials," she said as he was tucking in the tail.

"You sharp-eyed thing, you." He actually smiled. "You're staying late."

"I'm waiting to talk to you."

How extraordinary, thought Malcolm, taken aback. A person under the age of sixty-five who was not a member of the health care profession was actually suggesting that they engage in a conversation! What in the world could she want? "I have to take Grace out," he told her. "Would you like to join us?"

They left together. Too late, he realized he would have to invite her up, and while they walked the few blocks in silence he tried in vain to think of an excuse for how he lived. The truth prettied-up occurred to him: we are maintaining separate residences. The expense? *Mon Dieu!* In the end, he let her in without saying anything and pointed up the stairs.

If, when he opened the apartment door, she was taken aback by what she saw, a bachelor's suite so crowded with furniture and boxes there was little space left to stand or move, she didn't show it. What she saw was a life diminishing and pushing the furniture together. Strangely, the mirrors were all covered, but she didn't have time to ask why; just then a rattish dog came out of nowhere and lunged at her shins. Alison, who in the great divide of humanity fell squarely on the side of cat people, barely managed not to scream.

"Grace!" Malcolm roared. "Down, you idiotic thing!"

The dog collapsed and began to writhe in supplication on the mat. Malcolm shimmied over to what, in less cramped circumstances, would have been the kitchen and from under the sink took a greying rag. Grace stopped swimming, sat up, and with hind legs open, licked her private parts.

"That is unconscionable behaviour," Malcolm told her. "What will our visitor think?" He dropped the rag over the wet spot on the mat and pressed it with his shoe. "She is dissolute," he told Alison. "Unreformable. God knows I've tried."

Alison didn't know whether he was serious or joking.

"I have concluded," he said, bending to fasten the lead, "that her blood is bad."

"I like the little bow," Alison said. "It's really cute."

"She insists I put it on her. I think it's going too far, considering her proclivities. Out, out, damned tart." He opened the door, holding Alison back by her elbow. "Let Grace go first. She always has to be first."

Christ, he was babbling. What would the girl think of *him*? Yet he was happy to take her along. His old dears would be delighted to see her. They knew her from the salon and liked her. They would appreciate the change of face.

After a short walk, they neared a park and Malcolm let the dog off the lead. She tore yapping across the grass, and when they had caught up to her Alison saw three familiar, wrinkled faces, all of them exclaiming when they saw her.

"Good heavens! Whom have we here?" Mrs. Parker warbled from her scooter.

"She's a little young for you, isn't she?" teased Miss

Velve.

"No younger," quipped Mrs. Rodeck, "than Malcolm is to you!"

They all cackled, pretending to be jealous, and Malcolm told them, "You've got it wrong. She has a very lucky swain. And I, I am likewise taken."

Plucked and redrawn eyebrows arched; faces leaned toward him, curiosity wiping off the years. Would he make a confession? They were dying to know.

"I have Grace," said Malcolm.

They all laughed. It was exactly the right answer.

"And what do you think of Malcolm's Gracie?" Mrs. Rodeck asked Alison.

Malcolm answered for her. "She saw immediately her striking resemblance to the late Princess of Monaco."

"Oh, get away!" cried Miss Velve. "I don't believe she said that!"

Alison hoped they would not ask her opinion of their own creatures. One had the torso of a pig. The chihuahua kept running into things. The other was dragging along the ground what appeared to be a long, misshapen penis.

Miss Velve came up beside her. "It's only a growth, dear."

"I suppose he told you Grace understands three languages," said Mrs. Rodeck.

"No," said Alison. "He didn't."

"She has a comprehending vocabulary of one hundred words in English, French and German. *Halt die Schnauze du altes Dreckschwein!*" he called.

Grace looked up, startled. The old girls shrieked.

"Ladies, I need your advice," Malcolm announced. "Something is wrong with Grace. I fear she is regressing." He had caught her pulling the stuffing out of the pillows, he explained. "She makes a sort of pap to suck. I had a bag of clothes sitting on the floor. She ripped that open, too."

Mrs. Rodeck was surprised. "How odd! That's cat behaviour."

"She was weaned too young," said Miss Velve. "What have you been doing to discourage her?"

"I shout, 'For God's sake, Grace! Pull yourself together!'"

"Spray her with a water bottle," said Miss Velve.

"A rolled-up newspaper doesn't hurt."

"Does she have a rawhide toy?"

"How about a wet-nurse?" suggested Malcolm, to titters from the ladies. Then Mrs. Rodeck and Miss Velve leashed their dogs to go. Malcolm helped Mrs. Parker back on her scooter, as he'd helped her off.

"Madam? Do you have a licence to operate this vehicle?"

"Oh, Malcolm," she giggled. "Stop!"

"And what are you wearing on your feet, Mrs. P? Bedroom slippers?"

"It doesn't matter. My feet rarely touch the ground."

She waved as she drove off with the chihuahua in her basket. Mrs. Rodeck owned the pig. "I hope you'll join us again," she told Alison. Miss Velve invited her to come around to her china shop.

As soon as they had gone, Malcolm suddenly seemed exhausted. "Come," he told her, heading for a bench. "The first twenty-five years, you can stand all day, then suddenly you can't."

The girl sat down beside him, so close he felt her warmth. Grace, without her canine friends, came and stood in front of them, full of hope. It sprang eternal from the beribboned fountain on her head. And the way the goop in her eyes stained her fur gave her a satisfyingly melancholic expression; he liked to believe she was just slightly more miserable than he. From his pocket, he took the bone-shaped biscuit. She cocked the ribbon and yapped, though, naturally, he couldn't torture her in front of the girl.

Out of the blue, she asked him about Denis. Was he still in the hospital?

"Actually, I'm not sure where he is any more." He meant that he didn't know if Denis had been sent back to the ward. The girl didn't know that, of course. By her pained, sympathetic expression, he saw that she thought Denis had left him. If only Denis *could*! But you couldn't leave someone you'd forgotten. All the difficult decisions were left for Malcolm to make, for Malcolm to suffer over.

She told him, "I don't know what to say. I'm sorry."

"Sorry is enough." No one else had told him that.

They sat in silence, the girl staring straight ahead and frowning. She was thinking, he could tell; she wore her mental processes on her face, charmingly. "I'm still upset about what happened to Christian," she said at last.

"It's not something," he told her, "to get over easily."

"We're the only ones who haven't."

There was an uncharacteristic bitterness in her voice. He didn't agree, but didn't say so. At night, the others surely sweated in their sleep and woke from bloody dreams, as well. She was so young, she didn't know yet that people had other, inner lives, of which they did not speak.

"I keep thinking about those boys I saw in court. I have a little brother, see?"

"I used to live in Europe. Maybe you knew that. I used to believe that, by virtue of their history, Europeans had a monopoly on these predilections. Absurd, of course, and simplistic. History, as you know by now, is not perpetuated in buildings or artifacts or on defunct battlefields. It does not belong exclusively to the place in which it occurred. It is borne along on currents of air and on the Internet and in genes."

The girl stared at him. The dog, too. He was, he realized, speechifying. He pressed his eyes, suddenly embarrassed.

"I'd like to go to Europe," she said, and began to tell him about a plan she had. He watched her move her hands in the air excitedly. Now and then she even touched his arm for emphasis, but he was not listening. He was thinking about Denis and fiddling with the biscuit, marking it with fingerprints of sweat. For some reason his heart had started pounding, as if on a great set of doors in his chest. What is wrong with me, he asked himself, alarmed and trying to draw a breath. How animated she was, how imploring. Do I love her? he wondered. Oh, Christ! Could I have sunk to that? Or am I dying? Is this a heart attack?

Grace, meanwhile, had wandered over to the sidewalk where she stood waiting abjectly for a passerby to rescue her. No one came.

"You understand, don't you?" Alison asked. He looked at her blankly from under his crow-dark hair and she saw he had not heard a word of what she had so agonized over saying.

"My dear, I am acutely distractible these days."

Sighing, she fell back against the bench. Now she would have to say it all again.

Malcolm held a finger up, then pointed to where the dog stood some distance off wearing a curious martyred look. "Excuse me." Taking from his pocket a plastic bag, he went over and, after a moment, gingerly stooped. He came back and stood in front of her—a tired man with dyed hair concealing behind his back a bag of poo. For the first time she saw what he was—not sarcastic, not bitter or indifferent. What really he was, was sad.

And why, Alison wondered, why had it taken her so long to think of Malcolm as her friend? Of everybody, he was the only one who seemed to understand how she felt. He would go with her. She would convince him.

"It's a museum now."

"I beg your pardon?"

"Auschwitz."

He heard her out. He reeled. First she had proposed a conversation and now a European holiday—together, just the two of them. How romantic! "What a coincidence," he said. "I was just reading the *Inferno*."

"I couldn't go alone," she said.

"What happened to your boyfriend?"

Her eyes, widening at the suggestion, were very blue. "Oh, I couldn't go with him!"

"I should show you my bank statements," he said, mildly hysterical. Then Grace came whingeing back, and by accident he threw her the dampened biscuit. She could not believe her luck.

For a long moment they watched the dog's strenuous champing, then the girl began to cry. He remembered her telling him that she didn't think he had liked Christian. It had bothered him at the time. Stricken by her words, he had turned away: because she had come close to the truth. The tears he had been holding back had not been for Christian, but for himself. Bent over, face in hands, shoulders heaving, the girl was no rocket scientist, true. But surely there were qualities equal to intelligence. A line from *Mrs. Dalloway* came to mind. *What did the brain matter, compared to the heart?* He thought it marvellous, marvellous she could care so much.

AN DIESEM ORT FÜGTEN MENSCHEN
MENSCHEN SCHLIMMSTE GRAUSAMKEITEN
ZU. LEIDEN UND TOD VIELER SIND MIT
UNS AUF DAS ENGSTE VERBUNDEN.
ZUM GEDACHTNIS DERER DIE HIER LITTEN
UND STARBEN BITTE BEGEHEN SIE DIESEN
ORT IN RUHIGER ANGEMESSENER WEISE

Pull the van up in front of the building, a boxy stucco apartment, a "villa" or "casa." Take the clipboard off the dash. Double-check the number and when you've confirmed that this is, indeed, the place, get out and take your tool box from the back. Head up the walk, whistling; it's your last job of the day. All along the walk, on either side, the open tulips are the various colours of flame.

It's a villa. VILLA CONSTANCE, it reads on the door in gold slanting script. Through the glass you see the burgundy leaf-patterned carpet and the leaves of all the plants. Find the manager on the intercom list, press the button next to her name. A moment later a voice barks out, Gestapo-like, "Who is there!" Startled, snapping to attention, stammer the reason that you're here. She cuts you off. "Come in!"

A sharp nasal buzz signals the door release. Step into the mirrored lobby and watch yourself lugging the box to the elevator. Press the "up" arrow, and while you're waiting, straighten the collar of your uniform. The front door is still buzzing, agitated, fretful, even as the elevator arrives.

It takes you to the penthouse, opening across from the apartment door. You are just reaching for the knocker when the door swings open on a face that perfectly fits the voice: scowling and leathery with stiff grey hair that may or may not be hers. "Who is Hermann?" she demands.

Tell her it's not you. You don't know any Hermann.

"Nor do I!" she cries. "Then why would she say such things to me and make reference to this Hermann person whom I do not even know?"

Are you in the right place after all? Where did you put the address? Set down the tool box and pat your shirt pocket. You must have left it with the clipboard in the van.

"Another thing! She left a message, very upsetting and untrue. I did not know at the time that it was she, but now I know. Why? Why did she do it?" She glares at you, accusing, waiting for some manner of reply.

"Is your fridge broken, lady?" you ask.

"Yes! It is broken!" she shrieks and, all at once, starts to cry.

Step back, surprised. Look at the old crone. It's terrible, pathetic. She needs an arm around her, someone to straighten up her wig. Joke with her a little, tell her, "Don't take it so hard. I can fix it." She seems to like that, a little tease. See her wrinkle around the eyes? Out of her sleeve comes a hankie and she daubs her *Nase* with it, still choked up, but managing to tell you, "I am sorry. After many days, I am still upset. I will go and get the keys now."

"It's not your fridge?"

"Yes. Across the street."

A desk right behind her, she goes over to it and, opening a drawer, takes out a key ring. About to turn, she stops instead to look at a picture on the desk. She stares a long time, a full minute maybe, so you are just wondering what she sees in it—it must be familiar enough—when the old lady suddenly swings around and asks, "Does she mean Dieter, do you think?"

She brings the picture over. "Look. This is me—"

"You?"

"Yes. And this is Dieter. Dieter, not Hermann."

Take it from her. It's black and white, a portrait from a long time ago. What does she expect you to say? Tell her it's nice. Tell her, "That's a good-looking man."

"Yes. Dieter, he was good." This seems to distress her all the more. "Dieter!" she cries, "Dieter!" and more tears flow.

Tell her she should sit down. Say, "Come on. Let's go sit."

She shakes her head and waves a hand and, after a second, calms down. "Dieter was distributing tracts, yes?" In order to tell you this, she has to take a deep breath.

"Yeah?"

"After the *Anschluss*."

"The what?"

She frowns. *Imbecile*, her look says. She is, you realize, explaining something very important, something she is proud to tell. Of course she's senile, or living in the past, but even so, lend an ear and try to sympathize.

"Then they caught him. They came for me, too, but Dieter would never tell me anything, just in case, so very kindly they only broke my mouth and I have not had my own teeth since age twenty. Look." She opens wide.

Oh, lady, you think, I am a refrigerator repairman, not a denturist.

"When you go over there," she tells you sternly, "if she says to you anything about Hermann, tell her I do not know him. Tell her about Dieter, that he was a good man, yes? Tell her that I thought she was a good girl, too. I was very kind to her. I gave her strudel."

Tell her you will. Say, "Sure. I'll straighten everything out."

"Oh, thank you!" Eyes filling up, with gratitude this time, she grabs at you; she has quite a pull on her for an old girl. All at once, though, she's embarrassed. You, you feel it too: an awkwardness. You are two strangers holding hands. "I am sorry," she says with dignity as she lets you go. "What do these things have to do with you?"

Tell her it's all right. Give her back the picture. She returns it to the desk and when she stands it up, it falls right over on its face so it looks for a second like waterworks again. But no, she sets it up without a fuss. Tell her, "I consider it, you know, part of the job. You'd be surprised what people tell me."

"Do they? Do they tell you all their woes?"

"Sometimes, yeah."

"Nobody cares about me, you see."

"That's not true."

"I have nobody. I have lost everything. Even my teeth."

You don't quite know what to say to that. Then she winks and you laugh. Opening the desk drawer again, she gives you a sneaky little glance. Out comes a photo album, the kind that holds only one picture on each page. She brings it over and starts flipping through it, showing you snapshots, all of them of children. Chinese kids. Black kids. Brown kids. Ask her if they're hers.

"Oh, no! It is the Foster Parent Plan. I only share them."

"Yeah? They're very cute."

That did it. Now she's really smiling, showing plastic choppers, the works. "This is Mira. This is Jean-Luc who writes very charming letters. And look! Look!" She beams down at the child. "This is *Ping*."

Nod and smile. Glance at your watch.

"Oh, I am sorry. I am making you late." Miracle of miracles, she presses into your hand the keys. "Thank you. Oh, thank you. You remember what to say?"

"Dieter, not Hermann."

"Yes. The big house across the street. With the tulips. This key is for the front. This one is for apartment number two."

Back down the elevator you go, chuckling to yourself. Chuckling as you leave the building, as you cross the street. A firewalker with a tool box, head up the tulip-bordered walk. It's a nice old place, you see, unlocking the front door. It opens into a vestibule of mahogany wainscoting, a big staircase, windows leaded with diamond-shaped panes of glass. Here, on the left, is apartment number two.

Knock. There is no answer. Go ahead and knock again. You are just going to use the key the old lady gave you when you hear the lock turn and see the door open a crack. An eye, blue and round, then squinting, looks out over the chain.

"Yes?" she says.

Tell her you're the repairman. "I've come to fix the fridge."

A huge sigh. She undoes the chain and, exasperated, tells you, "She never calls! She's supposed to give us a day's notice, right? Well, she never does." She steps aside to let you in.

The curtains are drawn. Someone has been sleeping on the couch; a shucked-off comforter lies crumpled at one end. The coffee table is piled with magazines.

"This way," says the girl.

She's not what you expected; except for the deadly platform shoes, she actually looks sweet, not at all the type to menace an old lady. "Have you ever been to Europe?" she asks, leading you down the hall.

Tell her, years ago.

"I'm going."

"Yeah? Where?"

Walking ahead of you, she stops at the kitchen.

"On holiday?" you ask.

"No. Sorry about the mess. If she'd called to say you were coming, I would have cleaned up a bit."

It's not so bad, just a lot of dirty dishes in the sink and a pool of water on the linoleum, probably from a plug in the drain line. Tell her that it won't be hard to fix. But she's staring off distractedly, at nothing, and does not seem to hear.

Pull the cord on the radio that sits on top, then stand in the puddle and drag the fridge out from the wall. All the stuff that's behind there, you just do not believe. It's always like that though. Things people don't know what to do with, they put on top of the fridge. Eventually it all falls down behind, forgotten, unmissed.

"Business?" you ask.

"What?"

"Are you going to Europe on business?"

"Oh, no," she says, either in reply to your question or because, from the other room, someone has just come in. The girl covers her face briefly, her eyes darting bluely back and forth. "Don't mention what I told you," she hisses.

"What?"

"The trip." She calls, "What are you doing here?"

"I live here," replies a weary voice.

"You're early."

He appears, baseball cap reversed on his head, very young, very curly, very cute.

"Look who's here," the girl says flatly.

"Hi." He barely glances at you getting in behind the fridge. Already you sense tension, something very much unsaid, ready to be spoken. "Fight of the century today," the boy tells her, and you wonder if he's announcing the opening round or what. He interrupts himself. "Can I get in here and grab myself a beer?"

Tell him sure. Go ahead. "Get 'em while they're cold."

He pops the tab and tells the girl, "Stuart 'The Stub' Little versus Fritz the Rat." Off they go down the hall. You can still hear them in the other room. "Picture it. The Stub alone in the enclosure, white lights glaring. He's nervous, quivering. He's not stupid. He knows something's up."

With the screwdriver, start on the plate.

"Suddenly he wheels a one-eighty. Fritz! Fritz! How the fuck?"

Barely audible, her mutter. "Billy?"

The drain line is plugged, just as you thought. The water's not hitting the tray. Take it off. Ream it out.

"The Stub stretches himself and starts creeping toward Fritz, Fritzie looking edgy."

"Billy," she says, louder.

"The Stub circles round, sniffing Fritzie—his fur, his arse. Fritz doesn't like it, but that's just tough. That's how it goes in Ratland, right?"

The girl says she has something to tell him. She says it very clearly, certainly loud enough for you, but still the boy acts as if he didn't hear. "The Stub rears. Fritz crouches—frozen, tense. Then the Stub starts that grooming thing. He's grooming Fritz."

"I thought it was a fight," says the girl.

"It is. That's what they do."

"What?"

"They give each other perms and trim each other's bangs. No, they do, sort of. Then things get vicious. The Stub goes for Fritz's left ear. Fritz screams, wrenches himself free, minus a piece. And they're both up and boxing! Left, right! Left, right! You hardly ever see stuff like this in the WBC!" He gives her the cue to laugh, too, a little expectant pause.

Nothing.

You though, you are chuckling to yourself.

"Where are you going?" he asks.

"Actually," she tells him from the hall, "I'm going to Poland."

You decide to put in a new line altogether; the old one's pretty brittle. The girl passes the kitchen in a hurry and the boy follows a moment later.

"I didn't hear you," he says.

They should close the door now that they are in the bedroom, but it happens like this all the time. As soon as you step behind the fridge, it is as if you, too, had fallen down the back. They don't remember that you're here. The arguments you have heard, the confessions, even a couple going at it, no holds barred, when you were right there in their kitchen.

"Poland."

"You're kidding, right? I thought we were, like, going to Mexico. What happened to Mexico?"

"I can't."

"So what's in Poland?" he asks, then, before she can answer, says, "Oh, no. Not *that*."

The line in, do them a favour: drag out all the stuff behind the fridge—the pizza boxes, the flyers and receipts, the single earring, the full prescription bottle of pills, the mousetrap sprung, but empty. Leave it there in the middle of the floor. She'll be glad about the pills, at least.

In the bedroom, the girl is sobbing; it breaks your heart to hear it. You hate to interrupt, but your tools are packed and you should tell them that you're leaving.

Walk down the hall and knock on the door frame. Say, "Excuse me."

They both look up, startled, surprised to see you there.

"It should be all right now," you tell them. "The fridge, I mean. It's fixed."

And you, you're surprised as well because, sitting on the edge of the bed curled forward, wet face lifted out of hands, it's not the girl who's crying, but the boy. It's the boy who looks bereft.

Tenues Sine Corpore Vitae

A SOUL IN THE LOWER WORLD

1

If love could actually be measured, she would have said that she loved Billy more. He was her first real boyfriend and before she'd met him, she hadn't known you could be so absorbed by another person. Gravely, she'd given him her virginity; he joked about it to this day. For Billy, even their most tender moments had a punchline. Nothing was sacred.

How surprised she was then to realize she was the one leaving and to see him so upset. He was actually crying and, at first, she did not know why. "It's only for a week." She tried to take his hand, but he pulled away and got up off the bed.

"Who are you going with?"

"Malcolm. The older man at the salon. He went to court with me, too, remember?"

"No," said Billy, glaring. "I don't remember. You never told me that."

It was in that moment, with Billy standing before her, accusing, that she caught a glimpse of her own future and knew he would not be in it. Shocked, she stared at him without seeing how ugly his anger made him—

crimson, sneering—without seeing him at all. Prescience had cut around the outline of his body and removed him from her sight. Instantly she missed him and all the things about him that she loved—the wayward curls, the indentation in his chest, his sense of humour, even the sex. She would never find another lover with Billy's appetite. She thought she would never have another lover again at all, that she would always be alone with her dark thoughts from then on.

"Why didn't you ask me to go?"

She almost let slip a disbelieving laugh. It inflamed him all the more. He stepped forward and pushed her, shoved her so her head snapped back and thudded against the wall. Concentric rings of pain, a skullcap of hurt. Wincing, she put her hand to the back of her head. Billy hurried off.

Should she follow him, she wondered, hearing him in the living room, crying again. After a minute she got up, but passing the kitchen and seeing the sodden mess in the middle of the floor, she stopped there instead. In a drawer she found a garbage bag. All the wet papers and junk she lifted into it. She might as well wash the floor, too, she thought.

"If you go with him, don't come back here!" Billy called.

She went to the living room, found him hunched miserably on the couch, face in his hands. "You're not jealous of Malcolm, are you?" she asked.

"You heard what I said?" He wouldn't look at her. He talked through the cracks between his fingers.

"Yes."

"I mean it." Peevish.

She went back to the kitchen, had just filled the bucket with hot water when she saw something soar past the door. It landed with a clunk, out of sight. A moment later, another came flying: her shoe. "Are you going or not?" he shouted, sending another airborne.

"Yes," she answered and went to pack.

"Ho ho," said her father, coming in the kitchen wearing his fez. "Look what the cat dragged in!" He popped the fez on her head.

"Hi, Dad," said Alison.

"Where's Billy the Kid?"

"Ali," her mother said, "is going to stay with us for a while."

Her father frowned and pulled a chair out, a long hiss of air escaping from the vinyl seat as he sat. She rarely saw him serious, except shouting at politicians on the TV, and it took him a minute to formulate the words. "He didn't do anything—?"

"No," said Alison. "We just weren't, you know, seeing things eye to eye."

"Ah," he chuckled. "Men and women hardly ever do. You'll patch things up."

"She's going to take a trip," her mother said.

"A trip? That's a good idea." Satisfied, incurious, he made to stand. Alison took the fez off her head and balanced it on the crest of his gut. "Hey, hey. I get the hint," he said and hobbled out of the room on his sore feet.

Alison excused herself as well. "I'm going to bed, Ma."

Her mother kissed her. "Sweet dreams, if that's possible."

In her childhood room Alison lay down on her childhood bed. Everything was the same as the day she'd moved out to live with Billy: the white-and-gold furniture, her patchwork quilt, the stuffed toys staring down from the shelf. Only she was different. Innocent the last time she slept here, now she looked up at the plush animals and saw their heads lolling, like they all had broken necks. Half of them had missing eyes or were in some way maimed. And in the next room, Jeffy was still up and playing on the computer. Through the wall they shared she could hear the click, click, click of the mouse.

2

Grace's claws ticking along ahead of him at the end of the red lead. Oh, Brute Time, Malcolm thought. For some the clock ran backward, for some it just stood still. The clock in Grace was winding down, and very shortly would unspring.

She rode the elevator showing her pink slip of a tongue, eager, as if she knew who she was coming to see. When the doors opened, she hurled herself out. "Mr. Firth!" someone called and Malcolm was glad to see it was Nurse Health towering behind the nursing station desk, not her officious twin. He came over and held out his hand. She took it warmly and smiled below her trace moustache.

Grace, overjoyed and twitching her little stump, lost all control. "Regrettably," said Malcolm, "I haven't fixed that leak."

Nurse Health laughed. "Denis's having another quiet day," she said. "He's been very subdued since he was sick. Did they tell you?"

Malcolm nodded.

"You'll see a change. He went downhill fast."

Haven't we all, thought Malcolm, or was it just that the world had tilted?

"Are you ready for it?"

"Yes," he chirped falsely.

"He's in his room. Do you want me to come with you?"

"That won't be necessary. I have Grace."

Tick, tick, tick went her claws on the linoleum. They entered the lounge where the television was on, though not for the benefit of the old lady Buddha propped up in her wheelchair. She was turned the other way and her cardigan had dropped to the floor. A woman who must have been her deadened daughter was watching a game show while two young children sported with Granny, the boy holding in the air her prodigious arm, the little girl swatting at the dangling wing of fat.

"What's that?" the old lady croaked.

Immediately, the giggling ceased. The grandchildren gaped and even the daughter seemed astonished. Turning glazed eyes from the sequined wheel on the television screen, she looked over the back of the couch at what had miraculously caused the idol to speak—Grace.

They moved on, brushing past the lanky grove of dieffenbachia, the dusty palms, into the corridor where halfway down someone staggered out of Mr. Stavros's room. His shirt was buttoned incorrectly, dentures missing in action, his hair a tragic mess. What was he doing in Mr. Stavros's room? Surely not *that*. The man looked so driven as he moved toward them, so strange that he set off the alarm in Grace. Oblivious to her yapping, he reached out to Malcolm.

"Daddy?"

Sidestepping him, Malcolm jerked the leash to shut up Grace. "Daddy's dead," he said.

And so was Mr. Stavros, he suddenly remembered.

And Mrs. Ross. Even Mrs. Mikaluk; death had silenced her incessant prayer.

The dog knew Denis's room, could perhaps smell him over the scent-screen of Lysol. Malcolm dropped the leash and watched it snake around the door. Ecstatic, Grace's barking: high-pitched yelps that sounded almost as if she were in pain. Perhaps she was. Malcolm himself was pressing his eyes to stop his tears. A full minute passed before she decrescendoed. It was almost unbearable to hear her giving up.

Stepping into the room and seeing Denis at the window, Malcolm was once again reminded that one of the autonomic functions of the human species was hope. Surely by now he had been disabused of such imaginings. Optimism should have died in him long ago. Yet Denis looked just the same. Showing no sign of his recent illness, he looked more the same now than he had a year ago. As Malcolm crossed the room, he felt his rage dissipating. He felt once again as if he were walking into that most amiable of places—Denis's arms.

Except they did not open. They dangled at his sides. At least they did not throw a punch. When Malcolm greeted him, Denis only stared and Malcolm's rage came back.

"Did you miss me?" he asked in chilly French.

Very slowly, with a decided hauteur, Denis turned away from Malcolm to the window.

"Ah," sniffed Malcolm. "The silent treatment."

The view was down on a courtyard where a cherry tree was in frothy bloom. Thinking he would try another tack, Malcolm clapped his hand across his forehead and pretended to reel. "Oh, my dear! I understand now! We are trapped together in a Chekhov play! No wonder I feel so wistful all the time!"

To this sudden outburst, Denis made no comment. Malcolm cleared the embarrassment from his throat. "I've come to tell you something." Denis didn't deign to turn. "*Je m'en vais.* On a holiday of sorts. That doesn't interest you? Not in the slightest? You don't give a damn what I do?" Peevishly, he looked down to where Grace was splayed, licking herself. "*Tiens,*" he said with sarcasm and lifted her. "Your *true* love."

They made a better match—an incontinent dog and a man who shat in drawers.

Denis took Grace. Expressionless, he held her to his breast and, in his arms, Grace writhed with pleasure and stretched up to lick his face. Malcolm looked away, jealous, so only out of the corner of his eye did he see her fall. Instinctively, he reached out to catch her. Her foreleg wrenched the wrong way unleashed a histrionic stream of yelping.

"What happened?" asked an orderly, poking her head in the door.

"Butterfingers," Malcolm said.

"You want me to take her? I'll show her around." She swooped down on the whimpering dog, Malcolm calling cheerily after them, "*Bon débarras!*"

He turned and saw Denis staring at him again, eyes pale and glassy. What Malcolm had taken for aloofness he saw now was vacancy. A chill washed over him.

Here was the ghost, at last.

What was it Denis saw? A person—Malcolm— vaguely familiar, moving his lips, each word overlapping the preceding so nothing he said made any sense. Likewise, all moments that preceded this one had been obliterated, so he didn't know where he was, or how he had got here, or why he was here at all. Something squeezing his shoulder. He looked and saw a hand, then looked past the hand, instantly forgetting it, forgetting even that there was another person with him in the room.

In the corner was a chair. This at least he remembered: that a four-legged object with a back was a chair. He shuffled toward it. What was it again? A dog? He had no idea that there had been a dog in his arms a minute ago or that the person he didn't remember—Malcolm—was behind this impulse to sit, was actually leading him to the dog that was, in fact, a chair. He simply felt impelled to sit. He saw his own hands feeling all around the chair, desperate to recall the act of sitting. All that came to him was that his body had to be somehow on this object which he no longer remembered the name of. Nor did he understand why he was hurling himself over the back of it, or why he was now lying on the floor. And who was this man staring down at him? How did he get in the room?

Tsking, Malcolm helped Denis to his feet, led him over to the bed and sat him on the edge. Denis, staring at the wall, his face beautiful and empty, had already forgotten his spill. Malcolm sat beside him, took his hand, hot and limp. He stroked it. This close, he smelled a sourness in Denis's hair and on his skin.

There was a soft knock on the door. Malcolm dropped Denis's hand. "Come in."

Nurse Health entered, tentatively, compassion flushed across her broad cheeks. "Does he understand you?"

"He doesn't seem to."

"Between us, the staff know a few songs. *Moi, je ne regrette rien*, that sort of thing. He used to catcall us, but now he doesn't respond at all." She paused. "Are you all right, Mr. Firth?"

"Peachy."

"You don't look it. Are you sure?"

He pressed his eyes. "Quite."

"I can give you the name of a counsellor. We also have our little group."

Probably he flinched. "Thank you. I appreciate your concern."

She left the room, a big woman with delicate foot-work. Before she closed the door, she told him. "Don't you stop talking, Mr. Firth. It will help you, telling him what's on your mind."

As soon as she was gone, he pulled his cuff back to expose a wrist and sniffed. He shook his head and looked at Denis whose mind was filled only with that second. Malcolm's flowed over with the past.

The salon that Malcolm had gone to Paris to see in 1959 turned out to be far from ready. The windows had been masked with newspaper, which Denis began tear-ing down once he had ushered Malcolm inside. Light poured in in mote-dense shafts and Malcolm started coughing. There had been an odour, too, something ran-cid. Rat, Malcolm thought, seeing the scatter of drop-pings on the floor. A plan was laid out on the floor, marked in wear and discoloration, of what had been removed—a long counter. As Denis moved about the empty space, pointing here and there, Malcolm heard in his exuberant monologue a reference to *la boucherie*.

Behind them, hanging from a hook, was an apron, bloodstained and forgotten.

"Here is better. For the sinks," Malcolm had said. He mimed it out.

Denis looked at him, pondering a moment. "*Vous avez raison.*" And where would Malcolm put the hair-dryers?

"Here."

"*Ici?*"

Denis was impressed by Malcolm's judgement, Malcolm could tell. Already, Malcolm badly wanted the job. More to the point, he badly wanted Denis, but doubted Denis would deign to consider a moody Canadian with acne on his back, with whom he had to communicate in pantomime.

That odour had to come out. The place had to be cleaned and painted. Malcolm, eager to prove himself, set to work. Over the next three days, on his hands and knees scrubbing or reaching with a paintbrush, he didn't rest. Denis came downstairs occasionally to stand with his small clean hands on his hips, watching Malcolm sweat in the Paris heat. He would point and make graceful gesticulations, which Malcolm interpreted as Denis drawing attention to his faults. Denis was entreating him not to debase himself another minute. It was ridiculous! A *nettoyeuse* was coming on Tuesday!

Malcolm didn't learn that until later.

What Denis did was cook. He made *omelette aux fruits de mer, ris de veau aux pointes d'asperges*, a salad of lettuce hearts. Every evening when Malcolm staggered filthy and aching up the stairs, Denis greeted him with his only English sentence: "*Are you angry?*"

On the third day, Malcolm's clothes were ruined. He'd gone through both trouser knees and camouflaged himself in paint, but the salon was ready to be equipped. To celebrate, Denis ran him a bath and invited two friends to dine with them. He prepared his specialty: *matelote d'anguille*.

Sitting at the table, Malcolm felt very young and very sorry for himself. The three Frenchmen were all much older and blond, models of sophistication. One smoked his cigarette in an ivory holder. They laughed a lot and Malcolm couldn't understand a word. When the *matelote* was served, the two friends each took a sip, then leaned across the table and kissed Denis on the lips.

Turning to watch Malcolm lift his spoon, they all waited with their perfect eyebrows raised.

"*Bon*," said Malcolm, an understatement. The men laughed trillingly.

Exhausted and morose, he told them good night, then slunk off to the sofa where he'd been sleeping the last two nights. He couldn't sleep now for their voices. The room was hot enough already without his burning jealousy, without his holding a pillow over his head to block out their good time. Suddenly, he kicked back the sheet and sat up panting. He had fallen asleep after all, and dreamt of fire, and now his undershirt and shorts were drenched with sweat.

But it had not been a nightmare: awake, he still smelled smoke.

The guests had gone and the only light now came through the open window, brightening, then strangely fading. He went over and looked down in the courtyard where, tomorrow, Denis would leave for the cats the leftover *matelote* in a newspaper hat. The restaurants were still open, but with only a scattering of diners. Nothing appeared to be on fire.

Then he noticed, next to the tree that was the leafy axis of the courtyard, a ragged figure swigging from a gasoline can. Suddenly dashing toward a couple sitting under the restaurant awning, he lunged and let gush a flame. Watching, Malcolm could not help but recognize himself. For the last three days he had been smouldering. If he had opened his mouth, he would have had a blowtorch for a tongue.

After accepting a gratuity from the diners he had so scorchingly entertained, the figure retreated to the tree. Still Malcolm smelled smoke. It wasn't coming from below, but was with him there, in the room. Turning, he saw in the corner the bright tip of a cigarette bobbing, a cinder floating in the dark.

"*Point de feu sans fumée.*"

Malcolm tried repeating the words. He might have actually learned some French if he hadn't suffered these pyrotechnic moods.

Denis joined him at the window. In silence, they watched the tattered man at his startling, irradiant craft. It was an act beyond language. The next day Denis would invite him upstairs and give him dinner, then trim the singe off his bangs. Now he dragged on the cigarette and passed it to Malcolm, who did not smoke but took it anyway for the chance it offered him to put his lips where Denis's had been.

Soon Denis left the window and went to switch on the lamp. He sat down on the sofa, on Malcolm's crumpled sheets. "*Venez,*" he said, patting the place beside him. Malcolm came over and sat at the other end of the sofa, his heart beating audibly, at least to him. Anything might happen, he thought, though inevitably it wouldn't. He glanced sidelong at his bemused host. Just then, something in the space between them caught Denis's eye. He reached over to pluck it off the sheet, leaned away from Malcolm, under the lamp, squinting as he held the wiry hair close to his face.

"*Quel trésor,*" Denis had whispered. "*Quel trésor.*"

"Every day," Malcolm told Denis now, "you asked if I was angry. Yes, I'm angry. I had nearly thirty years of memories I wouldn't have exchanged with anyone. In one year, you've ruined them all. Yes, I'm angry.

"I remember different things now, little things that make me angry, too. Like the time a client—Mme Moreau, I think it was—brought in that photo. Do you remember? Her young son in the Vichy-inspired uniform of the Front National de la Jeunesse. You passed it over to me and said, "*Comme il est charmant!*" It made me grim. It made me sick. I realized I could no longer say *Monsieur Le Pen in the Ass.* I had to be careful who I made such jokes to after that. You, you didn't care. You didn't see anything wrong with it."

He sniffed at his wrist again.

"We never did get that odour out of the salon." It had always been there, just faintly under the perm solution and the hairspray. Malcolm looked at Denis, longing both to strike him and to hold him. "I'm angry," he said, then, leaning over, smelled his hair.

"Come."

Taking Denis's hand, he helped him to his feet. Together they drifted out of the room, down the corridor to the lounge, where he left Denis while he went to get a towel. When Malcolm returned, Denis was rocking himself prayer-like among the dieffenbachia. Deep currents pushing and pulling, impulses, formless thoughts. To Malcolm's prodding, he turned, very, very slowly, as under water, as if the air were a fluid. He lifted his eyes to Malcolm.

"Come. I'm going to bathe you."

Words coming out bubbles, bubbles floating up.

Running the bath, Malcolm peeled the singlet over Denis's head, removed the padded pants, tugged off his socks. He ended on his knees at Denis's feet looking up, where he had figuratively placed himself through the years.

Under water, Denis's tiny pubic hairs swayed; his

penis floated, a sea cucumber above his thigh. Gradually, the room filled up with steam. It occurred to Malcolm then that Denis had reached the beginning again. Prelingual, asexual, mentally inchoate, he had crawled back into the primordial pool. Now he was innocent again, though maybe he had always been.

And Malcolm got an idea: to bring the tape recorder, plug it in the shaving outlet and toss it in the water. The shock would jump-start Denis. It would be like the original bolt that opened the story of Life. Denis would rise up from the steaming waters, reborn—his beloved. The tape would be Peggy Lee singing "Is That All There Is?"

Back in the room, Denis shampooed and fresh, Malcolm told him, "A terrible thing happened to a man I worked with. I was approached by a young woman who knew him as well. She asked for my help, asked that I accompany her on a pilgrimage of sorts." He shrugged. "That I be her Virgil."

Then he kissed Denis goodbye. He did not think he would see him again. First his sweet-smelling left cheek, then his right, as was their custom, then again the left. This third kiss was impromptu, an apology. It was for what he intended to do with Denis's dog.

3

The day came when he had to pack, but what? Deposited all around the apartment, like at a Salvation Army drop-off, were bags and bags of clothes. In the beginning he had been very careful about remembering which client had given him what; he liked always to be wearing something that would be familiar to each one when her appointment came, something that would make her smile and, musing, perhaps share a secret with him. In the end, he gave up trying. With no room to hang things up, no order could be made. He couldn't keep track of it all, couldn't even remember what he had used to wear before he came to work at Faye's. His own clothes were hopelessly mixed with the others, and with Denis's in the drawers.

Early in the morning he began to sort. He made himself be ruthless; some things—too much the wrong size, outlandish, stained—would simply never work. Then he would pull something interesting out of a bag and lay it on the bed, separate from the discard and the keeping piles, just because it struck his fancy. By the time he had finished, hours later, he turned and saw a museum spread across the bed.

"Tennis anyone?" he addressed the yellowing pair of flannel trousers pleated from the waist and its matching short-sleeved shirt, cotton knit and trimmed with piping—all the rage on the courts around 1938, though in 1938, they would have still been white. From the same bag he had been astonished to draw the uniform out. Who had given it to him? Had she really thought Malcolm could find a use for army khakis? The insignia torn off the jacket, he couldn't place the regiment or rank, but it was certainly of Second World War vintage. He laid it out next to the tennis outfit: how things change, and not just for Malcolm.

A post-war exuberance of ties, hand-painted with American skyscrapers or pin-up girls in silhouette, so optimistic. Then, from a more sober continent, the black cashmere turtleneck of an Existentialist. The Teddy Boy suit made him laugh, it was so like one he had worn himself in London with its narrow lapels and black velvet collar, its stove-pipe trousers. He found three ruffled blouses from Mr. Fish and a malodorous goatskin jacket—*très* sixties. Lapels went wide in the seventies, trousers flared, stripes turned clownish: from various bags he pieced a suit together. All his donors were too old to be influenced by any trend in the eighties. By the nineties they were dead.

What he packed was infinitely more sensible. Then he called a taxi and checked that the pills for the flight were in the pocket next to his heart. A last look around, at the clothes on the bed, the furniture wedged together, the Persian carpet rolled. It seemed more a storeroom than an apartment. Except what was essential, he had never really bothered to unpack. The Egyptian head was somewhere in a box.

Negotiating his way over to the door, he noticed that a fine layer of hair had settled over it all, as if he had disposed of the dog by plugging in a firecracker and exploding her in the room. The thought made him shudder. Picking up his suitcase filled with the clothes of dead men he had never known, he left without a backward glance.

Arriving at the airport, the girl nowhere to be seen, he joined a long line switching back through bands and posts. Intermittently he lifted his suitcase, shuffled a few steps forward and set it down again. At last, a briskly cheerful agent with a jaunty red bow under her chin beckoned to him. He gave her the girl's name so that they could sit together, and asked, "How long is the flight?"

"Ten hours to London. You'll have to clear customs at Heathrow and check in again with LOT."

Hearing this, his bag gave up completely. Handle tagged with a coded adhesive loop, it teetered and, thudding onto its side, was conveyed away.

He found her at the gate, remarkably composed, with a guidebook in her lap. "Are you okay?" she asked. "You look really pale."

It was just his shroud of skin contrasting with his hair. "I don't care for flying," he admitted, which started her rooting through her voluminous handbag for a piece of gum. She herself had never taken such a long flight, she said, hardly flown at all, but the day before Thi had given her an article about long-distance air travel. From it she had seemed to glean that chewing gum was some kind of cure-all. She held a stick out to him, but he declined and took a pill instead.

When they boarded the plane and found their appointed row, a man in a suit was sitting in the middle seat. "Are you together? I'll move over. No, no. I insist. Why break up a party?"

He stepped into the aisle and gestured chivalrously. Malcolm slid in first, thinking about the unlikely party they made, he a lachrymose and jaded chaperone, she a wide-eyed naïf. Why had he agreed to come? He would have been embarrassed to admit to her that he'd been flattered, that it gave him hope. His clientele, though they endured, they would not last. Despite his best efforts, he could do nothing to hold them back. When the girl approached him, he suddenly saw himself as he was to his biddies—a guide, a confidant—but this time to the young. There was a future, then, not just a past. Buoyed along for several weeks by this conceit, he had felt the dizzy thrill of peering into bankruptcy's abyss. He had even dared to take the towel off the bathroom mirror: she had made him feel needed.

When the video presentation of the emergency procedures began he was already dozy from the pill. The girl was sitting up straight watching the video, attentive as a child. She tightened the strap of her seat belt and looked up to see from where in the ceiling the oxygen mask would drop, as if she believed in a *deus ex machina*. He was touched and, for that instant, still glad he came. Then the plane began to move and the pilot's voice, staticky and omniscient, told them they were taxiing to the runway.

He clutched onto her, filled with dread. Briefly, when the plane came to a stop, he let go, only to grab her hand again. Acceleration, tilt and lift, the panicked heart, then the giddy lightening that he associated with death. When next he opened his eyes they were entering the clouds.

The lit seat-belt signs pinged and went out; a hundred buckles simultaneously unclicked. Already Malcolm was asleep, so Alison extricated herself from his grip. The window seat was wasted on him but, leaning over to peek down, the spectacle of unbaling cloud was all there was to see.

From her handbag she took the guidebook. "*Dzi-eń do-bry?*" she sounded out. Dz: "d" as in "day" rapidly followed by "z" as in "zoo," except at the end of the word, where it becomes "ts," or if the "z" is dotted, when it becomes "d-sh," or the "z" has a stroke above it, which sharpens the pronunciation, or at the end of the word when it sounds like "c" with a stroke above it. She sighed. It would take all day for her to say good day.

And here was fearsome cluster—*szcz*. A cluster with teeth. *Szczur*: rat.

"Ah," said the man in the suit who had changed seats with her. "You're going to Poland?"

"Yes. How about you?"

"I've got business in London."

She talked to him until dinner, which Malcolm slept

right through. Then more drinks were served and the movie started. She watched the moving picture outside the window instead: above the Northwest Territories now the cloud had finally cleared, though it took some time for her to realize it, mistaking for cloud the thousand tiny grey lakes floating in the darker grey of land. What she was watching then, while the rest of them watched the screen, was evening becoming night, the very edge of the sky slowly turning the colour of an old bruise or the inside of a rotten plum—that peculiar yellowy black. Gradually, the colour drained completely and the stars set in clusters in the pale sky blended with the clustered lights of the occasional settlements far below, so she could no longer distinguish where the sky ended and the land began. Now and then the businessman ooh-ed and clucked, as if marvelling at the night's plot.

Malcolm woke to the horizon's seam, visible now as a rusty streak, and the girl's head heavy against his shoulder, her snoring light. He only seemed to blink, but must have slept again; when he opened his eyes he was as blinded as by a photographer's flash. They were inside the clouds, the light reflecting brilliantly.

The flight attendant was offering a Continental breakfast.

"Yes, coffee," the girl muttered dopily. "Coffee, please."

The worst of the lines was the one at Heathrow customs where even the congenial businessman looked right through Alison when she waved goodbye. Malcolm staggered along behind her, pulling his suitcase on a leash.

"What did you do with Grace?" she asked.

He started at the name and stabbed his eyes. "Grace is taken care of," he said and turned away.

They boarded the bus to Terminal 2. It took them in a wide circle bounded by a wire fence topped with bales of razor wire strung with shredded litter, all set against a cement sky. Hell, Malcolm remembered from the *Inferno*, was a downward spiral. For the entire ride, the girl kept one hand on her heart, beatifically.

There turned out to be no LOT counter. LOT used a desk at Air France where a woman told them to come back in four hours.

"Christ," Malcolm muttered. And what sadist decided on bucket-style chairs, impossible to stretch out on? His watch said it was the middle of the night.

"Didn't you bring anything to read?" the girl asked.

"No."

"You've read it all?" she joked.

"No," he told her. "I haven't read Douglas Coupland yet."

Nearby, a huge board clicked out some kind of tally—numbers, hundreds of thousands, millions.

Flight numbers. Gates and times.

On the plane to Kraków, she took the window seat. Europe from the air looked to her like a concrete floor covered with puffs of dust. She opened the guide book. *"Kiedy odjeżdża pociąg do Oświęcimia?"*

"Come again?"

"When does the train leave for Auschwitz?" she translated for Malcolm. *"Czy muszę się przesiadać?* Do I have to change?"

He began, slowly, to thump his head against the headrest.

They landed, stairs wheeled up to the plane, the passengers herded down into the night. Walking to the terminal building, Alison was surprised it was so cold.

Once inside, the luggage started arriving on a conveyor belt and everyone pitched in to help unload it, grabbing a suitcase, any suitcase, no matter whose. Then, going through customs, every third person was made to step aside. Foreigners turned out to be exempt from official curiosity and Malcolm and Alison were waved on through.

To the currency exchange counter where a young man sat, blank-faced except for an extraordinary number of moles. Immediately, the girl began groping down her front which was, Malcolm realized with disappointment, where her money was and the reason she kept her hand on her heart.

"I am sorry," said the spattered man without sounding in the least apologetic. "We exchange only banknotes."

She stared at him, puzzled, as if by the connect-the-dots on his face. "But I only have traveller's cheques. Aren't they any good?"

"Certainly. Traveller's cheques you may exchange at a bank. In Poland, banks generally open at seven-thirty."

She turned to Malcolm. "Do you have any money?"

"A credit card," he said.

"How can we get to the bank?" she asked.

The man behind the counter told her, "There is a taxi stand outside."

"But we don't have any money for a taxi."

Naturally, she turned to Malcolm again. It panged him: they'd only just arrived and already he'd let her down. In desperation, she found her wallet in her handbag, opened the change purse and overturned it on the counter. Coins wheeled off in all directions. The young man, gazing on blandly, reminded her: "Bank*notes*."

"I say, come in our cab."

They turned and saw, shambling toward them, an

enormous loose-jointed man with a suitcase in each hand. The girl followed him at once and Malcolm followed her, outside to where a queue of taxis waited at the curb. Cabbies and passengers yelling, arms thrown open, probably in welcome, but in Polish it sounded like umbrage and rancour.

"Thank you," said Alison to their hulking saviour. "Thanks."

"Yoo-hoo, Clive! Clive! Over here!" A woman flagging. "Oh, *sharesies*! What a good idea!"

"They're in a bit of a spot," said Clive.

"Francuski! Francuski!" the woman told the driver loading the suitcases in the trunk. She was small and plain with fine, unclean hair. Enthusiastically, she pumped Malcolm's arm. "I'm Ronnie. Which hotel are you at?"

"Pollera," Alison told the driver.

"Pollera! Pollera!" Ronnie echoed.

Malcolm got in the back, drawing the girl in after him to buffer him from Ronnie, Clive in front, knees tucked up. From behind, his hair looked like the matted brown plush of a stuffed bear.

As soon as the doors were closed and the taxi had pulled away, Ronnie turned to Alison. "So what brings you and your father to Poland?"

"Oh, he's not my father."

A hand clapped over her mouth, Ronnie leaned forward to peek at Malcolm.

"We're going to Auschwitz," Alison said.

The hand came down. "Did you hear that, Clive? Auschwitz-Birkenau!"

"Ghastly," said Clive. "Birkenau means 'a grove of birches.'"

"Do you have some connection there?"

"A friend of ours was killed."

"There?" asked Ronnie.

"No. Where we're from. Canada."

Ronnie looked puzzled.

"What about you?" asked Alison.

"Tell them what you're up to, Clive."

"Dendrology."

Alison said, "What?"

"Trees," said Malcolm.

Ronnie giggled. "He's a clever one. Tell them about the conference, Clive."

Where the road intersected with the lit highway, the taxi turned. Clive said, "International conference in Kraków next year."

"Clive's the principal organizer. They're all dying, you see."

"Who?" asked Alison.

"The trees."

"Are you a dendrologist, too?"

"Me? No! I simply tag along. I love Poland. I love the Poles. They've been through *so much*. Haven't they, Clive?"

"Yes, they have," Clive agreed and when Alison glanced up, she saw the silhouette of his hunched form against the spreading lights of Kraków.

Fifteen minutes later the taxi was shuttling through the narrow streets, the stone buildings plated silver where there was a lamp. They stopped first at the Pollera with its pretty mustard-coloured façade. Across was an empty parking lot and beyond, darkness.

When the cabbie got out to take their bags from the trunk, Clive got out, too, flexing at the knees. He shook their hands.

"Much appreciated," said Malcolm.

"Don't mention it."

"We'll pay you back tomorrow," said Alison.

Ronnie shrilled, "Don't you dare!" from the car.

Taking both their suitcases, Malcolm left the girl to say goodbye to Ronnie.

"The Francuski, right?" Alison waved to her.

The cabbie was still standing on the curb, Malcolm saw as he waited in the hotel doorway. He was wearing a tweed cap and a leather jacket, his eyes on the girl, yet deadened and unexpressive. The whole long drive he had uttered not a word so Malcolm had assumed he couldn't understand them. Absurdly, he had even forgotten he was there, an actual living specimen of the long-suffering Pole. But as the girl was about to walk away, the cabbie stopped her. He touched her arm and held her back.

"Miss, I can bring you."

She stared at him, uncomprehending.

"To Auschwitz. Four hundred thousand *złoty*. I can bring you."

4

Thi had honeymooned in Paris so knew to warn Alison about jet lag, how helplessly and at weird hours she was likely to wake or be overcome by sleep. Switching on the lamp, she saw by her watch on the night table that it was 4:00 a.m. There was no toilet in the room and, too weary to dress, too nervous to walk in her T-shirt and panties down the corridor, she got up and dragged the wooden chair over to the sink instead. She balanced precariously, backward, over the basin, then, falling back on the lumpy mattress, she fell asleep.

Hours later, she woke again. Filtering through the gold curtains—dull light and a soft rhythmic whimpering like the dénouement of someone's weeping. She reached for the corner of the curtain, tugged. It opened to an explosion of dark wings on the sill outside. Lying there, she thought of Billy and wondered if this feeling was missing him. No, she decided: it was something worse. It was the sickening hollowness of waking in a country where the Holocaust had happened.

She forced herself to get out of bed, stood a long moment shivering at the window, looking down into the courtyard where, in the rain, little box-like cars were parked around a dying tree.

To leave the room she had to unlock the door from the inside with the key. It was one of those old-fashioned keys that delighted her when they put it in her hand last night, though was less romantic now that she knew how awkward it was to work. She finally got herself out, only to have to struggle with the lock again, and more self-consciously because, at the end of the hall, a door was open on a windowless storeroom where two maids stood smoking. Their uniforms were possibly the ugliest Alison had ever seen—purple knit dresses with black stripes that on the older, plumper woman fit like a sock, on the younger a sack. Silently, they watched Alison's every clumsy move through eyes narrowed to slits.

The staircase, with its intricate wrought iron banister, split parenthetically on this floor, the two sides meeting again on the landing below before descending to the lobby as a single broad flight—a cascade of faded threadbare leaf-print.

The desk clerk sullenly pointed the way to the restaurant, which turned out to be a pretty, high-ceilinged room with ten little tables covered in white linen and a fireplace tiled green. Malcolm was already in the corner by the window, his breakfast barely touched. "*Dzień dobry*," she told him.

He raised an eyebrow.

"That means 'good day.'"

"Oh." Pressing his eyes, he looked away.

A waitress with peroxided hair and a cross expression came through the French doors. When Alison tried "*dzień dobry*" on her, she fared no better. The waitress froze, eyes darting around the room, looking everywhere but at Alison. She opened the menu and stabbed a finger at the first page. "*Polski.*" Turned the page to the menu in English. "English." The facing page: "*Deutsch.*" Then: "*Français.*" Those were Alison's choices.

She nodded. "*Polski! Dzień dobry!*"

Muttering, the waitress hurried off with Malcolm's plate.

Malcolm was staring out the window, his face rubbery in the grey light, like a mask, unalive except for the nick near his ear stuck with tissue fibres.

"Did you sleep all right?"

"No," he said.

"They left me a bottle of water. Is that what I'm supposed to drink?"

He didn't answer, so she turned to see what he was looking at. "Ugh. It's like winter in Vancouver." Except in Vancouver the streets were not cobbled, or half so narrow and picturesque.

Two women about her own age entered and took the other window table. The room was small enough for Alison to hear their twangy English and guess they were American. "They're going, too," she whispered.

"Who?"

"The women behind me. I just heard them say they're going. Do you want to go today?"

To her relief, he shook his head and told her, "Tomorrow." She felt reprieved. "Tomorrow then," she agreed.

The waitress returned with Alison's coffee. Alison pointed to what she wanted on the menu, eggs, and motioned for her to wait while she dug in her handbag for the guidebook.

"*Dziękuję.*"

From the ferocity of the waitress's glare, Alison guessed that in mangling the pronunciation she had said something off-colour. Quickly, she pointed to the word in the book.

"Ah! *Dziękuję!* Yes. You are welcome!" the waitress sneered in perfect English.

Alison's face prickled. She couldn't think what she had said to cause such offence. She took a sip of coffee, lukewarm, syrupy with condensed milk, and looked at Malcolm. "Why do you keep doing that?" she asked, suddenly annoyed at him instead.

"What?"

"Pressing your eyes like that?"

"I'm staunching my tears, you silly girl. I'm trying to prevent myself from weeping."

She set down the cup and stared across the table at him. Look how she suffers over every tongue slip, he thought. Then, telling him that she was sorry, she took her spatulate fingers from around the cup and laid her hand down in the middle of the table for him to pick up if he wanted.

"Grace is dead," he said.

"What?" said Alison, surprised. The dog had seemed young the time she saw her. "Was it an accident?"

"No. On purpose. It's better this way. It would have been crueller to let her live."

The waitress set down Alison's plate, two runny eggs, a bun, a blob of red jam like a clot of blood. Malcolm got unsteadily to his feet. "I need to go to the bank."

"Me, too. Can't you wait?"

He seemed to balk, then told her, "I'll meet you out front in half an hour."

Climbing up the stairs, he wished he hadn't told her about Grace. Now she would keep sending him achy, blue, sympathetic glances that he did not deserve. It would torment him and he wouldn't be able to spend the day with her after coming all this way.

He wished he'd taken a pill last night. After installing himself in his closet—it had been a grand hotel once, with expansive suites, but they'd thrown up walls everywhere and put him in the closet—he had wanted to take one, but worried he would not be able to get up if he drugged himself again. So he lay there thinking about the dog. She was haunting him. In every creak, he heard her yelp.

What he'd done was wrong and now, in his regret, he realized he had been wrong about her, too. He'd had nothing but contempt for her fawning when, in truth, there was no greater fawner than he. He'd considered her brainless and pitied her. All animals he tended to pity— because they cannot read. But can't they? Thinking back on their many hours in the park, he recalled how, let off the lead, she would fly off on a course of delirious sniffing. It reminded him of how he liked to race home to a book. Was it not a form of reading then, this picking up a scent trail, akin, say, to Braille? Braille for the nose. Splashed up on the tree trunks, put down in trickles in the grass, there were epics and sonnets, novellas and pornographic tales. Grace had been voracious for it all; she had really been a perfect little companion.

On her last night, Malcolm had allowed her the pleasure of sucking on a sock. Then, in the morning, before leaving for the vet, he had tied a new bow on her and wiped her eyes with a cloth. Her pink tongue washed his hands; no end to her forgiveness.

"Tsk, tsk," he had told her kindly. "It's too late for that."

In the waiting room, she sat shivering on his knee. A portly gentleman, a Santa Claus off-season, was also waiting, a Siamese cat in a carrier at his feet. "What's the matter with your dog?" he had asked.

"Nothing," Malcolm had said. "Her number's up. Her end is nigh."

The Siamese let loose an unholy yeowl.

He had not gone in with her to watch them put the needle in. He wouldn't have been able to stomach that.

When he looked at the clock, it was three in the morning, too late to take a pill.

Rain came straight down, as from a bucket overturned. Alison, under the umbrella, looked left and right, then at the open guidebook. Half a block down was some kind of palace. "It's the opera house. Which makes this street *Szpit—Szpitalna*." It sounded like how the waitress had spoken to her at breakfast.

They stepped out of shelter of the hotel doorway, Alison telling Malcolm, "You carry the umbrella." Down the cobbled street, all the ornamented buildings looked newly painted, warm brown or gold or terra cotta. Behind walls almost flush with the street were secret places: through an arched portal she glimpsed another portal, then a puddled courtyard and a door. It was all so pretty, yet eerily deserted.

Turning a corner, they suddenly emerged upon a square. After the narrowness of the streets, it felt vast, a flagstone expanse. Empty of people too, it seemed larger still. Only one man had not rushed for cover. He stood in the rain on a pillar wearing a long bronze cloak.

She stopped to flip through the guidebook and found the page about the square: the long arcaded building in the centre was the Sukiennice, a medieval cloth hall, and the statue was of a poet with an unpronounceable name, though not the original, which was toppled by the Nazis during the war. She read that phrase again—*toppled by the Nazis*—and only then did she really grasp that it was here, on this very spot. This was where history had happened.

She knew the bank before they were even across the square because the shorter word on the sign was "Bank." Inside, all the people standing against the wall or crowding the wooden benches reminded Alison of the Mission. Perhaps it was their furious restlessness, or that everyone was wearing a drenched raincoat. A man opened his wide—only to wrap it tighter around himself—but for a brief second she expected to see that underneath he was wound up with coloured lights.

They joined the line at the currency exchange. "Passport," said the clerk and Alison wondered how he knew she spoke English.

Next she got behind a man speaking Polish with a teller, stood there trying to figure the receipt, was shocked to realize that the number that looked halfway to infinity was what she had coming to her. The man ahead folded his wallet and Alison stepped forward, but the teller looked right through her and shouted something out.

"They're calling by number," Malcolm said, pointing to the metal token they had given her.

They went and stood with everyone else along the wall. Seeing Alison yawn, the woman on the bench next to her said, "Go on. Get some shut-eye. I'll wake you when they call you—in about eight years." She peered at the number on Alison's token. "One-two-two? You're a goner! Mine's ninety-nine and I've been here forty minutes!"

Alison laughed and, looking down on the woman, could tell that she wore foam rollers to bed. "Where are you from?"

"Chicago. You? Is this your first time?"

"Yes," said Alison.

"We came once before, in the seventies, but it was just awful. The lines were even worse and you couldn't get any meat." Her husband, she said, was Polish and a bastard when he didn't get his meat.

Alison took the guidebook from her handbag, turned to the page that explained the numbers and asked the woman to tell her what 122 would sound like. Just then a number was called. The woman rose to her feet. "Hallelujah! There is a God!" she cried, flashing her token all around.

Close to an hour later, they finally left the bank. Malcolm, holding the door for Alison, told her, "You look terribly sincere." He meant her hand pressed over her heart, where all her millions were concealed.

They headed back across the square, Alison carrying the umbrella now. The rain had diminished to a solemn drizzle and somewhere close by a bell started to toll. "I can't believe," she said, "how cold it is." People were milling under the shelter of the Sukiennice's arches. Across the square was the Mariacki Church with its unmatched towers, the gold crown shining on its steeple. "It must be eleven," she said. The bell was still tolling. "I'd like to drop the money off for Clive and Ronnie."

Malcolm stopped and took out his wallet. "I'm very tired," he said. "I'm going back to the hotel. Do you mind dropping off my share?"

The bell stopped and a long mournful note sounded. It came from on high, from one of the church towers. They both looked up and saw the trumpeter tiny in silhouette. While waiting in the bank, Alison had peeled apart the wet pages of the guidebook and read about the watchman who, spying an invasion, had raised his trumpet and played this eerie song as an alarm. That was back in the thirteenth century. He got an arrow in the throat.

Abruptly, the tune ended.

"Okay," Alison told him, trying not to sound abandoned. "I'll see you later then."

The address of the Francuski was in the guidebook. Alison found it just across from one of the arched gates in the city wall, through which she saw a broad band of dripping trees. Clive and Ronnie were not in, so she left the money in an envelope and hoped that they would get it.

She had thought to go back to the square and look around, but turning onto Floriańska Street, she was suddenly too cold and tired. She walked on past the take-out pizza joints and kebabarias, weaving through the tourists who had all come out now that the weather seemed finally to be clearing. She knew they were tourists, not Poles. Already she could tell the difference. They were laughing, for one, and did not seem half so bitter. They had not been to the museum yet, she supposed.

Going back to the hotel was a better idea. Sleep was stalking her, sleep and something else.

Entering the hotel lobby, Alison saw one of the maids pressing her purple uniform against the front desk as she and the clerk conversed. They didn't acknowledge Alison in any way so, to Alison standing there ignored and waiting, their Polish sounded like the drawing of phlegm. At last the maid broke off, laughing—a cold, sardonic laugh—and slapped a big chapped hand down on the desk.

Alison took the opportunity to politely interject. "Could I get my key, please?"

They fell silent so abruptly that, even though no word was uttered, Alison could truly say that they were curt. All the way up the stairs, she felt their hostile gaze against her back. What she had done wrong this time, she couldn't guess.

The lock was another taunt. She got it open, only to have to lock it behind her again. Over to the tucked-in bed she tripped. The room had been made up, but the chair was where she had left it in front of the sink. Was that it? Just that? That she'd peed in the sink? She pressed her face into the thin pillow. No matter how absurd the reason, it felt awful to be hated.

In the bank, the wretched purposelessness of everyone, their blank suspended stares, the one domineering voice, American, nurse-like and over-loud, had reminded Malcolm of the ward. He would go back to his room and sleep off his misery. He did not think it would be necessary to take a pill.

On his way back he found a store, simply rounded a corner and saw through an open door sausages stacked like cordwood in an ancient refrigerated display case. All at once he remembered he was rich, a veritable millionaire in *złoty*. He was even in costume with someone else's monogrammed silk aviator's scarf hanging loose around his neck. Flinging the matted tassels over his shoulder, he stepped inside.

"Is vodka consumption still the national pastime?" he asked the shopkeeper as he handed over the bottle of *Polonez*. He didn't expect a response, but the shopkeeper, wrapping the bottle in brown paper, told him, "*Tak.*"

Stopping on the sidewalk to fuss with the scarf again, when he looked up, he saw he was being watched. Across the street, a man in jeans and boots and a drab-coloured bomber jacket was leaning against a wall, smoking under the shelter of the eaves. The second they made eye contact, the man waved and threw down the cigarette. In hurried, deliberate strides, almost running, he crossed the cobbled street and, closer now, Malcolm saw he was not much more than a boy, eighteen or nineteen, perhaps, and very blond. Breathing accelerated when he reached Malcolm, cheeks aglow, he looked a veritable Polish prince, except for the shabby clothes and greying teeth.

"Excuse me?" he said. "May I speak with you a moment?" and Malcolm marvelled at how they always seemed to know who spoke English.

He began to tell a long story in formal, heavily accented English, evidently learned at school. All the while he kept his eyes coyly lowered, but betrayed himself with a pair of dimples that kept appearing and disappearing, as if he were trying not to laugh. The gist of it was that he had just arrived by train from a place called Katowice; in the station, someone had stolen his bag with everything he owned in it. He was just a poor student from Kraków University. He looked up at Malcolm and, dimples vanishing, put on an expression that reminded Malcolm of Grace.

He had, of course, seen Malcolm turn in the direction of the hotel a half block away. Likely he was trying to earn a few *złoty* at the same time he practised his English. "You've picked the wrong man," said Malcolm. "You're the prince. I'm the pauper."

The young man did not understand. He blinked and, regrettably, his eyes were a pale, almost luminescent blue.

"I haven't any money to give you," Malcolm told him, straight out.

The youth muttered something and, stuffing hands into tight jeans pockets, kicked the wet ground. Malcolm walked on, the paper-clad bottle under his arm. The boy was following, he sensed even without looking back. At the door of the hotel, something made him turn, a silly fancy, and the boy, flashing his grey teeth in a beguilingly disingenuous smile, hurried to catch up.

"What's your name?" Malcolm asked.

"Waldemar."

If he were going to pick an alias, Malcolm wished the boy would have picked one a little more melodious in English. "Would you like to join me for a drink, Waldemar?" He raised the bottle and the boy perked right up. Ever chivalrous, Malcolm held the door for him.

The desk clerk handed him his key with the usual sour impertinence and a scathing look for Waldemar. Appalling rudeness in the service sector was not something Malcolm thought he'd ever miss, but after Vancouver, where you would have to run all over town to find a clerk or waiter to abuse you, he appreciated the nobility in refusing to grovel or even smile. So far, it had been the highlight of the trip—seeing how close they could come to actually telling you off. The girl, tireless in her effort to be friendly, seemed especially to provoke them.

He climbed the leafy staircase with the boy, so blond, beside him. "Are there a lot of thieves around now?" he asked, referring to the loss of the boy's imaginary suitcase. Maybe he really was a student. He was at least intelligent, for he grinned greyly at the irony of Malcolm's question.

"The state," he said, "no longer guarantees us jobs."

Malcolm's room was at the front of the hotel overlooking the opera house and the treed belt called the Planty. He opened the door for Waldemar who, now that they were alone, was putting on a different walk— big boots, but tiny steps, and buttocks tight as if he were carrying a dime between them. There was only the bed and the chair. Malcolm pulled the chair out for him to set the dime on. He unwrapped the bottle and turned the two glasses on the little table right side up. Vodka splashed the clear sides, oily.

"Cheers, Waldemar," he said. "My name's Malcolm."

"Malcolm, cheers."

They threw back the drink in what Malcolm assumed was the Polish style. After a second shot, the room felt warmer and both of them removed their coats. The boy, who was wearing an old stretched sweater over a T-shirt grimy at the collar, took out a cigarette and came and sat next to Malcolm on the bed, keeping his eyes demurely lowered and smelling very headily of sweat.

"Aren't you going to ask me what I'm doing in Poland?"

"No," said Waldemar. "I don't care."

"Ah. A little nihilist."

"What is nihilist?"

"It is what you are, darling."

Waldemar sipped the vodka and leaned back on one arm, smiling and holding out the cigarette. "Do you have—?" He searched for the word. "Cinder."

Malcolm laughed, which made Waldemar pout. He got up, fished a matchbook from his coat pocket and lit the cigarette himself.

"Tomorrow we are visiting the Auschwitz Museum," said Malcolm as Waldemar resumed his reclining position on the bed. "Have you been there?"

"Of course." He exhaled smoke. "They take us for school trips."

"How is it?"

He shrugged. "I am tired of all that."

"Ah." Malcolm pressed his eyes. "Do you speak French, by any chance?" When Waldemar shook his head, a lock flopped into his eyes.

"Is your name really Waldemar?"

"Is your name really Malcolm?"

"It doesn't suit you, that's all."

Waldemar lifted the cigarette gracefully and, between grubby fingers, offered it to Malcolm.

Three hours later Alison woke the opposite of refreshed—groggy, headachy, confused. She curled up tighter under the thin blanket. A hot shower would warm her better, but she didn't want to go back outside with wet hair. When she finally did get up, she dressed herself in layers, in all the sweaters she'd brought.

In the lobby, the desk clerk told her where the tourist office was. "Across the Planty. Just down from the train station."

The Planty, Alison discovered, was the green ring surrounding the old, walled part of the city. She walked through it, thinking that nothing seemed to be the matter with the trees. In fact, nothing had seemed to be the matter with any of the trees she'd seen so far, with the exception of the one outside her hotel window, which might simply be late to leaf. Something in the branches of one caught her eye. She strayed off the path to look, then hurried on when she saw the mutilated pigeon hanging there, crucified on the twigs.

She came to a concrete pedestrian underpass lined with vendors of leather slippers and bulky hand-knit sweaters, brightly painted wooden boxes, fat knots of pretzel. Two Gypsies were begging—a mother and a child. Alison knew instantly that they were Gypsies because they looked exactly like those in the pictures that she'd seen in the book. The mother, squatting on the concrete, cocooned in a dirty shawl, droned at passers-by while the girl flitted around tugging sleeves. Alison found herself staring at them, standing there and marvelling that they were still here. Nearly all the Jews were gone, the guidebook said.

The little girl skittered over, fluttering fingers in Alison's face. When Alison tried to fend her off, the girl reached out and pinched her. "Ow!" cried Alison, bringing her hand up to her cheek. "Ow! Ow! Ow!" cawed the girl, capering and mocking.

Emerging on the other side of the tunnel, she stood a moment rubbing the stinging spot. The buildings here looked different, she noticed. They were discoloured almost to black. Overcast like this, too, it seemed that outside the city walls, Kraków was in black and white, while inside, where most of the tourists confined themselves, was in colour.

She crossed the street.

"Miss? Miss? Pretty miss?" Leaning up against the sooty stone, a chameleon in his black leather jacket, face blank as the wall. "Miss? I take you to Auschwitz. Four hundred and fifty thousand *złoty.*"

She kept on walking, her hand on her breast now, staring at the wet sidewalk, ignoring him. The next one droned the way the Gypsy woman had, "Miss? Ausch-witz? Ausch-witz. Four hundred thousand *złoty.*"

In a long line at the curb, the cabbies were milling, scavenger-like, waiting for the tourists to come out of the tourist office. Another followed close enough to touch her. "I drive you there. I drive you back. I give you a tour. Four hundred thousand. Three hundred fifty. Miss? A tour."

She fled inside the office, got the bus information, but was almost afraid to leave. How to brave that sinister gauntlet? Just outside the door, they were hawking a nightmare. In the end, she simply pressed through them, keeping her head low and rushing past.

She did not return to the underpass where the little wasp girl was, instead walked through the Planty again and up another street, ending back in the main square where the cafés along the perimeter had set up tables and umbrellas and the arcades of the cake-like Sukiennice had become a promenade. At the closest café, she threw herself down. She was shaking. The waiter came over and she ordered tea and *pierogi,* the only recognizable items on the menu.

In the square, an old man emptying a paper bag of bread crusts onto the flagstones became the instant vortex for an iridescent swirl of pigeons. Never in one place at one time had she seen so many people in religious costume. She started to count them—three nuns in habit, two priests in their collars, a brown-robed monk on a bicycle. The church bell struck four, echoed by her teeth against the cup. The same tune they had heard earlier sounded from the tower, bittersweet. When it ended, the people sitting around the statue of the desecrated poet looked up and applauded. Way, way up, the trumpeter took a bow.

The waiter set before her the plate of *pierogi*, onions fried to translucence and giving off a warming redolent steam. "Have you been to Wawel?" he asked, in English, naturally.

"Where?"

"To the castle."

"I didn't know there was a castle," Alison said.

"You must go. It is wonderful. It is medieval. Certainly, though, you've been inside," he pointed at it, "the Mariacki Church."

"Not yet."

"The altarpiece is very famous. They open it every day at noon."

"I wanted to go earlier. Maybe tomorrow. No." She winced. "Tomorrow I can't."

She ate and only afterward did she realize how hungry she had been. Stuffed now with dough stuffed with potatoes, she did not feel half so empty.

"You are going to Auschwitz."

She started and looked up at the waiter who was suddenly speaking so coldly to her and holding out the bill. Like all the others, he seemed to be condemning her to go.

She would go into the church now, she decided, getting up and crossing the square. Down three worn steps, she stumbled into darkness and, when her eyes had adjusted, she saw walls and huge pillars covered with faded frescos, patterned as on the painted wooden boxes sold in the streets. The front wall, where the guidebook said the best of the stained glass would be, was entirely covered with scaffolding and sheeting.

In the carved pews on either side of the main aisle people hunched in prayer. She passed gloomy little side chapels, then came to a painting of a blackface Madonna above a small altar, lit all round with votive candles. The famous high altar was set in a chapel at the back of the main body of the church, but the windows there were also draped and the wood so dark it was impossible to make out any details in the carving. The entrance roped off, she couldn't get up close.

She came back down the opposite aisle and sat down in a pew. Before her Christ hung on a stone cross, sinews, joints and tendons grotesque with straining. His crown was a twisted branch with finger-long thorns, though no less fearsome was the halo. The hair lying on his breast was wavy, so at first glance the crimped spikes of the halo seemed to be hair too, raised terrifyingly and electrically around his head. A bronze background, a bas-relief of a tippy medieval city, a fulminating sky. Staring at it, Alison was reminded once again how the force of suffering knocked the world off-kilter.

By the time she left the church, it was just beginning to drizzle. The street lights were coming on, but, few and far between, they shed about as much light as a votive candle.

The desk clerk didn't look up, even when Alison was right there asking for her key. She went right on leafing through her papers, deliberately ignoring Alison. Suddenly too weary to care what they thought of her, Alison said, "You know, I'm paying almost *two hundred million złoty* to stay in this hotel. I think you should try a little harder to be nice."

The clerk looked up. "Pardon me? Someone is not nice?"

"You're not. Nobody is."

"But we like you very much. This afternoon, I was talking here to Magda. We were saying you have such pretty hair."

"Oh," said Alison dully, quite sure she was about to cry, though really, what did she have to cry about but her broken circadian rhythms? The clerk turned to get the key just as the telephone rang and handed it over without a word.

She was halfway up the stairs when the clerk called to her. "Did you find the tourist office?"

"Yes. Thank you."

"Do you want to go to Auschwitz?"

Cringing, Alison told her, "Yes."

"As I thought. My brother can take you. He makes a tour. I will tell him to come in the morning."

"No," said Alison, holding back the sob now. "Please don't."

On her way down the corridor, she paused at Malcolm's room and, first looking left and right, put her ear to the door. She heard a faint percussion to which she added her light knock.

"Malcolm?"

No reply, but when she put her ear to the door again, the sound had stopped.

He turned over on his side, opening his eyes. Had something barked? Had someone called him? The girl, he thought. Sitting up groggily, he retrieved the glass from the floor and poured another drink, looking around the room and suddenly not seeing Denis.

They'd finished half the bottle, Malcolm on an empty

stomach. He'd grown unused to alcohol. It was too pricey a vice. Sloppily, he served himself another now, raising the glass to toast this vestige of Communism, cheap vodka, and Poland. Out the window, the rain was coming down in smearing streaks.

He had to relieve himself, badly. Setting the glass on the night table, he attempted to stand, tried again, succeeding unsteadily, then staggering over to the door. It was unlocked, but the prospect of stumbling down the hall to the toilet did not cheer him. Instead, he felt his way sideways to the sink and urinated in it.

Circumambulating the room to make use of the wall's support, he stopped, remembering. Felt his back pocket for his wallet which, naturally, was missing.

The bed was spinning. Clumsily, he chopped at the pillow, leaned back half propped up, his chin in the glass to catch his drool if it came to that. One hand he kept on the night table trying to still the gyre—uselessly. The night table, too, started turning, spinning down.

The room was dark when he woke again. He woke because he thought he heard someone pounding on the door. "Who is it?" he called. "What do you want?"

He had shouted out in French.

5

THROUGH ME ENTER THE CITY OF WOE
THROUGH ME PASS INTO ETERNAL PAIN
THROUGH ME COME AMONG THE PEOPLE
OF LOSS
ABANDON ALL HOPE, YOU WHO ENTER
The bus suddenly stops at the start of a long road between two high brick walls. Confusion, a babel of

tongues, faces pressed to the windows, but no one moves. There is a sign, but what does it mean? The driver pulls a lever and the door opens with a slap, or maybe it's just the way he bawls out the name of the place. Everyone getting off stands, gathers up guidebooks, bags, ineffectual umbrellas, and stumbles down the aisle—the quiet couple up front whispering Swiss Italian, the clean American boy naïve in face and socioeconomic theory, the two distressed Dutch girls he's been expounding to for the entire hour-and-a-half ride through the green acid-and-history-tainted countryside, the young Canadian woman with long dark hair, travelling with—an uncle? The driver had yelled at her when she could not understand him asking in Polish if she wanted a return ticket. You all climb down and in a dark blast of instantly wind-dissipated diesel the bus continues on toward the centre of town with only downtrodden Poles aboard.

Much windier here than in Kraków. Briefly, spontaneously, all of you turn inward in a circle, almost as if to commune a moment or pray, the Canadian woman's hair lifting and for a second staying lifted around her head. But you are only zipping jackets and wrapping scarves tighter and when the gust rallies again, it lashes the hair across her surprised face. Her mouth is open and hair fills it like a gag. No one makes eye contact, not even, it seems, those who have come together. At once the circle breaks, dispersing, and only you and the sour dandy of an uncle are left looking at the sign.

MUZEUM, it reads. MUZEUM.

He says something, recites it, but not to you.

Join the trudging, windward-canted line. Across the road, all that can be seen of the convent behind the wall is rooftops and a metal cross on a brick tower. Pass the

Canadian woman holding her hair at the back of her neck as she turns to see what is keeping her uncle. The Dutch girls hurry ahead, trying, it seems, to shake off the American. They round the wall and disappear, and when you reach the same point you see that the wall ends where the road meets a parking lot, half full, mostly with tour buses, placards propped up behind windscreens: *Auschwitz-Birkenau*. The sidewalk makes a right angle. Ahead is THE STATE MUZEUM IN OŚWIĘCIM, its banal brick-and-glass and concrete entrance just across the parking lot, beyond the taxi stand.

First you must pass a row of little shops. Stopping, you enter the last one, where books and pamphlets are on display across a long counter, covers grimly illustrated with barbed and twisted wire, train tracks, guard towers in silhouette. The American boy is just now paying for a set of postcards and making a joke about the absurd denominations of the bills, but the woman behind the counter, stolid, potato-fed and dour, only blinks. It is you who laugh, out loud, so the boy turns to you and grins. Mistaken, his conspiratoriality. You are laughing because of his lecture on the bus—how the Poles have to change, have to learn that in a market economy people expect to be served promptly and with courtesy, just as they are at Disneyland. Suddenly pictured: the woman handing him in a plastic bag a T-shirt that reads MY BOYFRIEND WENT TO AUSCHWITZ AND ALL HE BROUGHT ME WAS THIS LOUSY SHIRT and *still* not smiling.

The wind is waiting just outside the door. As you pull the handle toward you, the wind shoulders up against the glass, shoves the door open and storms in past you, straight for the books. It riffles through them, contemptuously—*a denier*—and the woman behind the counter barks. Close the door, she's saying in Polish. Close the door!

Approaching the entrance, you see a tour bus drawing up. It disgorges passengers, a long silent file driven forward by the truncheon blows of wind. Where are the men in black boots? Where are the dogs? Last is a priest, wind swelling his cassock and whipping it about his ankles, trying to make him dance. He holds the door, gesturing, "After you."

On the way to the station, Malcolm spoke at last. "We are leaving the first circle," he said and Alison, looking back over her shoulder, wondered if the curved remnant of the medieval wall was what he meant. They managed to find which bus to board, Alison stumbling down the aisle and taking the only empty seat, sliding in first so she wouldn't have to suffer Malcolm thudding his head against the window all the way. Almost immediately the bus pulled out, so maybe the driver had yelled at her because they'd made him late. Incomprehensible, his fury. It did not subside; every time she glanced up at his reflection in the rear-view mirror, she saw his lips still moving, forming curses.

Another circle was the ravaged rest of Kraków surrounding the Planty. In the lower town, some of the buildings seemed no less than charred, crucifixes set in smudged lintels, a decapitated statue of the Virgin and Child sooty in a recess by a door, again and again on disintegrating walls the blackface Madonna from the Mariacki Church, head tilted at the precise angle of compassion. But soon they were in the countryside, passing farmhouses, some thatched or wooden with carved, brightly painted staves along the eaves. In a flash of field, Alison saw a dwarf scarecrow berserkly windmilling its empty sleeves, and behind a grove of trees, on the rise of a hill, three copper church domes floating like balloons. A woman in a babushka, a rake over her shoulder as she marched through a ditch, comically interrupted and made bolt a shitting cat. It all seemed innocuous and green. Alison could even smell it. It smelled like spring.

She was smelling her own hair. Last night, she finally showered, then sat before the atonally clanking radiator with her head bowed, wet hair flipped over her face, a dark tangled veil. She sat combing with her fingers; more than two hours it took to dry.

After nearly as long a time, the bus stopped and the American finally shut up. For most of the ride he'd been jawing opinions that Alison thought she shared until she heard them voiced over-loudly and *ad nauseam*, with Polish country-and-western twanging in the background. "Sure everything's cheap, but not when you factor in the wait. Time is money, right?" Then, passing the silently imprecating driver and stepping down from the bus, she saw she had been mistaken about him. He hadn't been cursing her at all, but singing with the radio.

Instantly the wind made her hair fly. Standing in the open, she had trouble restraining it even, it whipped so wildly about her head. Alive, she thought. It is alive. She gathered it at her nape, then set off walking the wind-tunnel behind the others.

> *No sense of feeling is found in the:*
>   *a) skin*   *b) fingers*
>   *c) hair*   *d) lips*

Back in hairdressing school she had had to memorize a cross-sectional diagram of a hair follicle, epidermis pushing down into dermis. It had looked like a crocus before it flowers, which was not so romantic an analogy: at the bottom of the follicle there is a bud. The soft precursor cells are nourished there as they grow and divide. Pushed upward by more cells growing beneath, they die. When she first learned this, Alison could not believe it, that hair, the very growing, shedding, shining, tangling thing which seemed to her most alive about a person was, in fact, dead.

She rounded the wall. Ahead, a row of little shops; in the window of the first, flowers and votive candles. The smell as she entered was funereal and sweet. To the freshest of the limp white carnations the clerk added a sprig of fern browning at the tips, then tied the two stems together with a ribbon curled against a scissor blade and presented it, upside down, to Alison. Malcolm was just coming around the wall as she left the shop, the direction his hair was blowing abruptly changing as he turned; she waited for him to catch up and took his arm.

Just who, thought Malcolm, is leading whom?

The entrance had obviously been built later as part of the Muzeum. A long wide hall, coat check, book-stand, and behind a glass wall an empty cafeteria, the way it was lit discolouring and surreal. On the wall, the plan of the camps was painted, rows of small rectangles inside a large rectangle—*Death Block, Extermination, Execution Wall*—then the more complicated circuit-board of Birkenau. After a second set of glass doors, they had to get in line to register. Alison hadn't wanted to come today, would have preferred to wait one more day for the intermittent delirium of jet-lag to pass. Yet here she was, feeling exactly as she should: as if she had been dragged off in the middle of the night to a place spoken of only in dire whispers.

"Two Canadians," she said.

"Do you wish to see the film?"

"Yes."

"It will be shown in English in half an hour."

In the cinema foyer was a tableau of Gypsy prisoners photographed in the three familiar poses, but for some reason they were not in uniform and their heads were unshorn. They could even have been passport photos, each child scrubbed, men in suits and ties, the women's hair variously styled, lustrous and black. None were smiling, though neither did they look afraid. What impressed Alison was their dignity and how seriously they took it. Turning, she saw people milling, also looking at the tableau or talking hushedly or simply waiting in silence though no sign in four languages commanded quiet. The last and only other time she had been in a room where solemnity had seemed physically present was waiting for Christian's memorial service to begin. Then, too, she had felt this queasy foreboding.

Malcolm had wandered off somewhere. She remembered from the courthouse how he was wont to do this, but hoped this time he would come back. Returning to where she had seen a sign for the bathroom, she went down a flight of stairs to the tiled echo-chamber of an anteroom where three heavy-breasted, ill-permed Furies in cardigans sat collecting two thousand *złoty* notes. As a child, Alison had always been afraid to go down to the basement alone and she wondered now if that fear was a presentiment of this very moment.

"Here is plan of Birkenau to where we shall go to next ..." she overheard in the hall when she came back upstairs again. It was the same taxi driver who had brought them from the airport, talking to the two American women she had seen yesterday in the hotel.

326

"Let us go! We start now the tour!" Clapping fat hands together, he waved them on.

The double doors to the cinema were open now, but Malcolm was still nowhere to be seen. She took a seat and saved him the one beside it by laying the wilting carnation on it. In the foyer, the two American women were arguing with the taxi driver, loud enough for everyone to hear; they wanted to see the film, but he wanted to start the tour. Even after the lights were dimmed and the film began, their disputing voices carried in every time the door was opened.

Many of the pictures in the book turned out to be stills taken from this very film. Just as she had used to lie in bed staring up at the white rectangle on the ceiling and see the individual images projected from her mind as a slide-show, now she stared straight ahead and watched her imagination flipping, rapid-fire, the pages of the book. What she couldn't have seen—the way the twins teetered as they were herded in pairs out of the laboratory, or the liberating Soviet soldiers flinching as they stared down in the pit.

When the lights came back up, Alison noticed a family sitting in front of her, among them a little boy. In profile, she saw his cogitating face. He kept scrunching up his nose, as if he were sniffing. Every time, his glasses lifted.

"That wasn't a nice movie, was it?" said his father.

The boy swung around, glaring. "No! It was a dead movie!"

Alison stood. There was Malcolm, leaning against the back wall, waiting for her. She came over and, once again, offered him her arm.

Double doors led from the cinema directly outside where, diagonally across the green, the wooden tower of the guardhouse was. She saw the black-and-white striped posts on either side of the gate and, although she couldn't make it out from this distance, she knew that above the gate the wrought iron scroll read ARBEIT MACHT FREI.

In preparation for the onslaught of wind, she collected her hair in her free hand, the one not holding Malcolm's arm and the flower. She looked at Malcolm. He nodded and, together, they started along the path toward a sign.

ZNAJDUJESZ SIĘ W MIEJSCU WYJĄTKOWEJ GROZY I TRAGEDII. OKAŻ SWÓJ SZACUNEK ZACHOWUJĄC SIĘ W SPOSÓB GODNY, NALEŻNY PAMIĘCI TYCH KTÓRZY TUTAJ CIERPIELI I GINELI.

Then in English, French and German. You are standing beside the two Canadians, the woman holding tightly to her hair, though it is sheltered here in the quadrangle. Now you see that you were mistaken about their relationship, that if he is her uncle, he is her great-uncle. The dye fooled you. He didn't seem quite this old getting off the bus.

No one else you rode in from Kraków with is around. When you arrived the film was about to start in German and the Dutch girls were heading for the cinema. Probably the Swiss Italians watched it then, too, so all of them would have a head start. Where the American boy is, you don't know, but as they weren't selling popcorn and the film is black and white, he likely skipped it.

People leaving the cinema, then reclustering in the quadrangle around their guides, remind you of how

328

they were grouped before as "fit" for work or, most often, "unfit." Today, though, no one is stripped naked. No detour to the gas chamber. Like you, the Canadians seem to be waiting for a less crowded moment to start, and though you don't intend to intrude upon their privacy, you overhear her ask a question, which is not so strange except that you were sitting right behind them on the bus, and for the whole long ride they exchanged not a single word. Now you hear her asking if it's true that a person's hair can turn white overnight, but you step discreetly away before he answers.

Just before the gate stands an enormous weeping willow that, tousled by wind, appears to be shaking its head dementedly. Pass by it, then under the flat black letters—ARBEIT MACHT FREI. Stop and look back. The Canadians are following, the woman slowly leading the old man. In the quadrangle, another tour group forms. The gate has not slammed closed behind you, no distempered canine nightmare brings up the rear, no black boot delivers a coccyx-cracking kick—yet look at the tree. It keeps on rustling, insistent.

No, no.

Before you is a wooden building, beside which a group falls into a listening circle around the guide. Take the pamphlet from your pocket and find out what the building is.

e) Camp kitchen

Mounted behind glass on the wall, a poster-sized enlargement of the very spot you are all standing on looking at the photograph. THE CAMP ORCHESTRA IN 1941 reads the caption in Polish, English, French and, this time, Russian. Macabre, the shorn musicians in their stripes, the conductor on a wooden box in pyjama bottoms and tails. See the emaciated concertmaster, the percussionist with rickets. What are they playing, you wonder. Wagner?

"Marches," says the guide, who has a Polish accent but is speaking near-perfect English. "They played as the prisoners left the camp to work and also as they returned, often carrying their expired comrades."

In the pamphlet, red dots and arrows map a route, but instead of going straight, turn where no one is, down an avenue of tossing trees and identical red-brick blocks, each with its own little lawn and numbered Art Deco lamp. Except for the guard tower at the end and the triple barbed-and-electrified fence, it's almost pleasant, like pristinely maintained council housing. Two people emerge from the last building and begin walking toward you arm in arm. As they near, you recognize the Dutch girls. According to the pamphlet, the blocks in this row house national exhibitions and the one the girls have just left is shared by Italy and Holland.

But instead of going in, you walk on until you reach the triple wires at the end of the avenue, the concrete posts arching inward to discourage climbing. Who would try, you wonder, with a current running through and, right behind, the guard tower and the dogs? Sick-makingly eerie, the wind against your back, trying to push you against the wires. When it lets up, it is only to gather strength for another shove.

Continue walking. Ahead, between the last two blocks, is a dead end—quite—a courtyard where a large rectangular something stands against the brick of the back wall. You can't make it out yet, but there is a scattering of shiny objects on the ground in front. The facing windows are boarded up on the one side, and bricked in on the other, preventing anyone from looking out.

Entering the courtyard, you see flowers wrapped in shiny cellophane and candles flickering in a row and, coming closer, a panel made of some curious sod-like, bullet-absorbing material. Turn the page. The block on the left, Block 10, was boarded up so no one could see *in*. Dr. Mengele worked here with his dwarfs and twins. Dr. Mengele. Why has no one named a disease after him? Because, you suppose, in pathological circles that is the ultimate compliment. Imagine saying, "You don't look well," and hearing in reply, "No. I've got Mengele's disease. I am *sick, sick, sick*."

Block 11, to the right, is quaintly named the Death Block. A tour group just now arriving, the guide monotonously counts off in French each person crossing the threshold. Wait for her to enter or you'll be counted in.

On the main floor is where summary sessions of the Gestapo court were held. The walls retain their original paper, a marbled brown and green shot through with rusty streaks that bring to mind dried blood stopped in veins. The furniture is still here—sturdy wooden chairs, a monolithic desk. Missing is the gavel that precipitated with a doomish thwack each prisoner being bullied down the corridor to the second room, which you come to now, where they waited for their verdict—a flogging in the yard or a suspension: on a post, hung by wrists tied and wrenched up behind the back. Next are the rooms where they were stripped before being led out to the courtyard and the Execution Wall of grey sod. If they weren't taken outside, they went downstairs, as you go now.

The stairwell is so crowded that the line comes to a halt until some of the visitors already in the cellar come back up. You stand watching, looking at the faces of those mounting the stairs. There is no comprehensive reaction, but something does strike you. Oddly, it reminds you of how as an adolescent, in the tumult of self-definition, you began to recognize secret signs and gestures and would make pronouncements in your head like: *This one is like me, this one isn't.* Then the line starts to move and you descend, to where it is palpably colder and damper. Down here, an echo—the reiterated shuffle and whisper, the nauseating ring of a full sole on cement.

Long dark corridors lined with cells, some with doors regrilled in the motif of the Muzeum, some piled high inside with cellophane-wrapped flowers. People press up behind you trying to look through the tiny barred windows. According to the pamphlet, most of these concrete closets were for the ho-hum routine of torture and detention, but Cell 18 was one of those reserved for particular torments—a "starvation cell." Cell 20, windowless, was a "suffocation cell." In Cell 22, they have opened the wall of the "standing cells" to show the yard-square cubicle where four people were wedged in cosily for the night.

Here at the end of the hall a small crowd has gathered. No one is talking, but the way those in the rear determinedly push forward, you can tell there is something in that cell that everyone wants to see. Wait for them to clear away and when a young man butts in ahead of you, let him. He comes right out again.

Stoop and enter. You have to look twice to notice the protective square of plexiglass. Under it, a crude crucifix scratched into the plaster.

Climbing back up the stairs, you pass the people waiting to go down. Now they study your expression, as you studied others while you were waiting to descend. Do they see that you are thinking of that prisoner-cum-artist, shivering in his stripes, waiting for the stamp of boots to recede down the hall? What had he found for a tool—a bent and priceless nail? Did it dig into his own palm as he worked? Did he perish for it, his self-expression? Then you think of the young Frenchman ducking into the cell fifty years later and ducking smugly out again.

Leave Block 11 now, and as you go, recall the old Queen of Uncles reciting back when you were getting off the bus—*this way enter the Museum of woe* ... And watch the people entering, their varied expressions of outrage or grief, the blank faces of those in shock, the profound weariness, the revulsion. At the same time there are people coming through who seem undeniably detached. Perhaps they are simply unprepared; they skipped the film, or history in school. The sceptics and deniers, the imaginatively impoverished, the perversely curious— they are visiting, too.

Continue along the avenue, against the flow of people and wind. A couple walk slowly toward you joined at the hip, the man the woman's very sight and volition. Encircled in his arms, she moves along with both hands over her face. Then, sheltered between the blocks, four teenagers from a school group huddle around a communal cigarette.

Entering Block 7, you find yourself in a corridor lined with women's faces, their expressions worse than blank—gaunt and hauntingly restrained. *Aurelia, Emilia, Hana.* A flower hangs from a photo, tied with a long curled ribbon. *Teresa, Allegra.* "Living and Sanitary Conditions" the theme of this block, some of the rooms are glassed in. Stand and look inside, where, on the floor, straw and filthy blankets have been shaped into loose fetid pallets. Farther along—*Luzie, Flor, Katarzyna*—is a room with ten crude and unprivate toilets in a row.

Bożena, Bondi, Irena.

This next room you can walk through: three-tiered bunks strewn with straw and blanket scraps. "*C'est affreux*," the woman behind you mutters. "*C'est comme une installation.*"

Leave, walk down the steps and back out on the avenue to Block 6 where, in the corridor, you are met with the tearless eyes of men. *Edward, Józef, Michał, Stanisław, Emil.* In the first room off the corridor, a chart explains the triangular badges: red for Politicals; two in yellow, one reversed and overlapping, to form a star for Jews; for Gypsies and the Mentally Ill black; Jehovah's Witnesses purple; Homosexuals pink; Criminals green. Slowly, you turn and see at the far end of the room a display of prison uniforms and, for the first time, recognize that a colour is missing from the abject spectrum. You hadn't known that the stripes, seen all along in photographs in black and white, were blue.

Now it occurs to you that you have been following the official route after all, but in reverse. "Material Evidence of Crimes" reads the legend for Block 5. So it's like this: first photographs and drawings, reconstructions, models; now actual, contemporaneous objects. You are moving from the abstract to the personal and, as a result, your increasing agitation. Following the route backward—Block 7, Block 6, Block 5, Block 4—it makes a kind of countdown.

The first room in Block 5 is empty except for a wooden case under the window just inside the door containing nothing but round dinted tins of shoe polish. Turn now, look across the long room and, as you stare at the hill of brushes behind the glass there, the physical emptiness of the room is filled with the suggestion that the room itself was once filled with brushes.

Hair brushes
Nail brushes
Shaving brushes
Tooth brushes
Lint brushes
Shoe brushes
Scrub brushes

Step out into the corridor where the walls are lined with photo murals—pictures of the stores. Here is the very Everest of brushes you just imagined and, here, a magnitude of combs. Pause now to think of your own brush, the lost hair woven in a mat around the bristles. Give thought, too, to your toothbrush, flaring from overuse—a toothbrush that will be casually discarded, that never stood for anything but dental hygiene. Continue on past prayer shawls suspended like sails, mangled eyeglass frames, enamel dishes, pots, sieves, tubs, basins, all stacked to the ceiling, trusses, crutches, wooden hands, artificial legs and arms amassed like the limbs in the pits.

At the bottom of the stairs, another photo mural shows clothing spilling out of a two-storey warehouse door. Climb the stairs and, at the top, turn left and enter the room there. The clothes you brought with you are in your suitcase back in the hotel in Kraków. Overwhelming the bank of suitcases you find before you now, the whole long length of the room a slope of battered brown leather stopped by glass. Whereas downstairs, looking at the brushes, you were seized by the horrific made obvious— that each brush represented the person who had brought it—here you find, lettered in white, who that person was and where he or she was from: *Herman Pasternak, Marie Kafka, Liese Morgenstern, Jnese Meyer, Denis Gelbkopf, Irene Hahn* from *Prague, Köln, Westerbork, Paris ...*

How long you have been standing here you don't know, but now a tour group begins filing in. Leave, slip past those entering and cross the hall to the other room.

A narrow aisle runs between two enormous cases. The contents of the cases declining precipitously from the ceiling, the effect is that of being trapped in an avalanche on both sides, of shoes tumbling down to bury you alive. You feel as if you are burrowing along through them as you go, and heightening the claustrophobic panic is the German tour, still leaving as the tour in Hebrew crowds in. Pressed together like this, almost up against the shoes, everyone instantly smells everyone else and wants to bolt. Stop and wait for the others to clear out and when a man elbows you trying to get past, ignore him. But isn't he a bastard? He elbows you again, deliberately, it seems. You turn to face him. He points the outlandish horns of his eyebrows at you. Fuck off, you think, shaking with anger.

Fuck off, *Kraut.*

Turn back to the case. Slippers, clogs, sandals, brogues, work boots, overshoes, dancing shoes, every kind of sole, heel, strap, lace, all sizes from an infant's bootie to the galoshes of a giant. Breathing hard now, you fog the glass, then something stops your breath. The shoes were once all colours—here a red slipper, there a white Cuban heel—but only just. Most are now a near-uniform lustreless brown. Gradually, they have blended together into a mass, indistinguishable and, again, impersonal. They are becoming, once again, abstract. The shoes are fading as memory is fading, melding as they disintegrate. And the names on the suitcases in the next room grow fainter year by year, and the suitcases themselves are almost the same dull brown as the shoes, and the brands on the shoe polish tins have been effaced completely, the eyeglass frames rusted black, lenses fragile shards or crushed to powder, and on the handles of the brushes steadily losing bristles, only flecks of paint remain. What preservation is acceptable here, where altering anything amounts to tampering with evidence? How to put ourselves into these shoes, when these shoes no longer exist?

Shuffle forward now with the disconsolate rest, out of the shoeslide, sweating. As you descend the stairs, your sweat cools and, all at once, you feel the cold. Colder stepping out into the wind, onto the avenue of flailing trees. Pause and, with unsteady hands, take the guide from your pocket once more to read about Block 4. It is the first block on the official tour. It is your last. Afterwards, you will intercept the others *en route* to the crematorium.

As you enter, you immediately put your hand over your mouth and nose. A small group stands before a map of Europe that shows the asterisk of rail lines converging here, but they are all breathing normally. So, too, is the couple staring at the urn of human ash behind the glass. You, you are almost choking on the odour.

Stepping into the hall, you nearly collide with the Canadian woman, who is carrying a sorry white flower upside down. The uncle is not with her and from the anxious way she peers into the room beyond you, you guess she's looking for him. She crosses the hall, then turns suddenly.

"Do you speak English?" she asks.

Tell her yes. For a moment she just stands there, as if she can't decide what it is she wants to ask. At last she blurts it. She asks the obvious. "What is that awful smell?"

Tell her you think it's probably naphthene, "Or some kind of preservative—" but stop because she doesn't seem to know what is upstairs.

Dazedly, she turns and heads back down the corridor. Watching her go, it occurs to you that, rightly, you should have told her it was the smell of evil.

Approaching the gate, Alison was still clutching white-knuckled to her hair. Finally letting go, her fingers uncurled with stiff reluctance. "But you hear about it all the time," she said.

Malcolm insisted it wasn't so. What actually happens, he said, is the hair falls out in patches as a result of stress or trauma. White hair, hair that has lost its pigment, is coarser, its roots more resilient, so it holds. When the pigmented hair suddenly goes, it gives the impression of colour draining overnight.

"Oh," said Alison. "I didn't know that."

"Don't they teach you anything at hairdressing school any more?"

How to wash, to hold the scissors, to cut, colour, curl. To keep the armpits dry, the breath fresh. To always smile. Seeing the wind in the tree before the gate, she was reminded of something they didn't teach: that hair has its own capacity for expression. In terror, it rises on the nape and limbs. It falls out in grief or sorrow, or is torn out. Dishevelment is a sure sign of insanity. The tree looked insane. Walking slowly, Alison and Malcolm together, they passed right under the tossing branches and the familiar wrought-work maxim.

She had not expected the deep red of the brick, or that every leaf would be a chlorophyll flag; the photographs had all been in black and white. And the trees in the photographs were fifty years smaller, but they had flourished. Here, she thought, if anywhere, the trees ought to look like they were dying.

They stopped before a photo of an orchestra mounted on the side of a wooden building; at once Alison thought of her brother playing the piano every Christmas, though the rest of the year he rarely touched the keys. All her life she'd heard how special it was to be musical, but only now did she fully understand. Jeffy would survive here. Kevin Milligan would rule. Then she drew her hand out of her pocket to blink at her own strange fingers. She would, too, of course. She would be doing the shearing.

They turned away from the crowds, walked to the end of an avenue where they came to a double perimeter fence, cement posts studded with insulators through which ran sharp knotted wires.

VORSICHT!

They passed through the opening, walking on until they came to a set of steps up to a gravel platform where a wooden gallows stood. Just beyond, a tall chimney rose out of a bank of grass. A door in the side of the bank; they entered it.

With the only light coming from two mesh-covered windows across the long room, it took a moment for her eyes to adjust, standing as they were, blind, in the peculiar grave-like silence under the hill of earth. Then from the darkness, dark emerged—walls and ceiling black with human soot. Here were the ovens, the charred brick boxes in a row. Black iron doors, the arched one for the body and the smaller one below for the ash. The trolleys for the bodies were strewn with flowers. There were flowers in the ovens. It looked like a place for incinerating flowers.

They came out on the undisguised concrete side of the building, the grass slope stayed by a low stone wall.

Malcolm let go of her arm and sank down with his fingers to his eyes.

"I've got aspirin," said Alison, rummaging through her bag. When she passed him the little bottle, he shook out four tablets, popped them in his mouth and chewed until a white froth formed around his lips.

Two people came out of the crematorium. Malcolm waited for them to pass, then made to stand, but couldn't.

"Wait," she said. "Let's wait a bit."

Stabbing at his eyes again, he was breathing hard and the wind, ruffling his hair, showed the grey roots untreated by the flat black rinse.

"I'm sorry I asked you to come," she said.

"It's just the irony of it," he answered.

He hoped she hadn't passed his door yesterday and heard the boy in there with him.

He had not thought the boy would allow himself to be kissed, not the way Malcolm smelled; he had thought the boy would push him away. Waldemar had, of course, his own very potent odour, but it was the smell of sweat and sex—of life—while Malcolm smelled of death. Commerce before scruples. The boy was a hustler, after all. Lifting his face to Malcolm, he had puckered wetly. Malcolm, leaning over him, recalled that the last lips he had kissed were Christian's.

But he would not do what Malcolm asked. He had had nothing but contempt for Malcolm's suggestion: that they lie down in each other's arms and, while Malcolm muttered endearments in French, fall asleep.

"They tell me I should pick up my life where it left off," Malcolm told the girl now. "But I no longer have a life, you see." He flinched to say it here, sitting outside the Auschwitz crematorium.

Alison waited, saying nothing. Finally, he nodded

then, standing, took her arm again. Slowly, they walked around the green hill of the crematorium, back the way they had come. Twelve, thirteen, fourteen—the numbers on the blocks. They intersected with the stream of visitors, and, turning, continued in the direction everyone was being blown.

Malcolm, patting her hand, asked, "What are you most afraid of?"

She answered right away, "Being the same when we leave. And you?"

He was most afraid of what had happened to Denis, afraid that if it happened to him too, he would spout the same vile things. Everyone had a little Auschwitz inside. He was afraid that was what he believed.

The girl was looking at him, expecting him to speak. What he said was, "Being alone." And that he wanted to go in first.

"Of course," she told him. "I'll wait a few minutes."

At the other end of the avenue, the crowd was passing through the gate in slow-moving waves, like a procession of the wounded and the sick. Stopping to look at the picture of the orchestra, they seemed to be recovering their breath. But as they neared, then passed, Alison, she saw that most of them were fit. They climbed the steps to Block 4, only to balk in the doorway before entering. She waited, watching long enough to see the whole cycle: coming through the gate, staggering along the blowing avenue, entering Block 4, then leaving. She was anxious to see how they were different.

When she finally crossed the avenue and mounted the steps herself, the first thing she saw was that they weren't hesitating to enter, but stopping to read a sign in white on black. *The one who does not remember history is bound to live through it again.*

No, they were *recoiling*. There was a terrible smell in the room.

She hurried through, but the smell was in the next room, too, where she found a number of glass-topped wooden cases. They contained handwritten record books, plain, leather-bound with ruled pages. Each looked exactly like the appointment book at Vitae. She could even read the dates and names and addresses—*09.10.41 Pinette, Daniel, Paris 2, rue Richelie, 59*—just as if he'd come in for a cut.

He got that cut. Before her, another tableau, heads crudely scraped raw with a razor. Unlike the Gypsy tableau back in the cinema foyer, what struck Alison now was how generic people seemed when they were shorn. She would have thought the opposite, that the features would become more prominent on the face. But no: unframed by hair, they seemed to recede instead. And where looking at the Gypsies she had sensed in each a personality, she didn't here, couldn't begin to guess a thing about them, bald and uniformed. It was as if their personalities had been left in hanks on the shearing-room floor.

She began to look for Malcolm, but couldn't find him anywhere. Almost colliding with another person in a doorway, she realized she was wandering in and out of the same rooms, and the smell was sticking in the back of her throat where she could taste it. The man in the doorway was someone who had ridden with them on the bus, so she stopped to ask if he spoke English. Had he seen Malcolm, she was about to ask when she remembered that he wouldn't know who Malcolm was. Momentarily flustered, she asked instead what the odour was.

He started to explain, but she was not really listening. Reading her mind, he fell silent and glanced up. At the ceiling. Upstairs.

Malcolm was upstairs.

Stairs worn like the medieval stairs in the Mariacki Church. She turned on the landing, started up the second flight, climbing with one hand gripping the banister, the other the flower. The smell was coming from the room at the top, she discovered as she entered it. At first she didn't see Malcolm, yet she knew he was there. She knew, because this was where the hair went.

The room was perhaps fifteen metres long. One third of the width and the whole length was taken up by a glass case, the whole case filled with hair, the whole room filled with the sickening smell of the hair. They had packed it into twenty-kilogram bales and sold it to make thread and mattress stuffing, fuses for bombs, tailor's lining, felt insulators for army boots. That was what she'd read. That the average human head held approximately one hundred and twenty thousand hairs.

And this was where it went.

Standing in the doorway, she was thinking that somewhere tangled there was Mrs. Soloff's hair. Mrs. Soloff's hair and, somehow, Christian's, too. She started to come forward, numbly, until she was near enough to lay the flower on the sill. This close, she saw that the hair behind the glass was actually nothing like what she had been sweeping off the salon floor. Balled up, matted, like sheared dreadlocks or dull brown fleece, it was so mixed and faded that there were no more gilt strands, no blond hanks. There were no shades of auburn or aubergine, chestnut or silver. They had come just in time, come before it was too late. The hair was like something under the bed and as fragile. Hair is dead and

343

this was the dead hair of the dead. It was the dead and the dying, becoming dust.

6

At the hotel, Malcolm told her to leave him. "No," said Alison. "Let me help you in."

They climbed the staircase together, but when they reached his room, he wouldn't give her the key. Neither could he get it in the lock. She simply took it, and for the first time opened the door effortlessly. She helped him across the room to the bed, where he sank down. Seeing the vodka bottle sitting on the table, she poured him a drink.

His room looked out over the Planty, gloomy now in the concentrating dusk. When she turned from the window, he had already emptied the glass and was trying to get up.

"Let me help you take off your coat."

"No." He pushed away her hand. "Please go."

She stepped back, hesitating, not sure if she wanted to stay for his sake or hers. She didn't want to be alone. Closing Malcolm's door behind her, she went downstairs.

In the lobby, the desk clerk looked up as she passed. "Did you have a nice day?"

Alison refrained from replying.

Szpitalna Street was empty, but as she neared the corner a few people were meandering in the direction of the square. In Floriańska Street there were queues outside the pizza joints and a crowd had formed around a pair of busking Gypsies. Their music competed with Metallica blaring from a stand where pirated cassettes

344

were being sold. Loitering and commerce. Life was going on; she marvelled.

She ended up back at the Mariacki Church, lit from within now, stained glass luminescing across the high dark wall, as if the church were a heavy lantern with the wick turned low. Down the worn steps she went, entering next to the chapel of the blackface Madonna. Though night, it was much easier to see than yesterday when the little votive tongues of flame were the only illumination. Now the electricity was on, and in the part of the church around the high altar the lights were blazing. Someone was singing there, where it was brightest.

She made her way between the pews, walked up the aisle, stopping when she came to the crucifix. Light caught on the bronze relief and flared. Something she hadn't noticed yesterday: the wound below his ribs was rimmed with pearls, the deep red centre like an eye staring out. Do they see us? she wondered. Do the dead see us?

A priest was singing in the chapel, which was half full of worshippers. Now she could see the altar, even from the last pew where she took a seat. It was not what she had expected, this famous altar. She had thought it would be a kind of table, but it was instead a huge dark wood cabinet with panelled doors. Standing on top were near life-sized figures: a woman, the personification of demureness; boyish musicians; saints in parabolic hats. Carved into the door panels were more images of suffering.

The man in the pew ahead of her suddenly turned and extended his hand to her. For a second Alison only stared at it, then she saw that this was a mass, that this was how a mass ended; all around her, people were shaking hands. Hot, his hand when she took it. He said something in Polish and laughed. Somehow she understood he was telling her that, with hands that cold, her heart must be warm.

The priest came down into the aisle to chat. His brocaded robe and linen smock rounded him out and, the way he rocked on his toes as he talked, he looked like a toy punching bag. The man in front of Alison called out a question and the priest, pointing at the altar, gave an answer that prompted a spontaneous burst of laughter from them all. He left, but no one else did and soon a dour little nun appeared, beetling up the aisle in her black garment. Pausing to genuflect, she climbed the steps to the altar, disappearing a moment behind it before coming out again with a long hooked rod.

Not a cabinet. It was a book. She hooked the base of the dark wood covers—one, then the other—and swung them open.

Everyone gasped.

Dazzling, the gilt and colour. Alison put a hand over her heart.

If the beginning was carved on the outside in the near-black wood, and the middle on the two carved and vibrantly painted inside covers, then the ending was the entire huge central panel: a woman falling on her knees. She was the size of a living woman, the crowd around her life-size, too. Life-size and seemingly inspirited— Alison saw veins pulsing in legs, throbbing arthritic knuckles, pouching skin. One man was holding the woman as she sank; one, fingers twined together, made a gesture unreadable and strange. Another recoiled, two stared, one staggered. Above, angels winged like birds. The painted middle scenes on the doors were of angelic visitations, the poignant docility of livestock, gifts being given, a radiance in the sky. But the beginning, in the dark wood on the outside panels, was a taunting and a flaying, a ghastly drawn-out death, wounds bared then disbelieved—almost the same story she had pored over all winter.

She'd only once been to church, as a girl, with a neighbour, and all she remembered was the Sunday-school teacher telling them that God had counted every hair on their heads. Appalled by the thought of a stranger touching her, she had gone right home and told her mother.

"Gosh," her mother had said, "you'd think he'd have better things to do."

How could Alison ever believe in God when not even her mother did, her mother who, of everyone Alison knew, came closest to being a saint? How to believe in God after Auschwitz?

How to believe in anything after the Auschwitz Muzeum?

Her mother had said, "I just add that extra letter. I believe in Good." Alison thought: Oh, that I could even believe in Good.

The little bug-like nun came brisking back and perfunctorily closed up the altar. One by one the lights of the chapel were extinguished. All the people rose to go.

Back through the crowd on Floriańska Street, Alison wound her way. She thought of Malcolm, alone, and began to hurry. Entering the hotel lobby, she nodded quickly at the clerk. Climbed the leafy stairs. At Malcolm's door she paused first to listen, tried the handle and opened it a crack.

Inside a light was on and Malcolm was sitting on the bed in his coat, as he had been when she left him an hour ago. He seemed to be staring at the leaves strewn in a pattern on the carpet. "Can I come in?" she asked.

He nodded weakly and whispered for her to watch where she stepped. A dark wet stain on the carpet, flecked with white powder and broken bits of half-dissolved pills.

"What have you done?" she cried, seeing the bottle in his hand.

He said, "I'm sorry."

He allowed her to help him out of his coat. She took it over to the wardrobe and hung it on the hanger, pulling his bathrobe off another. In the mirror inside the door, her own reflection confronted her. Then she smelled that smell again, here in the room, and saw her face crumple. Grabbing a handful of her own hair, she sniffed it.

"What are you doing?" he asked when she came over.

"I'm smelling you. That smell from the museum, it's in your hair."

He grabbed her hand. "So you smell it, too!"

On the edge of the sink, she found his toilet bag, and a travel-sized bottle of shampoo. She left the tap running while she took off her coat.

"Lift your arms," she told him.

He did. He would do, she knew, anything she asked now. When she pulled his sweater off, he just sat there, shrunken-looking, ashen, his hair standing on his head.

"Oh, Malcolm."

She smoothed it down. Her fingers opened the row of buttons, slid the shirt off his shoulders. "Here," she said holding out the robe for him.

With difficulty, she got him to his feet and, dragging the chair along behind them, led him slowly across the room. She made a shawl with the towel and helped him to lean back. "Is that all right? Are you comfortable?" She pushed up her layers of sleeves and touched her wrist to the running water. A glass on the ledge under the mirror. She filled it, and very carefully, shielding his eyes, poured the water over his crown, feeling the skin on his forehead grow suddenly and minutely less taut.

He must have taken the little bottle of shampoo from some motel in another decade. The paper label had nearly worn off. Poured into her palm, it was a pink over-scented nectar until she rubbed her hands together and it frothed. Looking in his face, she saw gravity's kindness—pulling the loose skin back instead of down. She lifted his head and stood cradling it.

She had never really thought of it as washing. When she pressed her thumb into his temple, his jaw unstuck. His head grew heavier, would become more and more difficult to hold. But she would hold it despite the effort, while the other hand worked circles, drawing the blood to the surface, dispelling hurt. His lips parted. Leaning over him, she felt his warm exhalation on her throat.

She filled the glass again. The water went down in a foamy swirl. It went down grey. After the lather was gone, she tipped the glass and still the water was discoloured. The black dye was coming out. She was rinsing it away. When she looked in his face, she saw, by contrast, that the water pooling in his eye sockets was clear.

"Shh," she whispered. "Shh," and put her arms around him and raised him up. Clutching her, he pressed his face into her neck, but did not make a sound. Something wet trickled down between her breasts—his tears and water from his hair.

He was being lifted up, he felt. The terrible weight of all that had happened was being taken from him, if only for this moment.

"Shh," said Alison.

In the mirror, she saw herself rocking him.

The first thing you notice is that the room is nearly empty, which is strange for a train station at this hour. Before you are rows of wooden benches, the ticket booths and, at the end, high up, a huge clock reading exactly 6:30. Yet there is almost no one here. A single soul hunches on the benches and only one of the ticket booths is occupied. Here, by the door, two young travellers stand reading together from a guidebook, their backpacks at their feet, but except for them and you, there is no one else.

An airlessness about the place, you feel it as you walk over to the ticket booth, how everything seems so curiously static. Then, passing the benches where the lone passenger is waiting, you notice how he is folded up: legs crossed, one arm clutching his middle as he bows over himself, the other arm propped on his knee and reaching around his head. His clothes, his hair, suggest a profound dishevelment and, in this tangled posture, he is rocking, rocking and muttering to himself. Somehow you sense that he has been doing this for hours and, alarmed, you walk on, afraid to look back and see his face, afraid to recognize him from the Muzeum as another visitor, not a lunatic. Afraid his reaction is quite sane.

At the ticket booth, fish for the guidebook in your bag. In the glossary is a list of useful phrases from which you find Kiedy odjeżdża pociąg do Krakowa? When does the train leave for Kraków? Read it out slowly, labouring over the nonsense of each sound. "Kiedy odjeżdża pociąg do Krakowa?" Look up, probably expectantly, though the pummels of experience have long since taught you not to expect communication the first time.

The woman in the booth stares at you through lashless, pink-rimmed eyes. With her pointed nose and combed-up bangs, she reminds you of a battery hen ruffled in her coop and about to squawk. Miracle of miracles, she has caught your meaning. Sourly, she ejaculates a reply. But now what? To save your life, you couldn't decode her answer.

Turn back a page in the guidebook and look for a suitably

mollifying phrase. "*I don't understand,*" is self-evident, as is "*I don't speak Polish very well.*" So try this: "Proszę mówić trochę wolniej."

Please speak a bit more slowly.

Oh, the disgust! The utter, cowing contempt! You feel yourself shrinking before her sneer, blushing with shame as she fires back a volley of sarcastic syllables. You almost want to duck. Certainly you flinch, then, in a panic, hold the guidebook to the window with your finger on the phrase for her to read.

That *did it. That* was absolutely the last straw. *Glaring, she slams the window down, leaving you standing there astonished. Rap on the glass.*

She turns her back!

"Proszę," *you plead,* "Proszę. Just give me a fucking ticket!"

And so you find yourself stuck, for all intents and purposes stranded, in the train station at Oświęcim. A garbled announcement over the loudspeakers: presumably a train is arriving or departing, but no one moves toward the door that leads out onto the platform and no one comes in. There is a news stand, you observe, at the bottom of the stairs that lead up to the mezzanine, but it is unlit, the glass door shut. Nothing is newsworthy after what happened here. More recent wars and war crimes, the camps and slaughters since—all of them only hark back to those primal crimes, they are reflections in a mirror; here, at the Oświęcim train station, they do not warrant print. The young man on the bench has figured this out already and all day the poor bastard has been trying to get a ticket. And look at the moon-faced clock. Surprised? It's 6:30 exactly. Your own watch reads 5:43.

Nevertheless, you do not completely believe this is a nightmare. You march past the benches and back over to the door where the two travellers are still studying their guidebook. It does not occur to you that they, too, might be searching for an escape. Have they got their tickets, you ask them, and, if so, are they going to Kraków and when does the train leave?

Blank, their doubled gaze. Barely older than teenagers, they shake their heads in unison and shrug.

Ask, "Do you speak English?"

"No," says the taller boy. "We are Germans."

You back away. Then, by chance, you happen to glance up and see the letter "I" in the blue circle on the sign posted on the railing of the mezzanine.

At the top of the stairs is the information desk and, sitting behind it, someone's grandmother. She frowns as you approach and, reluctant to lay her knitting down, cranes to read the phrase you point to in the guidebook. She runs a knitting needle along one column of a yellowed schedule taped to the desk, stopping on a time. Take a pen from your bag and write it on your hand then, to be absolutely certain, point in the guidebook to "What time is it?" She motions with the needle across the station to the paralysed, slack-handed clock.

Downstairs, you secure your ticket with surprisingly little fuss. It is as if the woman in the booth doesn't recognize you as the same person she treated so appallingly just moments before. Which is not to say she is in any way congenial. She simply hands the ticket over without a glance. Slip the ticket inside your wallet, the wallet in your pocket. Press the place to feel its shape. Surprisingly, no sense of triumph or relief accompanies this gesture. In a way, you even feel worse, for now you have nothing to do but kill time until the train leaves, nothing to do but to wait.

Next to the entrance to the platform is the cafeteria. Here is where all the people are, clustered around the tables in the surreal yellowish light of the room. A few look like locals, stout men in tweed caps with doughy hands around their mugs of beer. The others have just come from the Muzeum, you know because there is no other reason to be here. No one is talking. What is there to say? Though almost all younger, there is something old about them, too, something profoundly weary, as they sit slumped and motionless, mostly staring straight ahead. It is as if this is not a train station cafeteria at all, but a hospital ward for catatonics, or a room preserved perfectly in amber.

The smell of onions frying rushes up to meet you at the door. Even here, it is the very smell that reminds you of love, of being warm and replete. It lures you over to the counter, where a menu is posted. Since seven-thirty this morning you've had nothing to eat; there you stand, cross-referencing the menu with the glossary in the guidebook, but the moment you lift your eyes from the page, you forget the order of all the z's and y's and k's. Suddenly nothing seems to correlate. Dizzying cyphers, the Polish words. You clutch the counter.

"Proszę Pana?" someone tells you. "Proszę Pana?"

Look up. At first, you believe yourself to be hallucinating for before you is a genuine bouffant, a platinum back-combed miracle, the poof the waitress materialized in, a line of discoloured lace perched in the pillowy centre of it. Gummy strips hold her outrageous eyelashes in place. She shows a full mouth of grey teeth— an actual smile, here, of all places. Queasy, you close your eyes again and, after a moment, feel the guidebook being pulled from your sweaty grip. When you look up the second time, the waitress is scanning the glossary and frowning with painted lips. She ponders, making one incomprehensible suggestion after another before pronouncing, "Frytki!" with a finger decisively held up. On the end of it, a long plastic nail is glued. Waving all ten of them, she shoos you off in the direction of the tables.

An hour later, when you are on the train hurtling to God knows where, it will occur to you who she is. You will even make up a name for her, and, in the years to come, think again of her face, round, open, marbled with foundation, and her tawdry crown of lace. In the church in Kraków and in the sham icons in the market she looked different, muddy and serene. Like a chameleon, all her guises depend upon the place in which she appears. Today she is Our Lady of the Oświęcim Train Station, though others would naturally call her something else. Most might not even recognize her.

This very evening, before a mirror peeling the insect legs off her eyelids, she might not even recognize herself.

She sets a heaped plate before you. "French fries!" you exclaim and grab her hand to hold her back. "You are the first person to be nice to me in Poland."

Laughing, she pulls her hand away. Eat, she seems to be telling you. Eat. And you do, greedily, using your fingers, then wiping them with a napkin. By the time you return to the counter to pay, the waitress has disappeared and in her place is a bloated cook in an apron calicoed with grease.

Several people begin to stir. They stand, the ones with packs swinging them wordlessly onto their backs. Follow as they shuffle out onto the platform. A train is just now easing in, exceedingly slowly, as if blown by the wind. Another waits on the tracks and both have passengers on board. Turn to the person closest to you, a flame-haired woman in Gore-Tex who turns out, from her accent, to be Australian.

"Are you going to Kraków?"

"Yeah," she drawls.

"Do you know which train to take?"

"No." She turns away.

Stung, you stare a moment at her back, though perhaps you are in the wrong to have spoken at all. In the Muzeum, except for the hushed, multilingual lectures of the tour guides, silence was the rule.

A conductor is leaning out of the train that has just come in. Cross the tracks and call to him. "Kraków?" He nods. You get on board.

Enter the first compartment and take a window seat facing a heavy-bosomed woman with a wicker basket in her lap, a cloth tucked around its contents. Through the window, you watch the Australian woman and her friend, a blond boy, and wonder why they aren't getting on the train. Everyone is still standing there, mute and grim. Barely perceptible, your departure. You don't, in fact, feel it. The station simply slides away before your eyes. Then it occurs to you that you must be the only person retaining any volition. Everyone else has been left behind, possibly forever, but you, you got away.

At the far end of the compartment, the conductor enters and with a hole-punch begins making confetti down the aisle. Take out your ticket: Kraków Główny. The bosomy woman across from you has a broad country face, raw-looking from the web of veins under her cheeks. Lean forward and tap her knee; wake her from the beginning of a doze. Her eyes fly open and she puts a hand over the basket. In gestures, tell her you want to see her ticket. At first she thinks you want to see inside the basket and, fearfully, she shakes her head. Wave your own ticket at her. Point at hers and nod and smile.

"Ah!" she says and holds it out.

Płaszów, it reads.

You're on the wrong train. Show her your ticket and ask, "I'm on the wrong train, aren't I?"

Puzzled, she cocks her head.

The conductor is approaching. "Never mind," you say and, holding the ticket out to him, ask, "Do you speak English?"

He arches a wiry eyebrow and squeezes the hole-punch.

"Am I on—"

The compartment door clatters closed behind him.

Accelerating, the train begins to jostle from side to side. Past sodden, unplanted fields, its clacking rises to a crescendo and, with it, your agitation. You are going to Płaszów. Where the hell is Płaszów? Why does it sound so familiar? The best you can hope for is that it is on the way to Kraków. Past woods, past empty stations without a soul on the platform, past farmhouses with duvets hung out the windows in surrender. A monstrous factory rears in the distance, all stacks and smoke. You can smell it, acrid and sour, in the compartment of the train.

Staring out the window like this, swaying back and forth, the rhythmic clacking of the wheels always in the background, under-standably you will drift off in your mind. Again and again, images from the Muzeum. You try to shut them out, to marvel instead at the countryside beyond the window coming back to life. But it is impossible. Impossible to forget.

By your watch, over an hour has gone by when you finally near a city. The woman with the basket has slept the whole trip. Tap her knee again. She starts awake, jarring the basket; under the cloth, something squirms.

"Where are we?" you ask. "Is this Plaszów?"

She nods, and with one hand on the churning cloth, puts a finger to her lips.

Plaszów looks a lot like Kraków, the blackened cladding crumbling off the walls, exposing the stone and brick. The train decelerates and you see on a brick wall a freshly painted sign that reads ZLIRT. A slow glide into the station. Everyone stands; they begin to gather up their things. The woman with the basket hur-ries out of the compartment first, then, one by one, the others. You, you stay where you are in your seat hoping that the train will move again. But soon the conductor reappears and, glaring, motions for you to get off.

Show him your ticket again. "I don't want Płaszów."

He makes a violent gesture toward the door. Rising, you stum-ble past him, out of the compartment and down onto the platform. A sign says Płaszów, so this is Plaszów indeed. Helplessly, you look around, but cannot see an information desk anywhere.

In your hands is the guidebook. You blink at it, as if had just appeared there on its own. Using it all week as a phrase book, you didn't think to look up Płaszów in it.

Płaszów is not listed in the index, but when you flip to the chapter on Kraków, you find a small subsection with "Płaszów" as its title. On the emptying platform, you stand and read while passers-by jostle past you, almost knocking the guidebook out of your hands. Again, you read it, and again, starting from the *beginning, so you are reading in a loop. And though your eyes remain on the page, in your peripheral vision, it seems the people have formed a crowd that is swirling around you. All of you spinning, spinning downward. And this is what you read: that* Płaszów *is a suburb of Kraków. That there were mass graves in* Płaszów.

That Płaszów *was a concentration camp.*

Acknowledgements

I wish to thank Zsuzsi Gartner, Ingrid MacDonald and Mary Tilberg—my three Graces—for their advice and encouragement. For their translations, I am indebted to Tobi Panter, Joëlle Régnier, Margaret Stefanowicz and Christina Gerber. I thank the Canada Council for its financial support. To Patrick Crean and John Metcalf, extraordinary editors—my gratitude, my admiration, my respect.